SWEET ACHE

A DRIVEN NOVEL

K. Bromberg

A SIGNET SELECT BOOK

SIGNET SELECT
Published by the Penguin Group
Penguin Group (USA) LLC, 375 Hudson Street,
New York, New York 10014

USA | Canada | UK | Ireland | Australia | New Zealand | India | South Africa | China
penguin.com
A Penguin Random House Company

First published by Signet Select, an imprint of New American Library,
a division of Penguin Group (USA) LLC

First Printing, June 2015

ISBN 978-0-451-47393-6

Printed in the United States of America
10 9 8 7 6 5 4 3 2 1

Praise for the Novels
of K. Bromberg

"[A] highly emotional yet satisfying series; oh, and let me not leave out SEXY." —Guilty Pleasures Book Reviews

"Well-written and with a great balance of dialogue and description." —Love Between the Sheets

"An emotionally charged, adrenaline-filled, steamy, and passionate read. . . . K. Bromberg deliver[s]." —TotallyBookedBlog

"This series is *everything* a true fan of romance would want or need." —Sinfully Sexy Book Reviews

"An intense, emotional, riveting ride [that's] sexy, romantic, heartbreaking, and uplifting. This is the kind of book you don't want to put down." —Aestas Book Blog

"K. Bromberg has created wonderful characters that you just can't help but fall in love with . . . beautifully written and a very emotional read." —Ramblings from This Chick

"K. Bromberg is nothing short of an absolute genius . . . so real and raw that you truly feel every single emotion." —Romance Addiction

"An irresistibly hot romance that stays with you long after you finish the book."
—*New York Times* bestselling author
Jennifer Armentrout

"Captivating, emotional, and sizzling hot!"
—*New York Times* bestselling author S. C. Stephens

Also by K. Bromberg

Slow Burn

Acknowledgments

This book was a labor of love that had to be completed in a very short time frame. It tested and pushed me, and there are most definitely a few people I need to acknowledge and thank for their encouragement while I wrote it.

To my family: Thank you so much for your endless support as I take this crazy ride.

For understanding when I'm frustrated or sleep deprived or for taking the kids for a bit so I can hit a word count or work through a plotline. I can't get back the moments I missed but I can make up for it with how much I love you all.

To the bloggers: Thank you so much for all of your support to make my books visible to readers. My success is due in part to you.

To my readers: You have shown me so much love and support that I'm overwhelmed most days. Without you, these books mean nothing. Thank you a thousand times over. I race you!

To my peers: Lauren, Laurelin, Pepper, Corinne, Whitney, E.K., J.E.M., Raine, M. Pierce, Claire, B.J., Katy, Adriana, Gail—thank you for the camaraderie, the ideas, the answers to my numerous questions, and most of all the friendship. No one understands this journey better than you guys, so it is nice to have like minds to speak with. A special thank-you to C. D. Reiss for the phone call that kicked my butt in gear when this book almost broke my confidence. I owe you one.

To S. C. Stephens, Samantha Towle, and Michelle Valentine: Thank you for allowing me to use your beloved rocker boys in *Sweet Ache*.

To Amy Tannenbaum: Thank you for your guidance

through this crazy minefield of publishing. I'm lucky to have you on my side.

To Kerry, Jessica, Erin, and the team at Penguin: Thank you for making my first foray into traditional publishing not too scary.

Prologue

"If you really want someone to manhandle your ass, I'm sure I could arrange for it to happen discreetly for you."

I whip my head up and choke on the M&M's I just swallowed. Did he really just say that? I meet Ben's unamused eyes staring from behind his glasses and he just raises his eyebrows. His out-of-character comment causes me to stutter, while Vince chuckles at my friend's dig.

"You're my lawyer—get me out of it." I shake my head and match him glare for glare. "Earn the big bucks you charge me. . . . Now, wouldn't that be something?"

I know I'm being an ass but I'm fed up with everything right now. The lyrics that won't come to complete the album, Ben sitting across from me daring me to tell him the truth so he can scold me like the kid I was when we first met years ago, and fucking Hunter and his bullshit that has me in this predicament.

Again. But this time with a helluva lot more on the line.

"You want to be an asshole, Hawkin? I can play that part real well too in case you've forgotten. How about you come clean? How about you make Hunter pay for his own mistakes and you stop risking everything you've worked so hard for?" He leans forward, props his elbows on the massive desk, and continues our visual pissing match over his folded hands. The truth in his words hangs heavy in the air between us.

"I told you—the jacket was mine." I grit my teeth on the lie. "I don't know how the blow got in the pocket. . . . Shit, I was drunk off my ass. I set it down for a few minutes—some groupie probably stuffed the baggy of the shit in there or something. I don't remember. Party got out of control, cops came, shook us all down, and it was *just there* in my pocket."

"You mean it was in Hunter's pocket."

This conversation needed to have ended like ten minutes ago. Or better yet, never have happened.

"Nah. It was me. People kept mixing us up all night long because we both had on jeans and dark T-shirts. My jacket, my pocket, my fault." End of story, Ben. Drop it.

My mind flashes back to the look Hunter gave me and the desperation in his voice as he tossed me his jacket when the cops came barging in. *"Please, Hawke. It's not mine. I swear. I can't go to jail for this stupid mistake. It'll kill Mom."*

"Convenient theory." He breaks through my thoughts and brings me back to the here and now. "But you're forgetting the simple fact that there are pictures from the party and not once were you wearing that jacket . . . but Hunter sure as hell was. Your martyrdom is admirable, but I still call bullshit," he says, leaning back, with contempt in his eyes.

And I hate putting it there, hate seeing the obvious disappointment and knowing that I'm letting him down, but I can't do what he's asking. I can't risk Hunter being locked up for the long haul under California's Three Strikes law for some stupid coke. Mom's health is bad enough as it is—losing her baby might just push her over the edge. Might be the last straw.

And besides, I don't go back on my promises.

Vince snickers again and Ben's eyes shift over to glare at him. "You think this is a fucking joke, Vinny?" Ben says, reminding Vince of the hoodlum punk he once was and the nickname he's distanced himself from as much as possible.

The laughter stops immediately, the tension ratchets up another notch, and their inherent dislike for each other rears its ugly head. "You want your boy here locked up? Your new album and tour to go to shit because he's getting some love in cell block G? Can't sing to the groupies then, now, can he?"

Vince sits forward in his chair and just shakes his head. I can see his anger vibrating beneath the surface, but thank fuck he reins it in, because I sure as hell don't need more to deal with.

"I know what's at stake, *Benji*. No one has to spell it out for me." He raises his eyebrows, the *come at me* taunt written all over his face.

"It was mine," I reassert to break the hold of our shared history and bring their attention back to the shit I need over and done with.

"I'm still not buying it. You ready to perjure yourself and have both you and Hunter end up in jail? Protecting your brother is one thing, but hell, Hawke, *you*," he says on a cough, and I sure as hell know he means Hunter, "were carrying enough grams to be charged with intent to sell. We're talking hard time here if you get convicted."

"I won't be convicted." I make the pronouncement with certainty, although internally doubt slithers into the cracks of my resolve.

"You said you'd never have a number-one single on Billboard either," he replies, eyebrows raised, "and I believe you're sitting on four of them in the last two years. . . . Never say never, Hawke."

"You made your fucking point, Ben. Now get off my case and quit passing judgment on me. I—"

"I'd love to get off your case. In fact, there shouldn't even be a fucking case because it should be Hunter and not you sitting here." The silence practically suffocates me as his eyes dare me to correct him. To confess I'm taking the rap for my brother.

I want to say fuck this shit, storm out, and go beat the hell out of Gizmo's drums until my arms are sore and my ears ring, but that won't fix a goddamn thing. Instead, I lean back in my chair and rest my head, eyes to the ceiling and fingers pinching the bridge of my nose.

I'd bet my ass that a judge isn't going to throw the book at me. There's no way.

"And before you sit there and start thinking that a judge

wouldn't give you hard time for your first real offense, think again."

How in the hell did Ben know what I was thinking? "Fuck that. I'm as clean-cut as they come besides the shit we all did as kids."

"You mean as clean-cut as rockers come, right? Because let's face it, the Abercrombie & Fitch look works in your favor, but you still have a documented press record of being the hotheaded rebel: club fights, paparazzi run-ins, a penchant for fast cars. . . ."

"And your point is what? Being hotheaded and being a fucking drug dealer are two different things, right?" Vince speaks up and shifts forward so his elbows rest on his knees. The guy would go to bat for me in a goddamn football game if I asked him to.

But of course so would Ben. At least my back is covered from all angles.

Then his comment about prison hits me again and I shudder at the thought of who else might want my back if I was to be convicted. Fuck me.

I blow out a frustrated breath and close my eyes, knowing I'm going to piss somebody off regardless of the decision I make. It sucks when doing what's right and what is required of you are two completely different things.

So let's add a few more people to disappoint to my list. Save Hunter and then possibly my mom and keep my promise, or let him sink, lose my integrity, but make everyone else happy?

But what makes me happy? None of the fucking above.

"True, but a judge would just love to make an example of that pretty face and your public status. The women screaming they want to have your babies may boost that ego of yours but they aren't going to do you an ounce of good influencing a judge on the length of your sentence."

Vince snorts beside me. "I wouldn't put it past his fangirls. . . . I'm sure a few would offer the judge their blow job services in order to save this asshole. Gives a whole new meaning to the phrase 'Meet me in my chambers,' right?"

I roll my head against the back of the chair to glare at him but he ignores me. And I know he's pissed, know he's fed up with Hunter's bullshit affecting me and in turn the band.

So I stare back at the ceiling, head and heart in conflict but only because I know this is wrong, that I'm just as guilty for enabling Hunter. Know that when I tell myself this is the last time I'm going to save his ass at the expense of mine that I have to really follow through.

Blood is thicker than water but you can still drown in it all the same.

I lift my head up and look at Ben again. "What are my options?" I refuse to talk about whether it was really me or not again for the umpteenth time. Subject's dead.

Ben twists his lips as he looks at me with confused disbelief over why I'm standing my ground but he shouldn't be, he knows my history. *"Man . . ."* He sighs in resignation. "I wish you'd reconsider, but I knew you weren't going to, so I spoke to some associates of mine who know the judge on your case and well . . . and there is a possibility . . ."

"A possibility? Dude, I need something concrete here," I tell him, glancing over at Vince, who's staring at Ben in anticipation of how he's going to fix the impossible situation.

"Well, the judge is an alumnus of USC and likes to make his status and success known by giving back to the school in unique ways."

He's fucking lost me here. What does this have to do with me? "And . . . ?"

"Well, my associates suggested that maybe if you agree to do a seminar about public media and the pressures on the modern-day public persona—"

"A seminar?" I swear to God Ben's lost his mind. Does he not remember that school was not my strong suit? Shit, I was so busy daydreaming about song lyrics and escaping into their notes, I never paid attention. Well, unless she had a short skirt, a tight top, and an appreciation for the backseat of my car. I sure as fuck paid attention then. "Like teach, lecture, whatever one class?"

"More like twelve classes," he deadpans and pushes the jar of chocolate across his desk, using my notorious sweet tooth to try to soften the blow.

"Hell no!" I say the same time Vince bursts out laughing hysterically like a goddamn hyena. Did Ben take the blow from evidence and get high? Because hell if he doesn't sound like it with that suggestion. School was a sour note played on an out-of-tune guitar to me, and now he wants me to teach?

Clearly Ben doesn't think our laughter is very funny, because he just sits and stares at me until our laughter dies down. He's just about to speak when the intercom on the desk beeps. "Yes, Jennifer?"

"Mr. Levine's here to hand deliver the contracts and wants a quick word with you if possible?"

"Tell him I'll be right there but I only have a minute because I'm with a client," Ben says as he rises from his chair, holding a hand up to me. "I'll be right back. It'll give you time to think this over . . . and you do need to, Hawke. You're in some serious shit here. Twelve lectures and you're in the judge's good graces, meaning the possibility of a lighter sentence if any at all." He buttons his suit jacket as he moves from behind the desk toward the door to his office. "Your options are limited: no band and jail time or teach the seminar and finish up the album."

He puts his hand on the door and turns to meet my eyes again. "Don't toss the idea. You need this, Hawke. If you're protecting Hunter to help your mom, what do you really think will happen to her if you're gone? The one person who's really looking out for her?" And with that he opens the door and leaves the room as I bite back the expletives I want to hurl at him.

"Fuck man!" I exhale the words once the door is shut, put my hands behind my head, and slouch back in the chair, his low blow hitting its mark dead on.

"Dude . . . you teaching? That's hilarious," Vince says, words interspersed with laughter. "Professor Play. Sounds like a bad stage name for a porno."

"Shut it, Vince." Even if I had any intention of saying yes, what the fuck would I talk about? I mean I'm sure the judge isn't looking for someone to lecture about the women who ask me to sign their tits or who hand me their panties as a proposition. I shove up out of the chair, needing to move, to chew over all of this.

"Well, if you're not sure what to do, man, I'd say you should just tell the truth and quit cleaning up Hunter's shit."

"I am telling the truth!" I grit the words out with my jaw clenched, hands fisted momentarily as I control my urge to punch the wall beside me. They need to stop making me repeat myself.

"Yeah. Uh-huh."

"Vince." It's the only warning I can give him because he's right, and I don't have anything else to convince him otherwise. He's my best friend for Christ's sake, knows me better than I know myself, and yet here I am, spinning a web of lies, hoping he can't see right through them.

"Look, do what you've gotta do, man. I'll stand behind you whatever you decide and for whatever your reasons but . . ." His voice trails off as my shoulders droop under the weight of the guilt I carry around with me like a second skin.

"But what?" I ask even though I already know the answer. "You're siding with Ben on this?" Fuck, if that's the case, I know he's serious.

"No, man, just siding with simple logic. We've all worked so damn hard for this. . . . It's all we've eaten, slept, or drank for the last ten years. To have Hunter almost lose it for us once and now possibly fuck it up when we're finally making a name for ourselves?" His voice breaks for a moment and I know there's more coming, know he has something else he wants to say and in typical Vince fashion is taking his sweet ass time getting to it. "I get and don't get all at the same time your loyalty to your brother, but fuck, man, what about your loyalty to us? To everything we have riding on you? What about letting us down?"

And of course he went in for the kill with that line.

"Yeah, no pressure or anything. Thanks," I say quietly, having no one to blame but myself for the drama swirling around me. I catch a glimpse of my reflection in the window and hate the person I see because once again, Hunter is getting exactly what he wants at my expense: big brother protecting little brother at all costs.

I just happen to think that this cost might break the bank in all senses of the meaning.

We're both quiet as I try to figure out my next step, my next chord, the next lyric in my life's song.

"Well, the bright side is that you'll be on a college campus, which means tons of fresh-faced college coeds for you to take your pick from, lure in with your pretty-boy smile, and then corrupt with your fucked-up ways." He turns to look at me for the first time and I see the plea in his eyes for me to do this, to take the offer to lecture. Throw the band a fucking bone when they've put their money on me while I'm busy trying to use mine to save my brother. "We missed this rite of passage being on the road so much, might as well take advantage of it while you can, right?"

When I run a hand through my hair, I catch a glimpse of the tattoo on the inside of my wrist. A treble clef and an okodee. My ever-present reminder of where I came from and what I need to do to get where I want to go.

If I'm honest with myself, I already know what I'm going to do despite the reluctance and my irritation at having a decision to even make.

If I thought it would fool him, I'd put on my stage face to convince him of my absolute certainty about going forward with this but we've been friends for way too long and have been through way too much shit together for me to pull one over on him. I infuse enthusiasm in my voice anyway.

Fake it until you make it. Sounds about fucking par for the course to me.

"I do love the classy, intelligent type," I murmur.

"Who the fuck are you kidding?" Vince says, relief in his voice since he knows my comment is my way of telling him I'm going to do it. Sell myself to save everyone else. "If they have a pussy, they're your type."

I can't fight the smile on my face. "True but dude, give me some credit here. You make me sound like I'll play with any kitty that wants to be petted."

He raises an eyebrow, a smirk of amusement on his lips. "This being said from the ringmaster of his own three-ring Cirque du Pussy."

"You're so wrong." I laugh at our long-running joke about lead singers and their inherent draw for female fans. And thank fuck I'm on the lucky end of that deal. I'd best be happy that doing this seminar will keep me on the other end of the microphone instead of the wrong end of a jail cell. I roll my shoulders and feel the weight of the decision I've made begin to lessen some as the idea settles. Shaking my head, I walk back to the chair beside him and just stand there as I meet his eyes. I never doubt my decisions so I'm not quite sure why I'm doing it now.

"This is the right thing to do, right?" And I'm not sure if I'm talking about covering for Hunter or agreeing to do the seminar when I throw out the question, but he doesn't ask. He just nods his head with unwavering support when he reads the turmoil in my eyes.

"Prison or pussy? Sounds like an easy decision if you ask me."

Chapter 1

"Whoever thought to put a race in wine country sure as hell knew what they were doing." I take a sip of wine and glance over to meet my sister-in-law Rylee's amused gaze.

"They did indeed," she agrees, a laugh falling from her lips that sounds slightly on the giggly side, making me believe she's riding the road to tipsy right beside me.

I lean my head back to appreciate the unprecedented cool breeze in the Sonoma valley mixed with the sun's warmth on my face. It's a welcome feeling compared to the endless hours in the classroom that wait for me in the coming weeks. Fluorescent lights, tedious hours researching for my dissertation, and the always draining sessions where I fulfill my teaching assistant duties loom on my mental calendar.

So I enjoy this, appreciate the downtime to spend with my family here at Colton's race before I return to the crazy schedule of my graduate studies. An engine hums in the distance, the reverberation vibrating in my chest and the wine in my glass, as it approaches our location.

I lift my head back up just in time to see Rylee's head snap to the left when my brother's car moves past pit row, easing with a skilled finesse around the road course where we're currently sitting in the infield. Her relaxed features immediately pull tight as she watches Colton's open-wheel Indy car navigate the turns of the course until he goes out of sight again.

"Still worry you?" I ask her although I know the answer since the sight of him in the car makes my heart pound with anxiety despite the amount of times I've sat and watched him. Because regardless of how many times he's crossed the finish line safe and sound, it's the one time he didn't that still holds my heart hostage. The crash when we almost lost him.

"Yes and no," she says, a soft smile spreading on her lips, the love for my pain-in-the-ass brother evident there. "Yes because of the nature of what he does. The speed he goes. No because he loves it. I can't tell him not to do what he's so passionate about."

And it's as simple as that. Incredible that he found someone who could handle his flaws and soften all his hard edges.

Someday. Way far off I'll find a person like that . . . but romance is not on my current horizon.

"You deserve a medal for putting up with his shit," I tease her, our long-running joke causing her to laugh again.

"He has his merits," she teases in return, her words reinforcing the affectionate smile on her lips and love written across her face. "So what about you? How's things in the man department?"

I roll my eyes with a sigh. "I've written off men for a while."

She snorts out a laugh. "Uh-huh." She looks over her wineglass, eyebrows raised, eyes telling me to talk.

"I'm the furthest thing from a doormat—"

"You can say that again!" She laughs.

I just shake my head, wondering why if that's the reaction I get from her, why does every man I choose treat me like one. "It's just too much work, honestly. You know me—I want some fun. I want some good sex. I just don't think the cliché 'happily ever after' is for me."

"Well, sometimes, right in the middle of everyday life, love gives you a fairy tale when you least expect it." Of course she thinks that way after the way her courtship with my brother has turned out.

But she's not me.

"I doubt it in my case," I say, "but I've been kissing a whole helluva lot of frogs if it is." My mind flickers to my last few boyfriends and how I've been completely blindsided by the shit they've pulled. It's almost as if the easier sex is to get, the harder love is to find for me.

"Well, I guess I'm not one to give advice since I was told to have some wild, reckless sex with a guy and look where that landed me." She smiles as she holds up her hand and wiggles her ring finger, the diamond reflecting the sun and sending prisms sparkling all around us.

Our laughter is drowned out as Colton loops back around the track. The noise of the engine fades, and I'm just about to speak when I hear someone knock on the door of our observation booth.

"Well, if it isn't Quinlan Westin." The voice sends a slight thrill mixed with irritation through me.

I meet Ry's eyes briefly, and her lips fight to hold back the knowing smile as she stands. She's heard some of the heated discussions between Colton and me over Luke and his determination to take me out. She's even intervened a few times to explain that just because they competed for the same girl way back when doesn't make him a bad guy. Her comments fell on deaf, testosterone-plugged ears.

"Hey, Luke," she says, tone void of any kind of hospitality. "I was just going to find my glass slipper. Excuse me." The expression in her gaze tells me she's escaping to save herself the drama that will ensue when Colton finds out he sought us out.

Smart lady.

I on the other hand couldn't care less what Colton thinks of Luke Mason because I have my own opinions. I'm just still trying to figure out what they are but, hell, if his persistence isn't admirable in trying to get a date from his archnemesis's baby sister.

He must have balls the size of cantaloupes walking in here and purposely poking the sleeping bear. I have to give him some credit though—he never fails to find me at the track, never neglects to ask one more time even though he knows the answer is going to be a resounding no.

As I turn to face him I can't help the hitch of my breath

at the sight of him leaning against the doorjamb, black and silver fire suit unzipped and sleeves tied around his waist. The plain white T-shirt he wears is that perfect combination of not too tight and not too loose to give just the right hint of the corded muscles underneath. Can't say the man doesn't wear clothing well.

And I'm sure when they're off he wears what's beneath even better. Too bad I won't be finding out.

"Well, if it isn't Luke Mason," I mimic him. A slow, lopsided grin spreads across his face, and as All-American, boy-next-door handsome as he is, nothing stirs inside me. Hell yes he's as good-looking as they come but something that pretty needs a bit of a rough edge to him to attract me, and all I see and hear from him are smooth lines.

He takes one step into the room and both of our eyes reflect the appreciation for our mutual attraction. "Gorgeous as ever." He says the words like he's testing them, trying to sense if this time around my interest is piqued more than with his numerous other attempts.

"Thank you but the answer is still no." I say it with a smile, but I might as well head this off at the pass. No need to beat around the bush when he's going to get there eventually.

He chokes out a laugh, his reaction causing my smile to widen. "Pretty presumptuous when I don't believe I asked you anything."

"Just because you didn't speak doesn't mean you weren't asking with your eyes." I raise my eyebrows at him, my own eyes speaking for me as well.

He shakes his head very subtly, and exasperation resonates in his sigh. "Good to know you think so highly of yourself that you think I'll keep coming back for your punishment." His smirk tells me he's joking but there's still the question in his eyes. "Well, now that that's out of the way," he says, leaning his shoulder on the wall beside where I sit, "how are you doing, Q?"

I shot him down, again, and he's standing here like a champ. The optimism is commendable. "I'm good and you? How's the car running?"

He looks out toward Colton's car as it approaches and passes by once again, speaking when the noise of the engine abates into the distance. "Fast," he muses. "Fast enough to beat him."

I snort and raise my eyebrows. "Luke, I do believe you just insulted my brother."

"Not in the least darling." He winks at me and normally that would creep me out but for some reason it's charming on him. "If I were to insult your brother, you'd most definitely know it from my word choice alone. . . ."

"So noted," I say, our eyes continuing the flirtation without words, and I find myself questioning why even though he's attractive, the chemistry is a few beakers short of the right formula for anything to reach combustion. I sigh, knowing he's waiting to see where I go with this conversation so I figure, fuck it, might as well. "How's your girlfriend doing?"

His lips curl up on one side; his eyes dance with mirth. "Well, she's refusing to go on a date with me even though I've asked her seven different ways from Sunday, but I'll keep at it and let you know when she finally says yes."

Shit, I walked right into that one didn't I? "She must not know what she's missing then," I offer up.

"Hm, I'd say she's missing about ten thick inches but you never know, it might be too much for a girl like her to handle."

Cocky bastard. I keep my face impassive while my mind wonders how much he's exaggerating—or if he is at all—and make sure my eyes don't drift down and give him the satisfaction of knowing that I'm even curious.

"Well there's your problem Mason," I say as I rise from my position. Colton's car veers down pit row, and I'm relieved and annoyed that our conversation is coming to an end. "The digits you should be talking about are the ones to call her with. A woman knows when a man talks in inches he's only doing so to boost his ego. We always assume we need to cut the number by half," I lie and then return the wink he gave me as I walk past him and head to the door, fighting two urges, the one to look and see if he is indeed packing all those inches and the other to not burst out laughing from the look on his face in reaction to my bald-faced lie.

"Well, if we're playing by your rules, I should have told you it was twenty, then."

I hear him stifle a chuckle behind me and am glad that he's not getting his dick in a twist over my verbal dis. I descend the stairs to the infield heading toward the garages where I know the rest of my family will be to greet and shoot the shit with Colton when he gets out of the car as is our usual custom as of late. Luke's boots echo off the metal steps right behind me, and I'm curious just how much he's willing to tempt fate by following me.

He falls in step beside me in silence but the sounds and sights of time trials for pole position filter in all around us. "Hey, Quin?" he says as we approach the mechanic bays.

"Hey, Luke?" I mimic him again.

"What do you say you come join me for a victory celebration tomorrow night?" He angles his head to the side and waits for my answer.

And I can't resist, he's making it too damn easy. "You're throwing Colton a victory party? How sweet of you!" He snorts out in disbelief and runs a hand through his cropped hair. I place my hand on his chest momentarily. "Thanks for the laugh and the walk down but—"

"I know, I know," he says, raising his hands in surrender and taking a step back. "Can't fault a guy for trying."

I can hear Colton talking to Becks a few yards away, something about wing adjustments and lap times and although Colton's preoccupied, I prefer for the peace to be kept and punches to remain unthrown.

"I think it's best for your sake if you vacate the premises before my brother notices you're here."

"Ah see, true love. You're looking out for me, but in case you forgot," he says, pointing to his name on his fire suit, "I have every right to be here."

I purse my lips and hold his gaze. "Well, not exactly here," I reply, pointing to the yellow line denoting the garage boundaries for each race team.

He takes a step back so that his toes are just to the edge of the painted delineation and looks back to me with a smirk on his face. "Better?"

"Much," I say as we hold each other's stares a bit longer. I flick my hands at him in a shooing motion. "Now quit causing trouble and go." I love the fact that he doesn't react right away, that he has a mind of his own and isn't going to let me persuade him. Maybe there are some rough edges to him after all. Food for thought.

"I love causing trouble. In fact I'd love to stick around and watch your big, bad brother protect you from the likes of me," he says, and pulls at his shirt, which is beginning to stick to the middle of his chest from the heat sweltering off the asphalt track. I watch the movement and let my eyes drift down to the crotch of his race suit and hate myself for looking and still wondering.

And I curse the race suit for being so damn baggy.

"I can take care of myself just fine. No need for my brother's help," I tell him, challenge in my voice and amusement in my eyes.

Luke works his tongue in his cheek. "Well, since your brother doesn't factor in, there's nothing standing in the way so why won't you go out with me?"

"Because arrogant race car drivers aren't my type." Maybe that will dissuade him.

"Well, since I'm more of the good-looking, financially stable, athletic type, I guess I'm golden." His smile widens, proud of his answer.

"Far from it. I'd say more like silver." I squint my eyes looking at the metallic color of his race suit as he steps toward me no longer blocking the sunlight and with blatant disregard for the line at his feet.

"Oh believe me, Quinlan, as long as it's hard as metal, that's all that matters," he says, suggestion lacing his voice.

Did he really just say that? "Jesus. That right there is exactly why I've rejected you the other forty-two times you've asked me."

"Well shit, I'm on number forty-three, so next time you'll say yes."

"Um, no," I say with finality, but I can't help the appreciation from coming through in my tone.

"Oh, Westin, I have your number, baby." He takes a step back, and I glance back down to the line he's cleared and smirk. "Actually, you don't."

He laughs deep and loud and I know Colton will have heard it. Thanks a lot. "You're right. I only have the number twenty but," he says with a shrug, "I'm sure you'd be willing to work with that. Later, Quinlan."

"Later, Luke," I tell him as he turns his back and starts to walk away.

"One of these days you're going to say yes," he calls over his shoulder.

"No I'm not."

"Yes you are," he says one final time, causing me to laugh and wish I did feel something between us because hell if his unrelenting effort isn't attractive in itself. Shit, it would be fun to take him up on the offer if not to just piss Colton off. Hm. Maybe I'll do just that next time.

"What the fuck did he want?"

Then again, maybe I won't. Not worth the trouble.

I turn to find Colton leaning against the wall, Gatorade in hand, fire suit unzipped, and chest grossly plastered with sweat.

"Um, you're married now. You don't need to flex your chest to try to get women anymore. It's nasty." Distraction at its finest.

"Didn't have to try to get them before," he says, emphasizing his point with the flash of a grin.

I just roll my eyes, first Luke and now my brother. I most definitely do not need to date a race car driver.

"You had to work to get me," Rylee says as she walks up behind him and swats him on the butt.

He laughs and places a soft kiss on her lips. She pushes him away when he tries to take the kiss further. "You see that?" Colton says, tone playful. "Married for a year and she's already starting to reject me."

"You poor baby," I mock.

"So did you say yes?" Rylee asks with a lift of her chin motioning to where Luke walked away.

Thanks, Rylee. I thought I was off the hook, but I guess not.

"Of course she didn't say yes. My little sister is not going out with that asshole," Colton says, toggling his head back and forth between us.

I've never understood what the big deal is. Luke and Colton went after the same woman. Colton won, big deal. Well, and then Luke threw a few punches because of it . . . and maybe, perhaps he let a bit of the hostility transfer over to the track a time or two.

"Cool it, Ace," she says with a raise of her brows, beating me to the punch. "She can go out with anyone she wants. You're not her keeper."

I can see the muscle pulse in my brother's clenched jaw as Rylee stands her ground with him—she's the only person besides his best friend, Becks, and our dad who can.

"He's an arrogant ass!" he spouts off, mouth agape like we're both crazy.

"I seem to know someone else who was just as arrogant and just as good-looking," she teases, holding her ground.

I can't fight my smirk from spreading into a full-blown grin from Rylee's comment that is right on target. Becks summons Colton to come over toward the car. He looks at me with the stern big-brother, *don't fuck with me* look. It's kind of cute.

And annoying.

"Relax! I told him no." The pronouncement earns me a flash of a grin before he pecks a kiss on Rylee's cheek.

He starts to walk away and then stops and turns back. "Keep it that way," he warns before continuing over to Becks.

Rylee tsks out a sound as she follows something over my shoulder, and I turn to see Luke walking farther down the pits. He flashes me a grin before continuing into a building.

"You can't deny that he is definite eye candy." My neck hurts from the sudden whiplash at her words. "Oh come on, Quin, I may be married but I'm not dead." She shrugs. "Don't act like you wouldn't see how many licks it takes to get to the center of his Tootsie Pop."

And she says the comment so matter of factly I just burst out laughing. I swear to God all of the hormones she's been taking to try to get pregnant have affected her usually demure manner.

"He wishes," I say, still laughing.

"Well, he is persistent. You've got to give him that."

"That's all I'm giving him."

Chapter 2

The Southern California heat mixed with the second week of school has really done a number on me. I'm ready to melt into the cool air-conditioning of the Fine Arts offices as I pull open the door, tired from a late night hanging out with Layla—my fault but still aggravating nonetheless—and having had to deal with some dipshit undergrads in the teaching assistant session I just came from didn't help matters.

Generally I don't mind if a student doesn't get a concept. I have no problem helping them so that they understand. But when the students are too busy chasing skirts and worrying about who the Trojans take on this weekend to listen, it's not my problem they received bad marks on their first pop quiz.

And it's not helping my mood that I need to get laid something fierce. And not by my own hand. There's nothing worse than a woman in need of a good orgasm.

Or two.

Or three.

I drop my backpack on the counter with a sudden resolve to rectify the situation with the first willing candidate who meets my discriminating standards. Then again I'm on the verge of being desperate enough that I might throw them out of the window for the right mistake.

I start rifling through the bazillion pieces of paper stuffed in my mailbox—such is the life of a graduate student in the Cinematic Arts. Shit, save a tree people, use e-mail. I automatically toss the ones about elective seminars into the recycle bin without even reading them because at the beginning of a semester the last thing I have time for is something that does nothing to further help me write my dissertation.

"Quinlan! Just the person I wanted to see!"

As I turn around to face my graduate adviser, the smile comes naturally to my face since I'm one of the select few fortunate enough to be under her tutelage. "Hi, Dr. Stevens." She gives me a stern look that causes me to laugh at the formality of my greeting, so I cave to her oft-repeated request and correct myself. "Hi, Carla."

"Better." She laughs the word out. "Now, I'm not looking for my husband when you say that," she says, referring to her spouse, who is a cardiologist.

I nod my head in agreement. "Why do I have the feeling that I'm not going to like the fact that you wanted to see me?"

Please God don't let her ask me to add something else to my already overflowing plate full of obligations, deadlines, and drafts I need to write.

"I'm kind of in a jam and I need your help." She scrunches up her nose like she knows I'm not going to be too happy with what she's going to say next. "Like I'll give you a three-week extension on your first draft due date kind of help."

I worry my bottom lip between my teeth and know that no matter what she asks, I'll say yes. She's my mentor for God's sake. Anything not to disappoint her. "Okay?" I draw the word out into a question, fearful and curious all at the same time.

"Well, Dr. Elliot has brought in someone for a seminar that is starting"—she looks down at her watch and winces—"well, it started about five minutes ago actually. Anyway, he's asked if I can help him. His TA, Callie, was supposed to do it, but she had a last-minute schedule change to accommodate one of her professors . . . and all of his other teaching assistants have classes right now. . . ."

I bite back the urge to make a smart-ass comment about how Callie's conflict is the need to flirt ridiculously with the professor she has the hots for, university protocol be damned. Instead I look at Carla and blow out an audible breath, certain that my expression reflects my displeasure.

I'm usually on top of all of the department's goings-on but my last-minute trip to the Sonoma race to watch Colton mixed with playing bestie to nurse Layla through her unexpected breakup and the usual first month of school discord has left me in the dark about course specifics. It had better be a damn good class if I'm going to have to be stuck sitting through it.

"You know I'm agreeing to this because I'm already behind on my draft and need those weeks, right?"

"Exactly!" She smirks. "I don't have that PhD behind my name for nothing."

"That's low." I just shake my head as I reach over to grab my bag. "So give me the details."

"You're a lifesaver!" She reaches out and pats my shoulder. "So the seminar is on sex, drugs, and rock and roll in a manner of speaking." She quirks her eyebrows up, asking if I'm okay with that.

Like I have a choice. I can just imagine some stiff professor giving a seminar about something so completely foreign to him. Now I'm going to have to waste my time mollycoddling someone when I have so many other things that would be a better use of my time. Sounds like a real *barn burner*.

"Who's teaching it?" I ask, my tone reflecting the cynicism I feel over the contradiction between teacher and subject.

"A guest lecturer. I forget his name but he's a member of some popular band." She rolls her eyes. Her musical taste includes only classical music and jazz. "Oh and he's cute," she says with a smile and then cuts me off before I can ask her any more details. "Now shoo—he's probably mangling the sound system as we speak. Microphone on upside down or something. Class is in the GFA building, room sixty-nine."

Mentally I roll my eyes at the room number, thinking how something else that number represents would be a much better way to occupy my time than listening to a monotone oration. And I wonder how big of a name he can really be if Carla's worried the he has his mic on upside down.

I shake my head one more time and sling my bag over my shoulder. "Thank you Quinlan," she says in a saccharine sweet tone that makes me laugh.

"Just so you know, I'm cursing you right now," I say over my shoulder as I open the door and begin the journey across campus.

I'm winded, hotter than hell, and cussing out Carla even more by the time I reach the closed door of the lecture hall. When I pull it open and step into the lobby, I can hear laughter from the students beyond the open theater doors.

Two coeds exit the bathroom across the foyer from me, both way overdressed for students attending a lecture, and one is applying lipstick while the other giggles uncontrollably. They walk past me and I hear hushed comments about how they "just had to see for themselves" if he's as hot in person and "damn security for kicking them out" before they push through the doors I've just entered

My curiosity is now definitely piqued. Who the hell is the guest lecturer if there is security here?

Maybe it's one of Dad's friends. Stranger things have happened.

"So you see, it was the Grammys—it's not like you can say no to him when he just won album of the year and asks you to hang out. Little did I know," the male voice says in a low tenor that's almost a contradiction: smooth like velvet but with a rasp that pulls at my libido and makes me think of bedroom murmurs and hot sex, "that I'd go with him and walk into a private club where everything is laid out like candy—drugs, women, record producers. He turned to me and said, 'Welcome to Hollywood, son.' Shit, I looked at Vince here and thought is this what I have to do to make it here? Play this game? Or can I do this the old-fashioned way? And I don't mean sleep my way to the top either."

The room erupts into laughter with a few whistles as I clear the doorway. I recognize him immediately. He may be on the stage at a distance but his face, his presence, is unmistakable. I've seen it gracing tabloids. *TMZ*, *Rolling Stone*—you name it, he's been on their cover.

He's Hawkin Play, front man and lead singer of the highly popular rock band *Bent*.

And according to his most recent press coverage, a man on the path to a drug-fueled destruction. So that exaggeration most likely means he was caught in possession of some drugs.

Why in the hell is he here?

I walk farther into the auditorium and falter at the top of the steps because just as my ears are attuned to his voice, my body reacts immediately to the overpowering sight of him.

And I sure as hell don't want it to.

I tell myself it's just because I need some action. That my battery-operated boyfriend is getting old and the visceral reaction of my racing pulse or the catch in my breath is just from my dry spell. Well, not really a complete dry spell per se, but rather a lack of toe-curling, mind-numbing, knock-you-on-your-ass sex that I haven't been able to find lately. It's the good lays that are hard to come by.

Don't even think about it. He may be hot, but shit, I grew up with Colton, the ultimate player, so this girl knows what a player sounds and acts like. And from everything I've seen splashed across headlines and social media, Hawkin plays the part to perfection.

But the notion that just like the drug rumors blasted across the magazines, his reputation as a player could be manufactured just as easily lingers in my subconscious. I stare at him again as the class laughs, his ease in front of a large crowd more than apparent, and I immediately wonder if I had a chance with him if I'd take it.

What is wrong with me? My head says to stop thinking thoughts like that, things that are never going to happen, while my body is telling my legs to *open wide*.

I force myself away from thinking such ludicrous thoughts and focus instead on finding a seat in the room packed full of coeds. I begin walking slowly down the aisles, glancing back and forth to try to find an open spot but there's not a single one available.

I glance forward to see a beefy guy walking toward me with an irritated expression on his face. It immediately hits me that I have nothing to prove I should be in this class, no paper, nothing to show to the security that appears to be bearing down on me that I'm not a fangirl and have a legitimate reason for attending the lecture. Well, maybe they'll kick me out and then he won't have a TA for the day.

Just one less class I'll have to sit through. And one less asshole I'll have to deal with.

He approaches me and reaches out a very muscular arm toward me. "Course paperwork?" He asks in a hushed whisper, trying to not disrupt whatever Mr. Rock Star at the front of the class is babbling on and on about.

I take in a deep breath, trying to figure how I'm going to play this. What I really want to do and what I know is right are two different things so I suck it up and take the higher road.

Reluctantly.

"I don't have anything," I whisper back. "But I'm the TA for the course."

"Sure you are." He chuckles with a roll of his eyes. "TA doesn't stand for tits and ass, honey."

I clench my jaw, reining in my frustration as we begin to draw the attention of those around us. "I just came from the department offices; I don't have —"

"Is there a problem, Axe?" His liquid sex of a voice booms across the room, causing all of the heads in the room to whip over toward us on the stairway.

Axe, I presume, turns his body to look back at Hawkin, which opens up his line of sight to see me.

"No problem," Axe says and before he can say anything else, Hawke speaks again.

"So nice of you to show up on time." Sarcasm drips from his voice, and my eyes snap up to meet his despite the distance between us.

And I swear I hate everything about myself right now because I feel a jolt to my system and quick bang of lust between my thighs as our eyes connect and that slow, I'm-a-god-you-can-bow-before-me smile curls up one side of his mouth.

And damn it to hell if that doesn't make him look even sexier.

But good looks sure as hell don't make him any less of an asshole.

My own lips pull into a tight, scowling grimace, thoughts firing but the damn words don't come because I'm still momentarily frozen by whatever just ricocheted between us.

"Well at least you're quiet, huh? Not one to disrupt unless you count arguing with Axe on the stairs."

How did I know he was going to be a prick? "I wasn't arguing. I'm not a—"

"Look," he says, cutting me off. "There's one seat left and it's right here." He points to a space right in front of the lectern when a man hurriedly stands and vacates it. I watch the occupant stroll to the side of the room and turn to lean his back against the wall, arms crossed, grin wide, as all the while he shakes his head at Hawkin like they have a private joke between them.

He seems vaguely familiar but I don't get a chance to figure it out because Hawkin speaks to me again. "C'mon now. I don't bite—right guys?" He says to the rest of the lecture hall and the audience erupts in a cacophony of hoots and hollers egging me on to go take the seat.

I also hear a few offers from the females that they'll take the seat if I don't.

I'm sure they would. Particularly a seat that's astride his hips if my hunch is right.

"Please, take your time. We like waiting." His voice floats through the room but grates on my nerves.

I grit my teeth as I move reluctantly, my anger escalating with each step I descend toward the front of the room. As much as I don't want to be here, dealing with the likes of a cocky asshole like him, my graduate career does have requirements, and I really don't think pissing off who I have a feeling will be one of the most popular lecturers of the year is the brightest idea.

But hell if I don't want to tell him to kiss my ass with that smart mouth of his while I stride up the steps toward the exit and flip him the bird instead.

But my degree is more important so I swallow my pride along with my anger, even though I'd much rather verbalize it as I reach the front row. Keeping my eyes fastened to his, I refuse to let him think he's gotten the upper hand despite me following his directive and taking the seat he so *graciously* offered.

I reach the seat and stop before I sit down and stand my ground, my eyebrows arched and eyes telling him everything my lips can't. He meets them challenge for challenge while all the while those lips of his smirk and taunt me.

I force my eyes to remain forward, not to wander and take in the whole of him because I don't want to see how sexy-hot he is face-to-face, don't want to notice his cologne that makes me think of fresh air with a subtle hint of musk, don't want to feel my cheeks flush because I know my nipples just hardened and I'm quite sure they're more than obvious through the thin layer of my bra's lace and my cotton T-shirt.

After a moment, when I know I have no point I can really make in front of several hundred students, I lower my eyes and take my seat. But instead of continuing on right away, he stands in front of me a few seconds more, making sure I know who won this ridiculous little show of control between us.

And of course as he stands in front of me with his hips right at my eye level, I can't help the two thoughts colliding: the one of him being in control with the one of just how well his worn denim jeans are filled out behind that button fly of his.

I immediately chastise myself. Tell myself that it's my sex-deprived brain—well, more like other deprived body parts—that is directing my thoughts like a nympho. And that alone fuels my dislike of Hawkin even more because I should be focused on being pissed off at him rather than wondering about how he performs in *other ways* . . . off the stage.

I'm pulled from my thoughts when laughter erupts in the room and I realize he's continued on with his spiel and is no longer in front of me.

"Isn't that right?" he asks and the classroom falls quiet causing me to glance his way.

His eyes are locked on mine and I know I've been caught not paying attention. His tongue darts out to lick his bottom lip as he waits for my response and I swear to all things holy when the girl next to me actually sighs. It takes everything I have not to roll my eyes. I have no clue what he's asking me and make that split-second decision between faking it or playing it off.

"What's that?" I reply, lips pursed, telling him if he wants to keep this game up, I'll play it right back.

He flashes me a bright smile and angles his head to the side for a moment, eyes narrowing momentarily before he delivers, "That being late for an event is a surefire way to make a bad first impression."

Bastard. I walked right into that one and I silently fume over it but hell if I'm going to let him know it. "True," I say with a measured nod of my head, his eyes dancing with mirthful victory when I continue. "It is better to stay silent and be thought a fool, than to open one's mouth and remove all doubt." I recite the proverb to him, expecting his brow to furrow and irritation to flicker across his face, but instead of anger in his eyes I see amusement, challenge.

The crowd falls silent, probably a tad shocked that I'm not bowing down to the rock god who I'm sure is used to getting anything he wants. But I grew up in a room next door to my brother and with the famed director Andy Westin as my father so I more than anyone know that I will not be getting anywhere near my knees to bow for Hawkin Play.

Or do anything else on them for that matter when it comes to him.

He just shakes his head, a curious look on his face before a student calls out a question across the oppressive silence we've created. He turns to face the fellow student and luckily leaves our unspoken sparring match unresolved.

I'm furious at him for calling me out again, and at the same time amused by his arrogance that he thinks I care. Risking a glance his way now that his focus is elsewhere, I take the chance to stare at and scrutinize him. I have to pay attention and figure him out if I'm going to try to get the upper hand here. I mean, it's *purely out of curiosity*. Good-looking guys are a dime a dozen in California.

But not all of them are rock stars that cause that tingly ache I have from simply imagining what he'd be like in bed.

His physique is lean, medium build with broad shoulders, but I can tell the muscles beneath are toned. Of course he takes the moment I'm watching him to raise his arm and point to someone, gifting me a flex of his biceps and the hint of a tattoo on the upper part of his arm hidden by his shirt.

And I'm a girl that has a thing for firm biceps, especially when they are framing my body on the mattress beneath me.

I trail him as he walks back toward the podium, taking in his profile, strong jaw, straight nose, and hair a little on the long side but somehow styled into a messy disarray that says *I didn't try to do this*. He fiddles with the overhead projector, the school's setup for it much more complicated than necessary. He continues on, speaking of something in regard to media expectations—a part of me curious what he's talking about because I've been so focused on not liking him and at the same time studying him I haven't followed a single word of his lecture.

The man leaning against the wall whose seat I took chuckles loud enough that the first few rows can hear him and it takes me a second to realize that Hawkin can't get the projector to turn on.

Serves him right. I sit in my chair and tuck my tongue in my cheek, refusing to help and enjoying watching him fumble. If he's going to call me out like he did, then I guess I'll act like a student and feign technological ignorance.

"And this folks is why I sing and play an instrument for a living," he says with a half laugh, brushing his hair off his forehead, his charismatic charm coming across even when he's frustrated. "Guess my reputation proceeds me and I'm too much to handle since the TA I was promised has yet to show and help me set everything up."

"I'll handle you!" a girl in the back yells, garnering a chuckle from him.

I'm sure you will, sweetie.

I watch him a few more moments until he gives up and says something I can't hear to his friend before turning to the class. "Well, I guess I'll have to rely on my many other hidden talents," he says rubbing his hands together and causing me to sigh like the girl next to me while the rest of the students chuckle, "but it seems they'll have to wait until next time. . . . Time's up for today." The sigher next to me makes a sound of protest, and I swear she's going to be stuck to the seat she's so desperate for all things Hawkin.

"Until next time," he says and students begin to shuffle their papers. I lean forward to pick up my bag when his voice stops me. "Ms. I'm-Too-Special-to-Be-on-Time? Please stay a minute."

I freeze more from disbelief than because I care. Seems to me by his arrogance that this whole I'm-a-professor kick has gone to his head. Then again, this is probably his norm, considering he's used to performing on stage in front of thousands.

I bite the inside of my cheek to stifle the smart-ass remark that is begging for escape, and lean back in the chair, arms and legs crossed, and raise my eyebrows at him. Come at me rocker boy. I'm ready for you.

Hawkin holds my taunting gaze, and I feel like we're on a playground having a staring contest. Guess things don't change much when you get older.

He leans his hips back on the table behind him and mirrors my posture. "Hey, blondie, what's your name?"

"Trixie," I tell him off the cuff. My mind immediately went to the name Layla and I use in a club when we're being hit on by someone we have no interest in.

"Trixie, huh?"

"Says so on my birth certificate. Is there something you needed?"

"Yeah," he says pushing his way off the table and walking toward me. My god, even his swagger across the short distance is sexy. He stops right in front of me and just stares. Chemistry I don't want to feel ignites between us.

You keep telling yourself that you don't want to feel that, Quinlan.

I look away, breaking whatever draw he continues to have over me. The one I don't want to feel. I just need to get out of here before those eyes of his and that cocky grin wear me down until I'm lying on my back with him above me. And thankfully he speaks because his words help all of those thoughts from finding purchase inside my mind.

"So was the lecture bad or something?" He angles his head and for some reason his body language does not reflect the simple question he asks. I won't walk right into his verbal trap of sarcasm again so I look back to him, eyebrows arched, fingers drumming on my bicep, waiting for him to continue. "Are you too cool to take notes?"

"Lecture about something noteworthy, and I'd be glad to take some," I fire back. And yes it's an unfair response because I barely listened to his lecture at all, more focused on ignoring him than anything, but he deserves it for his comment.

"Ooh," he says, bringing his hand to his heart like I've wounded him before flashing a lightning-fast grin. "I've got a soft spot for a woman who's beautiful *and* quick with her tongue."

I snort in exasperation. "Well, I'm sure you have the *soft* part down pat but I thought a guy like you'd prefer a woman without a brain or better yet, no teeth."

Hawkin's friend whistles to the side of us, but I ignore him, not needing any more of a distraction than what is in front of me. I rise from my seat and start throwing my stuff in my bag knowing that me and my smart mouth need to get up and leave before they get me in more trouble than normal.

"You think you have me pegged, huh?" His voice murmurs too close for comfort behind me. My body reacts instantly: goose-bumped skin, hitched breath, and my every nerve attuned to the proximity of his body.

Then again, trouble can be so much fun.

I can tell he's used to women begging to be played and hell if that's an option here. Chemistry or no chemistry, I'm smart enough to know he's one of those guys I need to steer clear of.

And I plan on doing just that. Marching up these steps and back to the department office to tell Carla that assisting this seminar is just too much for my class load. That even with the extension of time she'll give me on my thesis, it's still not enough. I'm sure she'll see right through the lie, know something is up, but will never question me on it.

But before I go . . .

"I know I have you pegged," I say with a small laugh as I throw my bag over my shoulder carelessly, silently hoping he is close enough to me that he gets hit by it. "And you sure as hell are proving me right."

"Oh, I can be all kinds of right, Trixie," he says as I turn around to find him still way too close. It's just a moment really but with our bodies so close and our eyes burning into each other's the pang of desire between my thighs turns into a full-blown ache.

I sidestep away from him immediately, hating the jump in my pulse and the lust coursing through me. I need to get out of here, away from him and his arrogant smirk and his *come fuck me* eyes.

"You were late," he states matter-of-factly as I begin to walk toward the stairs. "Don't let it happen again."

His taunting dare causes my foot to falter on the first step, my quick temper getting the best of me. I turn around and stride back toward him, stopping only when I'm well within his personal space. "No worries there. Must be nice, though. . . . Stroll in here, act like a wannabe teacher for a few lectures, and that power trip you seem to be needing gets an unwarranted boost for that ginormous ego of yours."

I see the surprise flicker through his eyes with temerity following closely behind it. He takes a step closer, our bodies a whisper away from each other, and I have to tilt my head up to hold his gaze.

"Since you were late, did you miss who I am? *Wannabe* is something I surpassed a long time ago." He grates the words out, that velvet voice packed with grit and coated in an unhealthy dose of conceit.

"Well, excuse me *Professor Play*," I say, voice laced with saccharine, as his breath feathers over my lips from our less than professional proximity. "So what? You're just an asshole on a power trip then?"

A sliver of a laugh falls from his lips but there is anything but humor in it. I know I've hit a nerve and hell if I care because he needs to get knocked down a peg.

"So much hostility from such a pretty girl."

Girl? Guess he's not noticing my tits or curves. And why does that bug me?

"I've got a lot more where that came from," I reply, taking a step back from his cologne that's clouding my thoughts and the dark gray flecks in his eyes that mine keep focusing on.

"Thanks for the warning," he says with a nod of his head, "but I'm not quite sure what I've done to deserve it."

"Nothing." I snort. "Your type just rubs me the wrong way."

"I'll rub you any way you like if you want." His smile

widens and eyes wander down my body and slowly back up in obvious appraisal.

And as much as I'm glad he's finally taking notice, I hope he likes what he sees because it will be the last time he gets a good look at it. "Like I said, you're an asshole."

"I can think of worse things to be." He shrugs, smarmy look in place that tells me he's enjoying this. "I hate to break it to you but uh, I'm not going anywhere." He lifts his chin toward the podium. "I happen to be a wannabe professor." He licks his bottom lip and steps closer to me. "So we can play this two ways."

"Two ways?" I don't think I like where this conversation is going considering that fuck-all smirk of his just widened so big that tiny little dimples appeared. I hear his friend shift and sigh but don't look.

"Yeah. You know your hostility is obviously masking your true feelings."

"True feelings?" And there I go again, repeating what he says. How has he reduced me—a woman always confident and quick with my wit—to two-word sentences? I don't have much time to think about it because he steps closer, causing me to retreat so that the backs of my legs hit the seat behind me. I have nowhere to go now.

"Mm-hm. That you're hot for teacher."

I cough out a laugh, choking on my own words with the knowledge of hierarchy of student to professor. I tone down my response before I respond. "I'm sure you'd love to think that, except not everyone is mesmerized by your dazzling charm. Besides, there's a school policy against fraternization between students and wannabe professors." I purse my lips and wait for his response.

He glances over to his friend and gives him a look I can't quite see before running a hand through his hair and focusing back on me. "For some reason I don't think you care if you follow any rules or not."

Well, at least he's got that right because I'm probably breaking several right now with the way I'm speaking to him and I couldn't care in the least. "You said we could play it two ways," I say, suddenly remembering the comment from moments before that his cocksure comeback distracted me from. "What's the second?"

"Drop the class," he deadpans, eyes daring me to, body telling me not to.

"I can't."

"Hm," he murmurs. "You most definitely aren't doing it right Trix, if you can't."

"Does everything with you have to be sexual?" I ask even though I know damn well the reason I'm hearing the innuendo is because of the supercharged sexual tension I suddenly realize is zinging between us.

"Yes." He nods but it's not the matter-of-fact way he says it that causes my libido to stand at attention but rather the predatory way his eyes own mine. "Like I said, if it bugs you that much, be my guest, transfer out."

"I'm sure you're not used to being told the word but I'll gladly say it to you." I step even closer, our eyes locked, our bodies reacting to the lack of space between us. I swallow down the lust I don't want to feel that's lodged in my throat and whisper the word to him. "No."

He shakes his head and stares with those storm cloud–colored eyes of his, trying to figure out how to take me. "Why not?"

"Because I'm your TA."

Chapter 3

My TA? What the fuck?

She stares at me with defiance in her caramel-colored eyes and a victorious smirk on those full lips. I love the fact that she has the balls to play me like she did when everyone else simply complies either from being starstruck or intimidated.

Gotta love a girl with brass ones.

Our verbal duel ends abruptly when she turns and walks away without another word. So why do I find myself wanting to ask her to stay even though she obviously detests me? The woman is intriguing and intense and . . . a bitch, but shit, there's just something about her that has my dick commandeering my thoughts.

Damn her for pointing out my sexual innuendos because now as she stalks out, her fine-as-fuck ass in that short skirt that keeps giving me a glimpse of tan, toned thigh with each step, sex is all I can think of.

Sex with her in particular.

I blow out a breath as she strides out the door without a backward glance and even though I hear the outer door to the auditorium open and then close, I still keep staring.

Vince draws out a long, low whistle to the left of me.

"Now, that's a coed worth getting schooled by. Bet your ass she'd be feisty as hell in the sack."

I tear my eyes from the doorway, a part of me hoping she'll come back through it for some reason, before turning to face him. And I can't pinpoint what it is that he said that irritates me but I'm irritated nonetheless. But I shake off the notion just like I wish I could shake the desire riding rampant through my system. "She might be sexy as hell but some kitty-cat claws aren't worth the scratch." Even as I'm speaking the words, my body calls me on the lie.

"Sexy? Dude, that's the understatement of the year. She's smokin' hot. Her curves were banging, her—"

"Banging is definitely something I'd like to do to her," I mutter under my breath, her face immediately flashing in my mind even though it's been only a matter of moments since she's left. I turn to retrieve my bag where it lies.

"Since when is hostile your type?"

"You know me, Vince, the only type I have is *willing*," I say over my shoulder although right now I'm thinking hostile looks pretty damn attractive.

"Truth." He falls silent for a moment, which leaves me alone with my thoughts of how the lecture I was anxious to give turned out more interesting than I'd expected because of her presence. How focusing on her allowed me to calm my nerves on what to lecture about when I never get nerves on a stage. "And she was so far from willing she just might be the one woman on this campus whose hand job would be a fist in your face rather than wrapped around your dick."

"What?" I ask around the Skittles I just tossed into my mouth, annoyed that he's questioning my prowess. "You think I couldn't get her to go out with me?"

He laughs and scrubs a hand over his jaw. "Even your charm has limitations Hawke . . . and that woman is most definitely one of them."

"Bullshit." I snort in response as I glance down at my phone for messages. I can't remember the last time I was turned down.

"Dude, there's no way in hell she'd go on a date with you."

"Bet me." I snap the words out in reflex, my damn ego

stomping its feet in protest, and then cringe when I realize what I just said. How I just carried over the go-to response within our band to prove a point about this, over her. *Fuck*.

"Nah, that bet's not worth it because she'd say yes just to get easier access to knee you in the nuts." He purses his lips and then his smile spreads wide to match his eyes lighting up. "But sleeping with her? Now, that's a bet I could sure as hell win."

"You think I couldn't get her in bed? Are you kidding me?"

He pats me on the back roughly. "Nope. Even the ladies' man Hawkin Play can't have a perfect record, and she's most definitely the chick who will ruin it for you."

I jerk my shoulder to get his hand off me. "No way in hell. I'll have her eating out of my hand by the end of this seminar. *Watch me.*"

"That'll be funny as fuck, man. Watching you get shot down repeatedly. Hell, this might even be a record or something."

"Put your money where your mouth is then, huh, Vinny?" I taunt as we begin to make our way up the steps. I make only bets I can win and *I know* I can win this one.

"In a heartbeat but man, last bet, what was her name?" I shrug in response because there have been so many women involved in our band bets over the years they all kind of run together after enough time. "It doesn't matter but shit you swore you won, sealed the deal with her, and there was no way for me to prove otherwise."

Her face flickers before my eyes, the beautiful redhead from our *blow job bet*: who could get sucked off first from the gaggle of groupies at an after party. "Damn she was good," I reminisce, thinking about that little tongue technique she used. "You're just jealous the chick you picked—"

"Don't remind me," he groans.

"It's your fault you didn't outline the terms of your bet better. Besides, we didn't make you get the tattoo dude. No harm, no foul," I say, referring to the stakes of all of our band's bets: If the challenger loses, he must get a heart tattooed on the inside of his wrist. Each bet lost results in the heart being outlined and made bigger.

Thank fuck I've never lost. The few tats I have are for a reason, a reminder of my life's lessons in some abstract way or another—not because I lost some dumb-ass bet like they all have.

He glares at me, still cross over it. "All I'm saying is that if we're betting, then I want proof this time that you sleep with her."

"Sure thing. Hop on in with us if you're that desperate for proof," I offer without any conviction.

"Perfect."

I snap my head over at him as we stop for a beat in the auditorium's foyer to finish our conversation. "Fuck no. I was joking!"

And it's not that we haven't done something like that before—two of us with one or a few more girls. A tour bus is only so big and there's only so much time you can kill playing Halo or Guitar Hero.

"I know you were but my bet, my rules. I want proof. And it has to be done by the last day of the seminar." He raises his eyebrows before slipping his own sunglasses on, smarmy smile in place.

"Piece of cake," I say as I glance out the windows to where a small crowd is gathered past where Axe and his guys stand, waiting for autographs and pictures.

"I want in on the action with the little hellcat. I'm there or there's no proof and you, my boy, finally get a goddamn pansy-ass heart on your pretty-boy skin."

And therein lies his motive. He thinks I'll back down, afraid to lose and finally get inked with the stupid image we all decided was our band tradition over ten years ago . . . when we were young and dumb.

I sigh and just shake my head. Maybe it's the need to prove I can get the girl and avoid an idiotic, meaningless tattoo. Or maybe it's because I really want to figure her out, understand why those golden eyes and long legs of hers are still on my mind. Why I keep wondering if she's really as feisty in bed as she is out of it.

Regardless, the die is cast. And I'll just have to hope I'm not revisiting the young and dumb phase with this decision.

"You're on, Vinny boy!" I say as I push open the doors with gusto. Immediately excited screams, the soundtrack of my life this past year, fill the air around us.

Chapter 4

The seminar has been over for thirty minutes. So why am I still sitting in my car, forehead pressed against the steering wheel, and mind going a million miles an hour as I try to process the riot of emotions coursing through me? I'm always even keeled. I may have a hot temper, definitely have a smart mouth, but I'm always able to process my thoughts and respond intelligently.

So why in the hell do I feel like a flustered mess who knows I definitely made an ass out of myself in that stupid lecture with Hawkin?

And why do I even care?

I groan out in frustration knowing full well the mistake I made.

How I told Hawkin I *was* his TA when I have no desire to see him again. My plans were to hoof it across campus back to Carla's office and tell her no way in hell I was going back—so why am I sitting in my car instead?

And why did I give the upper hand I battled for away so easily with that stupid parting statement? I basically implied I'll be sitting here next week with bells on waiting to assist him in any way possible.

Now I'm just being dramatic.

I groan in frustration because I damn well know that I

made a mental slip with my comment, but I'm pretty damn sure parts of me secretly wanted the chance to assist him in all sorts of ways.

I'm so frustrated with myself, especially since my mind won't stop envisioning him, smirk on his lips, challenge in his eyes, or the rough edge to his pretty-boy looks. I swore off men. Told myself I needed a break, that I needed to focus on my thesis rather than getting hurt again, so why am I sitting here thinking about him? I stare at the ceiling for a moment in an attempt to convince myself that there's no shame in being attracted to him, in wondering about the sound of his voice and if he talks dirty in bed. None of that matters because he's an asshole and I may be drawn to the bad boys but they are not mutually exclusive.

Acknowledging that he gets me hot and bothered doesn't mean that I still can't drop the class.

Time to pull on my big-girl panties and go tell Carla I can't do this. Save yourself from yourself.

Pep talk in place I put my hand on the handle of the car door and look up before I open it to see Hawkin and his friend whose seat I took walking about twenty feet in front of me down the row of cars. My breath hitches and I tell myself it's just because I'm surprised at seeing him there.

And of course I sit and stare, observe without him knowing. Take in the faded jeans worn in all the right places, the black T-shirt tight on his biceps with a Rolling Stones emblem on the front, and the black combat boots. I watch him push the brown hair off his forehead and smile that lopsided smirk that makes parts within me clench that shouldn't be clenching.

He throws his head back and laughs, obviously at ease with the guy who accompanied him to the lecture. I take a closer look at his friend, as Hawke's physical presence is far enough removed that I can pay attention to something other than him. Then my thoughts snap into line and I recall vague tabloid images of the band to realize that it's Vincent Jennings, Bent's bassist.

I watch them a few more minutes as they laugh. Hawkin pulls out a bag of Skittles and pours them straight into his mouth, and I just grin at the little-boy gesture in a grown man. They bump fists a couple of times before I notice the bodyguards not far behind. Just as I'm sinking into the idea that he might not be too much of an asshole, that I was overreacting to being called out, I watch two female students wearing their sorority letters approach them.

I'm immediately conflicted because a part of me wants to watch the exchange while another larger part doesn't want to because I already know deep down that I'm going to be jealous.

And the notion that I even care pisses me off, but in true female form, I can't bring myself to look away.

The girls giggle and flirt as they introduce themselves. Hair is twirled, eyelashes are batted, and backs are suddenly arched so that tits are front and center between them and the men. I roll my eyes at the sight, then narrow my gaze when that lopsided grin tugs up Hawkin's mouth in a way that makes him the perfect combination of sheepish and wolfish. As he signs something for the sample-size brunette with boobs proportionate to a Barbie doll's, I watch her make her move.

She reaches out to touch the cuff of his shirt on his bicep. He hands her back her pen and then laughs as he pulls up the sleeve of his shirt so she can see the tattoo she's obviously asked about. I cringe when her hands immediately reach out to trace the ink that I can't see because she's now blocking my line of sight. I shift my gaze to Hawkin's face, watch him watch her coo over his tat.

"It's just ink, honey. Got a pen in your backpack with some don't you? Get over it already," I mumble, knowing damn well I want to know what the tattoo design is. And before I finish saying the words, she's lifting up his shirt to see if there is another tattoo there. "Brazen little hussy."

I grit my teeth at the sight of her hands touching as much of his bare skin as she can while he just grins at her—and Vince is equally occupied with the other way too perky Delta Sig girl. Seconds turn to minutes and before much time passes, Hawkin's arm is around Barbie's shoulder and the four of them are walking somewhere off campus.

By the time they disappear, his hand has conveniently slid down her back and is resting comfortably on the curve of her ass.

Shaking my head, I start telling myself I shouldn't be

surprised, can't be angry at what I'd already pegged him for. Once a player always a player.

Time to go visit Carla.

"Ugly Heart" plays through the speakers as I flop back on my couch, research notes scattered all around the table in front of me and the cushions beside me. I hum along, trying to decipher my scribble that made perfect sense when I took the notes but now seems like a jumble of incomprehensible mishmash.

It doesn't help that my talk with my adviser was fruitless. Every attempt to explain the exact reason why I couldn't assist Hawkin's seminar fell on deaf ears until the conversation ended with the one word everyone dreads hearing: Don't *disappoint* me, Quinlan.

And then of course my mind shifts toward *him*. "Go away!" I mutter and begin to sing the lyrics to drown out the unwelcome thoughts.

"Maybe I'm just crazy; maybe I'm a fool. . . ."

I sing the words on autopilot, my thoughts scattered and loneliness setting in. It's been six months since Rick and I called it quits. Six months since I walked in on him in bed with another woman naked and moaning after being with him for a year. The player who swore he'd changed just for me obviously hadn't. So I took his key off my ring, then walked away from his apartment with a promise to never be that girl again.

After working so hard at my relationship with him and it ending the same way that my previous two relationships had, I vowed to revisit my undergrad days of casual dating where it's fun and uncomplicated. Sex without strings, without happily-ever-afters. To never date a player again.

So now I ask myself: Why have I been fine for the past six months, not a day spent moping since my ego was bruised yet again and I swore off men, but now I'm sitting here wanting a guy to keep me company? And a complete player nonetheless.

The song switches and of course it's a Bent song. *The irony*. The person behind the voice on the radio is the reason I'm feeling this way when I don't want to be. He's irritated me enough to get under my skin and that takes a lot to do.

Rylee's words sift through my mind. I need to have some wild, reckless sex. The funny thing is I have been, so why do I feel so unsatisfied? Just as quickly the answer hits me — because it's sex without emotion. It's akin to having the ice cream to make a sundae and then realizing you don't have any toppings, cherries, or hot fudge. You eat the ice cream nonetheless, but you aren't fully satisfied.

My phone rings and I welcome the distraction from my pathetic thoughts that compare sex to sundaes. Yes, I'm in desperate need of help. Or an intervention.

"Hey, Layla!" I greet my oldest and dearest friend.

"I need to get drunk," she groans.

"And I need to get laid," I confess. Then I toss my pen on my open book next to me, thinking that maybe the physicality will clear my head from thoughts of a particular rock star.

"Well shit, that sounds like the perfect combination to me." She sighs, my ever-ready partner in crime.

"True."

"But I'll stick to the drunk part. . . . Last time I wasn't too successful at the getting laid thing. I'm no good at it. I was with Sean way too long to remember how to play this game."

"Lay, you played the game just fine . . . but I think you scared the shit out of the guy you determined was your fun for the night." I laugh as I recall the look on the poor guy's face.

"You think it was too much?"

"Telling the guy your vagina needed a hug and could his penis provide it? Yeah. Just a tad much." She starts laughing with me because the deadpan expression she had when she asked the question was so damn hilarious.

"I was drunk. And horny. Can't fault a girl for trying." I love her and her *take no prisoners* attitude.

"It was one for the record books," I confess.

"So let's try again tonight. I promise I'll be on my best behavior this time around. Let's go find some hot guys and have a fun-night-stand."

"I'm just, ugh . . ." I laugh. "It sounds so easy, but it's always more complicated than that."

"Like what? The hangover or the walk of shame the morning after?" she asks.

"Both. Remembering names, that awkward moment when you randomly see each other on campus . . . Shit, I'll take the hangover and get myself off to avoid all of that. After Rick the Prick," I say with a sigh, "I'm done for a while."

"Yeah that's funny. I think I heard that before him and the guy before him," she teases with nothing but the truth. "Besides, never date a guy with a name that rhymes with prick or dick. There's just something wrong with that. . . . It's like you're just asking for him to be one or something."

"It makes dirty talk easy though in case you forget his name in the heat of the moment," I explain, knowing from experience.

Her contagious laugh fills the line—the one that gets me every time. "So you in? Wanna go drink away our sorrows?"

"Sorrows? Since you can't say happiness without saying penis, I'm assuming it has to do with a man. . . . What's going on with you?" I ask, immediately concerned although I think she's handling her breakup rather well considering the length of time she and Sean dated.

"Ugh! I had my first help session today, and I already want to stab my eyes out from giving the same explanation over and over," she says, referring to her question-and-answer session for students who need help grasping the concepts in the main lecture. But then again, I don't understand what a TA session has to do with a man.

"We were probably just as bad when that was us."

"I know! But add to that Sean stopped by to make sure that I was okay—like he really cares—and all I really wanted to do was knee him in the nuts."

"Well," I muse, finally getting to the heart of her trouble. "At least you're progressing from wanting to cry over him to wanting to inflict the pain he deserves for dumping you."

"I know," she says, then the line falls silent for a moment. I know she's trying to sound strong, like their breakup hasn't hurt her deeply, so I give her the silence to regain the fraudulent resolve in her voice. She sighs, her sadness palpable. "So see, we need to go out and have a drink. Celebrate us not being whiny first years and maybe have another three or four to make us forget the fact that we both need to get good and laid."

My smile spreads wide until I look down at the papers littering my lap. "Layla," I groan, "I wish I could, but I've gotta get moving on my first draft. . . ."

"You're seriously going to leave me high and dry?"

My mind flashes to how I'd rather be wet and low with Hawkin, and I hit the heel of my hand to my forehead to stop the insanity. "It's so tempting because it's been a fucked-up day for me too. . . . I just really need to make some headway here before I seriously screw myself with procrastination."

"I know . . . but it's still a helluva good idea. Well, I'm going to—oh my God! I totally forgot! Did you hear who was on campus today?" She says in a rush and from the excitement in her voice I'm really hoping she says Brad Pitt or something but I have a feeling I know exactly who she's talking about.

"Who?"

"Hawkin—come-to-momma—Play. What I wouldn't give to *play* him," she murmurs as if she's fantasizing doing just that. "I guess he's doing some kind of seminar that I'm going to have to crash just so that I can—oh shit! A cop's behind me, call you right back!" She ends the call abruptly, not willing to risk another ticket for talking on her cell phone and driving without a Bluetooth device. Guaranteed she's most likely lost the last one she bought like she did the five before that.

I lean back and exhale, thankful for the momentary break in conversation so that I can figure out how exactly to tell Layla about my run-in with Hawkin. And then I wonder why my immediate reaction is that I don't want to confide in her. Don't want to knock him off the pedestal she's set him on even though it's not warranted. Just because he has a voice begging for sin doesn't mean he's the stellar guy she thinks he is.

Besides, it's not like I'm going to see him again anyway so why am I even stressing over it?

My phone rings in my hand and startles me so much I answer it without looking. "That was quick, Lay!"

A masculine chuckle fills the line. "I'm anything but quick, but the lay part I can make sure of."

What is it with men and everything being turned into

sexual innuendo today? And of course as much as I want to roll my eyes, my lips form an involuntary smile.

"Luke? How—"

"You told me I was focused on the wrong numbers . . . so I found the right ones," he says and I can't help the little flutter in my stomach from the thought that he went the extra distance—like he always seems to do—to try yet again.

I emit a nervous laugh, unsure how to really feel about his continued pursuit. I fall back to my standard use of sarcasm whenever I'm uncomfortable. "Oh, how sweet of you! Were things going so well for you that you needed some rejection so you searched me out?"

"Charming as always," he replies, humor in his voice so at least I know he took my comment how it was intended.

Unlike a different asshole from earlier today who couldn't take a hint to save his life.

"You know you can't resist me."

"The answer's still no, Luke." I know he can hear the fondness in my voice.

"Don't believe I asked but thanks for shooting me down . . . again," he teases.

"And again and again." I laugh. "How'd you get my number?"

"I have my ways," he responds, and I have a gut feeling that Rylee is meddling here, handing him my phone number on the sly.

"Are those ways going to end up with my brother's fist in your face?"

"If it did, would you come kiss it and make me feel better?"

I sigh into the line in response to his relentless pursuit. "Hm. Probably not. I'm not very gentle."

His laugh is deep and rich and full of suggestion. "You're such a goddamn tease, you know that? Maybe I like it a little rough."

"Walked right into that one didn't I?" I chuckle, feeling a sincere smile on my face for the first time since meeting Hawkin earlier today.

"Sure did."

It dawns on me that he might be calling for a real purpose, and that I've made an incorrect assumption. "So . . . what can I do for you?"

"You sure you want me to answer that?"

"Give me the PG version," I state.

"Ah, now that wouldn't be any fun now would it?" The line falls silent for a beat. "How about we go out sometime?"

One of these days the man is going to wear me down to nothing until I relent. We've been following the steps of this dance for so long.

"You sure are tenacious. . . . I think you need to find a hobby or something to occupy your time besides racing." It's so fun to tease him, and in fact it makes me miss Colton and our constant banter.

"Tell me about it. We've got a three-week lag until the next race. I need something to chase now since there's not a spoiler in front of me, so once again I've set my sights on chasing you."

"Well there's your problem, Mason."

"Problem?"

"Why you're having a little dry spell on the track."

"A dry spell?" He coughs the words out.

"Yep. You can't cross the finish line in first place if you're always chasing. You need to figure out how to lead, cowboy, then you just might have a chance at taking the checkered flag." I hear his laugh and know that I've had enough of cocky, overbearing men today. "Maybe next time, I'll say yes. Good-bye, Luke."

"I'll take that as a maybe," I hear as I end the call.

I immediately dial Layla. "Did you get a ticket?" I ask when she answers.

"Thank God, no." Relief floods her voice.

"Good because I've reconsidered. Ready to go get liquored and laid?"

"Well, at least one of them," she laughs out.

"I'm aiming for both."

Chapter 5

Campus is buzzing from the combination of a break in the relentless heat and students finally settling in for the long haul of the school year. It's comforting to me and hell do I need the feeling because once again I'm heading to the department offices, but this time I've been summoned.

And somehow it has to do with Hawkin's seminar.

After biting the bullet and accepting the fact that I was going to let her down, I was finally able to talk Carla into getting someone else to cover the rest of the series, starting with today's lecture, so now I'm worried why all of a sudden she needs to talk to me about something we decided upon five days ago. Did another student—or Hawkin himself—report my insubordination in the last lecture and it's just now trickling down through administration?

I don't know what to expect but I can't deny that my nerves are humming and I'm mentally chastising myself for my inability to just shut my mouth.

When I head toward Carla's office at the end of the hallway, laughter sounds from within and she waves me in upon seeing me approach.

"Professor Stevens, you wanted to see me?" I hate that my voice sounds unsteady as I stand in the doorway, partially obscured by the half-opened door, but there's no way that I can mask it.

"C'mon in Quinlan," she says as I push the door open, my eyes meeting hers.

"Quinlan?" Hawkin's voice hits my ears before I see him sitting very comfortably in a chair opposite her desk. He says my name in a tone that's both a question and a statement at the same time.

Shit.

My body jolts with awareness from being back in his proximity. I'm sure it doesn't help that even though I'd dropped the lecture, I've spent a shameful amount of time on the Internet checking him out, watching his interviews, and the band's music videos. Learning about the band's history and antics before researching him personally. I scanned his dating history, which can only be described as an ever-revolving door of women who are more than willing to brag about him and his abilities even after splitting up. I admit I allowed myself to be hypnotized by his voice.

Purely out of curiosity.

But hell if the sight of him in the flesh—the lazy smirk and bedroom eyes laden with secrets—doesn't cause all my research to rush back and clog the space between us with the hint of desire and possibility.

And that's before he even utters a word beyond my name. In silence he still exudes arrogance and sex appeal—I don't think that's something he can help—with his nonchalant posture and the easy expression on the sculpted lines of his face. But he also looks dead serious, which ratchets up my discomfort with the situation when all he does is nod his head and then glance over to Carla and raise an eyebrow.

Yes, it's her office but clearly he's running the show, and I've just been told not so subtly that my opinion in whatever matter is being discussed is of no importance.

How come they were laughing moments before and now they are both so somber? I glance back and forth between the two of them, his eyebrows asking the questions his voice doesn't. *Quinlan, not Trixie? Really?*

So I focus on Carla. Hawkin's too distracting, and if I answer his questions honestly I might just have to face a few truths I'm not ready to. That he irritates me, unnerves me, turns me on, and turns me off all at the same damn time. He makes me want when I don't want to. Tempts me to go back on my decree of never dating anyone like my brother again.

Because there is just something inherently sexy and clichéd about a man who can play a guitar, and, damn it to hell . . . it's making me want to go back on those same promises to myself.

It's not worth it. Think of your brother, think of how you've observed too many things during his single, playboy days that have made you shudder when it came to the women he dated. At least Hawkin's not a race car driver—he's got that going for him.

Carla's cheeks flush under my stare, and she quickly averts her eyes from mine. Apparently he's worked his effortless charm on her for some reason, and the question I fear is for what purpose?

And if he's won her over, why am I the only one he's treated differently with his flippant comments and unwarranted attention?

"I called you in early because Mr. Play asked if you could spare some time to show him the PA system and overhead setup before today's lecture."

My head must snap up because she looks at me strangely. Does she not remember our conversation several days ago when she agreed that I was off his service? "I'm sorry?" I ask, confusion laced with disbelief in my voice.

"Well, I know we discussed that you needed to drop assisting Mr. Play's seminar here because of your course load, but . . ." And the way her voice fades off tells me that he has definitely worked his magic charm on her.

"I told her I couldn't do it without you or the cool *tricks* you had to make class more interesting." I don't even want to turn my head to look at him because if I do, I'll risk either sarcastically commenting that he's full of shit or falling momentarily comatose to his good looks.

I don't want to give him the satisfaction of either of those reactions.

Plus, I know he's bluffing but I'm not exactly sure why. We were hostile toward each other, not flirtatious, combative not friendly. . . . So why would he request me when he could most likely have all of those things I'm not with another TA?

Sure he's attractive and could probably serenade a pair of panties to fall off without a person even knowing it, but if our first meeting was any indication, he knows I'm sure as hell not going to let that happen.

In disbelief I keep staring at Carla, my mind buzzing all the while trying to shove my libido back into hiding. And the crappy thing is that I'm more mad at myself than anything else because I'm standing here like a doormat not arguing my case when normally I'm like a battering ram knocking the door down.

"Quin, there's no one else available and there's really not a lot of assisting required beyond class time," Carla says with a sheepish smile when she finally tears her gaze from his to meet mine. The look in her eyes acknowledging she's throwing me into the fire.

"But . . ."

What can I say to that when she's perfectly right? *Sorry Carla but he was a prick and I don't think it's safe for the two of us to be in close proximity because one of us is bound to get physical with the other—in some form or another.* Yeah, *fist or fuck*, because that screams professionalism.

When my only response is to nod my head in silent resignation, she shifts her focus back to Hawkin. "See? I told you she'd reconsider. Now, you guys need to get going so you have time for Quin to give you the complete rundown."

Of course she has no idea the double entendre she's just given him about me giving him a complete rundown, but I know Hawke catches it. I manage to resist the urge to stomp my feet in frustration and storm out of her office like a toddler. Instead I give her a tight smile before turning and walking out of the office and then the department.

I stand there in the sunshine, waiting for him to get his ass in gear and quit wasting my time. When I finally hear the door open I just start walking and the sound of his boots is the only indication that he's following.

"I've got longer legs than you Trixie," he chides from a few feet back. "But feel free to keep swinging your hips like that, and I'll stay right here behind you and enjoy the show."

I bristle at the comment. At the moment there's no authority to be respectful of, no damage that can't be undone.

"A show?" The pitch of my voice escalates as I whirl around to face him—sunglasses on, hair disheveled, and I wish I hadn't turned around because *damn*, he's just that devastatingly fine. I'm quiet for a beat as we both appraise each other from behind darkened lenses. His dark hair, tanned skin, and cocky smirk pull at those parts of me I don't want to be pulled. "You want to talk about a show." I grit the words out, trying to push my physical attraction to him from my mind. "Let's talk about your little performance for Dr. Stevens."

"I know. I'm good, huh? Sorry, but a man's got to do what he's got to do. . . . Besides, I wasn't done with you yet."

My mouth falls lax and I'm momentarily flabbergasted. "Done with me yet?" I sputter the words when I've recovered my wits at his arrogance run amok . . . but I can't deny the little flutter in my belly at his comment. There's just something about him aside from the whole *I'm a rock star* thing that makes me desire him in a way I can't put into words.

"Yep," he says casually as he unwraps a Starburst and pops it into his mouth. And I hate that I'm fascinated with watching his mouth suck on the sweet candy. Luckily he speaks so I can distract myself from the captivating sight. "I'm pretty sure you have a usefulness. . . . I'm just trying to figure out what that is." He licks his lips. "Well, besides the obvious, that is . . ." Smirk is handily in place and I hate that ache starting to simmer in my core.

"Why don't you go suck a—"

"Relax," he says, angling his head to the side and emitting a laugh as he steps closer to me. "I'm just teasing you. You're so damn easy to rile up and so hard to resist. Plus you're even hotter when you're pissed. I like it." He shrugs an apology, hands shoved deep in the pockets of his jeans with a sheepish grin that softens all those hard edges and makes me sigh with the contrast of characteristics. He holds a red Starburst out to me as a peace offering. "C'mon, you know you want to be the star to my burst."

We've stopped, my hands are on my hips, and the sun falls around us as he waits for me to react to his innocent little comment. Deep down I know I'm screwed. I feel an urge to smile but immediately realign my defenses. The contradiction he presents, the smooth with the rough, is the one thing that I always fall for when it comes to men.

And I'm not going to fall for Hawkin Play.

"More like the fruit to your loop," I say with a roll of my eyes before I shift my gaze elsewhere. I have to because he's one of those guys who when you look into his eyes you can see the ending before you even decide to begin. And hell, I'm all for fun and sex but something tells me the heartache he causes isn't worth the pain. Then again, he is damn fine.

Lock it down Westin. I shake my head in frustration—at me, at him, over this attraction—and turn on my heel, putting all my effort into getting to the lecture hall so that I can push that image of him standing like that out of my head. Because that look makes me want to walk up to him, fist a hand in his shirt, and kiss him senseless.

I have no shame about admitting it, or even in the idea of doing it because hell, being confident in wanting a guy is a good thing. I never shy away from a man when I want him . . . but something tells me that this one just might knock me off my feet. And while I'm all for having my world rocked, I'd rather it was not by someone used to playing women like a guitar and then disposing of them once the song's over.

His mocking laugh behind me breaks through my thoughts. But I keep walking, not wanting to give him the satisfaction of knowing he's gotten to me, that I can't take a frickin' step without him invading my thoughts.

"Quinlan! Stop," he says. "You're not going to leave me poor and defenseless against that fucked-up PA system, are you?"

"You're a big boy; I'm sure you can fend for yourself just fine."

I hear him snicker beside me and I roll my eyes, realizing the *big boy* comment I just handed him without thought. "You're right, on both counts," he chuckles, and the sound, smooth silk with a hint of strain, hits my ears and my libido in ways I don't want it to. "But a man likes to have some help every now and again."

"I'm sure you have plenty of willing candidates." I'm thinking of the sigher who sat next to me at the last lecture as I keep walking, trying to focus on anything but the man beside me.

"Well, I guess I'll just have to go back and tell Carla, then. . . ."

I slow my pace a clip but keep moving forward, knowing he has my number. "You handle complicated stage equipment regularly and yet you can't work a simple audio system?" I snort out a laugh of disbelief. "Sounds to me you're so busy being pretty that you don't like to get your hands dirty. Forget where you came from that quick, huh?"

His hand is on my arm and I'm spun around before the last word is out of my mouth. I guess that dig hit a little too close to home.

"Where and what I came from is none of your goddamn business." Our bodies are close, my eyes behind my sunglasses flickering back and forth from his lips to his eyes as he snaps the words out. He presses his fingers a little tighter on my bicep. "Who are you to judge anyway . . . ? *Right, Trixie?*"

Even though I can't see his eyes, I know they are boring into mine. I can feel the anger vibrating off him from the nerve I've hit. I don't say a word because I've pushed the buttons—and right or wrong—for no other purpose than to keep him at arm's length from me.

"What the fuck is your problem?" He finally breaks his silence and asks.

"Who says there's a problem? Just because you're intimidated by a strong woman doesn't mean there's a problem," I snip, trying to push this off on him when I know damn well that I'm carrying the chip handily on my shoulder.

"Sweetness, only boys are intimidated by strong women. Men find it attractive, a challenge, so why don't you pull another excuse out of thin air and see if it sticks."

I shrug my arm out of his grasp and step back, hating that he's right in every sense of the word. It's not like I'm going to let him know it though. "I know your type Hawkin. I know the games you play." I look across the campus for a moment before looking back to him.

"Who said I'm playing any games?"

"Ha." I laugh. "Your type always does, don't they?"

He pulls a hand out of his pocket and runs it through his chocolate-colored hair, jaw clenched in frustration at the bitchiness I'm directing his way. "If anyone's playing games, I'm pretty sure it's you considering you go back and forth between hot and cold quicker than a faucet. So like I asked, what's your deal?" He repeats himself, irritation laced with a trace of sadness in his soothing voice. "You can't handle me?"

I swallow over the lump of confusion in my throat; the blatant conflict between lust and obstinacy runs rampant within me whenever I'm near him. "I'm not handling anything on you, no worries."

"That's what you say now, but I'm patient. . . . You'll come around." He licks his lips, and unless it's my imagination, I can tell he's fighting back a smirk.

And I have to give it to him—he's as relentless as Luke. Almost. But the difference is he has my blood pumping whereas I've never felt overly attracted to Luke. I shake my head in an effort to clear my thoughts.

"I just don't understand why you're here. Why you agreed to do this seminar . . . One and one doesn't exactly equal two on this one."

He works his tongue in his cheek as he processes my statement. "I thought it would be fun. A change of pace to help me work around some issues I'm having . . . with a few songs on the new album. A new perspective . . ." He nods his head and glances over to where someone yells out on the grassy quad area.

The way his voice drifts off, combined with the shifting of his body, tells me something's off and as much as I know I should leave well enough alone, I'm not buying it. He wants to call me on the carpet, I'm going to match him, challenge for challenge.

"That's too perfect of an answer, Hawkin," I say, recalling the image of the Delta Sig girls from the other day and his hand on her ass. "I know your type and if there's not easy sex, fast crowds, or loose women to get lost in, you lose interest so—"

"What's wrong with easy sex?" he asks as he falls into step beside me.

"Nothing." I turn and start walking again toward the lecture hall. "Easy sex is most definitely fun, but why—"

"Whoa!" He reaches out to touch my arm, and I ignore his subtle request to turn and face him. In my periphery, I see him scrub a hand over his shaven jaw and shake his head. "You can't say shit like that to a guy like me and expect me to gloss over it."

"Shit like what?" I glance over at him. "Easy sex? Why deny it? Sex is great; sex is fun. You just won't be the lucky one. . . . Now, tell me what's in this lecture for you."

He laughs aloud, producing a sound that's laced with strained desire and disbelief. "Fuck Quin. With statements like that, you're making me hope it's you I'm in it for."

"Keep dreaming, rocker boy." I roll my eyes even though he can't see them, although a small thrill surges through me from his comment. What girl wouldn't want to hear that? Then I have to control my runaway thoughts, reminding myself over and over again that this man wears an *I'm going to break your heart* warning like a tattoo. "You still haven't answered my question—why the seminar?"

I'm not backing down on this because something tells me the truthful answer is going to divulge "the something" about him that I need to know. And hell no, I don't deserve the honest truth from him considering our shaky start, but I know if I keep him on his toes, then he'll spend less time trying to get me off mine.

"I told you—I'm struggling on the album. . . . Never got the chance to go to college and the opportunity arose for the lecture so I took it." I hear the disconnect beneath the words he speaks more.

"My bullshit-o-meter is zinging here."

"Are you always this combative, trying to be the badass?" He shakes his head. "Lips like an angel, body made for sin, and feisty enough to rival the devil's fire?"

My step falters momentarily as his depiction knocks any coherent thoughts from my head. And I'm not sure what it is about his assessment that causes that ache within me to begin to coil again. "You like to play with fire, huh?"

This time his laugh is free and suggestive. "Oh Quin, the hotter the better."

I don't respond, just keep walking as the air between us

thickens with unspoken and yet undeniable chemistry. I can feel the heat of the glances he steals my way but I ignore them, focusing instead on the murmured whispers in the groups of students we pass. And it must be the look on his face or our defensive posture but no one approaches us as we walk the last few feet toward the auditorium where Axe stands, arms crossed over his chest and back against the doors.

We're just about to enter when Hawkin says, "Hold up," and walks to the right of the building toward a food vendor cart.

I follow out of curiosity, wondering what could have caught his attention in the midst of our discussion. "What are you . . . ?" My voice trails off as I see the little-boy grin light up his handsome features. Something about the look on his face, pure joy mixed with the hint of shadow on his jaw, has me staring a bit longer than I should.

"Ice cream!" he says, eyes wide as he peruses the list of flavors.

"Ice cream?" Ice cream is what made this gruff rocker turn into an adolescent? "Sweet tooth much?" I ask.

"The sweeter, the better," he says, giving me an appraising once-over.

"Guess that leaves me out," I say with a smirk that causes him to laugh.

"I have a feeling you have a sweet spot beneath that tough exterior, Quinlan," he says as he points to a flavor and motions for me to pick one myself.

"No thank you," I reply, a little dumbfounded by this new development. I must still be staring, trying to figure him out as he waits for the vendor to press the scoop of cookies 'n' cream on the cone because he glances over to me and feels the need to explain.

"It's my vice . . . my habit." He pays the vendor, takes the cone, and then brings the ice cream to his lips. Parts deep within me stir as I watch him close his eyes momentarily and savor his first taste. My thoughts automatically wonder if this is what he looks like when he goes down on a woman.

When I refocus after shaking off the image, he's staring at me. My obscene thoughts must be written all over my face because a knowing smile spreads over his lips. His eyes tell me *yes*, it's the same expression.

And now I have to wonder how exactly I'm going to get that look out of my mind.

"I thought rockers were supposed to prefer sex, drugs, and alcohol," I stutter, trying to deflect his intense scrutiny. And then once the words are out, I see anger flash through his eyes and realize what a stupid comment it was on the heels of his drug charges.

But he pushes whatever it is aside and takes a step closer to me. He angles his head to the side, and licks around the ice-cream cone where it is starting to melt. "I do love the sex and the alcohol . . . and let's not mention the drug part," he says with a strained laugh, "but my daily habit is sugar. My favorite is ice cream."

"Seriously?"

He takes another lick and then starts to walk back toward where Axe stands guard but stops when we are shoulder to shoulder. He leans in so that his mouth is near my ear and I can feel his breath chilled by the ice cream as it hits my skin. "Are you really going to complain about a man who likes to use his tongue?"

And before I can regain my wits or the blood that has flooded to the delta of my thighs, he walks toward the auditorium's entrance without another word. I feel like a groupie as I turn around and scramble after him, trying to tamp down the lust after he just knowingly lit the flame.

"Let's get this over with," I mutter to myself as Rylee's *have wild, reckless sex* comment flickers through my mind.

Because damn it, Hawkin just threw me for an unexpected loop. The *throw caution to the wind* part of me stood to attention. The skeptical part of me flipped him the bird.

And despite myself, I know who I want to win.

Chapter 6

QUINLAN

Concentrating on teaching Hawkin how to operate the PA system is difficult with his comment running loops through my mind. Add to that, he's taking his sweet-ass time savoring his treat while we're both in the confines of the small alcove off to the side of the stage where the controller resides. The space is minimal so each time I demonstrate the switches on the board it causes him to lean in closer.

And with each brush up against my back—the thin cotton of my tank top does nothing to mute the feeling—I'm getting more turned on. And more irritated with him.

"Make it count," he murmurs behind me, his breath feathering over the exposed skin and I immediately know what he's talking about. I suck in a breath when his finger traces the small and delicately inked words in the space between my shoulder blades. The only tattoo I have. "What does it mean?"

"Pretty self-explanatory," I bite out but when a sigh of disappointment falls from him, I relent and quickly elaborate, finding that I want to tell him the truth. "I . . . I think it's important to make every moment count. Every friendship, every lover, every broken heart, every decision, every everything—they all need to count for something or else they're pointless and when all is said and done and you look back at your life, you'll have regrets." I shrug, feeling a tad too philosophical over a damn tattoo but I'm being honest. "Regrets suck. Making it count lessens that for me."

He's silent behind me, mulling over my comments I assume, and I hate that I can't see his face. Suddenly I feel extremely vulnerable both emotionally and physically so I finish flicking the switches over so that he can see what I'm doing. I need to get out of this small space and his proximity. Like pronto.

"See, simple," I say, stepping back and into his chest. I expect him to move immediately, since the full contact of our bodies is anything but professional, but he doesn't. And it's his immobility that lets me know he's doing this on purpose.

Irritation escalates to full-blown anger. I don't like my hand being forced. He wants to flirt, fine.

No, it's not fine.

God, he's got me flustered when I *never* get flustered and now I can't think straight. I just want to get this over with.

"Not simple, no," he says, breaking through my internal debate, his mouth close to my ear so that his breath tickles my bare skin. "Is there a reason you're trying to rush this?"

So many words fill my head but I know I need distance from the heat of his body clouding my thoughts. I step back again, aiming to free myself from the small space but only succeed in pressing my ass further against his groin.

I sidestep immediately, our bodies separating as I bump my back against the wall behind me in an ungraceful escape. "I'm not rushing," I lie. "Just making sure I show you everything you need to know before class starts. I can slow it down some if you'd like?" I ramble the words out, choosing to focus on the Def Leppard logo on his black shirt instead of meet his eyes.

"Nice and slow is always good—don't you think, Quinlan?"

I snort out a laugh, nerves front and center so that the quip is off my lips without thought. "Guys like you wouldn't know slow if it hit you in the face." The comment gives me a little better bearing, and I arch a brow at him, daring him to respond and grant me the argument I'm pushing for. A confrontation that will piss him off so he'll steer clear of me and the trouble we'd cause each other.

"You think you have me pegged, don't you? I assure you, square or round, I don't fit in any predetermined hole." With our sunglasses off, I can't deny the question in his eyes like I could on the way here. Just as I can't hide the truth in mine.

But I'm damn well going to try.

"You don't have to fit in any hole for me to be right. My brother used to be just like you. . . . Hell, I probably know your game better than you do." I quirk an eyebrow, waiting for the comment I can see on the tip of his tongue.

"Maybe I only want to fit in one hole," he says softly as he takes a step into me, our bodies close, eyes locked, and libidos begging for the physical connection that we're both fighting. I should be pissed at his comment, should think it sounds corny, but holy hell that melodic tone to his voice makes it sound anything but. "Go out on a date with me."

My breath hitches and mind consents but my feet step back, reminding me I have nowhere to run. I falter against the wall behind me, emotions whirling and warring at a breakneck pace.

"Bet you didn't guess I was going to ask that now, did you?"

I hope he doesn't notice the slight hesitation before I respond with a laugh. "Smooth, but uh, no thanks." Despite the words, my mind says *yes*.

He angles his head and his eyes lock onto mine—daring me to look away. "Then why do I make you so nervous?"

I can't help but glance down at his lips and then back up to his eyes as every part of me wonders what they'd feel like on mine. My tongue darts out and wets my bottom lip in reflex and the slow curl of his mouth tells me he notices it.

The grip I have on logic weakens in the confined space, my fingers restless to reach out and draw him into me.

"You don't." I murmur the words, captivated by the proximity of his lips and the hunger in his eyes. I close mine to break the connection for a moment before opening them, resolve firmly back in place.

"Mm-hm, and yet earlier I asked you why you didn't like me and you ignored it. Your lack of an answer leads me to believe just the opposite. Why fight it? You do like me don't you?"

"Like I said, I've been surrounded by guys like you my whole life. No thank you."

"I bet none of them have done this."

His moves into me at such a slow pace that he grants me every chance to reject his advance. *But I don't*. My quick inhale fills my lungs but nothing else fazes me because I'm completely focused on the descent of his mouth.

He brushes his lips against mine. Once. Twice. I'm so lost in the feeling that I don't even realize his hands are gently cradling my face. Fingertips calloused by guitar strings angle my head to the side the same time my lips part, and the need to taste him is my only focus.

Our tongues meet in a gentle caress of heat and desire. A mixture of curiosity and lust, need and hesitancy. My hands are on his biceps, fingernails digging into muscular flesh as he deepens the kiss.

My body reacts instantly to his subtle claiming of my mouth. It might be light brushes of lips and licks of tongues but the ache deep within me burns so strong I emit a pained moan. There is just something about Hawkin that has me wanting so much more than a stolen kiss.

His thumb brushes over the line of my jaw as his other hand runs down the length of my back, pulling me into him. Our bodies battle the desire, wanting more but not taking it.

"Stop!" I cry out when something in me sparks to life. I can't explain the feeling but it scares the hell out of me and has me pushing him away with a half-assed protest that sounds less than convincing. But how can it sound otherwise when my thoughts, my senses, my lips are consumed by the taste of him.

He leans back, lips parted and eyes wide with confusion. All I can do is shake my head back and forth to express my rejection. "I just . . . We can't." I fumble for the right words to say and then just say screw it. I turn on my heel and run up the stairs of the auditorium as he shouts my name behind me.

I push open the doors, needing the fresh air to clear my head and help with what I can only describe as a mini panic attack. I don't know what the hell is wrong with me, but I wave away Axe as he starts to approach me and walk a few more feet to a bench near the shade of a tree.

I sit down, lean my elbows on my knees, and hang my head down to try to calm myself. I close my eyes, welcoming the cool breeze on my face, when it hits me why I'm so freaked out.

I've kissed a lot of men. But never have I been so lost in a kiss that when I closed my eyes I saw tomorrows and ever-afters. Certainly not with Rick, and not with any man I've been with. Shit, I'm the last one on the planet to believe in the fairy-tale crap and yet there they were, vivid and in my face.

Frustrated and confused, I blow out an exhale and lift my eyes. Everything around me—students, buildings, bikes—blends together as I try to wrap my head around the irony of it all. I don't usually think this way, don't want these type of things—marriage, monogamy, kids, the death of spontaneity—at this point in my life, if ever. It's just not my driving force. I've been in school forever, am about to grad-uate and dive headfirst into my dream career in film pro-duction, so they aren't even a blip on my radar.

So why was I thinking them? And more important, why was I envisioning Hawkin Play as being the center of my universe when we butt heads like siblings and verbally spar like enemies?

It has to be because of his goddamn kiss.

Hell yes I wanted it—won't deny it even to myself—because damn, the man can kiss. I shove the thought away that he's probably had many women to practice on to get that kind of skill; it was so mind-blowing, I don't care so long as I got the benefit of it.

His lips were the perfect combination of firm and soft, he used enough tongue but not too much, and then added to it the gentle coaxing of his fingertips to get me to open up to him, and ugh, I want more.

But therein lies the problem. I'm sure wanting more means different things to him than it does for me. For him it's probably a quick fling that would run the duration of his seminar. And while I'm all for quick, fun, and meaningless, the way I just reacted to his kiss alone scares me into thinking that I might not be able to keep it on that level, promises made to myself be damned. That I'd be falling headfirst into something serious without a moment to enjoy it before heartbreak crashes down around me.

I roll my shoulders, stand up, and do something uncharacteristic of me. I'm usually a go-for-it, damn-the-consequences-later type of girl . . . and yet as I head back toward the auditorium with thoughts of how to play this with Hawkin, I tell myself not this time, not with this guy.

He may embody all of the things that call to me on so many levels—and I'll probably curse myself later for it—but with the start of my career on the horizon, I need to be smart.

And walking headfirst into heartbreak is not smart.

"You okay?" Axe asks, his expression stoic, and his eyes hidden behind dark lenses scanning the students beginning to line up for the lecture.

"Yeah. Thanks," I tell him as he opens the door for me. I walk through it, head down as I try to figure out how to handle this. Do I take the blame, apologize, and then hide behind the facade of hostility that helps me to resist him?

I'm still deciding what to do when I'm startled by a scuffing sound ahead of me. I look up to find Hawkin leaning against a pillar, arms across his chest and a condescending smirk turning up the corners of his mouth. "Well, well, well. So good you came back for more, huh?"

His words startle me. And not in a good way. I came in here willing to apologize, worried about everything, and he greets me like that? Pretending to be hostile is no longer a necessity because it's a reality.

"Excuse me?" I take a step closer, eyes narrowed and disbelief undoubtedly written all over my face.

He straightens up some, and the smarmy look stays on his face but he drops his hands. I briefly notice he's changed his shirt to a white button-up—and I can see the hint of another tattoo through the open collar—but my frazzled state leads me to not give it a second thought. I'm too busy watching how rejection doesn't sit well with the rock god Hawkin Play.

Well, he'd better get ready for more of it if he thinks he

can be an asshole to me. So what if I kissed him and then changed my mind? And standing here, eyes locked on each other's, I'm dismayed by the way he's handling this. Stupid me thought he'd be more hurt and less jerk. Guess I thought too highly of myself. The reality check that I really am just another in a long line of women to him is welcome.

Good thing I found out now rather than in a month when my heart's already invested. I use my own hurt, the revelation of truths I didn't expect—the spite in his glare—to keep my guard up. But guard or no guard, I become uncomfortable under his intense scrutiny when he just stands before me, posture in itself threatening, and doesn't say a word.

"What do you want?" I snap, shifting my feet.

"You for a start." He ghosts a smile and where before I found it sexy, right now, the sight of it mixed with the look in his eyes unsettles me.

"If my actions didn't say it earlier, then my lips will say it so you can understand: *Dream on*." I take a breath, eyes flickering over my shoulder to see if Axe is still there just on the other side of the door, because for some reason alarm bells are sounding in my head.

He laughs low and mocking and if he's trying to freak me out, he's doing a damn good job. I'm done here. Carla can pull my thesis for all I care but I refuse to work with this schizophrenic asshole. In the span of one minute we've gone from flirting to kissing and in the next making me uncomfortable.

I start to walk past him to go grab my bag I left when I ran away and he grabs my arm, fingers digging in. A shocked gasp falls from my mouth but I refuse to give in and meet his eyes.

"Believe me, any dream I have of you will be a wet one."

I yank my arm from his grasp, disgusted by his comment and how far off the mark I was in judging him. How did he go from hot and desirable to cheesy and creepy?

I ignore his laugh at my back and all but jog to the open doors of the auditorium. I rush through them, head turning to glance back at him, and find myself colliding into someone.

"Jesus!"

I'm shocked by the voice, the scent of cologne, and the face when I look up to see Hawkin's surprised expression. *What the hell?*

"Hawkin?" His name comes out in a flustered gasp as I try to process the fact that he's standing before me when I thought he was behind me. I push back from him, adrenaline hitting me now so that my hands are a little shaky and take in his black Def Leppard T-shirt and the hair mussed earlier from my hands.

How can? . . . And then it hits me. I recollect an article I read during my intermittent cyberstalking about Hawkin that he had a brother. It definitely didn't say he had an identical twin.

He stares for a beat, trying to figure out what's wrong, when his eyes lift to over my shoulder. Hawke's gaze immediately turns hard, jaw clenched and shoulders squaring in irritation as he delivers an unspoken warning to his brother before falling back on mine and softening with concern.

"You okay?" His focus is solely on me, hands reaching out to touch my arm in a reassuring manner.

"Yeah?" I say it like a question, asking him if the man at my back is really who I think it is.

"I'm sorry." Hawkin murmurs the apology, somehow realizing that his brother has unnerved me, and he positions himself so that he's standing between us.

"What are you doing here, Hunter?" The two men stare at each other, animosity palpable between them as they speak without words.

"Wanted to see my big bro's new gig. Got quite a nice surprise though when I came early and went looking for him. Alcoves can be fun places, no?" Hunter says with a chuckle, giving me the chills that he was watching us. He lifts his chin toward me and raises his eyebrows. "She yours?"

As much as a part of me wants to speak up, assert my position, the obvious discord vibrating between the two of them has me biting my tongue.

"New gig's courtesy of you, right? If you wanted this for yourself," Hawke says pointing to the auditorium behind him, sarcasm all but dripping from his voice, "all you had to do was have a little integrity."

"Integrity is overrated. Contracts, a man's word, family bonds—nothing holds anymore these days. But you already know that, dontcha *brother*?" Hunter chides him with a wink, and I notice Hawkin clench his fists. Hunter's eyes glance over and meet mine, a ghost of a smirk playing on his lips.

"Leave her alone, Hunt. She's with me."

And I'm not sure if it's the fact that he seems like he's protecting me from his brother or if it's him saying I'm his, but hearing those words pulls on some inherent female part of me, a part that longs to be someone's. Despite the tension of the moment, I find it sadly comical that my resolve to keep Hawkin at arm's length crumbles with that simple statement.

"Does *she's with me* have a name?"

"Trixie," Hawkin states, beating me to the punch when I was going to give my real one. And then I wonder why he's giving his own brother my fake name but in the same breath I'm glad he does.

"Trixie." Hunter rolls the false name around on his tongue before nodding in acceptance. "Aren't you going to introduce us?"

Hawkin's sigh is audible and his voice monotone when he speaks. "Trixie, this is my brother, Hunter. . . . Hunter, this is Trixie. *Satisfied?*"

"Very," he murmurs, eyes finding mine again and I have no problem being the first to look away this time as he takes a step closer. "So Trix—"

"What do you want, Hunter? If you wanted to be here, I know a surefire way you could be." The derision in Hawke's voice is frigid.

"Testy, testy. Do you let him talk to you like this?" Hunter directs the question at me, and it's more than obvious he's enjoying taunting his brother.

"Answer my question, Hunt." Hawkin's tone tells me he's had enough of whatever game his twin is playing. I just wish I knew what exactly it was.

"I need to borrow your car."

Hawkin physically startles at Hunter's request. "You have your own."

"It's in the shop. Besides"—Hunter shrugs, completely unapologetic—"I like yours better."

"You always like mine better."

"Yes, I do," he drawls the words out, a predatory gleam in his eye as he glances my way, "since you seem to enjoy taking what I deserve."

"Cut the crap," Hawkin orders, authority resonating in his voice as it echoes around the empty theater. "Why do you need it?"

"Mine's in the shop so—"

"So you thought you'd trek halfway across town to a place you'd never go otherwise to ask me for my car? Ever heard of a taxi? Kind of presumptuous to just assume I'd hand it over, dontcha think?"

From the way they glare at each other—testosterone mixed with what I can guess is familial bad blood—I can't help but wonder what else they are speaking about because it sure as hell isn't a car.

"You'd do anything for family, isn't that right?" Hunter angles his head at his brother, lips pursed, attitude prevalent.

"*Try me again.* Seems my generosity is running thin." Hawke's body vibrates with anger.

"Hmm." Hunter laughs, the sound in itself mocking. The two spitting images stare each other down, animosity and irritation dueling between them. "Mom needs me."

The simple statement causes everything about Hawkin to immediately alter despite the cocky raise of Hunter's eyebrows that says, *see, I told you, you'd bend for me*. His shoulders fall and he glances back my way for a split second, indecision mixed with concern marring his face, before walking closer to his brother. "She okay?" he asks in a hushed whisper, his back toward me now.

I can't hear the rest of what is said, just bits and pieces that don't make sense as Hawkin digs in his pocket for his car keys and hands them over. He gives him some sort of instructions, and then puts a hand on his shoulder and squeezes.

The mirror images look at each other for a prolonged period of silence before Hunter nods his head and walks out. The students, in line waiting for the lecture to start, call out "Hawkin"—mistaking Hunter for his brother—as the door shuts behind him.

I study the lines of Hawkin's back as he watches his brother's movements outside, shaking hands, posing for cell phone pictures . . . acting as if he is his twin. It vaguely crosses my mind to wonder how often he does this, impersonates his brother. I turn my focus back to the man himself. His demeanor seems altered now, so far from the arrogant, self-assured man from earlier or the clips I've seen of him performing. A part of me wants to ask what's wrong, figure out what can affect him so quickly, but I also understand that I know absolutely nothing about him besides the image he feeds to the media.

And growing up in a household under the scrutiny of the Hollywood magnifying glass, I know better than most how image can be a manufactured product.

Standing here beside Hawkin I can feel his angst, sense his restlessness, and I want to know more. Every person has two sides, the side they let everyone believe and the side they let few see. Usually I couldn't care less because each person deserves their own story, but for some reason with Hawkin, I want to see that private side. The man has been making me question my own sanity with the reactions he's pulling from me. Maybe the rest of his story will explain why I respond so strongly to him.

His audible sigh pulls me from my thoughts. "Everything okay?" I can't help it. I know he won't answer, but I have to ask anyway.

"Fucking stellar," he snaps, and then hangs his head with a self-deprecating groan. When he turns and faces me, I can see the lines etched in the sculpted perfection of his face, the remorse in his eyes that melts my heart. "Sorry, I just . . ." His voice trails off as we stare at each other. Just when he's about to explain, Axe pushes open the door and peeks his head in.

"You ready for them, Hawke?"

Hawkin holds my gaze for a second longer, relief flickering that he doesn't have to explain further, before glancing over to Axe. "Yeah, I'm ready."

He walks past me and down the steps to the podium without another word. Students file in and do a double take when they take their seats and realize the imposter outside was not really him. You can hear the hushed buzz grow louder until Hawke clears his throat and a hush falls over the room. When he begins to speak, the students hang on his every word.

But it's the words he's left unspoken that captivate me the most.

Chapter 7

I watch the lecture from the cheap seats near the very top of the hall. This time I pay attention, listen to his lessons buried under the glamour and glitz of his stories. His charisma comingled with his star power mesmerizes the other students in the room. They laugh with him, groan in the right places, and are rapt with attention.

I see the attraction now, why they hang on his every word because despite telling myself he's off limits, I'm doing the exact same thing.

The lecture ends and while everyone stands, I remain seated as student after student approaches him to get their five seconds of personal attention. He comes off as approachable and yet after about thirty minutes and a line that never ends, I catch the glance Hawke slides to Axe in a practiced move so smooth that most wouldn't notice it.

"Okay, folks! We've got to clear the room for the next lecture. Those who need to speak to Hawkin can do so through the Fine Arts department Web site or after the next lecture." Axe starts ushering the stragglers out, walking behind them up the steps to assure that they keep moving toward the exit.

The minute they clear the door, Hawkin takes a deep breath and runs a hand through his hair before reaching for his phone on the podium shelf. Irritation flickers on his face when whatever he's looking for isn't there.

When I start to stuff my papers in my bag, his voice booms, echoing through the empty theater. "What do you mean Hunter hasn't been there?" I jump when his fist pounds on the podium, obviously not happy with whatever answer he's getting on the other end of the line. "She's okay, though? . . . Okay. I will. . . . Later."

He shoves his phone in his pocket and hangs his head down for a moment. "Do you need something?" Impatience, irritation, annoyance—so many emotions laced in the tone of the question.

I didn't realize he knew I was still here and now feel like a voyeur, unsure of what to say or do. He lifts his head to meet my eyes across the distance of the room as I stand and lift my bag to my shoulder.

"No, I—uh—was just gathering my stuff." I apologize without saying the words.

"You good if we take off, man?" I'm startled when Axe speaks behind me.

Hawke's eyes shift from me to him. "Yeah. No. Fuck, Hunt's got my car so—"

"I can take you home." The offer is out of my mouth before I can think about it or the ramifications. "Or wherever you need to go," I correct realizing no way in hell is Hawkin Play going to let some random woman he knows nothing about take him to his house.

Then again, he is a successful musician, aren't random women a way of life?

His eyes move back to mine and although the agitation from moments before is still there, I also see intrigue. "You gonna drive me home, Trix?" He begins to walk up the steps as he asks the question. I don't even get a chance to respond before he lifts his chin to Axe. "I'm good. Thanks man."

Axe leaves without a sound. I wait for Hawkin, and with each step he takes, I can see him shed whatever it is that's bugging him bit by bit so that by the time he reaches me, he's the same man from earlier. Arrogant, enigmatic, and sexy as hell.

He stands in front of me, tongue flicking out to wet his lower lip, and all I want regardless of what I've told myself is to kiss those lips again. Screw caution because I'm throwing it to the wind when it comes to Hawkin Play.

"Are you afraid to take a ride with me?" I ask, knowing full well how the question will be received.

A dimple deepens with his lopsided smile, eyes dancing with mirth. "I assure you, I'm not afraid of riding anything with you." He gestures in front of him for me to lead the way. "Just be warned, I like to take shotgun."

"Good thing I'm great at driving a stick," I say over my shoulder as the welcome sound of laughter returns to his voice.

"I have to tell you I'm seriously turned on here."

The subtle change of subject from my question about whether he and his brother were close does not go unnoticed. I mean we've driven for forty minutes through traffic filled with idle chitchat, but the constant glances at his phone for a text he told me he's waiting for have caused the somber mood from earlier to settle back over him.

So I figured why keep dancing around it and instead I would just ask. And of course, he just delivered the comment that has my mind shifting gears faster than my car climbing up through the hills of Bel Air. So now I'm left to try to figure out what it is he's turned on by, hoping like hell it's by me.

It's one thing to be in a large lecture hall where there is space to move about, to step away. It's another to be in the close confines of a car where everything about him is mere inches away, causing my libido to go into overdrive.

I wet my bottom lip with my tongue and nod. "And . . ." I'll let him lead this conversation, see where it takes us.

"Between your choice of car and the way you handle her . . . damn." He lets the last word trail off and I smile smugly at his compliment. "Impressive and hot."

"Yeah, well, when your brother is a professional race car driver, you can't shame him by being a shitty driver." I recall the numerous driving lessons from Colton as a teenager, the constant ribbing that he was going to teach me to not drive "like a woman."

I catch his double take in my periphery. "Race car driver, huh?"

"Yeah. Indy." I navigate a turn up the windy road.

"Should I know him?"

"Colton Donavan?" I say his name like a question, my lips pursed as I wait to see Hawkin's reaction.

"No shit." He says it so casually that he earns major brownie points with me. But it's not like he's a slouch in the fame department either so my brother's public lifestyle shouldn't faze him—make him suddenly fawn all over me—like it does so many others. He falls silent for a minute as he thinks. "I don't follow racing but know who he is. So that's your last name, huh? I was wondering. Quinlan Donavan," he muses more to himself than me.

And here goes part two of the Quinlan checklist of whether a man can handle me.

"Actually, no it's not." I glance over to catch the perplexed look on his face. "Colton wanted to make it on his own accord, not on the family name."

"Go on." He draws the words out. I can hear the amusement in his voice as he tries to figure out what I'm going to say next. "What is your last name then?"

"Westin."

"Hm," he murmurs as I can all but hear the thoughts connecting in his mind. The ones telling him that my father is the renowned film director Andy Westin. His lack of a reaction is so refreshing compared to the usual barrage of questions and requests that follow someone finding out who my dad is. "You're like unwrapping a present. So many surprises to discover."

You can unwrap me all you like.

"The best parts of me are hidden," I deadpan, a lopsided smirk playing over one corner of my mouth. I love seeing his jaw fall lax in my periphery. Gotta keep him on his toes.

"Good thing I like to take my time when I open a gift. Nice and slow." He draws the words out, a whistle falling from his lips as the tingle begins anew deep in my core. "And I always take my time untying them when they're knotted tight. Always open the box by sliding my fingers in the seam first before I dive right in . . ."

How in the hell has he just seduced me and all he's describing is a damn birthday present?

It's best I don't respond right now because his cologne,

his unaffected responses, his just being normal is causing things inside me to zig and zag when they should be going straight.

"I bet your brother got in a lot of fights growing up."

His comment throws me. "Why do you say that?" He points for me to turn left on another street and I steal a glance at him from behind my sunglasses.

"Well, I'm sure he spent a lot of time protecting your virtue," Hawkin says, and I fight back the laugh that threatens when I think of the scuffles he got in with guys talking in the locker room about his little sister, then and now— Luke Mason, case in point. "Any good older brother protects their younger sibling. No questions."

There's something about the way he says it, the catch in his voice, that makes me feel like he's not just talking about Colton. And of course I want to delve deeper, want to ask about Hunter because I'm not oblivious to the fact that this whole conversation has focused on me when I'd much rather have it be on him.

"You're older than Hunter?" I ask in another attempt to learn more.

"Mm-hm . . . by four minutes," he says, pointing for me to take a left turn.

"Are you guys close?"

"We're identical twins." I bite back the sarcastic remark on my lips about the obviousness of his statement, and how he didn't answer the question. "Most people can't tell us apart, especially when we dress alike."

"I bet that was fun growing up. Does he—"

"So, you're a TA. . . . What is your master's degree in?"

"Film and television production." I glance over to see his eyebrows raised for me to explain further. And it's not lost on me that he's turned the topic of conversation back on me. "I grew up watching filmmaking behind the scenes. I find it fascinating—the egos, the money, watching ideas come to fruition . . . the stuff that no one thinks about."

"Well, it's not like you didn't have a good teacher," he muses casually with a slight nod of his head. "No acting bug then?"

"Being in front of the camera doesn't interest me." I shiver at the thought. The assessing eyes and unforgiving critics. No thanks. While I'm all for being front and center in my personal life, I prefer behind the scenes in my professional one. I think of watching the media chaos that used to surround my brother when the woman he dated changed or if he got in a fight in his testosterone-fueled bachelor days. The thought of all that attention is not appealing.

"Right here," he says pointing to a long driveway, ivy-covered walls on both sides as we drive up it. "It all makes sense now."

"What does?" I ask, slowly getting used to his habit of speaking his internal thoughts without giving me a direction which way they are going. With most people I'd be annoyed but with Hawkin for some reason I find it endearing, a sign that his mind is running a million miles an hour although he never divulges what the other things are that occupy it.

"Your smart-ass mouth."

"Come again?" I laugh as I pull my car to a stop in front of an expansive Tuscan-style house. I shift in my seat and remove my sunglasses so that I can study him, try to figure where exactly he's going with this. How a conversation about my degree, my future career, has led him to a conclusion I'm sure is all wrong about me. I know I have a helluva bite, but get beneath the surface and I'm a softie to those that really know me.

"Most people walk on eggshells around me, kiss my ass" — he shrugs without apology and offers up a smirk that tugs on every part of my body yet to be awakened by him — "or want to kiss other things . . . just because of the music, fame, whatever you want to call it." He looks toward the house and flicks his hand in front of him in a gesture signifying irrelevance and indifference over the whole attention aspect of his job. He brings his eyes back to mine. "But you treat me like anyone else. Give as good as you get. The chaos around me doesn't faze you because you grew up with it. It's kind of nice. . . . I like it."

I hate the little thrill that shoots through me at his ridiculous praise but it does nonetheless. Shit, he just praised me for not fan-girling over him but if he keeps making comments like that I just might start.

"Well, it's not like you're a big deal or anything," I tease with a wink. "*Billboard* charts are *so* yesterday." I roll my eyes, loving the flash of mirth in his eyes before he snickers.

His laugh continues longer than it should and he leans his head back on the headrest. I can sense his release from whatever was eating at him in the manic sound of it. When it finally abates he closes his eyes for a moment to regain his composure, and now my curiosity has been piqued even further about the secrets he holds.

"Thanks. I needed that." He shakes his head and then tilts it toward the house. "Want to come in?"

Warning bells sound in my head, alerting me that this is one of those first steps you can't take back while another side of me says I'm reading way too much into the invite and to hurry up and get out of the car. And of course, my body is reacting, hand on the door handle before my head can tell it to sit still.

We exit the car together and he explains that he and the guys are renting the house while they finish up the current album. He tells me that when they are all in the same place, they mesh better, write the music quicker, are more creative.

He leads me up the steps to the front door, his hand placed on my lower back. Just when his free hand touches the door handle, he pulls it back in what seems like a moment of indecision. I stand there waiting and am taken by surprise when within a beat Hawkin has my back against the wall, his body pressed close, and his mouth on mine.

I react. I don't allow myself to question it or him this time, don't worry myself about the ever-afters I envisioned earlier because he is here and this is now and I like to live in the moment. I don't even think I could analyze anything if I wanted to because desire clouds my thoughts, need overwhelms my senses.

I throw myself into the embrace. Tongues dance, lips claim, and hands fist as we pour the strange emotions of the day into our kiss. There's something different this time around and I'm not sure if it's my willingness or whatever he's struggling with internally but I can feel the desperation in him for some kind of connection, can taste the need as he skillfully knocks all of my senses out from beneath me.

His hands move from framing my face and slide down

my rib cage, thumbs brushing over my nipples through the fabric of my shirt causing the lick of desire to inflame. I moan into his mouth as one of his hands squeezes my ass and presses me against his dick that's begging to escape the confines of his jeans.

My body is on fire with need for this man to the point that this front porch is looking pretty damn good but I wouldn't know for sure because my eyes are closed and already rolling back in rapture. *Take me*, I want to tell him, because shame is so overrated right now. I want to lose myself to him so that he has no option to be the only person that can pull me out of his fog.

"We have beds inside if you want to keep going. Or not . . . and I'll grab some popcorn so I can enjoy the show. *Or some lube.*"

The voice shocks us apart, my heart hammering in my chest, my hands unwilling to loosen from the old-school Def Leppard logo fisted in them, but my eyes remain locked on Hawkin's and the lascivious thoughts flickering in his gaze.

"Fuck off Gizmo," Hawkin growls, his lips reconnecting with mine like there's no one watching. The desperation is insatiable now on our parts—we both need to draw out the last of this kiss since we know we're about to be interrupted.

"Popcorn it is then." He laughs and yet doesn't move because I can feel the weight of his presence still.

And shit, I'm all for exhibition, but for some reason, as hot and primed as I am right now from Hawkin's complete consumption of my willpower, I tear my lips from his. Our faces are mere inches apart, our labored breaths pant over the other's, and our eyes are locked—regret and desire a potent combination reflected back at each other.

But there's something else buried in Hawke's eyes. And I can't quite place just what it is. "You okay?"

Those flecks of silver in his gray eyes darken momentarily because he knows I see the hint of the secret he wants to keep hidden. He nods with a sigh, hands still flexing into the flesh of my hips.

"Did you need something, Giz?" he asks with a glance over to the door, breaking our stare. Reluctantly I drag my eyes from him and follow his gaze. I take in the man leaning against the doorjamb, hands stuffed in the pockets of his

jeans, bare chest covered in a dizzying array of intricate tattoos that I could probably spend a week studying and not
see all of them. His dark hair is shaggy down to his nape, ice
blue eyes a stark contrast to it, and a smile so warm and
welcoming when he offers it to me that I immediately like
him.

His eyes flick up and down my body before aiming an
approving glance back to Hawkin. "Yeah," he blows the
word out and brings a hand up to tug on the back of his
neck. The motion reveals a pink tattoo of a heart on the
inside of his wrist that looks out of place and contradicts the
coloring of his others but his words pull me from the observation. "Hunter called." The disdain in his voice matches
the sigh that falls from Hawke's mouth when he releases
me.

It seems as if Hunter is a real favorite around here. Can't
say I blame them because my first encounter with him was
less than favorable.

"Fuck." It's all Hawkin says before he glances back to
me, irritation and exasperation prevalent in the furrow of
his brow. "Quinlan this is Gizmo, Gizmo, Quinlan."

We say hello to each other and Gizmo moves out of the
doorway so we can enter the house. I can feel his assessing
eyes on my backside but whereas Hunter's perusal felt in-
trusive, Gizmo's is more of the *I'm a male—how can I not
look?* variety. The Old World decor of the house is warm
and welcoming despite its opulence, but I'm more interested in the conversation between the two men.

"You gave him your car?" The shock in Gizmo's voice
has me listening a little closer.

"Long story man." Hawke runs a hand through his hair
as we all move into the stainless steel and granite-slab de-
signer kitchen. He accepts a beer that Gizmo pulls from the
fridge and pops it open, the sound reverberating through
the silence surrounding us after I decline the offer. "He
showed up at the lecture, was fucking with Quin." I catch
the concerned glance Gizmo gives Hawke and then the
warning one he flashes Vince when he walks in the room.
Vince nods his head in acknowledgement as Hawke continues. ". . . And then said he needed my car to go see Mom . . .
but after class, I called and he never showed."

The room falls quiet as I try to decipher what it is that's going on, all of them pondering something serious I have no knowledge of. Vince glares at Hawkin in obvious chastisement, fingers drumming on the granite countertop, an unspoken message delivered.

"Don't give me that look Vince, I don't need you starting in on me right now."

"I didn't say shit, man," Vince says, holding his hands up and darting his eyes my way. I catch the look, know he's telling Hawkin *Not here, not now,* not with an outsider present and that makes me even more intrigued.

"Fellas," Gizmo breaks in with a laugh, walking into the space between them. He shoves a bowl of candy in front of Hawke before hooking his arms around their shoulders. "So much testosterone wasted on one another when it could be used on the lovely Quinlan here." He flashes me a playful grin like he has not a care in the world before walking out of the room toward where a cell phone chimes with a text in the other room.

"Quinlan?" Vince asks confused, and I scrunch up my nose, forgetting he doesn't know the truth about my name. "What happened to *Trixie*?"

Feeling a tad shy under the quiet scrutiny he seems to be aiming my way, I opt to shake my head while his hazel eyes assess and judge me. So I hold his stare, letting him know that I can stand my ground.

"Like he didn't deserve it for calling me out like that in the lecture?" I say, Vince nodding his head in agreement. "Trixie's for the assholes who aren't worth my time."

"Damn, woman," he says with a laugh, the intensity on his face easing some as his approval is granted. "I like the way you think. . . . And what? Now you think he deserves it?"

"Nah, he's gotta work a lot harder to get what he wants," I quip off the cuff, and it earns me an even heartier laugh from him.

The laughter draws Gizmo's attention from the text he's reading as he enters the room. "What's that? You gonna make Hawke work for something? Ah, a woman after my own heart," Gizmo says, beer to his lips against his smirk.

I glance over to Hawkin and he has his head angled to

the side, eyes steadfast on mine telling me he'll get what he wants despite the easygoing smile on his lips. And it's such a turn-on, the unspoken words on the heels of the kiss on the porch that left his taste on my lips and the damp patch in my panties.

I try to hold on to that resolve of mine that says I will not mess with another player again but I can feel myself faltering when he looks at me this way. And hell if he's not the perfect person to keep things casual despite my imagination running wild and wanting a whole hell of a lot more when he kisses me like he did.

The sound of an amplified guitar echoes through the house and draws me from my thoughts. It starts off slow and even, haunting and melodic, and then it hits hard and fast. The three guys around me transform at the sound, concentration etched on their faces, heads bobbing to the beat as the musician picks up the pace until his fingers are screaming up and down the notes.

Silence falls momentarily before he starts all over again.

The music is incredible but even more powerful is watching Gizmo, Vince, and Hawkin internalize the notes this time around and figure out their accompaniment to it, even if it's in the form of hands beating against the counter. I don't belong there in that moment but wouldn't step away if I could because there's something so captivating about watching it unfold.

In my periphery I see Gizmo hurry to grab a pad full of scribbled words from the kitchen counter behind him and start adding to the lyrics already there as Hawkin belts them out. And as much as I want to take them all in—watch them all do their own things—I can't tear my eyes off Hawkin.

Talk about aural foreplay.

The musician thing was never my hot button; I never understood the groupie thing but holy mother of God, watching and hearing Hawkin work through lyrics as the guitar riffs down the hall, I'm a converted woman. A very needy, horny converted woman.

I'm with the band. The clichéd phrase runs through my head, but I can't deny the pull I feel toward Hawke.

Hawkin opens his eyes, and they lock on mine immediately. The sudden jolt of arousal snaps through me, and the air between us practically crackles as it ignites from our unsated desire. He continues the song flawlessly all the while his eyes tell me to do what the lyrics he sings ask.

Play me. Beg me. Take me. Make me.
Be the one to make me fall.
Be the one to take it all.

The music ends, the house falling to silence. Hawkin and I just sit there until he glances over to his bandmates. The three of them all get similar smiles spreading across their faces, and then simultaneously they let out a whoop in celebration that startles me. They start giving one another high fives and slaps on the back.

"What? What did I miss?" A voice shouts from down the hall followed by the appearance of a tall, athletic blond guy, one arm sleeved, gauges in his ears, confused look on his face.

"Were you recording that?" Hawkin asks as the guys all stand still and stare at him, anticipation on their faces.

"Yeah, why?"

The guys start their celebration again, including the newcomer this time around. *Finally* and *it's about fucking time* is murmured between them as I stand there and put the pieces in place.

Gizmo looks over and lifts his chin. "Been working on that song for four months. Couldn't get it right. We were ready to scrap it from the album—and who the fuck knew that it would come together like that from Rocket fiddling around by himself in the studio."

"Ha. He's used to fiddling by himself, just not with a guitar," Vince quips.

I raise my eyebrows, excited to be a part of what they're creating here, the lyrics on repeat through my head for more reasons than how perfectly they complete the song. I feel like Hawke was talking to me, asking me, and I settle into the feelings they invoke within me.

Before I realize it, Hawkin's at my side, hand on my elbow as he leads me from the kitchen. His touch on my skin is intoxicating, his murmur in my ear telling me *"Let's go,"* even more so.

We clear the doorway and he tugs on my arm so that our

bodies crash into each other's the same time our mouths do. And hell yes the kiss on the porch was hotter than hell but this one is scorching. I don't know if it's the euphoric adrenaline of figuring out the song but Hawkin is a man taking what he wants and thank God he wants me.

His hands fist in my clothing and the kiss turns close to bruising as our bodies remain pressed and grinding into each other. I know we're at risk of being caught by the rest of the band, but Hawkin is kissing me like he sings . . . with a little bit of roughness to his smooth and fuck if I don't love the hard edge.

"Upstairs," he pants, hand in my hair, mouth moving down the line of my neck.

"Yes." There is no other response to his command. No concern that he's a player because all I can think about is him and me. Naked. Moving. Entangled. Breathless.

My body responds to his body's nonverbal commands. An intimate reaction to his every action, wanting more, needing more of everything he's giving me.

My back bumps into the banister of the staircase as we move clumsily up the stairs. We both laugh at our impeded progress between urgent kisses and desperate gropes. I pull back and open my eyes to look at where we are going, and I gasp in shock when I lock eyes with Hunter.

"Ahhh!" The sound bursts out of me and Hawkin jolts in reaction. He whirls around as a slow, smarmy smirk curls up the corner of his brother's mouth.

"What the fuck dude?" Hawkin's hands are off me in a flash as he whirls around to face him, the desire raging between us moments ago converting to disappointed anger. And I know Hawke's mad, I just can't figure out if he's pissed because his brother interrupted us or because he lied and took off with his car. Pride has me wanting to think one thing but reason has me knowing it's another.

Hunter lifts his hands up in front of him. "Sorry. I didn't mean to interrupt, really." His mouth says the words but his eyes say something different. "I was just bringing your keys to you."

"What's going on?" Vince comes through the kitchen door and stops when he sees Hunter. The look that passes between the two of them is less than friendly.

Hunter ignores Vince's question and lifts his chin my direction. "So this is more than just you being hot for teacher, huh Trixie? Got a thing for musicians too?"

It's impossible to miss the derision that laces his tone and wonder why it's directed at me. I'm not quite sure how to answer him, what to say, because while he may be the spitting image of Hawkin, he makes me uneasy.

"Who the hell is this Trixie?" It's Gizmo now coming into the foyer, and I'm thankful for him unknowingly breaking up the tension. Although I don't see Hawkin's shoulders ease at all. I wish I could see his face, try to read his expression.

Vince's chuckle and shake of his head pulls me from my thoughts. He slaps Gizmo on the chest. "Always late to the party dude and a few brews short of a six-pack."

"Huh?" I hear him say as Vince pushes him back into the kitchen but doesn't follow. He turns and leans his shoulder against the doorjamb, arms crossed over his chest and his eyebrows raised as if to say *continue* to the two brothers.

"Where were you? And don't say with Mom," Hawkin grits the words out.

"Yeah, sorry about that, I got sidetracked. Didn't make it—"

"No shit," Hawkin says stepping toward him, agitation in his voice and anger reflected in his posture. "Hard to show up when they didn't call you in the first place. After everything . . ." He rolls his shoulders as he tries to rein in his temper. "Can't you just follow through with a promise one fucking time, Hunter?" His voice is low and threatening. Vince's eyes toggle back and forth between the two of them as he assesses the situation.

"Relax," Hunter says with a roll of his eyes and a shake of his head as if the comment is irrelevant. His facetious attitude is a complete contrast to the humorless ones of Hawkin and Vince. "I'll hold my end of the bargain, *brother*." He says the last word with a disdained sarcasm that even ruffles my feathers. Hunter's eyes track over to me and stop. "You can always ensure that I will though by sharing."

"Come again?" The retort is off my tongue before I even think it through. If he's saying what I think he's saying he can move right along.

Hawkin is in Hunter's face within a split second of my comment, hand fisted in the front of his shirt, nose to nose. "Leave her out of the bullshit between us! You had your chance and blew it. *That's on you.* You want something I have again, you best figure out how to get your shit straightened out and get it yourself. Your second chances are wearing thin here, *brother*," Hawkin says, mimicking Hunter's tone, his voice quiet, yet the steel in his attitude more than obvious.

There is a tense few seconds where they remain toe to toe, their unspoken battle filling up the room, until Vince steps forward and grips Hawkin's shoulder. At first he resists Vince trying to force them apart and then relents.

"It's best you leave, Hunt," Vince says with a cluck of his tongue. "You're a bit outnumbered here, if you catch my drift. Door's that way." He gestures behind him, not backing down while Hawkin stalks down the length of the hallway, hands laced on the back of his neck, face grimaced in restraint.

"Ah, so cute you have your bodyguard to make sure you don't get hurt," Hunter sneers like a child.

"You've worn out your welcome, and I don't have any promises that I've made keeping me from plowing my fist in your face," Vince says with a shrug of his shoulders that's anything but apologetic. "I'd love nothing more than for you to give me a reason. . . ."

Hunter nods, teeth biting his bottom lip to fight the smirk playing there, like all of this is humorous to him. He looks over to where I'm frozen with uncertainty over what to do, and lifts his chin.

"You'll learn soon that these guys aren't worth your time. I look forward to seeing you again. *Soon.*" The shuffling of Hawke's feet on the wood floor instantly falls silent at the same time Hunter lifts his eyebrows, smirk bordering arrogant, before turning and heading toward the front door like he hasn't a care in the world. "You guys need to loosen the fuck up in this place," he throws over his shoulder as he strides out of the house, his mocking laughter fading with him.

The front door slams, but no one moves. Despite Hunter's departure, the tension still vibrates off the walls. I'm so uncomfortable, unsure what to do, but all I know is that the look on Hawkin's face calls me to comfort him. But I don't react right away. I barely know this man and as much as I want to fulfill my inherent need to soothe our ache—a quick fuck in the bedroom upstairs might fix him for a little bit—but it won't make me feel very good.

"Sorry about that," Vince says, breaking his stare away from Hawkin's and turning on me, trying to relieve the tension. *"Brotherly love."* He smiles, but it's strained and never reaches his eyes. "Will you excuse us a moment?" he asks but is already walking toward Hawkin before I can respond.

As Vince approaches him, I wonder what the hell that was all about and what has Hawkin so agitated that he won't meet my eyes. They stand face-to-face, their harsh whispers echoing off the wood floor, but only a few words at a time come back to me. And they are not enough for me to piece together the conversation.

"I'm Rocket." The voice startles me to the point that I gasp because I was so focused on them that I never noticed Rocket standing in the doorway.

My eyes flash up to his, and I smile. "Hi, I'm Quinlan," I offer, unsure what else to say as Hawkin's temper escalates, their words unmistakable now.

"I know what I promised, Vince," Hawke shouts.

"You know he's going to take what he wants just to fuck you over anyway," Vince says, glancing our way and then back to Hawkin before saying something I can't hear.

"Sorry about all of this," Rocket says, motioning to the two of them and sensing my discomfort. "Those two go way back. They're close. Closer than Hunt and Hawke are."

"They're not close?" I pry, asking Rocket what I should be asking Hawkin myself but given his aversion in the car to questions about him, I know he'll avoid answering.

Rocket's laugh is low and cavalier. "Do they look like it?" His sarcasm is overtaken by Hawkin barking *"Enough"* to Vince.

"You're dangling a motherfucking carrot in front of him, Hawke," Vince yells and then blows out a breath in frustration. "If he can't have X, then he's gonna take Y."

"Like you have to remind me. I've got it handled. Don't

bring it up again." Hawkin slams a hand down against the console next to him, the sound echoing through the room. He stalks toward me, anger vibrating off him, and I have a feeling it's from a combination of Vince and Hunter.

"Give me a minute," he growls as he passes me without meeting my eyes, his angst palpable. I watch him retreat down a hallway and when I look back, Rocket has his eyebrows raised and a look of resignation on his handsome face.

"Welcome to Bent," Rocket says with an exasperated laugh.

I smile awkwardly at him, feeling completely out of place after the transition from making out to being witness to the familial argument. Do I go? Do I stay? Rocket motions for me to follow him into the now empty kitchen where we both take seats at the island.

We talk for a few minutes about random stuff. How the band rents a house when they're writing an album because it allows the four of them to work all hours, pushes them to be more creative when they can't leave, and helps build their overall bond. He's telling me a story about Gizmo and an accidental drum mishap when Hawkin interrupts us.

"Quin?" Rocket falls silent as I look over to Hawkin, stress etched in the lines of his tanned face. The look calls on the mothering instinct I didn't think I possessed to soothe it all away. He nods his head over his shoulder, and I thank Rocket while I stand to follow Hawkin.

He doesn't say anything to me, just leads so that I'll follow him out to the front porch, where I assume he's wanting some privacy away from the rest of the guys, although I'm unsure why he's choosing out here to have it.

We stand there for a moment before he runs a hand through his hair and blows out an exasperated breath. "Look, I'm sorry about all of that, that you had to see internal band bullshit," he says, confusing me since as far as I know Hunter isn't part of the band.

"It's okay. It happens." I twist my lips, hands linking to prevent myself from reaching out and running a hand down his arm.

"Nah, it's bullshit and I'm sorry," he says again, meeting

my eyes. Something flickers through them and I can't quite catch what they say. "I've got some stuff to do though, so uh, thanks for the ride."

I guess it was indifference since I'm getting a thanks for the ride and nothing else. I stare at him for a moment, although he's not meeting my gaze, and try to figure out why I basically just got downgraded from girl he wants to have hot sex with to one only good enough to be his chauffeur. And it's not that I expect the hot sex right now, that mood is done and gone, but I don't expect to be brushed off without another thought either.

I have to be wrong here. I still feel the heat of his hands on my body and the taste of his kiss on my lips but right now he's as closed off from me as my brother would be.

"Hawke?" I prevent myself from saying anything more and sounding like a needy female . . . but at the same time I'm confused, trying not to be hurt but failing miserably.

He licks his lips, and averts his eyes before stepping back so that his physical distance emphasizes the emotional distance he's just established between us. "See you at the next lecture."

"Did I miss something here?" I can't help it, have to ask.

He shakes his head. "Nope. Just got work to do. That's all."

Our eyes meet, asking questions our mouths won't answer. The silence stretches until the brush-off I thought I was mistaken about is more than obvious. "Mm-kay," I say as I walk down the first few steps, trying to hold fast to my dignity. And I must be so used to watching movies where the guy calls after the girl when she walks away because I purposefully walk slowly to my car.

But he never calls after me.

Never says my name to let me know what he's thinking or that he feels sorry for the whiplash of emotions. I climb in my car without another word from him and head out of the Hollywood Hills, rejection bitter on my tongue and confusion forefront in my mind. The afternoon was a strong affirmation why I shouldn't believe in happily-ever-afters because let's face it, the girl rarely gets the guy in the end.

Chapter 8

The Jack and Coke quenches my thirst but not my anger. Or the sexual frustration.

Quinlan. The thought of her has my hands banging Giz's sticks harder and harder on the mid-toms. I suck at playing the drums but there is something about them and the unsteady rhythm I attempt to create that helps me when I'm stressed. Plus the physicality of it drives me to think only of the notes—nothing else—and fuck if I don't need to not think right now.

No Hunter and his bullshit disappearing act with my car doing who the fuck knows what.

No Benji and the lectures on my voice mail that I need to come clean and turn my brother in. No now that I've pleaded, I can't change my mind or else I'll perjure myself, and we'll both end up in jail.

No Vince telling me on one side that I need to keep this Quinlan shit under lock and key so that Hunter doesn't try to screw up this part of my life, and out of the other side of his mouth teasing me to let him fuck this up so that I can lose and get that first heart-shaped tattoo of idiocy like the rest of the guys.

No lecture where I stumble through stories to try to make it meaningful and memorable somehow for the students flocking in just because I'm Hawkin Play, the lead singer of Bent, rather than because I actually have something good to say. And oddly, it's quite rewarding, regardless of why they are there, to have someone actually listening to my words. Crazy how shit happens.

And lastly when I'm pounding the fuck out of the drums, there's no Quinlan tempting me with that hot body, smart mouth, and unaffected nonchalance. I take that back. She was most definitely affected. No doubt I could have seen just how affected if I'd gotten her upstairs.

Talk about a two for one: sex that I have no doubt would have been stellar and cinching the win with Vince and our bet in record time. Well, the first part of the bet anyway. His proof can wait.

Shit, I see Sledge's tattoo parlor in our near future for him. So why in the hell did I not so subtly kick her out like I did?

Because you're a pansy-ass motherfucker, that's why. I hit the high-tom harder, pissed at myself for the necessary brush-off. I'd tried to appease Vince and his fucked-up theory that Hunter would go after her just because I'm seeing her. Little does Hunter know the reasons behind my pursuit of Quin, and that's for the best, or Vince is right, he'd purposely try to be part of it.

And truth be told, I fucking wanted to drag her up the stairs to my bedroom, lay her out naked, and have my every which way with her. Fuck her like there's no tomorrow so that I could get all this pent-up shit out: anger, frustration, irritation, validation—all of it.

But no way in hell would that be fair to her. Being rough in the sack is one thing—the sting of a hand in a spank, the bite of a flogger—I'm all for it, but being aggressive because you're pissed off at the fucking world and the hand you were dealt isn't cool. There may be pleasure in pain but it's gotta come with the right motivation or you're just a sick fuck.

Hell if it didn't make me feel like shit to push her away, though. Partially to keep Vince at bay and his asinine claims about Hunter being vindictive, but more so because my balls ached so goddamn bad it was painful to send her off when they were begging for her to come and play.

I groan at the thought, the drums drowning out the sound and my shoulders starting to scream from the hour I've been doing this, trying to purge the need to punch my hand through the wall.

Because broken drywall means a hurt hand. And a hurt hand means I can't play the guitar.

But muscles screaming from the workout does nothing to abate the goddamn ache in my balls from wanting her.

I hit the last drum, sweat trickling down my forehead, and open my eyes, expecting to see Vince there but not sure if I would after we got into it earlier. He's a moody fucker and likes to dwell on things when we fight, so I'm surprised he's sitting at the soundboard, beer in one hand, feet up on an opposing chair and indifference in his expression.

"You get it all out? Feel better, now?" He lifts the bottle to his lips but keeps his eyes fixed on mine. The silent *fuck you* relayed in his unrelenting stare.

I grab my shirt that's lying on the floor beside me and scrub it over my sweat-drenched face. I hold it there for a minute as I catch my breath, waiting for him to start in on me but when silence remains, I look up.

"Rough day?"

I can't help but laugh at his accurate assessment of to-day's events. "Fucking stellar."

"Wanna talk about it?"

He knows I don't—I never want to—but I appreciate the offer. I rise from the drums without answering and toss the sticks in a case Gizmo has for them. I grab a handful of Sugar Babies from my tray and toss them into my mouth. For some reason I think of Quin, of her *fruit to my loop* comment and think *sugar to your daddy* would be a good one.

What the fuck is wrong with me? Oh my God, I have issues if that's the shit that I'm thinking of. But at the same time, I did find it so damn adorable when she said that, even when the only reason I should want her is the quick fuck to shut Vince up.

"I'm surprised your teeth aren't rotted out yet," Vince says as he plops down on the recliner we have in the pseudo-studio we've created here at the rental house.

Something's rotten in me, all right, but it's not my teeth.

I flop down onto the couch adjacent to the recliner and lie across the seat of it with my feet crossed over the armrest. Out of habit, I put my hands behind my head and stare up at the ceiling for a bit, the thought angering me. "Do you ever miss our old life when it was strictly music and chicks and ramen? When we had like five groupies and we thought we were the shit?"

He snorts. "You mean you had five groupies and we were just the assholes they had to get through to get to you."

"Those were the days." It all seems so long ago. The funny thing is I had all the same shit in my life back then—Hunter's antics, figuring out how to help my mom, trying to keep my promise to my dad—just on a much different scale, but it still seemed simpler back then somehow. Less stress, less pressure, less bullshit.

"Living the dream, man," Vince says.

"Yeah, living the dream." I fall silent, my mind running over the day and what exactly I'm going to do about it.

"Dude, the guys and I talked and we're willing to push back the start of the tour if we need to so you can take care of all of your shit." I hear the sincerity in his voice and it pisses me off. The guys have to keep adjusting and reprioritizing because of me and the shitstorm currently surrounding me. "We're just worried about you."

"Thanks, man . . . appreciate it, but I can't do that to you guys. I'll get it figured out, leave it all behind by the time we kick it off. Besides, man, I need this—to get the fuck away for a bit."

"New women, new faces, more just for the nights," he muses.

I grunt in response because normally that sounds more than appealing to me. An escape from the pressure here although I still worry about it all when we're on the road. I push away the thought that the only new face I see in my mind is Quinlan's tonight as I basically kicked her off the porch. I shake the image away.

"Offer stands," he reasserts as I sit up and rest my elbows on my knees so I can meet his eyes. "We can pull out of the benefit if need be as well. Might raise some eyebrows but you can have a nodule on your chords again and have to rest your vocals or some shit like that."

"You've got this all planned out, don't you?"

He shrugs. "Well . . ."

And as much as I'd love to blow off the upcoming fund-raiser, take a weekend for myself and get lost in a cabin in the High Sierras to clear my head, I can't be that hypocritical by abandoning the cause so near and dear to my heart.

"Family comes first, Hawkin. Always."

And it's the way he says it that causes the pang in my chest. *Family.* "Well that depends who you're talking about since you guys are more my family than . . ." I let my voice trail off and pause a moment before I continue. "I know with where my priorities are right now it doesn't seem like it, but you are. . . ." That's all I can say because it's been a shit day and fuck if I want to think about how someday I know Hunt will be in jail and my mom will be gone but the guys—Vince, Rocket, and Gizmo—will still be here.

Life and reality suck sometimes. I learned that the hard way a long-ass time ago and it still kicks me in the teeth on a regular basis regardless of how much success comes my way.

"I know. We know." The resignation in his tone is an echo of how I feel.

"Hunter has to get help, see a therapist, something. I made that a stipulation to all of this." That's as close to a confession that I'm going to make in regard to taking the blame for my brother's stupidity the night I was arrested.

"Uh-huh." And that inherent part of me that's always ready to defend my brother bubbles up before I rein it in. Yet Vince deserves to be skeptical after the numerous fall-outs he's had to deal with over the years. "Dude, if kicking him out of the band didn't sober him up, nothing's going to. Shit, it's almost worse now. Him being high, missing a rehearsal, being too coked out to perform is one thing . . . but now, it's like he has a vendetta against you to fucking take you down too, except he knows he can't get to us, so he goes after everything else he can," he says.

The urge to punch a wall returns; my hands fist, and jaw clenches as I'm reminded of the fallout years ago before we became successful. The decision the band ultimately left up to me when it came to my brother. The choice I made that still eats at me, still causes guilt, and that my brother uses every chance he gets to remind me of it. To try to pay me back for kicking him out of Bent because he couldn't control his habit and was risking our chance at a record deal.

One of the hardest decisions I've ever made was whether to push him away or try to help him and at the same time save me in a sense. I close my eyes momentarily, Depeche Mode's lyrics to "Halo" running through my mind: *You wear guilt like shackles on your feet, like a halo in reverse.* The words serve as a reminder that the one constant in my life, besides music, has been guilt.

And then I look at my other constant, Vince and his unwavering friendship. "Man, I'm doing the best I can." I blow out a breath, staring at my hands for a beat, knowing I'm going to say the words and Vince isn't going to believe them but I need to say them anyway. "I told him he has to set something up and follow through by next month."

Vince just meets my eyes with a disbelieving nod. "Whatever you say, Play."

"Fuck, I told him if he didn't, I'm going to Ben and telling him what happened that night. . . ." My words drift off as I realize what I just said. The combination of Quin and the fight with Hunt and the alcohol and . . . just fucking everything had scattered my thoughts and it took its toll on me in the form of a semiconfession.

Vince's eyes flash over to mine, the *I fucking knew it* written all over his face, but he doesn't say a word. He just twists his lips in thought and takes a deep breath as he digests the admission that he already knew. I know he wants to chastise me, get in my face over what he deems is my stupidity, but he knows me so well, knows that this was a slip I never intended to make, understands that I'll shut down and take the fuck off for a while so that I don't have to deal with everything, so he bites back the bitterness on his tongue.

Little does he know at this juncture I've fucked myself to the point that if I do change my story, there will be repercussions—perjury—so I just keep my mouth shut. The giant wave of guilt crashing into my conscience once again.

"I promise man, I'm not going to let his shit affect me or the group."

Vince sighs and the room falls quiet for a moment, only

the second-hand click of the clock hanging on the wall breaking through the silence. "You don't go back on promises and we believed you when you told us that Hunter's bullshit won't come into our house again. I don't know how you're going to do that man but we believe you will."

"Thanks for the vote of confidence," I say, lying back down and bending my arm over my eyes, wanting to shut this all out. Wanting to shrug out of the responsibility that fell on me at much too early an age to take care of my mother and Hunter.

It all flashes in my memory like it was yesterday—his voice, his words, the images. My dad's grown-up rant to my nine-year-old ears. How love makes the strongest person weak, can ruin them, make them lose their way. I remember my confusion, not understanding what he meant, why tears were streaming down his face as he told me over and over that love would make me weak.

That he was weak.

I can still hear my voice asking him how love can make you weak when Mommy loves him and he wasn't weak. The tears came harder then from him and me as he knelt down in front of me and looked me in the eyes, made me swear to take care of them because I was the strongest of all. He went on to make me promise that no matter what, I'd do all I could to protect them because weak people made stupid mistakes and only brave men—me—could try to help them.

And I remember how the nine-year-old me was so proud that my dad had called me a man that I nodded, I agreed with everything I had, I promised faithfully because I had no idea what would happen next.

So I swore to protect my own blood at all costs and if I didn't, I would be weak too. My only choice would be the same as his. He rambled on, scaring me with his words, his sudden anger that turned back to tears, shaking me by the shoulders to reinforce them. I kept glancing at the door, wondering when Mom and Hunter were going to come home because I didn't know what to do, how to calm him. All I wanted when I came downstairs was my Transformers and yet I was scared to move and go get them from where they sat on the fireplace.

I remember glancing at the hearth and then back to him

just in time to see him load the bullet in the gun I was never supposed to touch. The taste of the fear was like acid in my mouth and yet I couldn't swallow. He looked me in the eye and told me that if I was weak, if I let him down by not being strong and taking care of them, then I would have to do what a weak man does. And then he put the tip under his chin as I whimpered and cowered. He yelled at me to stand up, to show him how strong I was by watching because if I didn't, I'd be just as weak as he was and earn the same fate.

I stood tall, so afraid to let him down despite the tears sliding down my cheeks and the taste of vomit in my mouth from fear, and looked him in the eyes, and said the words, *I promise, Daddy*.

Then he pulled the trigger.

Vince calling my name shakes me from the memories that have scarred me like a brand, deep and irreversible. The Jack and Coke no longer sits well in my stomach and yet I'm sure as fuck going to have another to quiet the shit in my head.

"Yeah, what?" I ask as he eyes me, trying to determine whether I'm okay. I just shake my head at him to drop it as I scrub my hand over my face to try to rub away the memory that's etched in permanent ink.

"I'm gonna be honest, man. You're toeing that fine line with everything—Hunt, Quin, the other shit," he implies without acknowledging. "The sucky thing about lines though is once you step over the edge, you can't always find your way back."

I stare at him, unsure which of those lines he's talking about specifically but I don't even want to venture a guess because I'm just glad it drags my thoughts from my past. "Maybe I don't want to find my way back."

"You talking about Trixie now?" He chuckles.

I'm not talking about anything in particular, just that unsettled feeling in regard to everything tumbling out of control around me . . . everything except for our music. My one and only constant through life. And I don't really want to sit here and talk about this shit with myself let alone Vince so I hold on to the comment and use it as an out.

"I would definitely toe any line with her especially if I

can use it to tie her to the headboard and have some fun." The smile that graces my lips is genuine in what feels like the first time since the moment Quin left the house.

"You're a sick fuck but I love the way you think."

I laugh with him. "Living the dream, man."

He laughs harder. "You're going to be living in a tattoo shop pretty soon if you don't set things right with little Miss Q."

"Things are fine," I correct him even though I know I was an asshole to her. Fuck. What I'd give to have her here right now since my anger has been thoroughly taken out on Giz's drums. "I'll fix it," I say, and then realize I didn't tell him anything about how the two of us left things. I shift to sit up and stare at him, eyes narrowed, lips pursed so that I don't even say a word and yet he knows what I'm thinking.

"Yep. I spied," he confesses with a smirk. "Gotta know where I stand so I know when I'll be needed to step in. Dude, being a third wheel never sounded so fucking appealing. I still think she's going to grab you by the balls and add a little twist when telling you to fuck off after how you handled her tonight, but I'll gladly take the extra ring around my tattooed heart because she's *hot*."

"That she is." I blow out a breath and angle my head back against the cushion, thinking how I'm not too thrilled with the terms of this bet anymore. I'm not a possessive guy but fuck if I want Vinny in on this one. Then again, I'm not getting a tattoo of a heart like a pussy either.

Talk about being between a rock and a hard place. Shit, I'd much rather just be between her thighs.

But Vince might just be right. I might have screwed the pooch here in how I left things tonight. Talk about a hard row to hoe, kiss her like I want to fuck her and then shove her out the door without so much as a hug. Stellar, Play. Frickin' stellar.

The sad fact is I'm being protective of her as if I'm looking for something more than some fun between the sheets with a girl who readily admits that she enjoys sex. *But I'm not.* I don't have time for that in my life right now, and definitely don't want to invite the crazy in that comes with the steady woman territory. Jealousy over groupies, inability to handle lonely nights while I'm on the road, and the constant underlying feeling that they're with me for the wrong reasons. I have enough crazy already to last a lifetime.

Besides, *something more* means love. Love means weak. Weak means I've failed.

No, I most definitely am in this for the challenge, wanting to prove I can bed her as well as get a kick out of fucking with Vince.

Now I have to figure out how to do that since I just proved to her she was right in assuming I was the player she kept telling me I was. But I'm not worried. She hated me at first sight and came around, so it can't be that much harder to get her into bed.

Now, if I only had her phone number.

"I see you figuring your angles on how to fix this over there Hawky-boy . . . but it's going to take a whole lot more than you think. A woman scorned is a whole different animal than a groupie. . . ."

I laugh. "Yeah, they leave bite marks."

"Hey, a little pain never hurt anybody," he muses with a slow nod of his head and a tip of his bottle back up.

My phone breaks through our comfortable laughter. Vince looks down at my phone sitting on the soundboard next to him. "Westbrook," he says, holding the phone out to me.

Fuck. Dread rifles through me. They never call for good news. "Hello?"

"Mr. Play, please."

"Is my mom okay?" I ask like I don't know what's coming next.

"She's quite agitated. I've called your brother but he isn't answering. We can either give her something to calm her down or—"

"I'm on my way." I blow out a breath and give Vince a look he knows all to well.

I grab my keys on the run, the familiar burden of responsibility a son should never have weighing heavy on my shoulders. I just wonder how much longer I'll be able to carry the brunt of it before my back breaks.

Weak is not an option.

Chapter 9

HAWKIN

The beige walls are supposed to be warm and comforting to the residents but in my mind they do nothing but reinforce my mother's institutionalization here. The dreary color serves as a steady reminder that she's so far beyond my ability to help that I have to pay other people to do the job that I no longer can.

I can take the number one spot on every chart in the world with the songs I sing, the lyrics I write, the beats I create, but none of it really matters because I can't take care of my mother. When will the rest of the world realize that I'm a phony? That I've sold out as a son, failed to take care of her as I'd promised Dad, and that I've left her with strangers to deal with her so that I don't have to?

Riding shotgun beside my guilt is the relief. Even that thought causes more guilt to spiral within me as the soles of my shoes squeak down the monochromatic hallways. Because without the daily interaction I was so used to, there's no opportunity for her to unleash her disdain of me, her spite, her disappointment. Yes, I know it's her disease talking most of the time but that knowledge does nothing to abate the searing ache of the loss of my mother.

Of the mother who once loved me.

And of the only woman I've loved. I've spent a lifetime

building walls to keep everyone at arm's length and yet with a single phone call, a single word from her, she can bring me to my knees in all senses of the word.

She can make me weak.

I shake off the morose thoughts, force myself to push away the memories from earlier that are still clouding the edges of my mind.

"Hawke!" Hunter's voice calls from behind me, and as pissed as I am right now over all of his shit from earlier, a part of me is relieved that I don't have to do this by myself. It's better not to face her alone since he is the one that somehow calms her.

So I stop walking, letting the reprimands die on my tongue because this isn't the time or place, and wait for him. "Nice of you to show up. Next time pick up your damn phone." Those are the nicest words I have for him, so I stop there, before I turn and keep walking the familiar path.

Muted televisions play as we pass by rooms with open doors but for the most part there is a peaceful calm over the unit when we approach the nurse's station. The nurse, Beth, raises her head as Hunter and I approach.

"Thanks for coming," she says, repeating the same thing she says on my at least twice-weekly urgent visits here.

"What's going on?" Hunter asks.

"How is she?" I ask at the same time.

"Dr. Manning had thought the sundowning had peaked," she says, referring to the syndrome with dementia patients where they become more agitated, revert to a previous time period in their life, and in most cases it occurs from sundown to sunup. I know this is her polite way of saying my mom's Alzheimer's has progressed to a more advanced stage. "Tonight, though, she's been extremely distressed—more so than normal. We've been able to placate her by making sure she has all of her handbags with her."

I nod my head at Beth, grateful they've accepted my mom's need to have her purses with her—for some reason they help to calm her when she becomes agitated. The doctor doesn't understand why but has heard of it in a few other cases, and instructed the staff to let her have the purses if needed to calm her down and bring her back to the present.

"Okay, thanks," I tell her as Hunter moves ahead of us and toward our mom's room.

"It's almost as if something is really getting to her today," she says as I start to walk past the desk.

Hunter continues in, and I stop and hang my head for a moment before meeting her eyes. "I'm not sure but we're approaching the anniversary of my dad's suicide," I tell her, voice quiet, memories colliding in my mind. The day our lives changed forever.

The catalyst.

One moment in time when a person's inherent makeup can determine whether they are going to overcome or succumb to an obstacle . . . fight or flight . . . sink or swim. Too bad what most individuals don't realize is even if you swim, that doesn't mean everyone else around you will too. Regardless of how strong you are for them all. . . . You become the life preserver while everyone else holds on, fingers gripping, hands slipping, hope waning, until they drag you down with them.

Thanks, Dad.

The thought flickers through my mind and I struggle against the hostility toward him that slips through every now and again. It wasn't Mom's fault but I swear to God his suicide was the beginning of her undoing. They say Alzheimer's doesn't have a trigger, but she shut down after Dad died. Life was too much for her to cope with any longer. I swear she didn't want to remember so her mind turned against her.

I force myself to shake off the thoughts as I approach her room slowly, a lump of anxiety in my throat since I'm unsure which person she's going to be when I enter. The room decor offers more muted colors, as a soft glow emanates from the lamps on the walls, mementos of the family she rarely remembers scattered throughout it.

The sound of her humming has cautious optimism rising within me as she comes into view, embracing Hunter, her hand petting over his hair like she used to when we were kids. I strain to hear the song, but already know what it is: "Over the Rainbow."

My beautiful mother with the pitch-perfect voice. She had so much musical potential but she preferred singing lullabies to her boys over being out late and performing in the jazz clubs that begged for her and my father to take their stage. She feared the moments she'd miss if her sons woke up and needed her. All her life my mother was so full of laughter, love, and compassion. But a single gunshot silenced all of that within her—it killed her too in a sense.

Her brain is allowing her a moment's reprieve before it swallows her back into dementia's bitter clutches. I stand still and watch the woman she used to be, afraid to breathe too loudly and upset her and trigger her to turn into the woman I don't know.

"There now, Hunter. What did your brother do to you this time?" she asks him gently as a mother does a young child. Every time I come here I hope that she remembers me for the child she loved, not the one she blamed for not stopping her husband from killing himself.

Those glimpses of that mom who used to kiss my scrapes and tuck me in are so few and far between these days, her mind so warped that even when she does remember us, she remembers that Hunter was her baby, and I am the son who didn't *stop him*.

I know she doesn't mean the things she says to me, know it deep in my core, and yet it does nothing to lessen the hurt or damage the hope that for one fleeting moment she'll look at me and tell me it's not my fault. That she'll hold me in her arms, tell me she knows I couldn't have stopped it.

That she'll tell me something I've gone what feels like a lifetime without hearing, that she loves me. So once again I fight off the discord that overtakes me every time I visit her.

I shift my feet and she hears. She looks over and the familiar sneer appears on her face, the words like a reflex at the sight of me. "What are you doing here? I told you I don't want you here anymore." She hugs tighter to Hunter as she speaks to me, ice lacing her voice. It's amazing to me that even though we are twins she can still tell us apart even in her altered mental state.

The stupid fucking hope I get every time I cross into this damn room sinks to the pit of my stomach.

"Hi, Mom." It's all I can say really. "How are you today?"

"How am I today?" she shrieks, releasing Hunter to face me. "How am I? I'd be a lot better if you didn't let my husband kill himself, is what I'd be." Her voice rises as she stands from the bed. I glance at Hunter and it's the first time in a long time that I see compassion in his eyes for what he knows is coming next. The pain he can't stop for me. "You stood there like a pathetic little boy and didn't scream for help, did you?" Her words begin to slur as she steps into my personal space, and I know that means her mind is starting to pluck her memories away one by one.

I set my jaw, teeth clenched as I prepare myself for the verbal assault to come because as much as I'd love to scream and yell back, tell her she's full of shit and what in the hell can a little boy do to prevent a man with a gun—the words I've repeated in my head for years, the ones I've used to try to silence my own conscience—I keep quiet. It's not going to fix anything and by the time the words are out, she won't even remember what happened anyway.

And besides, she's still *my mom*.

"You stood there," she says, shoving me in the chest, "and let him take the easy way out. Ruined me."

I so desperately want to tell her it was in no way the easy way out. That obviously he was sick, and he needed help that he never got. But how do you explain to one sick person about another sick person and have it make sense? Especially when it doesn't even make sense to you all these years later.

Hell yes I'm pissed at my dad. Angry he robbed me of all the things in life I deserved to do and see with him. Angry that he left me with a bucket load of promises I don't want to keep most days and yet I do so that somehow, in some fucked-up way, he'll be proud of me. I still love him just like I still love her despite how much she hates me.

I brace myself for the slap that comes but welcome it to shock me from the slide show in my mind of all the skeletons in our familial closet. It stings like a bitch despite her weakening physical state but I accept the pain.

"Mom, stop!" Hunter speaks up for me, knowing this isn't my fault even though I'm sure over the years he's blamed me too at some point. He uses the rage inside him over being cheated out of a father and he uses the drugs to numb himself as fuel to get back at me subconsciously.

"Don't you protect him!" She whirls on Hunter, the pitch

of her voice shrill. "He ruined our lives. Your brother didn't try to stop it and ruined our lives." She's screaming now, loud enough that I hear the nurses call over the intercoms for a Code Gray in her room.

I fist my hands, the only reaction I can give when all I want to do is punch through the drywall beside me. She turns back to me, hands shoving, hysterics escalating, so that I can't make out everything she's saying but I do hear her say the comment that causes the burn of anger to comingle with the tears I refuse to shed. "You're weak just like your father was."

I grab on to her wrists as she continues to thump my chest even though they aren't causing any real damage. The orderlies come in and help Hunter and me try to calm her down some, her head thrashing and arms flailing. I know they're going to call the nurse in to medicate her if she doesn't settle down so I do the only thing I can think of, the one thing that sometimes helps.

I begin to sing.

An old song that Aya, our nanny, used to sing to me when I had trouble sleeping after my dad died. When the sound and smell and image of that day would haunt my dreams so that I wanted to stay awake all night so I wouldn't have to relive it. In my childhood naïveté I believed I could forget it. Fuck was I wrong.

I sing the foreign words that I held on to like a lifeline, some of their symbols inked on my skin still, and hope that it calms my mom so that she can forget: her cruel words, her pain, her mangled memories, her hatred of a tragic event a little boy had no control over.

I'm on the second verse when her resistance begins to abate. Her head sags down, her curses grow quieter, and then as we set her down on her bed, she begins crying. It's so soft at first it takes me a moment to hear it but I kneel down in front of her, her hands still gripped in mine so that I can look up to her.

Her gaze meets mine and I see the confusion flicker in her eyes followed closely by panic. Her head whips back and forth looking at Hunter and me in a frantic haze as the fear takes hold. "Who are you? Why are you here?" She yanks her hands from mine and reaches for one of her purses on her bed and clutches it to her chest, fingers trembling, breathing rapid. "Joshua?" She yells, the name crippling every part of me. "Joshua?" Her voice escalates in pitch and in terror as she calls for my father.

"Mom! Mom!" I try to get her attention, break through her fear but feel as helpless now as I did standing with my dad.

"Mom?" She says as she looks back. "You're not my son. My boys are young. Get away from me!" She yelps when I reach for her and scrambles as far away from me onto her bed as she can manage and curls into a ball, cowering.

"Mrs. Wilson," the orderly says, and hearing someone call her the last name she insisted we abandon after his death is a jolt to my system. But she whips her head up and stares at him, eyes wide and expectant. "Joshua had to work late. He'll be back later tonight." I watch her absorb his words, and she gives little nods of her head as her breathing slows down. "He said to leave the—"

"Bathroom light on," she finishes with a slight smile on her face that makes my heart ache so desperately I have to force the burn that's back in my throat away. "Joshy doesn't work at night though."

"He has a dinner thing tonight."

"Oh yes. With the Brooks firm. I forgot. Okay then." She smiles at the orderly again and she seems so young, even the tone of her voice has softened and taken on a youthful quality. "Can you please see these strange men out? Josh would not be happy they're here. You know he's been known to throw a few punches in my honor."

I'm a grown man—successful, famous, tatted up—and those last words, seeing my mom's love for my dad before it turned bitter and resentful, have just reduced me to a child fighting back the sobs that are warring inside me.

My chest constricts with the pain, with the weakness I feel because I can't bring him back. . . . I can't get us back. My eyes meet Hunter's and as we start to leave the room, I think of everything I can't fix lately. But at the same time I know I'm looking at the one person I still can help.

As we leave I glance back at Mom through the open doorway and a part of me just needs her to be my mom again so badly. The one I remember from *before*. And I'm so desperate for the feeling of belonging, for the love, that there are days I consider dressing like Hunter and coming here to see her. Maybe then she'll hold me in her arms and tell me she loves me. Maybe then she'll not look at me and think of her weak son who did nothing to stop her husband's suicide.

It's a ludicrous thought. Even I know that, but it does nothing to abate that need I have deep down to hear her tell me she loves me one last time before her mind slips away for good. I swear to God it's better to miss someone quietly than to let them know and get no response, because that lack of response? That's the one that kills you.

The nurse comes in to give her her medication, and her appearance saves me from wanting to go back in and tell her good night. I wanted to wrap my arms around her small frame and feel her arms around me like she was hugging Hunter. I feel like a pussy, still needing that connection with her but I don't care. It doesn't matter how old you are, how tough you are, what shit life's thrown at you, every fucking person still wants their mom at some point.

It's like losing her over and over each time I see her even though she's right there in front of me.

Chapter 10

The lecture hall is noisy as I sit down in the last row as part of my perfectly timed entrance. I don't want to see Hawkin, don't want to deal with his bullshit—or the unexpected pang I feel at wanting him to look up and notice I'm there.

Get over it, Westin.

Somehow I've become a sappy female, and I'm usually so far from sappy it's ridiculous. I wanted casual. Well, you can't get any more casual than a guy who rejects you. Besides, if a guy's not interested, I know how to brush it off and move on. Plenty of fish in the sea—one pectoral fin is the same as the next, just hopefully a little bigger.

I had thought Rick's irrefutable demonstration of how men are like bras—that they hook up behind your back—had hardened me some and made me not care. . . . So why are things with Hawkin affecting me so much?

That's the question I need an answer to but even after moping around like a lost puppy the past few days, I still don't get it, don't get him. We flirted, he made the first move when I was trying to show him the PA system, and so how am I left to feel like I'm the one inferring there was something more there than there really was?

He initiated the kiss on the porch. He led me from the

kitchen to go upstairs. And then he said *see-ya* like nothing happened.

Maybe I'm just stressed about the couple of snags I've had with my thesis. The writer's block that's made a permanent place on my creative doorstep needs to leave sooner rather than later. It has to be the stress contributing to my vulnerable emotional state.

Not Hawkin per se, just the combination of everything all at once.

So when his voice fills the room, I hate that I immediately sit up taller hoping that he looks up and acknowledges me like some road-battered groupie who follows him from city to city wanting any scrap they can get from him.

Pathetic. Yep, that's what he's reduced me to and it's not very attractive.

I keep my head angled down, pissed off at myself for how stupid I'm being. I don't want to feed the insanity if he does actually look my way. I busy myself with double-checking notes for a different class, purposefully ignoring him. If I could stick my earbuds in and get away with it I would.

Anything to tune him out because all I want to do is let him in.

An hour later I sigh in relief as a few students in the class clap when the lecture finishes. I did it. See, Quin, not a problem, you can be in the same vicinity as him and not fall to his charms. My confidence boost rings false seeing as how in a lecture hall filled with hundreds that feat is a little easier to accomplish, but I'll take what I can get.

When I rise from my seat I make the fatal error of looking down to the front of the room. And of course he's talking to some coed but his eyes find mine, causing that punch of carnal lust to hit me hard. I reason that I'm just horny and need to get good and laid. The kind of laid that leaves your knees rubbery and your body feeling like it's floating on a cloud while you wait to come down from its euphoric high.

The kind that allows you to lose your thoughts for a while.

We stare at each for a beat. Long enough for the jolt of chemistry between us to reach across the distance and attack my senses. That panicked feeling hits me chased by unfettered lust. I force myself to turn abruptly and walk the few steps up to the door and out of the auditorium, feeling like I've gained a bit of my good sense in walking away from him on my own accord, this time.

And yes I'm walking away but I do so knowing I'm most likely walking away from that rubbery-knee postorgasmic glow as well. Something tells me that Hawkin screws like his voice sounds, seductive, a little rough, a lot thorough, and with a lot of tongue.

A girl can't go wrong when there's a lot of tongue involved.

I groan to myself as I walk across campus to the department offices, the idea of a night with him making me want and need. The image of Hawke and his ice-cream cone returns to me. I chastise myself, tell myself that there are plenty of men out there who are skilled in bed and that I'm just too damn picky. The only conclusion I draw is that the only way to get over the repeated image in my head of sex with Hawkin is to have sex with someone else. Preferably mind-blowing sex with someone else. So I vow that I will accept the next offer made to me for a date—or a fuck—to get over the player that is Hawkin Play.

I welcome the cool air as I enter the department and toss my bag on one of the desks set aside for grad students to catch up on paperwork or miscellaneous tasks for their professors.

I text Layla and tell her to study this afternoon so that we can meet up later for some drinks and some flirting with strangers. I feel a bit more centered when she replies with a *hell yeah!* because it's a step toward burying any remnant of Hawkin from my mind, by either alcohol or great sex.

I know I'll find the first, at least.

Shifting through papers, I work at getting caught up with administrative stuff for Professor Stevens: class requests, grading papers, adjusting syllabi. I'm in the middle of entering grades in the computer when something catches my eye out the window. I glance up and see Hawkin standing a ways away on the grassy area surrounded by a few other students.

Despite telling myself to look away, to ignore the sadness I saw in his eyes after he argued with Vince the other day, I can't. Even though I know he doesn't deserve my compassion, a part of me feels for him anyway.

So I watch him make the group around him laugh aloud while they hang on his every word, and I'm sure there are stars in their eyes from getting his attention. I glance to the left to see Axe standing there, attention wandering as he waits for his playboy of a boss to finish making coeds' panties wet.

I hate the bitterness I feel that he's giving them attention when he gave me none, least of all any consideration toward me in explaining why he flipped off like a switch after most definitely being turned on. And then of course I'm mad at myself for being upset at him over a situation I clearly didn't understand.

This right here is why I swore off men. The schizophrenic combat of emotions they cause is something I don't want to battle right now when I have to worry about my thesis. I shake my head, frustrated at myself—and him.

When I shift my gaze back, a pebble of anger ripples through me. Most of the crowd has dispersed and yet two remain, the Delta Sig girls from last week.

I roll my eyes out of reflex, batting away that tinge of jealousy that I shouldn't feel. Hell, a few kisses don't hold any of the strings that bind two people into a relationship. And yet I watch: the flirting, the intimate body language, the looks she darts his way that lead me to believe they've shared more than just the kiss we have.

His hand slides down her backside again, fingers playing idly in her back pockets in a way that irritates me enough to force my attention back to my work, trying not to remember the feel of those hands on the bare skin of my own back. Damn if it doesn't sting to know he wants her and not me.

Go Delta Sig! *Not.*

When I glance back up a moment later, unable to resist the impulse any longer, the lot of them are nowhere to be seen. Thank God because my *bitter, party of one* was getting to be a bit dramatic for my tastes. To think there are women who thrive on this feeling, live their lives always wanting and never walking away, astounds me.

I'm just about finished entering the grades when I hear footsteps behind me. I'd heard Carla's voice earlier so I expect to see her when I turn around.

Boy am I wrong.

Hawkin's hips are resting on the empty desk behind me, arms folded across his chest so that once again I'm afforded a glimpse of the tattoos that call to my curiosity. His head is angled to the side, black boots crossed at the ankles and the smirk pursed on his lips also lights up the gray of his eyes.

"Can I help you?" I ask in a terse tone. He raises one eyebrow in response and that's about as nice as I'm going to get so he better take what I give him or he needs to turn around and walk right out.

"Well, good day to you too." His eyes narrow as he appraises me, trying to get a feel for my mood although he should clearly know why I'm upset. He unfolds his arms and toys with the wrapper on the Tootsie Pop in his hand.

"It was until you walked in."

"Oh! That's cold!" He laughs with a shake of his head and a lick of his bottom lip that has my eyes darting down to watch it, and my mind drifting to other thoughts about tongues and licking and . . . I have to make a conscious effort to look back up and meet his eyes.

"Well, you know all about being cold, now, don't you?" I lean back in my chair and cross my arms over my chest.

Something flashes in his eyes that I don't quite catch before it clears. "C'mon, Quin . . . don't be that way. Just do me a solid and let's forget about it. Why don't you come with me to an event I have this Saturday? Yeah?" He flashes a disarming grin that I'm sure would have most women's panties falling to their ankles, but not mine. I've experienced how quickly he can flip the switch from being interested to uninterested. I can't imagine how it feels when he's yanking the sheets off you, when his interest is gone, after just having had sex.

"Sorry, I have plans," I tell him knowing full well I told myself that I was going to accept the next offer that came my way that might possibly result in mind-blowing sex. Little did I know it would come from him.

And so goes my life.

"You have something better to do than hang out with

me?" That cocky smirk is back, the one that makes me want to fist my hands in his shirt and do dirty things to him, but I just shake my head, holding fast to my slowly weakening resolve.

"I know that's hard to believe but on Saturday I need to watch my paint dry," I deadpan.

His laugh fills the air, rich and deep, and even it sounds melodic. He points the sucker at me and just shakes his head and a part of me caves that he finds humor and not offense in my comment. "Friday then?"

"Paint drying."

"Sunday, then?"

"Paint will still be drying." I fight the urge to crack a smile at his playfulness and the way he's angling his head and staring at me with a boyish smile on those sculpted lips of his.

"Damn, I would have never guessed you led such a fascinating life."

"Yep. So you see, I don't have time to go out. Sorry." We hold each other's gaze and I know he sees my interest. And as much as I want to consent to going with him, I need to do this for me—say no so that I can look in the mirror when I go home and know I'm thinking with my head and not my Bermuda triangle—the place where my thoughts go to die and lust acts without recourse.

"C'mon, you know you want to see if the rumors are true." That lopsided smirk appears again and I hate the feeling it evokes in me—*giddy schoolgirl begging for attention* comes to mind and I just want to brush the thoughts off my shoulders. Too bad the only place they'll fall from there is in my lap and that in itself is the crux of this problem.

"Rumors?" There are probably too many for me to guess so I'll let him tell me what I need to worry about.

"Yeah." He nods his head, lopsided smirk now a full-blown panty-dropping smile. "If I play a woman like a guitar." He wiggles his fingers in front of him and raises his eyebrows.

Thoughts flicker through my mind that I don't want there. His fingers running over me, manipulating me into rapturous oblivion. Damn. "You really need to get some better lines. The women that fall for those are ones you need to steer clear of . . . like Delta Sig girl. I'm sure she'd love to spend some more time with you after you beguile her with witty one-liners like that."

I raise my eyebrows in a silent *Yes, I saw you* but then realize that in that one little sentence, I gave him the upper hand. I let him know that I was paying attention to him and his actions and by the derisive tone in my voice that it bugs me.

We both toy with the silence between us, him waiting to see if I'll say more and me wondering if he's going to call me on the carpet as to why I won't go with him on Friday but I'm pissed that Delta Sig just might.

"I'm sure she would," he finally says, "but perception can often be misleading."

What? Please talk female here because I'm not following your cryptic answers. "Yes, it can. Like when a guy kisses you senseless one minute and then pushes you off the porch the next. Something like that, right?"

I notice him register my hurt and his expression falters as he figures out how to respond. "Exactly like that. What could have been perceived as pushing off a porch may have really just been a guy trying to prevent a mistake from happening."

And the minute the words are out of his mouth, his eyes widen and my back straightens in incredulity that he really just went there. His comment stings in ways I never expected—and that tells me I'm way too invested already. I can tell myself till I'm blue in the face that I won't date a player like him, will date only casually, but the spear of disappointment that shoots through me tells me I want more.

"Well, thank God! I didn't realize I would've been such a horrible mistake—"

"No! That's not what I meant—"

"I don't believe I heard you stutter." Emotions run at a rampant pace through me, hurt, anger, disbelief. I shake my head and look out of the window as the sting of tears unexpectedly burns the back of my throat.

I'm not an overly emotional girl. I'm not one of those annoying criers who sheds a tear when someone looks at them cross-eyed, so why the hell does his comment create such a visceral reaction from me?

"Quin." His voice is low and apologetic, like gravel scraping my ears.

"Just leave it, Hawke. Point made. No worries about *that girl* wanting anything more from you. I've got to get back to my work." I turn my back without saying another thing, once again mad at myself for allowing him to cause such internal conflict within me.

And that's scary in itself because all we've shared are a few groping kisses. I should see the sign blinking HEART-BREAKER a mile away, but instead all I feel is that he's worth the risk.

He blows out an audible breath behind me and yet I don't hear any footsteps walking away. I busy myself, well aware of the heat of his stare burning in my back.

"Can I get your number?"

Sarcasm weaves through my laugh mixed with a quiet thrill that he asked. And then it's dashed when I realize he's only asking to save face. "Now you're just making me feel like a pity case. No need for you to scrape the bottom of the barrel."

"That's not it at all. Between Hunter and Vince . . . I just wasn't . . . I can't explain it here. It's complicated. . . . I wanted to call you to apologize but didn't have your number."

I hear the sincerity in his voice but at the same time can't be sure if it's real. "Mm-hm." It's the only thing I say, needing him to go and leave me be so I can go out with Layla, lose myself in someone else for a few hours—or more—and make that sweet ache I feel for him not so sweet.

"So can I get your number?" he asks again.

"Your charm isn't going to work on me this time rocker boy." I set my pen down so that I don't use it to write out my number and glance over to him.

"Yes it will," he says, that shy smile that calls to me turning up one corner of his mouth. He makes a show of putting the lollipop in his mouth before he nods and walks off.

Of course my mind veers to Rylee's comment in Sonoma about how many licks it takes to get to the center of a certain Tootsie Pop. *Different man, same thought,* I think while I watch every delicious inch of his backside as he walks with that swagger out the door. Gotta love a man asserting himself and then walking away with the confidence that he will get what he wants.

And I'm not going to lie, a little thrill shoots through me but only for a minute before I shake the idea off that has heartbreak written all over it in an extra thick Sharpie. The writing is definitely on the wall and no matter how pretty the ink looks, it will still bleed through and stain the layers beneath permanently.

Chapter 11

Traffic sucks so bad it takes me forever to crawl the few miles from the university to my house. To make matters worse, I keep hearing Hawkin's voice in my head and my level of confusion is at an all-time high.

I try to rationalize it all but realize that since I'm thinking of a man, there's no use in even trying to.

I turn down my street, anxious to get home and relax a bit before Layla arrives for our night of anticipated debauchery. My phone rings and after the day I've had, I can't help but smile at the one man that continues to prove time and time again that at least he thinks I'm desirable.

"Luke Mason," I say aloud for the speaker to pick up.

"Quinlan Westin," he mimics. "How goes it?"

"It goes. And you?"

"It'd go a helluva lot better if some hot little Cali girl would let me take her out this weekend since I'm going to be in her neck of the woods." I hear the hope laced with amusement in his tone and for some reason it's just what I needed to hear at this moment.

Something in me gives—maybe it's Luke's temerity, or a need to feel wanted amid Hawke's rejection, the need to defy my brother's orders, or the promise to myself that I'd accept the next offer that came my way—and I laugh. "You know Luke—*today just might be your lucky day.*"

The line falls silent and for a moment I fear I dropped the call and my dramatic little comment went unappreciated. "How lucky of a day?" he asks, finally breaking the silence.

And I can play off his comment so many ways but I'm suddenly feeling kind of like my old self, sassy and spunky. The bit of confidence I lost over the situation with Hawkin returns and I decide to just go for it. "Well, you're going to get lucky all right, it just kind of depends on you if the luck is on the platonic or on the good-morning level."

He clears his throat and my grin widens as I pull in my driveway, pleased that I've made someone happy today. "A girl who plays hard to get and then plays get him hard . . . Hm. I guess we'll see where the night takes us."

A part of me deflates at his response. What I truly wanted was for that alpha male side of him to come through and let me know exactly what will happen, just like Hawkin did with his confident *yes I will.* Damn me and my needing a little bit of rough in a man.

But I shake off all thoughts of Hawkin and remind myself that I just accepted a date with Luke. He at least deserves me to not be thinking about another man when I just suggested there is possibility between us.

We make plans to talk later in the week to finalize details and say good-bye as I climb from the car and gather my stuff. Once inside, I spend some time picking up, perusing my social media, and throwing in a load of wash. I respond to an e-mail from my brother, something about his best friend, Beckett, finally falling for someone, and tell him it's about damn time. I've just finished making a few notes of things I need to do for Carla and sit down with a freshly poured glass of wine when Layla opens the front door.

"Q?"

"In here!" I call out, settling into the couch and putting my feet on the table.

"Hey, lady!" She rounds the corner followed by an approving sound when she sees the glass in my hand. "That rough, huh?"

"It got better," I say and point to the kitchen counter for her to grab a glass herself. She's been here enough times that she knows where everything is so I let her help herself. Having a friend that's known you since middle school has its merits, like you're so comfortable around each other that they help themselves without thought in your house. It also has a downside too: that you know each other so well they can read your thoughts when you don't want them to.

And right now, I don't want Layla to just yet.

Wine in hand and feet curled underneath her in the chair opposite me, Layla looks over the rim of her glass. "So what's up? How's Professor Hottie Hawkin?" Her lips curl in a smile and she gets a dreamy-girly look in her eyes akin to cartoons where irises turn into hearts. Luckily she keeps going before I can respond with an answer I'm not exactly sure of yet. "Man, it's been two more lectures with him. Has he stopped being an ass and talked to you yet?"

"A little," I reply, figuring I can deal with the guilt of withholding information momentarily because I know I'll spill it eventually. And it's not so much withholding, it's more being unable to put into words the way he makes me feel.

"Man," she moans, "the things I'd love to do to that man. I'd bang him like a screen door in a hurricane, hard and repeatedly. Shit, why wait for Mother Nature when there are so many fun places in that auditorium I could explore with him instead. Naked. For hours. Damn!" She grins devilishly with a raise of her eyebrows while my mind drifts to the little soundboard alcove and the taste of Hawkin's lips on mine. "Sorry. I didn't mean to fantasize out loud—the man just makes the tingle in my lady parts turn full-blown earthquake."

Mine too.

"It's not hard to make your lady parts tingle," I tease with affection since I'm more of a serial dater than she is.

"True. Very true. I'd like them to be tingling later tonight if possible."

"Deal," I say, raising my glass in a mock toast to her, "because I sure as hell need something to get me out of this funk I'm in." Hawke's offer for a date on Saturday flickers through my mind as the potential answer but I push it out. I'm going out with Luke. He's safer.

But do I really want safe?

"Talk to me lady. Bad day? You need to get laid? What?" Her question pulls me from my internal tug-of-war as she squints her eyes to try to figure out herself what my problem is. "Definitely need to get laid more than anything."

"I'm working on it." Although I neglect to explain I'm working on it with one man while thinking about another.

Her eyes run up and down my body, taking in my ponytail piled high on my head, my capri-length sweat pants, and camisole tank top. "Looks like it."

"It's complicated."

"Men always are, Q. . . . But what's the deal? You usually have them eating out of the V of your thighs without so much as a bat of your lashes, so what gives?"

I fixate on my finger as it draws lines on the arm of my couch. "Well, I agreed to go out with Luke."

Her mouth falls lax but she remains silent as she tries to figure out what's caused my about-face. "Okay." She draws the word out, and I'm curious how long it's going to take her to figure out what I'm doing. "Your enthusiasm to go on a date with him is overwhelming. Really, please try to contain it." She snickers and then adds as an afterthought, "You know your brother is going to flip his lid when he hears about this."

"He'll never know. Besides, my life is my own. He was a manwhore his entire bachelorhood. He has no right to tell me what I can and can't do."

"Yeah, but we're talking about Colton here." She laughs with a raise of her eyebrows, garnering an eye roll from me in response. "So let me get this straight. You need to get laid. You agree to a date with a man who doesn't light your fire, and I don't understand why not . . . So what am I missing here?" I swear I can see the cogs turning in her mind and then click perfectly into place. "Who are you replacing Luke for?"

And bingo! That was in record time.

"Whatever do you mean?" I feign innocence knowing she's going to freak out when I tell her who I'm trying to forget about.

She scoots forward to the edge of her chair while my cheeks heat. "Quinlan?"

"Well, there's this guy. . . ."

"No shit, Sherlock."

"He made a move, we kissed some, brought it to his house where we kissed some more and then he up and said he had shit to do. Basically he told me to leave without saying those exact words." I give her the short version of the story, trying to keep details to a minimum.

"And you're wasting your time on him why, then? This isn't like you. I thought we weren't caring, doing the casual dating thing so we didn't have to do the high hopes crashing to the floor thing. If a guy loses interest, so do we . . . so this must be a serious contender to knock all that to the wayside." She sits forward, elbows on her knees as she studies me. "Who has your panties trapped around your thighs when you'd rather have them around your ankles?"

"It's stupid," I deflect, feeling like a teenager crushing on the popular kid in high school. "And that's exactly why I agreed to go out with Luke. He called at the perfect time when I needed to feel wanted and I said yes." I shrug as I take a sip, letting the wine slowly take the edge off the events of my day.

"The only man I'd probably give a pass on acting like that just because the Richter scale thing would be"—Layla's eyes flash up to mine, awareness lighting them afire as she connects the dots—"Hawkin."

Shit. Shit. Double shit.

It's not like I wasn't going to tell her. I was just hoping to downplay the situation first so I don't feel like such an idiot for wanting someone who is exactly what I swore I didn't want.

And of course it's this moment that the advice my mom always gives me decides to resurface in my head. *When you stop chasing all the wrong things, you give the right things a chance to catch you.* Did I stop chasing the wrong things and could Hawkin be my chance at right?

"Quinlan?" Lay's question brings me back from Hawkin-lost-in-thought-land and her eyes widen, her grin falters, and her mouth drops open. I finally meet her eyes but I can see that she knows the answer. "Holy fuck, Q!" She jumps to her feet, exactly the reaction I was hoping to avoid because I know she's not going to stop now.

There's never a way to stop her when she's excited.

"Wow . . . So Professor Hottie, huh?"

"I wouldn't exactly call him professor," I correct. The man may be fine but he does not need someone to give him a bigger ego than he already has.

"Girl he can call me whatever he wants to call me and I'll play the role," she kids and then stops herself when she sees my uncomfortable expression. "C'mon, you feel the same way, so what's the deal? He pushed you away but at least he tracked you down and apologized and asked for a phone number."

I snort. "It was a rough apology . . . and both actions were done out of guilt. The man's a player, plain and simple."

"Ha. You've never complained about rough before." She quirks her eyebrows and I can't fight the laugh in response to her very true statement. "No, seriously though. Was it done out of guilt? Possibly, but a player doesn't apologize, so tell me what's really making you keep your distance."

I look down at my finger tracing over the rim of my glass, the alcohol making the truths I don't want to admit come a little quicker to my lips now. "He's the one that I think can royally fuck me up."

"Figuratively and literally," she says, testing the waters to see if I chuckle or glare at her. I chuckle. And then glare. "But Q, why is that? Why him?"

I stare at her while I try to figure out the answer. "I don't know. He's like this big bad rocker with a sarcastic bite to him, but there's something else, something underneath. . . . I can't put my finger on it. It's almost a sadness of some sort that makes me want to make sure he's okay."

"Uh-oh, you're in momma-syndrome mode now?" she asks, eyebrows raised.

"No. It's not like that," I attempt to explain. "There just seems to be so much more beneath the surface than the image we all see . . . and it's intriguing to me."

"Bad boy, good heart. I can see that, but damn, that man is fine. I'm sure that doesn't hurt either."

The smile flashes quick on my lips. "No, but there's more

there. It's like . . . everything about him pulls at me. The good, bad, all parts of me. I've never felt that from someone before. And, ugh . . ."

"And what? You don't want to be pulled at because you'd rather be poked by him?" She laughs at herself and her witty comment.

"Well, that's a given," I admit, "but I don't want to feel this way. I need casual desperately right now, because if I get burned one more time, Lay . . . I don't know. . . . I just think it's best to walk away. Damage control. Besides, my heart's been bruised and battered enough, I don't need to walk into another situation where I hand him the weapons to hurt me with."

"I don't know what to tell you, sister, because his actions are confusing. But I say give him another chance. The whole thing with his brother and then the fight with Vince obviously doused his flame."

"This coming from the woman who moments ago told me to move on."

"Um, Hawkin Play? No more words need to be said." I have to laugh at her logic because lame as it may be, it's starting to pull me toward her reasoning. "Did you really think dating Chasin' Mason was going to sate that ache Hawkin created?" She shakes her head and the look on her face says I've lost my sanity. "Did Luke bust a nut when you accepted?"

I shrug in response. It's all I can do because I said yes, but I know in the end, I'll still tell Luke no.

"At least Luke is easy on the eyes as well as funny. Not a bad way to spend an evening," she says.

"Yeah . . ."

"But he's no rock god." She purses her lips, hearing the hesitancy in my response. "I get it."

I can't really explain it, so I just shake my head. If this is the response he normally receives, no wonder Hawkin has an ego the size of Texas. "He is *not* a rock god."

"If he's not now, he's well on his way to becoming one and fuck I'll consider his dick my rock god as long as it's rolling into me."

There's absolutely no response I can give to that comment except to take a long drink of my wine.

"You know you're thinking it," she chides me. "Hey, there's no shame in trying to use Luke to make you forget about Hawkin, but let's be serious here, there is no chance in hell you're going to forget about him."

"Thanks for your vote of confidence, Lay."

My phone rings on the end table beside me, and I glance over at the unknown number and mute the call. When it starts ringing again before I can recall my train of thought, my distracted mind immediately thinks that something's wrong with my family.

"Hello?"

"So is what you said the other day true?" And just like that, the voice that sounds like sex fills my ears and softens my resistance.

And I don't want soft. No. When it comes to Hawkin Play, I want hard.

"Not sure what you mean, but why don't we start with how did you get my phone number?" Irritation masks the rush of desire I feel just beneath the surface. I don't know what it is about this man that makes me feel like a damn virgin anticipating what her first time will be like.

Because I am far from virginal. And thank God for that because it means I know just what I need. I try not to acknowledge the voice in the back of my head that says *and what I need is him*.

"You're my TA, remember? Carla was more than willing to get it for me when I told her I needed to discuss some things with you," he says with victorious amusement.

"And then what? I don't answer so you were going to keep calling me back until I did? *Stalk much?*"

His laugh sounds low and rich. "I've learned from the best, just don't expect me to be throwing any bras at your feet."

I stifle the laugh as my eyes meet Layla's and she points to my phone and mouths Hawkin's name. I nod my head, which earns an arms up in the air in a touchdown motion.

"It takes a lot more than clothing at my feet to make me like you." Although the image of him naked is a mighty fine way to fill my thoughts.

"Well, Trixie, if my clothing is at your feet, that means you're in my bed and we're going to be doing a whole helluva lot more than *liking* each other."

Touché. The suggestive arrogance in his tone alongside the quiet promise of his words has me squeezing my thighs together to try to block him out. It's good in theory anyway. "Semantics," I tell him, trying to feign nonchalance and get the conversation back toward a neutral topic that will afford me a few more moments of self-restraint. "So what is it that you're asking me if it's true or not?"

"If you really are a girl who enjoys easy sex."

With you I'd be all kinds of easy.

"I don't believe I said I did easy sex," I refute. And then I think that if I really did say it, it's further proof he gets me flustered because that's not a comment a typical woman would say when trying to resist a man's advances.

"Yeah, actually you did say it. A man doesn't forget proclamations like that one." I can hear the amusement in his voice, the smile on his lips.

"What business is it of yours?" The bitchiness in my tone is part reflex, part resistance, and a huge chunk of losing grip on my resolve.

Hawke's chuckle again fills the line and saturates my senses among other places. "Well, I'm sitting here licking my ice-cream cone, and I can't stop thinking how good you tasted the other day with it on my lips . . . and it makes me wonder how other parts of you taste. And that begs me to wonder how fast I can make you come, how many times I can make you scream my name, how tight and addictive that pussy of yours will feel." His voice trails off and thank God it does because I don't think I can handle any more of his *wondering*.

"Um . . ." I search for words to respond and pray when I actually speak that they don't sound breathless and needy. And of course the sane part of my brain tells me I should be offended by both his assumption that I'll be sleeping with him as well as his comments telling me that he's even thinking about me that way.

I should be.

But I'm not.

I manage to pull together my thoughts while listening to the draw of his breath on the other end of the connection. I'm supposed to be resisting him, telling him to take a hike so I can forget him. Instead I taunt him.

"You're eating ice cream again?" I use humor as my fall-back, unwilling to let him know his words have unraveled my insides and at the same time coiled them so tight my body is vibrating with need.

"I'd rather be eating you out instead. . . ." His line should sound corny, should make me roll my eyes, but has quite the opposite effect. I left the door right open for him to walk through. I shouldn't have expected any less.

I fight the wanton smirk that wants to spread on my lips and emit a strained laugh instead. "This conversation is *so* not happening right now."

"You sound strained. Do you need a little release, Quin-lan? Do you need to be filled, stretched till it burns oh-so-good as I fuck you nice and slow and then pick up the pace and drive into you fast and hard?" His voice is as seductive as silk, wrapping around me, and sliding over my body. Words that I should be offended by turn me on—their ex-plicitness only serves to intensify the desire he's stirring within me. "Do you like to be tied up? Dominated? I told you you're like unwrapping a present. I'm curious what other surprises I can discover." He groans out a murmur of appreciation. "I can't wait to see which of these flavors you opt for because believe me, I've tasted all thirty-one of them but can't seem to get yours out of my head and off my lips."

I'm pretty sure my mouth is lax, I know my nipples are hard, and I have to consciously remind myself to draw in air because I'm at a complete loss for words. Did he really just say all of that to me? I'm seriously turned on, want to give him the answers to all of the questions he just asked but I know how easily this man can shift gears and change his mind.

"Ah, you're pulling out the dirty talk. . . . Must be feeling a little desperate, huh?" Irony at its finest considering I'm the one who feels desperate right now. "Look, I know you're a rock star, so you think you can snap your fingers, and all women within a set radius will hop in the sack—"

"Tsk, tsk, tsk . . . I don't think; *I know*." He waits for me to fall silent before he speaks again. "You talk a hard game sweetness but you know all of your soft places want my hard places."

"Now you're just proving to be the arrogant ass I knew

you were." And fuck if it's not turning me on something fierce right now. How am I going to play this game and not get burned by him? Better yet why does the burn not seem so daunting as long as my fire gets lit properly?

I'm pathetic.

"Hm. I know desire when I see it and damn it looks good on you, Q."

"You can't see me right now so how do you know what I look like?"

"Cute. But you forget, I've seen it on you before, felt it on your lips, and you can't argue with desire. Care to prove me wrong?"

"Good-bye, Hawkin." Hanging up is the best move right now seeing as I'm never one to back down from a dare, and yet at the same time I need to continually remind myself he's trouble with a capital T.

"Hey, Quin?" I haven't lowered the phone from my ear yet despite my brain telling my hand to do just that so I hear his comment.

"What?"

"You know you're going to cave in the end. Wouldn't you rather enjoy that time begging me to stop because it feels so good rather than fighting a losing battle?"

"You're a cocky son of a bitch, aren't you?"

"A man's allowed to be confident when talking about what he does best."

"What you do best? I thought what you did best was sing."

His laugh lights the phone connection on fire. "I think you should be the judge of that. You've heard me sing, now it's time you experience my skills in the bedroom."

"Good night." I hang up the phone while his seductive laugh rolls through the line. The problem is he most definitely got his point across, and now that's all I can think about. The heat of his touch, the taste of his kiss, the firm press of his body against mine are all things I can recall from experience and damn if they don't own my thoughts. I blow out an exasperated breath, toss my phone on the couch beside me, and look up to meet Layla's eyes and knowing smirk.

"That sure was one long conversation for someone you're not interested in," she muses.

"Yep. I'm not interested at all."

"Uh-huh. Make sure you remember that statement while you're screaming his name at some point in the near future."

Shit. I'm screwed.

Chapter 12

On Saturday night I glance over at Luke as we drive, the lights of the city flashing across his face. I've had a good time so far—cocktails, dinner, and now off to some event he's kept a secret but that he's super excited about. I get the feeling that he thinks wherever our next destination is, it will be the coup de grâce in impressing me so that I fall madly in love with him.

I'm trying, I really am, to feel something more for him, but I'm still getting the platonic vibe on my end. I promised myself that I'd push Hawkin and the dark promise of his words that have filled my dreams with different variations of their suggestions from my mind and not let him interfere with the possibility that tonight holds.

Luke must sense my quiet observation because he glances over and smiles, hand reaching out to rest on my bare knee. I smile tightly and look out of the windshield, silently chastising myself for my indifference. I should feel something. Our skin-on-skin contact should make my blood hum and cause that delicious anticipatory ache in my core. I should be feeling that fluttery feeling in my stomach and be thankful I wore the lacy, barely there g-string panties with matching bra for him to gasp at later in the evening when he undresses me.

Or when he rips them off me.

But right now I'm thinking I could have worn my period panties and felt the same way as I do now. Not a good sign at all.

I mean he's been a gentleman in all respects of the word: opening car doors, comfortable conversation, laughter, and flirty banter. He's the guy you think you want, but hell if I can get into him.

And lamely I kind of resent him for it right now. Call my resentment being moody or estrogen-fueled misplaced anger but I need him to give me all of those feelings so that I can forget about Hawkin. Shit, I even played hooky and feigned an illness so I could skip the lecture on Thursday in an attempt to not sabotage my chances tonight.

And yet here I sit beside him, enjoying myself, having a good time, but I feel like I'm hanging out with a friend, not a potential horizontal cohabitant.

Luke squeezes my knee. "You figure it out yet?" he asks, all but bouncing with excitement.

"I have no clue." I laugh because his enthusiasm is really adorable.

"Well, one of my sponsors this year is Verbz—the company that makes those high-end headphones. Anyway, there's this big benefit tonight to raise money for Alzheimer's research—a huge lineup of some of my favorite bands—and so they gave me tickets."

My smile comes naturally while my synapses start to fire as I try to place a comment that Layla made the other night in our drunken state about how she'd love to see Bent play this weekend at a local concert. And there's no way my luck can be so shitty that my date is taking me to see the man I'm wishing he was, perform.

"Sounds like fun—who's performing?" I'm on a fishing expedition; I just hope he doesn't notice.

"Shit, you name it, they're performing. The D-Bags, Bending Cupid, the Mighty Storm, Black Falcon, and my fav band is, like, the main headliner: *Bent*."

There you have it. How did I know he was going to say Hawkin's band? I smile enthusiastically and say something about how exciting and what great bands while my mind rationalizes that it's a concert where thousands of people will attend. I'll be so far away from Hawkin that I should be able to keep my libidinous thoughts under control with so much distance between us.

"And even better," he continues as we pull into the Staples Center, "we have backstage passes to the postshow meet and greet for the Bent guys."

And the hits just keep on coming.

Luke keeps talking incessantly, chattering away about his favorite songs of each band as well as random trivia about each one as we make our way into the arena. Each step closer we get, my anticipation increases. Those fluttery feelings I was missing when he touched my knee are finally making their presence known and it's all because of the man awaiting us inside.

"You're being so quiet, is everything okay?" he asks, concern lacing his voice as he stops me in the darkened shadows of the facility.

"Yes! I'm just so surprised by all of this." All the while I chastise myself for being so caught up in my own head and so selfish that I'm not doing the one thing I promised myself I would, leave Hawkin behind for the night.

And so maybe that's why Luke catches me off guard when he leans forward and brushes his mouth against mine. My startled gasp parts my lips and he mistakes the action for wanting more, and he takes complete advantage of my reaction by slipping his tongue gently between them. I react in reflex, not really urging him on but not being a dead fish either, because I'm not exactly sure how I'm supposed to react short of pushing him away. He's been nothing but polite and I don't want to ruin the evening with him but at the same time don't want to encourage him either.

The kiss ends quickly because being the gentleman he is, he keeps the first one as a way to gauge my interest and I'm hoping by my lack of enthusiastic reciprocation he might get the hint. A girl can hope anyway, because the thing is, Luke's kiss was soft and taunting; it should call to my desire on every level . . . but the fluttering I feel at the mere thought of Hawkin just doesn't compare to anything with Luke.

Luke smiles softly, a silent affirmation that yes, we did

just kiss, and then links his fingers with mine as we enter the arena and prepare to hear the bands.

The concert so far has been great. Our seats are incredible, located just a few rows back from center stage. I've been able to push Hawkin from my mind and enjoy Luke. I've laughed with him, danced with him in the confines of our close quarters, and sang at the top of my lungs to the lyrics of each set. But now shouts of increasing volume pierce the air as the crowd waits for the final band to take the stage, Bent.

And I can't help that I purposefully occupy my hands so Luke can't hold one of them as I prepare for the visceral reaction I expect to have to the sight of Hawkin. As the anticipation builds I can feel my legs leaning forward to try to coax him to come into view, my need to lay eyes on him increasing with each passing second like an addict knowing her next fix is just within reach.

And then his voice comes through the speakers as a single spotlight lights up the empty stage. A frenzy ensues all around us as women begin shrieking in epic decibels so that I can't hear his voice but can feel it somehow. The crowd must feel the same way because the shrieks calm just in time for him to hit the first chorus.

You killed my heart.
You snuffed it out.
You stole my hope.

He sings the notes to their biggest hit, "Stolen," and even though the fangirls are on an ecstatic high, the power of his voice a cappella silences them. Goose bumps chase over my skin despite the stifling heat of the arena. I've heard the song a hundred times on the radio and yet the raw emotion when he sings, like he's scraping the words from his core, captivates me.

The lights flood the stage in a blaze of brightness, and Hawkin stands there, head down, foot tapping, a striking profile dressed in dark clothing against all of the light. He slowly lifts his head to end the chorus and the guys kick in with their instruments.

And I'm lost.

I know he's entertaining thousands and has no clue I'm even here and yet I feel, as he peers into what I'm sure is a mass of blinding light on his end, that he's looking straight into me.

I tell myself to move, to dance and not act like I've just been struck by lightning, because as much as I'm electrified by him on stage in front of me, I did come here with Luke. And I might be a bitch for wanting Hawkin while I'm on a date with someone else but Luke's a good guy, we're just not right for each other.

"He has an incredible voice, doesn't he?" Luke says above the music, breath hot against my ear. I nod at him with a smile on my face before making the concerted effort to not just stand there.

Soon enough the song ends with a melancholy note in Hawke's voice that's almost haunting as his voice rounds out the solo. The crowd erupts into a riotous frenzy all around.

"Los Angeles!" His voice booms into the microphone. "How the fuck are you?" If I thought the screams were loud before, they are deafening now. He chuckles suggestively into the mic and—I'm sure like every other female in this arena—I feel like it caresses my skin and wraps hold of me. Screams of "I'd rather be fucking you" ring out and I bristle at the comments while he plays right into them. "Hey, I'm all for that babe but I've got a few more songs to sing before my mouth can be otherwise occupied."

Vince walks over to him and hands him a beer and they tap the necks together while more women scream, plus a few bras and panties hit the stage. I scoff at the desperation to be Hawkin's just-for-the-night-girl and wonder why the hell am I getting miffed at something he sees all the time. I mean shit, how can I even think he still wants me when he can have his pick of women.

I'd rather be eating you out instead. . . .

His words rush back and give me a slight feeling of advantage since at least I know he was talking directly to me. This sense of sudden insecurity and inadequacy I feel is ridiculous.

"Settle down ladies, the men in the house need to retain

their hearing so they can hear you screaming their names later if you catch my drift." He gives that lazy, lopsided smirk that makes my body respond to him instantly, even though I know better than to want him.

"Hey, Hawke, that man back there," Gizmo says into the mic, pointing with his drumsticks from behind his set, "says thank you."

The crowd laughs as Hawkin motions with his hands for everyone to settle down. "On a serious note, I want to thank you all for coming here tonight for a cause that's near and dear to my heart. Your tickets will benefit research to help our grandparents and parents and hopefully find a cure for this ugly disease before it can affect us. So thank you so very much for coming tonight and helping us donate all of the proceeds to this worthy cause."

The crowd erupts in cheers.

"Okay, so Noel and Kellan and Wethers already sang their asses off for you, now you ready for Bent to end the night with a bang?" The screams erupt again. "C'mon boys, let's rock!"

My ears are still ringing as we fight our way opposite the crowd leaving the arena. Luke holds my hand as he leads me backstage and into a holding room of sorts where a few other ecstatic fans are practically vibrating with anticipation.

I'm antsy too but for completely different reasons.

Luke is rocking on his heels like a little kid and it really is endearing to witness. "Oh my God," he says, pointing down a hallway where a mob of men are walking. "That's Black Falcon. . . . Noel, Riff . . ." His voice fades off as he smiles sheepishly. "Do you follow them?"

I shake my head no. "They were really good, though. . . . I'll probably start now." The comment earns me a huge grin.

Chatter in the room pulls our attention back and when I look up, I'm staring straight into Vince's eyes from across the room. And then a slow, sly smile slides across his lips before he shakes his head and looks away. It's only a momentary connection before he focuses his attention on the two fans in front of him but even in that quick glance, there's so much exchanged between us: *What the hell? You're with him?*

I'm confused by the whole exchange but luckily Luke caught none of it that I can tell.

We wait as Vince makes his way around the room. I fidget restlessly, nervous that Vince is going to acknowledge me and then I'll be left to explain to Luke that I've met him before when I've made no mention of it tonight. I track his progress and when it comes to us, he stares a beat longer than normal. "Hi," he finally says.

"Hi," we both say at the same time and Luke apologizes for talking over me.

Vince chuckles and looks me in the eyes again. "Sorry for staring," he says, "you remind me of a girl I know named *Trixie*."

Inwardly I sag in relief at his comment, a nervous chuckle escaping my lips as I avert my gaze, and mutter, "No." And thankfully Luke takes over, oblivious to the awkwardness of the moment, and begins to rain praise on Vince over his bass-playing skills. I wonder and yet am at the same time glad that Vince didn't call me out on knowing him or the rest of the band. I'm curious over it but tune their conversation out and glance back down the hallway where the Black Falcon boys had left, not sure what I'm looking for.

An escape? For Hawkin? Not for Hawkin?

Whatever it is I don't find it but when I look back into the room, there he is. Hawkin has on a white shirt that's sticking slightly to him as if he just got out of the shower and rushed to dry off. His hair's wet and a beer is in one hand while an arm is slung casually around the shoulders of a woman next to him.

Every instinct within me hones in on Hawke.

The woman stands on her toes and kisses him haphazardly on the side of his mouth, her body rubbing up against him way more than the action deserves, and I see hussy written all over her. I hope he sees it too.

Of course he sees it. That's why his arm's wrapped around her.

How was I so stupid to convince myself that he wasn't a player? That he really wanted me? That he would take my no-nonsense complicated over her no-hassle-spread-her-legs simplicity?

Her other friend sidles up next to them and they place

something in his hand with flirty little giggles that are so pathetic they make my ovaries cringe. He looks down at his hand and arches his eyebrows. He says something that earns him another set of giggles that not surprisingly make their proffered cleavage jiggle up and down.

I'm pretty sure it's a hotel key with an offer for double your pleasure, double your fun. Ugh.

Hell, most of the time I'm game for anything and would never judge someone else but something about the setting, about the random offer, about the whole damn situation is rather disturbing to me. Maybe it's the fact that knowing the person for a whole five minutes before sex is offered is of importance. Call me crazy.

I'm distracted from the eye-roll-worthy display when Luke puts his hand on my waist and pulls me into his side. I didn't even realize that Vince had moved on to the next fan. "That was so fucking cool!" he exclaims squeezing me in tighter. He starts rambling on and on and I look up to watch the animation on his features as he talks.

And then his voice falls quiet when he notices the lead singer mere feet away from us. I follow his gaze to find mine locked with Hawkin's.

I swear my breath is stolen momentarily; all I know is I have to tell myself to draw in air from the quizzical look he gives me, a mixture of surprise, disbelief, and *you're with him*?

Luke lifts his chin to Hawkin in an I'm-a-cool-guy kind of way and Hawke pulls his eyes from mine and acknowledges him with his own head tilt. He glances back to me and I just shake my head subtly as my eyes flicker to the roadhos beside him, my lips pursed in judgment. I know he reads the disdain in my eyes and yet his arms remain on the women.

As our connection is broken, one last glare passes between us—I know why I'm glaring but am unsure why he's pissed—when one of them asks for an autograph. I watch the three of them separate as Hawkin reaches for his beer with one hand and slides the hotel room card in his back pocket, which of course begs my eyes to take in the way the denim frames his ass.

He grabs the Sharpie offered and smiles big for the camera phone as he signs across the top of the woman's right breast. I watch, not surprised by the behavior of some of the women as he moves on from group to group greeting them, because it's not like I haven't seen women throw themselves at a man before. The difference is this time it's not my dad or my brother, it's the man I want.

Or rather the man I wanted before I saw this behavior. I get it's part of his job, but after Delta Sig and now the boobsie-twins, I'm determined to keep telling my hormones to quit humming over him.

I watch another woman offer herself to him, dignity obviously a foreign concept to her, and I look up to Luke. "I'm going to run to the bathroom really quick."

"What?" His eyes are wide and he shakes his head back and forth. "You might miss meeting *Hawkin Play*!"

"I'll be back in time," I tell him, secretly hoping I won't. "Don't worry, all that beer is hitting me all of a sudden."

I can see an internal tug-of-war going on within Luke. "Let me take you."

And I realize he's trying to be a gentleman and take me even though it means possibly missing meeting Hawke. Why can't I feel that buzz for this man and his considerate ways? Maybe it's one of those things that takes time when it comes to him. I wish I believed that.

"No. Really. I'll be fine. I don't want you to miss meeting Hawke in case I don't make it back in time."

"You sure?" His hesitancy speaks volumes of his character as a man.

"I'm sure."

When I start to walk away, Luke calls my name. "Quin?"

I turn to find his mouth meeting mine. It's a soft gentle brush of lips that he takes a bit further before stepping back. "Thanks for tonight. I'm having so much fun."

I smile gently at him and nod my head, wishing I felt something more for him than just platonic warmth. I turn to go in and in my periphery see Hawkin standing there, ignoring the women at his side to watch me.

I quickly avert my gaze and hustle down the hallway where I ask a roadie on the way where the nearest bathroom is. I'm confused and sick of the tumultuous feelings that are so foreign to me, the back and forth between sense and lust, head and heart, desire and prudence.

I go through a doorway that leads me into a dressing area of sorts and see the partially opened bathroom door across the room. I have my hand on it, pushing it open timidly, making sure that it's not occupied when all of a sudden a larger hand slams the door open from behind me.

A startled gasp falls from my lips as I'm jolted forward from the connection of our bodies. He pushes his way into the bathroom and then slams the door behind me.

I know I should be scared shitless, yet not an ounce of fear falls over me because every attuned nerve in my body senses it's Hawkin. It's the heady buzz and fluttering in my stomach that I get every time he's near that gives it away.

This. This feeling is what I should feel for Luke, but don't.

"Do you have any idea how hot you are?" He growls the words in my ear, the heat of his breath against my skin. "I can't take my eyes off you. You want me just as bad and yet you don't want him to know that you're going home with me tonight do you?"

Every part of me lights up in relief at his statement but at the same time I can't just up and leave my date. I may be a bitch for wanting Hawkin while I'm with Luke but I'm not that cold-hearted. "I can't," I tell him, voice strained with the desire I feel coursing through me, an obvious tell to him how I feel.

"Can't and want are two different things," he says, "and I'm not accepting a no."

I shake my head to contradict him, the "No" about to pass over my lips as he spins me around, backing me up not so gently against the door, and before I can even meet Hawkin's eyes, his mouth is on mine. I don't have time to think, only react, and oh how I react.

We become a mass of hands groping, lips bruising, and tongues tasting in a savage union of frustrated lust. Nothing is static for more than a beat as we try to feel our way into each others' lives. His hand squeezing my ass. My nails digging into his biceps. Teeth nipping lips followed by not so soothing licks because we are so desperate to claim and tempt and take.

All I can think of is more—all I want is more. I know minutes must pass but I swear it feels like fleeting seconds before he drags his lips from mine so that he can stare into my eyes, his labored breaths panting over my lips, swollen from his kiss. "You can tell me no all you want, Q. You can push me, pull my hair . . . bite me even . . . but you can't deny that you want me as much as I want you."

His words are an incendiary match to the emotions simmering within me. I want to act on them, but he's just annihilated my wits with his mouth—words and kisses. I shake my head side to side as I try to process, not realizing that he thinks I'm disagreeing. Before I can speak he leans in closer and says, "Make me believe you don't want me."

In a heartbeat his mouth is back on mine with a volatile intensity that even if I wanted to resist, I wouldn't be able to. My body tingles with need to the point where I feel like I can never get enough of him.

"Hawke?" Axe's muted voice breaks through our libidinous haze.

Hawkin swears out a curse, his forehead against mine. He removes his hand from where it was wrapped in my hair and forces my chin up as we separate.

"In the head," he yells out, irritated at being interrupted.

"You okay? Vince is asking. They need you back at the meet and greet."

"Yeah man, just zipping up. Tell him to hold his fucking horses, I'll be right out."

Hawke drops his head forward, eyes squeezed shut, hand still holding my hair hostage as we stand here in this suspended state of time. It's not long but just enough for reason to start seeping through the haze of what I'm doing.

And the women from earlier flash in my mind, but then Hawkin does something so unexpected and yet seemingly intimate that the images dissipate. He takes the tip of his nose and runs it from my collar bone up the column of my throat and to beneath my ear.

"You're coming to the after party. I don't care how, I don't care why, but I need more of you than this. You want me and then you don't want me and frankly I don't give a flying fuck anymore what your reasons are, because *I want you*. And I guarantee that once I have you, there will be no more back-and-forth because I'll leave your body so fucking high on me there will be no other option but to want more of me again."

I draw in a ragged breath as I try to take in his words that are erotic and possessive and downright assuming all at once but holy hell am I a trembling ball of need. And yet I say nothing.

He gently pulls my hair so that when he leans back he's looking straight into my eyes with unfettered intensity and unbridled desire expressed in his stormy irises. "It's taking everything I have right now not to tell Axe to fuck off, to tell them to wait so I can lift up this sexy skirt of yours, pull aside the panties you wore *for him* to discover, and finger-fuck you breathless. Claim you first. Show you just a taste of what we could be like together." He leans forward and tugs on my bottom lip gently with his teeth until they scrape along it and it falls free. "But I want to take my time with you Quinlan, edge you out so that by the time you come the only sound on your lips is my name, the only thought in your head is me, and the only thing you want filling you is this." He presses his dick that's hard and straining against the denim of his jeans into my hip.

My heart is pounding, and I gasp out when he roughly yanks down the neckline of my tank so that the lace of my bra is exposed. The possessive growl in the back of his throat is seductive and arousing and hotter than hell in so many ways. His eyes meet mine, then he lowers his head, fingers pulling the lace down farther before his mouth dips to the top part of my breast. I open my mouth again, the soft mewl of need falling from my lips as the warmth of his mouth glides over my skin.

His mouth sucks gently at first and then a little harder. I lean my head back against the door, my body zinging with so many different definitions of need that I can't focus on any one part at once. I'm losing myself under the haze of desire when all of a sudden he releases me, all contact lost so that a gasp escapes from my lips at the sudden loss of his warmth.

The electricity remains though.

I stare at him, his jaw tight in physical restraint, biceps tense as his fists clench, and I see so many things that contradict one another I'm not sure what to think.

But thinking is overrated when desire can be in control.

"That's so he knows that you're mine," he says, glancing down to my chest, intensity etched in his eyes. "And so you don't forget it." He takes another step back and turns to place his hand on the doorknob. "Wait a minute before you head back," he says with his head down, "and don't look so surprised. You knew this was coming." He opens the door.

"Hawke." His name tumbles brokenly from my mouth, a sound of desperation.

He looks at me, that devil-may-care smirk lighting up his face in triumph. "That just proved me right," he says with a shake of his head, and then leaves me behind with my mouth lax, cheeks flushed, and the knowledge that I just showed him I want him as much as he wants me.

I startle when the door shuts and the sound echoes around the tiled bathroom. But nothing rivals the pounding of my heart in my ears—or the juncture of my thighs—because the man just lit my fuse with his words and walked out without helping it catch flame.

I brace my hands on the counter next to me, needing a minute to catch my breath and collect myself. My mind whirls while my body still burns from his touch. I lift my head up and catch sight of myself in the mirror and can't tear my eyes away from what I see.

My tank is still pulled down below my boob, a dark red mark at the edge of my bra's lace from his mouth, but it's the look on my face that holds my attention. My cheeks are flush, my lips are swollen, and my eyes are more alive than I've ever seen them. I stare at my reflection for a moment, feeling like I'm looking at a stranger. Hawkin is the reason I look like this. The attraction between us is irresistible and combustible.

I force myself to look away, to straighten myself up—my shirt, my smeared lipstick, my disheveled hair—before taking a deep breath to steady the parts of me that feel alive for the first time in way too long.

And as I make my way back to Luke, I know. I know that I won't be able to resist Hawkin's pull on me any longer, that it's stupid to deny myself. To not take the chance to see where this may lead us because when all is said and done, we regret only the chances we didn't take, not the ones we did and failed at.

Make it count. My motto runs through my head and makes me question my morality between what is right and what I want.

I reenter the meet and greet with that resolve in the forefront of my mind and smile softly at Luke, suddenly cognizant of the length of time I've been gone.

"You okay?" Concern blankets Luke's face as guilt lances through me. Can he tell that I've been kissed senseless? I don't think so but I swear to God I feel like my hidden hickey is as visible as a scarlet letter.

"Yeah. Sorry. Got lost," I ramble and force myself to stop so that my lie isn't over-the-top obvious. I keep my eyes focused on him although I swear I can feel the weight of Hawkin's stare as Luke puts his arm around my waist and pulls me into him. My immediate reaction is to wriggle from his touch but I know I can't do it.

"It's okay. Perfect timing," he says. "We're next."

If he only knew.

I make a noncommittal sound and give him a forced smile. I feel his body vibrate with excitement even before I hear the voice over my shoulder.

"Hey, man, how are you doing tonight? Thanks for coming out!"

"Great show, Hawkin. You guys were incredible. That new song was killer." Luke falls all over himself as he tries to connect with Hawkin, and I wonder if I'm the only one who notices the tightness in his smile and arrogant lift of his eyebrows as he assesses Luke.

"Thanks. And you are?" Hawkin asks, reaching his left hand out to Luke. And it hits me. Hawkin's trying to get his arm off my waist.

"Sorry." Luke releases me to shake Hawke's hand eagerly. I watch that smirk return to Hawke's face as he gets the reaction he wanted from him. "Luke Mason, and this here is—"

"Luke Mason?" Hawke says, head tilting, eyes narrowing as Luke nods his head. "As in Indy Luke Mason?"

What the . . . ? He told me he didn't follow racing and yet he knows Luke's name?

In my periphery I can see Luke's smile widen to epic proportions at the notion that Hawkin knows who he is but I'm watching Hawke and not sure I like the predatory look he has in his eyes. "Yeah man, you follow racing?" The hope in Luke's voice is endearing.

"Not much," Hawke says with a shake of his head, "but I was just recently checking it out. Met someone that loves it . . . so Google was my friend."

The admission surprises me. So while I've been cyber-stalking him, he's been finding out more about what, my brother or my family? At least I know that he's curious enough to look.

"Well, if you ever want to check out a race . . ."

"Thanks." Hawke's eyes shift ever so subtly to mine. "And you are?"

"Qui—"

"Oh! I'm so rude. Sorry. This is Quinlan Westin." Luke shakes his head and places his hand on my back again, which doesn't go unnoticed.

Hawke reaches out to shake my hand, eyes lingering and hands held a beat longer than needed. "Hi, Quinlan," he says, rolling my name over his tongue. "Unique name. So you're into racers over rockers huh?" He raises his eyebrows in challenge causing me to shift uncomfortably but ready to play the game.

"It takes quite a lot to impress me." It's the only answer I can think of and I mean it as a warning, to back off in front of Luke, but all I get in response is that arrogant raise of an eyebrow.

He flashes me that lightning-quick grin. "I assure you rockers know how to leave their *mark* with more than just their music." He lifts his eyes to mine, reinforcing the innuendo in case I didn't catch it. A moment of awkward silence passes between the three of us.

"Hey, Luke," Hawke says, shifting gears and patting him on the shoulder as I try to figure out what kind of game he's playing now. "We're about to go to an after party at a club—the bands and a few others—do you guys want to come along?"

The devil inside me sags in respite knowing I've just been given the door to walk through to claim the pleasurable promise Hawkin threatened in the bathroom, while the angel cringes knowing if Luke accepts, he's walking us into a lion's den of disappointment that I don't want to be the culprit of.

And yet I don't think there's any way to prevent either thing from happening.

"No way! Really?" Luke's fingers tighten on my hip, and my eyes immediately flash to see if Hawkin notices. He doesn't. He's too busy whipping out his testosterone-laced gauntlet to throw down at Luke's feet.

"Yep," he says. "Axe, my security, will get you all the info. I've got to finish up here." He lifts his chin, indicating the next set of people in line to greet him. "We'll see you there though."

"Definitely," Luke says.

Hawkin starts to walk away and I'm far from oblivious to the look shared between Hawke and Vince before he turns back and looks at the both of us again, eyes shifting back and forth between us. "So you guys are a couple, right?"

"First date," Luke says proudly.

Hawke nods his head slowly as if he's mulling something over. "Well, you should definitely head on over to the club, have some drinks, relax, and party a bit, and you just might win her over." Hawke flashes a knowing grin at Luke that I sense means something more.

"Thanks man, we will."

Hawke chuckles as he turns his back to walk away, and I swear I hear him say, "Then again you might just lose her to a rock star."

"What?" Obviously Luke hears it too. His body stiffens beside me and I can tell by the condescending tilt of Hawke's head as he looks back at us that he meant every word he said.

"Sorry man, we're big on bets here within the band," Hawke says, waving over to Vince and Gizmo before turning back to us. "Making them is just kind of a habit. No harm, no foul."

So why am I screaming foul?

Chapter 13

The bass thumps in my chest, a constant drum of vibration, and out of habit I tap my fingers on the glass in my hand like I do my mic on stage. I glance around to where dark lights reflect off glass-littered tables, and take in the fact that there's enough talent between the four bands partying here to sell out any house.

Then I lock eyes with Jake, lead singer of the Mighty Storm, and tip my beer to him. He nods with a slow smile and by the look on his face, alcohol is his friend tonight. He relaxes with one arm around his wife and the other thrumming the beat on his leg. Like minds.

The song switches on the floor below, one that has a wicked beat, and I sink back into the cushion behind me, closing my eyes for a moment. The couch is comfortable enough but it's not like I'd want to pass out on it—no, not here with the rumors of what happens on the VIP floor of Scandalous—although I'm well on my way to doing just that.

Especially because *she's* not here. But why should she be? Why would she choose me over him? Yeah, I talk a good fucking game but when it comes right down to it, he can offer her so many things that I can't.

Sex I can do—I've certainly imagined long, sweat-inducing sessions of our bodies engaged every which way. Love on the other hand—the stability, the longevity—no fucking way.

So why do I keep looking at the stairway for her?

Talk about an unexpected surprise to look up from the quick-and-easy twins who I had a unique and interesting time with last month to find Quinlan standing there in the meet and greet room. With *his* arm around her.

And *his* lips on hers.

Her fucking perfect tits in that tight tank top and her sexy as hell legs, bare and long, beneath the short skirt that begged for me to yank it up around her waist while I discovered her perfection beneath. *Goddamn.* Talk about wanting to go over there and rip his hands off her, let him know where things stand between us, but shit, a make-out session on the porch and a one-sided phone call doesn't make her mine.

Yet.

Then she gave me the chance, rabbiting down the hall to escape after displaying the tiny flash of emotion in her eyes that I didn't have enough time to read. And I couldn't resist, had to follow her even with the opportunity for the twins again—shit, with any of the females in that room—sitting right in front of me, because I want only her.

I wanted to ask her so many things, most important what the fuck she was doing with that guy, but there was no stopping me from sampling her mouth the minute I pressed up against that ridiculous body of hers. Fucking hell, the woman kisses with every part of herself, like an R&B song that demands you to think of making slow, sweet love to someone. The kind of sex you can't shake long after the condom's tied off and your sheets fall cold.

I groan, the sound lost in the noise of the club, as I think of how fucking hard she made me with that selfish desperation she responded with. Nothing wrong with a woman going for what she wants. Talk about adding to her sex appeal and then some.

Take me. The thought has been on constant repeat since our first kiss. Pathetic, maybe. A necessary one, definitely.

And of course to make matters worse, I had to leave the sweetness of her in the bathroom to go back and watch that fucker's arm go around her. I'm not a possessive guy—shit, in my business chicks come and go in and out of our lives like on a constant lazy Susan—so it's not a feeling I'm too familiar with.

I sure as shit felt her react, tasted the need in our kiss, heard the way she called out my name, so where the fuck is she? *Rocker trumps racer every time.* Hands down.

What is it about her that has me wanting more? Ice cream is ice cream, so you need to keep sampling flavors so you don't get sick of the one you like the most, and yet she seems like a new flavor that I can't get enough of.

Addictive and has me craving more each time I get a taste.

You're so fucked in the head, I tell myself, comparing her to ice cream, all the while thinking of just where I want my tongue to lick her. *Damn.*

I lean forward and set my empty beer bottle down to pick up the glass where my Jack and Coke sits half gone. And fuck if I know what causes me to take note of my tats, the symbols telling the sordid story of my life when my shirt pulls up my bicep, but I do. To others they're just permanent ink on my skin; to me they are symbolic of everything churning inside me, past and present. All of them have their meaning, all of them tell of my hurt, my heartbreak, my motivation to move forward, to prove that I'm worthy of the things he robbed me of.

I draw in a deep breath, and try to shake the memories, the images that have forever left their indelible mark in my mind. It must be the mixture of alcohol that has me so contemplative. Quinlan not showing up.

It's all eating at me, spurring on the self-doubt that always lingers just beneath the surface. Singles hitting number one on the charts, more money than I can spend, fame . . . They do nothing to replace the emptiness or the need to prove to everyone that I'm worthy of it all. If I can't win over the one girl I want, then I sure as fuck am not enough to save the two people left in my life.

Fuck this. I down the rest of the drink, resign myself to the thought that I'll go find my own fun for the night. Get lost in someone else or call up the girls from earlier, I think I have their number somewhere. Fuck, or find a fangirl who'll be thrilled to be with me so that I can close my eyes and think of Quinlan.

I toss back the shot of Jäger on the table in front of me and when I slam the glass back down, I resolve that I need to take this back to where it all started, get my head on straight and simplify the situation. This is a bet, a challenge. Nothing more. Nothing less. A bet I have to win because fuck if I'm getting a tattoo of a pink damn heart.

Vince plops down on the other end of the couch and jars me from the shit fucking up my head and just eyes me up and down. "She show?"

"Who?" I play dumb even though I know he can see right through it.

"Your only hope at not getting a pussy pink heart tattooed on that wrist of yours." He throws his head back and laughs.

I'm about to tell him, *fuck you*, because hell no, I don't want to lose the bet. Won't lose. But immediately the thoughts about *after I do* sneak in, the ones that give possibility to the things I'll never allow in my life because they'll make you weak. Jesus Christ, I haven't even fucked her. Talk about a pussy predicament. Griff from the D-Bags beats me to it. "Fuck you, Vinny boy. The only pussy pink my man, Hawkin, here wears is on his lips."

I double over in laughter momentarily before I fist bump Griff. "Classic," I tell him. "Hey, Kellan," I say over his shoulder when I notice their band's lead singer on the other side of him. "You guys heading out?"

"Pussies," Vince mutters, making a show of checking his watch to tell them they're leaving way too early in the night.

"Well, yeah, that's next on my agenda," Griff says, all four of us laughing. "And definitely in the plural sense too."

"Early flight back to the tour," Kellan explains as he shakes my hand. "Thanks for letting us play tonight. My best to your family."

"Thanks for playing, man. Appreciate it!"

The guys finish saying good-bye to Vince and when they clear the space in front of us, I look up and my eyes lock on to Quinlan's. *Goddamn.* She's a few steps behind Luke, her hand's in his, but he's leading so she has the freedom to hold my stare.

And fuck the jolt that hits is like a live wire running rampant through my every nerve. It's like I'm seeing her for the first time and shit, it's not like she's doing anything other than walking, but it's as if she just made so many things that are off-kilter inside me even out.

The thought unnerves me enough that when they approach, I focus on Luke with glances aimed her way intermittently. But it's not enough.

I love the feistiness that sparks in the golden color of her eyes, the desire too, but I'm also intrigued to recognize her uncertainty over whether or nor I'll keep the promises I made earlier. And that tells me so much: that she's all-in with whatever this is between us. So I give her the only response I can with Luke present. I dart my eyes down to where my mark on her breast is hidden to let her know I'll live up to my words. No doubt there.

Even better is the hitch in her breath when she understands my intentions.

We make niceties for a bit and I just want to buy Luke a drink to occupy his mouth so he stops talking for a minute. He's a decent dude and all . . . just currently sitting with his arm around Quin. And she's mine.

Between the subtle and fleeting meeting of our eyes and the way her tits bounce beneath the tank as she moves instinctively to the music's beat, it takes every ounce of my effort to be attentive to whatever Luke is trying to talk about. I just nod and smile, pretend I'm more drunk than I really am because I learned a long-ass time ago that gets me out of having to converse with people when I don't want to. All the while my mind fixates on the aggressive desperation in her touch in the backstage bathroom what feels like a lifetime ago.

"Let me buy you a drink," Luke offers as he stands up. "What's your poison?"

Fuck if I'm going to tell him in the VIP lounge we have servers bring us our drinks, that we don't have to make a trip downstairs to the bar. Because now I get to be alone with Quinlan.

"Jack and Coke. Thanks." I nod to him.

He holds his hand out to help Quinlan up and I swear it

takes everything I have to not tell him she's staying here. "I'm gonna stay here," she says, reading my mind. I bite back the laugh when Luke glances back and forth between the two of us, my comment about losing the girl to a rock star from earlier obviously having left its impression. "My feet hurt," she explains, lifting up her tanned calf in a move that has thoughts of running my tongue up its inseam clouding my mind.

I lick my lips and when I look up from her sexy-ass heels, Quin's eyes are focused straight at me and are now full of libidinous hunger. It's almost as if the longer we're within each other's proximity, our attraction is irrefutable, growing stronger. And she must sense that the desire in her eyes is unmistakable to Luke as well because she averts her gaze suddenly as if she knows she's giving too much away.

But the damage has already been done. I'm sold. *Check please.* Time to go.

My dick's already rising to the occasion because if the look in her eyes showed me just a smidgen of the tigress beneath, I'm already done for.

But Luke remains and stares at her momentarily, confusion in the narrowing of his brow while he mouths to her *"You sure?"* to which she replies, "I'm fine. Really."

I can feel him looking but I just keep my eyes focused on the mix of lights flashing over the crowd of gyrating bodies below. I continue to gaze elsewhere because it's easier than looking into Luke's eyes and lying to him.

Shit, I'm nowhere close to being a saint but usually if I steal a man's woman, it's not literally right from under his nose. The crux of the matter though is that Quinlan definitely isn't his — to anyone on the outside it's easy to see — but obviously he still thinks it. And I don't want to be a dick or rub his face in the fact that she'll be going home with me tonight and not him.

By the way he looks at her, it's gonna sting enough, so I don't need to rub salt in the wound.

He's stuck in an awkward position, where he doesn't want to recant on his offer and lose the cool-guy vibe he's been trying hard for the past hour because he's nervous *his girl* is going to want to be played by me. He's definitely right on target with his thinking, but staying here or getting a drink at the bar isn't going to change the fact that I'm going to kiss Quin the minute he's out of sight.

I bob my head to the beat and continue to ignore him until he walks past Axe holding guard at the top of the stairs. Axe nods softly to me, and my body remains stationary as my eyes follow Luke's movement. The after-show adrenaline rush is still riding high within me but fuck if it's not being overwhelmed by the lust storming through my system.

He disappears, and I don't even have a second to think before Quinlan and I meet halfway across the distance separating us on the couch. The unsated need drives us. Without speaking we both know that time is fleeting between us and our mouths find each other's through the darkness.

The urgency of this stolen moment serves only to intensify things between us. There is no hesitancy, no words exchanged, no preamble because it's clear what we both want and need from each other right now. Contact. Skin to skin, tongue against tongue, fingertips to bare flesh.

There's no thought given to my voyeuristic bandmates scattered around us or the fact that we're in a very public place because the fuel to our desirous fire has already been lit. There's no turning back now.

Take and sate and claim. Those are the thoughts that fill my mind as her mouth brands itself to mine.

Without prompting she climbs atop my lap, her skirt hiking up as she presses herself against my dick that's already rock hard and begging to fuck her. And shit, it feels like heaven. The heat of her pussy grinding against where I want it the most. And I love that she's not shy, love that her hunger to sample is as riotous as mine right here in the wide open, because there is nothing sexier than a woman who refuses to give a fuck what other people think of her.

I've done the sex-in-public thing before, done the drunken plunge on a couch without shame, but there's something about Quinlan right now—the muted sensation of what could be between us, her fingers fisted in what she can grab of my hair, her tongue taking just as much as she's giving to me—I don't know what exactly holds me back but as much as every ounce of testosterone in my body is begging for me to unzip my fly and go for it, I can't. Fuck yes, this is only a bet I reaffirm in my mind between her tongue obliterating my thoughts but I know a quick fuck on the couch won't be enough for me.

Not with Quinlan.

From the pounding in my heart and the constriction in my chest I know I'll just want more. I might only get one shot at her alone without Luke there and I'm sure as fuck going to enjoy every goddamn second of it: to watch her parted for me and take me all in, watch her eyes roll back in her head as I make her come, hear her voice yell my name as she loses control.

And fuck yes I want her—now, later, every which way possible—but not here. Not like this.

It takes everything I have to make my body respond to my brain's request. To ignore the question running through my mind on why Quin's different and that this—fucking on a couch—isn't enough for me. To ignore the tightening of my sac as she grinds herself on me, to disregard her tits pressed against my chest or the taste of her on my tongue.

Every last ounce of restraint. But I do it.

My hand is fisted in the mass of her blond curls and I pull the strands just hard enough so that she notices and complies. A gasp falls from our mouths as our lips separate. Our faces are inches apart, eyes glazed with desire and searching each other's for any explanation of how this attraction vibrating between us can be so strong.

I see the minute she understands that I'm not going to take this any further—*fuck am I stupid*—because her lips form a *no* and she tugs her head against my grip.

"Not here. Not like this," I groan as she presses down against my lap, her body begging for what I'm withholding and fuck if she's not making this harder than it already is. "Ditch him. Come home with me right now." I grit the words out, pained to even have to ask.

She reaches down between her legs and rubs her hand over me. I grind my teeth, so amped up that I swear to God I feel like a damn teenager being touched for the first time. "Hawke," she moans my name into my ear, and hell if it's not the sexiest sound on the face of the earth. *"I want you."*

How the fuck is a man supposed to resist when she says that?

Our mouths are back on each other's, greed winning and hell if I'm going to repent for this sin because I plan on making a whole helluva lot more of them by the end of the night. We don't bother to speak, since the music is so loud that even if we did, the only thing we'd be able to feel is the vibrations against each other's chests and there's something innately hot about the notion that we're talking through actions only.

My hands slide under the back of her tank top and find purchase against her soft skin as she holds tight to my neck in what I take as a possessive show that she won't let me pull away from her again.

And shit, I'm a guy who loves to be in control but this—right here, right now, with her taking the lead—is seriously hotter than fuck.

The music may be loud and my blood is hammering in my eardrums but I hear Axe's warning whistle across the distance. It takes a moment for me to stop our kiss so that Quinlan can understand that Luke is on his way upstairs. A part of me doesn't want to stop, wants him to walk up, see his date currently dry-humping my dick and consumed with an urgency to have me. I know it's a bastard of a thought but it would mitigate the complications and choreographed dance we're stepping to not hurt Luke's feelings.

And why do I care? Why do I give a rat's ass about the shock value of him seeing this when I'm going to end up with the girl in the end? I know the reason, and it bugs the shit out of me and causes me to tear my lips from Quin's.

Because it's something Hunter would do.

"Quin. Luke. Coming," I pant into her ears as I physically lift her off my lap but have a hell of a time removing my hands from her arms and breaking the connection. I stare at her, her lips swollen, cheeks flushed, and those eyes of hers a dark storm of desire staring wide-eyed and inviting.

And something about the look on her face and the god damn dub step of my heart tells me that this is so much more than a bet.

I shove up off the couch and walk away from our section

toward the railing overlooking the floor below, my head spinning from the alcohol and the potency of her addictive fucking kiss. I catch Vince's sly grin from his seat and he just shakes his head at me and taps the heart on the inside of his wrist. The fucker. Gizmo has his arm around a hottie as well from the meet and greet. Looks like he's at least going to get lucky because by the way this shit is going tonight, my balls are going to be so goddamn blue I might as well pick up the sport of handball.

I brace myself on the railing, and blow out a breath as I try to figure what the hell it is about Quinlan Westin that's reeling me in like no chick has before. Women come, women go in my life without much thought. I've had steady relationships, monogamy isn't the problem, it's when they start having feelings that I start shutting down. And yet right now I'm ready to raise the white flag before I've even parted her thighs.

Not gonna happen, Play.

But then when I look over my shoulder to where Luke is handing her a drink and raising mine up to me all I can think of is him out of the picture.

I run a hand through my hair, determined to focus on anything else besides the clusterfuck of my thoughts—the killer performance we gave tonight, the fact that my vocal chords feel incredible even after the extended set we did, or that I can still taste Quin's lips and smell her perfume on my hands.

Get the girl, Hawke. I laugh out loud to myself. That's the funniest fucking line I've ever said because I always have the girl, normally no work needed and yet now I'm seeing how the other half lives—and this shit sucks.

It's just all of this shit with Hunter and Mom not doing well and now this bullshit seminar I have to do to prevent further damage that's fucking with my head. The disturbance in the force crap is not for me.

And neither is she, but sometimes you can't fuck with fate.

Time to get the girl.

Chapter 14

I'm listening to Luke but secretly watching Hawkin under the cover of the club's darkness. His drinks have been coming at a steady pace for the past hour.

I don't know what it is that Hawke does to me, but it took every ounce of restraint I had not to mount him right then and there on the damn couch. His dick was so hard and felt so good rubbing between my thighs, never mind the way he kisses—the complete obliteration of senses and thoughts—all of the sensations made it so difficult to pull away even though I knew Luke was coming.

Now I'm in such a clusterfuck of a position—seems like a constant since Hawke's come into my life—of hurting Luke in order to take what I want . . . but denying how I feel, how Hawkin Play makes me feel, is not an option.

My mind's been running scenarios all night long and I just can't seem to find a way to make this all play out without anyone getting hurt and that's a shitty feeling all around. I've been in his shoes before and it sucks, it hurts, but I try to rationalize that I've been there after months of fidelity rather than a single date. But it doesn't matter, I still feel guilty.

So I've had a few more drinks than normal, laughed a

little too loud more times than I care to count to feign like I'm having a blast instead of sitting with damp panties and wondering just how Hawkin fucks. He's a contradiction in so many ways—the cocky asshole, the rock star player, the protective brother, the consummate band member, and yet underneath all of that I can't get a read on the side of him that he lets slip every so often. The side I want to know, intimately.

Luke leans in again to kiss me and while I've tolerated it several times, I can't do it anymore. To not feel is to be dead and this girl likes to be made to feel alive. I'm sure it's the alcohol bolstering my actions but instead of kissing him back dispassionately as I have the other times, I push up out of my seat and wiggle my hips.

"I want to dance! You want to come with me?" I ask, knowing damn well he won't after catching snippets of his conversation with Rocket earlier about his two left feet.

"No. Nah. Not me," he slurs, his alcohol intake making its presence noted as he holds his hands up in front of him despite the resignation in his eyes that tells me he wants to be the one grinding up against me on the floor.

I scrunch my nose up in apology and wish that Layla was here—a little girl time on the dance floor is always fun, especially to protect your backside from drunk bastards trying to make advances you don't want. For when I have to use the name Trixie.

The music changes as I hit the floor, completely ignoring the several male hands that have already touched my arms asking for me to have a drink with them, and a David Guetta remix beat slams through the speakers. The alcohol, the unrequited sexual tension that's controlled my body the past three hours, leaves me with each step that I push through the throng of people. I claim a small space in the middle of the floor and begin to move amid the undulating mass of clubgoers. The lights play over the people around me and I let myself get lost in the beat and from my thoughts.

I dance a few more songs, glad I've pushed far enough into the crowd that I've been left alone by the guys trolling for action on the fringe of the floor, when I become too hot, my feet too sore in my heels, and decide I'm done. The beat of the music, the energy vibrating through my body, has only served to reinforce that I have to take this chance with him.

Making my way back up the stairs, Axe nods his head in greeting when I clear the landing. I walk on steadier feet toward the crowd of guys around the table where we've been sitting all evening.

Hawkin's eyes find me first and a shameful smirk tugs up one corner of his mouth. The sight of his reaction to me does funny things to my insides. As I approach, I hear Luke groan out while the rest of the guys begin a chant I can't quite make out. I swear to God it sounds like *make it count*—the irony of the saying Hawkin no doubt put to their game is not lost on me—but I'm unsure because they stop as I get closer.

"A bet's a bet, man," Hawkin says, shifting his attention toward Luke, who is obviously on his way to getting plastered right now, judging by the glaze of his eyes and the ridiculous amount of empty shot glasses lined up on the table in front of the band.

"Fffuuuccckkkk!" Luke slurs and lifts the glass to his lips with a defeated laugh. "Remind me never to challenge you to this again."

Gizmo erupts into laughter. "Dude. You never challenge musicians to a shot contest. We have hours on tour buses to build up tolerance to this shit—we'll win hands down every time. Especially that fucker!" he says, pointing at Hawkin, who just leans back with his half-empty Jack and Coke in one hand and an empty shot glass in his other and watches with amusement.

"Rocker trumps racer every time," Hawkin laughs, his eyes glancing over to Vince as Luke chugs the shot back.

"Fine by me," he says, pointing his finger at Hawke, "because racer gets the girl in the end."

The two men lock eyes—a nonverbal pissing match is waged between the two of them. I wonder what in the hell I've missed by going dancing and think maybe I don't want to know the parameters of this little contest that's going on.

"Just a little dick-dueling," Rocket says into my ear as he slings an arm around my shoulder. I bite back the chuckle I want to emit when both Hawkin and Luke unbeknownst to the other narrow their eyes at Rocket for touching me.

"Looks more like a big dick contest," I muse, my thoughts drifting back to Luke and his *ten inch* comment from weeks ago.

"Now, that? I'm not going to be the judge of," he laughs with a shake of his head and plops down next to Luke, whose head is now resting on the back of the couch, not looking so well.

The night wears on a bit longer, the contest slows down, but as I watch from the sidelines, I notice that Hawke is not downing the shots like Luke is. He's picking them up and then just moving them full to the table beside him where one of the others in the VIP room takes and downs them.

I cringe thinking what Luke is going to feel like in the morning—well, later in the morning—when he's done being passed out because that sure as hell is the way he's headed. And as much as I want to be pissed at the guys for whatever the bet is that's going on, I can't be because they continue to tell Luke the game's done, and yet he still feels the need to play. I have a slight feeling I know what the prize is and just why he's fighting so hard.

Last call comes and goes and it's decided by someone in our group that Axe is going to drive all of our drunk asses home. Luke disagrees and wants to stay and drink some more despite being unable to stand up, but it's closing time.

We are all zoned out in the limo bus, the evening's adrenaline and alcohol high slowly fading into exhaustion. We've dropped Luke off at his hotel room where Axe and I made sure he made it safe and sound inside and onto his bed. I felt like shit for leaving him there like that but he passed out on the bed before I could even take his shoes off.

When it comes down to it, whatever testosterone-fueled game he was playing is only going to result in a lot of puking tonight, and I really don't think he's going to want to end our first date that way.

And call me coldhearted but this squeamish girl doesn't really want to see it.

I left him a note to call me in the morning so that I can

make sure that he's okay, that I had a good time, and thanks for the invite. What else am I supposed to say? Thanks for making this easy on me, for passing out, so that I can go screw the man I really want?

At least for now his dignity remains intact in more ways than one. . . . Too bad I'm going to add to the wicked hangover he's going to have in the morning when he wakes, calls, and I tell him thank you for the nice evening, but there's nothing there on my end.

Axe is cautiously making his way through downtown LA traffic—present at all hours—toward my house. Gizmo went home with his raven-haired hottie and Rocket is currently making moaning noises a few rows behind us doing who knows what with one in a trio of women. Or maybe with all of them.

"Keep it down, Rock," Hawkin scolds. "Lady present." I can't help but laugh at the comment and love it all at the same time because it's cute. And then I wonder how offended I'd be if I were one of the trio but I figure their mouths are a bit too busy to pay attention to insults.

Sinking into Hawkin next to me, the alcohol hums through my blood and helps dull the guilt over abandoning Luke and leaves me charged with anticipation of how I want to spend the rest of the night.

I know Hawkin feels the same way because his body tenses up every time I rub against him, and I know it's taking a strong hold on his restraint to prevent himself from taking me right here and now. And the idea sends a slight thrill through me, fills me with a wanton desire to see just how far I can push him.

Shifting in my seat, I watch the lights of the city play over his face as we move through the night, my mind trying to process how we got from a combative first encounter to here. I slide my hand across his thigh, notice the hitch of his breath and the snap of his eyes over to mine. Oh yeah, he wants this just as bad as I do. Hell if that notion isn't a heady feeling.

The tips of my fingers graze the top of the crotch of his jeans, the seam already straining and begging me to relieve the pressure against it, soothe the ache with the warmth of my mouth. My sex throbs from the thought, and unsated need drives my actions.

As I lean into him, his eyes watch me all the while until I kiss the side of his neck before running the tip of my tongue up to just below his ear. The salt of his skin is on my tongue and the smell of his cologne is in my nose but it's the pained groan of restraint that turns me on more than anything. I'm a girl who loves a good dare and I'll be damned if I'm going to back down from this one.

I want a reaction from him right now—the fist in my hair, his mouth claiming mine, his hands parting me and dipping inside to ready me for the one thing I really want—to prove to myself that I can make this player lose his control.

"How hard are you going to fuck me, Hawkin? Are you going to play me like your guitar? All fingers strumming my strings till I react or are you going to use me like I'm your mic and use your mouth to make me scream like all the women in the crowd do?" As I whisper into his ear, my own words are turning me on. "Or am I the lucky one for the night? Will you let me watch as you part my thighs and slide your dick into my tight, wet pussy? Will you make me come with your kiss on my lips?"

I tug on the lobe of his ear with my lips, and he holds me at arm's distance before I'm able to connect with his lips. His eyes blaze with lascivious need and yet his head shakes subtly back and forth. I'm not sure what he's trying to tell me. His eyes say one thing and his body shows another right down to the expression on his handsome face.

"Go ahead, Hawke." Vince's words cut through the bemoaned silence of the bus. "I'll just watch from over here . . . unless you want me to join in, that is," he says with an amused chuckle.

I feel Hawkin's body tense further if that's even possible, and my mind begins to work overtime. Is that why he's acting so weird? Is that what Hawke wants and he's afraid to ask? Me and him and Vince together? I swallow the discomforting thrill of the idea, something I have never done before. This will be my first time with Hawke, no one else needs to be there while we memorize each other's bodies and sounds.

"Maybe some other time," I reply, hoping to add some levity and ease whatever tension remains. Fight fire with fire and all that. "Sorry, Vince, lead singer trumps bass player."

Hawkin erupts in a fit of laughter at my comment and holds his stomach as the hysterics take over his whole body. "Oh God! That's fucking classic!"

Chapter 15

The walk to my front door feels like a mile, but at least we're both sobering up some. Anticipation of what's going to come next assaults us with every step forward. My nerves hum, my core burns with that sweet, delicious ache, and I tell myself to expect nothing more than the moment. I laugh softly knowing no matter what I tell myself I'm already too attached to Hawkin and nothing has really happened yet.

I fumble with the key in the lock, the expectation adding to the heady moment, until Hawke steps up behind me, my back to his front. He pulls my hair off my neck with one hand, fingertip tracing over my inked motto, and places a kiss on the curve of my shoulder that is so unexpected it heightens the fluttering sensations in my belly. Nerves and expectation ruin my dexterity so he reaches out and places his hand over mine so that we both unlock the front door together.

And I'm so far from the flowery, Hallmark moment girl, but there is something that touches me with the action, and I can only hope he's unlocking more than just the front door and maybe opening up the possibility of letting me in.

When the door swings open and he follows me in, the silence stretches so tautly it only enhances the desire as we make our way through my darkened house straight to my bedroom. I don't think to ask if he wants another drink, a bottle of water—it never crosses my mind—because I'm driven by pure need at this point. Besides, we've had enough foreplay tonight that without even asking him, I know neither one of us wants to wait any longer.

So I step into my bedroom with confidence and when Hawkin's hands immediately find my waist and pull me back into the muscled heat of his chest, I close my eyes and allow myself to memorize the feel of his embrace before he renders my body senseless and my thoughts incoherent. He's already hard for me and I'm so turned on by the fact that I haven't said a word to him, I haven't shed my clothes, and yet he's ready.

His hands begin to move over my torso. They snake under my tank top, and I gasp in a breath at the feeling of skin on skin, at the sensation of rough to smooth that tells me this is real, this is about to happen. He smooths his hands up my rib cage so that my tank pulls up with them, and he cups my breasts as he goes. We both moan in unison as his fingers brush over my nipples. I gasp out as sensation swamps me, my head rolling back onto his shoulder behind me as I surrender my body to his hands, my emotions to his manipulations, and absorb the pleasure he's giving me.

He rubs my nipples between his fingers and thumbs through the lace of my bra before continuing to slide my tank up to my shoulders. He gestures for me to lean my head forward and he lifts my tank over my head but lowers it over my arms, stopping it so that they are held in place.

Chills race over my body; the ache he's building inside me intensifies with each touch feeling like a pleasurable pain. My sex throbs with each beat of my pulse and my muscles tense to prevent myself from twisting around, ripping the tank top off and jumping him. God yes I want him with every fiber of my being, but there's something innately arousing about turning yourself over to someone. Trusting someone with your body, your sexual pleasure, openly handing them your vulnerability—it's all a very intoxicating feeling.

Add to that the lack of any words between us. Our only communication is the dance of his fingers over my sensitized flesh. Hands urging in silent command, minds running wild.

He draws in a ragged breath from behind me and I love the thought that he's just as affected. Hawke's hands begin to move back down my body now, sliding between my breasts where he unclasps my bra before moving to my back and down the length of my spine to unzip my skirt. It falls to the floor and pools around my feet so that I'm wearing nothing but a fuchsia lace thong with nude heels and a tank top holding my arms motionless.

My skin is hot, the air is cool, and his breath feathers over my neck in a whisper of a touch. My thoughts forget the notion of the casual sex I told myself I could have with him because I already know that there is no turning back now as he runs his palms back to my abdomen so that his fingers dip beneath the band of my panties. He lowers them to the top of my cleft, parting me slightly so that his fingertips graze the top of my clit, causing my pelvis to buck into his hand as I beg for more.

The chuckle he gives me in reaction spurs me on, tells me he likes a woman to react, and good thing because I'm not one to take my passion quietly. Then his lips press lightly to the curve of my shoulder in an unexpected action that feels surprisingly intimate and coaxes a soft moan from my lips.

The heat of his body against my back disappears as he takes a step away but his hands command me to stay still when I try to turn toward him. His calloused fingertips begin to trace over my body: up my rib cage, skimming the underside of my breasts before heading up the midline of my chest, and then tracing the line of my collarbone out to my shoulders.

There's something about the way that he's touching me, almost as if he's learning the lines of my body like he would an instrument. It's intimate, sensual, and languorous, like he wants to take the time getting to know me before he claims me. It's surprisingly erotic and not what I've ever experienced in a first-time encounter with someone who hasn't already professed his love for me.

I push the thought from my head, ignore the questions his actions evoke: Is he always like this? Is he like this because he wants more? Parts of my psyche hold on to the hope that I know I'll need after tonight is over and decide to focus on the fact that he needs to fuck me soon. My body's on fire and so attuned to his touch that when he finally does I'm going to come in a matter of seconds.

The scrape of strong fingers up the curves of my shoulders, featherlight touches up the base of my neck and into my hair, quiet my thoughts, tell me to shut it down and enjoy the moment. My head falls forward and I moan in ecstasy as he kneads my muscles softly. His hands begin a seductive descent down my shoulder blades to the swell above my butt before slipping his fingers into the fabric at my hips. He pushes my panties down the length of my legs—slow and purposeful—smooth and rough in a devastating one-two punch to my nerves. I lift my feet as they fall and then stand motionless, our excited breathing the only sound in the room.

I'm not sure at what point he silently requested that I not speak and I decided to comply, but the combination only adds to the sexual tension snapping through the air. The notion that I am at his every whim heightens the sensations.

I stand motionless, Hawkin still behind me, and yet he's not touching me. Curiosity and desire wage a feudal war within me as I debate whether to turn around and take what I want or to play out this little game that has me willing to beg if he doesn't touch me soon.

And I *don't* beg.

His fingertips begin again, whispering a trail up my inseam, gentle pressure urging my legs farther apart. I suck in a breath as the cool air of the room bathes the heated skin between my thighs. He brushes his hands ever so slightly over me before they once again leave my body.

I close my eyes, wondering where to next, while goose bumps race over my skin in expectancy as I hear him move behind me. And I find out quick enough when I feel the warmth of his mouth on the nape of my neck again. Desire mainlines from everywhere within me as his fingertips touch the apex of my thighs, causing that sweet, pleasurable ache to burn with a heightened intensity.

He presses close against my back again, his erection

thick against me. "Open your mouth," he commands, his voice sending chills down my spine.

I part my lips without hesitancy and he murmurs in approval before slipping two fingers between my lips.

"*Suck.*"

How can that single word evoke such a visceral reaction from my body? Nipples hardening to the point of pain, my sex swelling, my mouth reacting. I respond, body vibrating with the desire that increases with each passing moment.

"Do you have any idea how bad I want you right now? I'm hard as a rock and it's taking everything I have to not lay you down on your bed and fuck you into oblivion," he says in a pained voice that only turns me on more knowing he's suffering as desperately as I am. "You deserve better than that, Quinlan, and fuck if it's not taking everything I have to give that to you. . . . I've never wanted to be more selfish than I do right now."

His teeth nip my shoulder, which causes me to open my mouth where his fingers still remain. His words stoke the flames of desire even brighter knowing that I matter enough to him in whatever this is to try to give me what I deserve.

I begin to respond, to tell him *Thanks but right now all I want is you in me, on me, pleasuring me*, but he stops me. "Uh-uh, don't talk." His mouth brushes against my ear, that raspy rhythm an audible pheromone. "Right now I'm going to take these fingers and fuck you with them. I'm going to lick your clit and finger fuck you into a frenzy until you're just about to climax. I'll hold you there. Make you ride that fine line between frustration and desire. Make you beg, make you moan, make you scream my name. And then I'll stop because I want to be in you when you come."

I close my eyes and let his words sink in, allow my body the visceral reaction—the sudden tensing up and then slow release of muscles—as I wait in that suspended state of hazy desire for him to begin. He crosses his free arm over my chest, lower rib cage to opposite shoulder, and pulls me roughly against the front of him so that there is no mistaking his want of me. His chuckle reverberates against my back and into me. "Oh, believe me. I know you think you'll come even if I stop but, sweetness, I assure you, you won't until I'm in you. You'll hate me, then love me and fuck if when you come it won't be the strongest orgasm you'll ever have." He runs the tip of his tongue along the side of my neck, making me forget my thoughts of how he knew what I was thinking. "Now bend over and get ready to beg."

He withdraws his fingers from my mouth, murmuring an approval as I obediently lean forward and place my chest onto the top of the mattress. And the funny thing is most of the time I'd tell a guy to screw off if he was going to give me orders, deny me my orgasm, and not let me touch—this girl likes to give just as good as she gets—but there is something about Hawkin that makes me want to earn the orgasm he gives me.

"Damn, woman," he murmurs the moment the finger I've just wet with my mouth slides between the already slick lips of my sex. My body is so on edge from this foreplay that there is no way he'll be able to stop my orgasm because the beginning of it is already bearing down on me like a freight train and he's barely touched me.

I feel him against my knees and it takes me a minute and a glance down to realize that he sat down on the floor, his back against the foot of the bed I'm bent over so that his face is right where it needs to be. He positions his hands so that when he grabs the roundness of my ass and pulls gently, the tips of his fingers skim over the backside of my cleft. The sensation is strangely arousing but it's taken to all new heights when his mouth closes over my pleasure. His tongue splits me and slides down to where his fingers have now pressed their way inside me.

The cry falls from my lips, my hands fist, and I work the tank top that's still holding my arms hostage up some so that I can bend my arms and fist them in the top of his hair. Pleasure swamps me, owns me, and has me begging for more. "Oh God Hawke." They're the first words that I speak in I don't know how long but they're all I need to say because I'm swamped with sensations.

I'm an *it takes time for me to come girl* but hell if he just hasn't blown that all to smithereens because the way his mouth is working my clit mixed with the slow slide of his fingers in and out has me climbing that peak faster than ever before. I can't catch my thoughts when usually I'm having to push them away as his tongue owns every inch of sensitized flesh between my folds.

The room fills with the commands he vocalizes, the vibration of his voice only adding to his delicious torment, my labored breathing and the slick sound of my wetness being expertly manipulated. My body begins to tense, that slow flush of heat beginning to bathe my body in its warm glow as my orgasm rises from the depths of my body. I start moving my hips, grinding back and forth onto his fingers and tongue, his previous decree of edging me out lost in my quest for release, so just as I can feel it wash over me, all movement from him ceases.

I gasp out and squeeze my eyes shut to try to will my orgasm to fruition, but without my hands or his, nothing's going to happen.

"Hawkin!" I say his name like a curse into the sexed-up air and it earns me a taunting laugh from him.

I clench my muscles, desperate for so much more of him than just this orgasm. The thought scares me momentarily but I can't think about it right now. I need to focus on the here and now and not the mess my heart will inevitably be in after he casts me aside.

I step back from where he's positioned between the confines of my legs and his hands slide up the outside of my thighs to my hips to my waist as he stands. He reaches my neck, and I look up and meet his gaze for the first time in what feels like forever since we arrived at my house.

The look in his eyes—burning desire and the wild need to sate it—makes me feel like he wants to take every single part of me, memorize me, use me, and then start all over again, and hell if I'm not down with this game. I want his kiss, his body on top of mine, his hands braced on either side of my head while he's driving into me.

And I want it now.

I step forward this time, my flanks into his, his legs pressed against the edge of the bed, and we just stand there. Our torsos are touching chests to thighs, our breaths mingle, and our eyes speak a language exclusively our own. *I want you. Take me now. Fuck me. Wreck me. Make me yours.*

A mutual exchange of needs and desires that I initiate when I lean into him and brush my lips to his. His hands slide around my back and pull me into him harder as our mouths part and tongues unite. I feel my heart slip a little toward the edge of no return and lose myself in the taste of my pleasure on his tongue and how there's something so strangely arousing about it that I just want more of what he's offering me. His hands move over my bared skin like his tongue does—skillful, urgent, a little rough, and a lot needy—and hell if the mixture of motions isn't a potent cocktail of desire that we're getting drunk on.

He groans my name into my mouth. I want to pull away, strip off his boxer briefs, and taste him, but right now he's savoring me and there's something endearing about it. As much as I want to order him to give me what I want like he has me, it's not possible because my independent streak is out the damn window right along with my control.

I'm all for equality between a man and a woman but right now this woman doesn't care about being equal, she just wants to come.

I know without a doubt that Hawkin owns the keys to that toe-curling orgasm I've been without for some time and hell if I'm not going to submit so he can find the lock and use his key to unleash it.

Our kiss grows possessive. I writhe against him, trying to tell him that I need him to push me off that ledge I'm walking precariously on just like he said I would be. His hands slide down my biceps and remove my tank top from my elbows.

And the minute my arms are released from their cotton confines, *it's on*.

My hands go immediately to the back of his neck, fingers tugging in his hair, pulling him into me. My hands match the urgency of his and yet we still stand there and express our desire with our hands and mouths when so many other men would have already been in, out, and done by now.

I snake one of my hands down his abdomen and slip it inside his underwear. I find his dick immediately, it's hard to miss it really, and the minute my fingers encircle his girth, a pained groan falls from his mouth. His hands leave my skin momentarily as he pushes the fabric down to grant me unhindered access to pleasure him.

My fingers dance over the length of his shaft, causing our lips to part and his head to fall back as he absorbs my reciprocal foreplay. I lean forward and kiss the underside of his jaw. He tastes of salt and soap and the scent sears itself into my memory as my tongue licks and hand slides back and forth over his cock.

"Quin." I love the grate of his voice over my name, desperate and defiant.

"Get ready to beg," I murmur against his skin, rough with his five o'clock shadow, tossing his comment back to him. His body falters a moment, a strained but amused laugh falling from his lips that turns into a groan of desire when I gently scrape my nails over the underside of his dick.

His hands find my shoulders and grip tightly as he tilts his head down so he can meet my gaze, a chiding smile on his lips and everything I want reflected in his eyes. "Sweetness, as much as I want you to wrap your mouth around my dick and make me beg for it, you can take me there next time because right now, I want you," he says, his tongue wetting his lower lip and distracting me from focusing on the fact that he said next time. And telling me there will be an again when he hasn't even had me yet makes places in me stir that have nothing to do with having an orgasm. "And I'm going to have you." He says the last statement on a melodic whisper that reminds me of the song earlier but this time he's not on stage in front of thousands of women, he's standing here in front of me.

I breathe in deeply, needing the air to help clear my head, and all it does is the opposite because it smells like him. I keep my hands on his dick but with my eyes on him, lean forward and take the flat disk of one of his nipples in my mouth and graze my teeth over it. He hisses in a breath, eyes darkening with lust as my own taunt him to do just what he's promised, to take me.

Two can play this game. My hand slides up and down him again, his dick pulsing in my hand from the stimulation. "What are you waiting for, Hawkin?"

I take a step back slowly, my eyes running up and down his body, my first time getting to see the whole of him. And holy mother of God . . . if Hawkin Play fully clothed is hot, a naked one is breathtaking. And being a man used to women staring at him, he stands still and lets me get my visual porn.

His shoulders are strong, pecs and abs defined but more from constant physical activity than a guy who lifts for bulk, and in the moonlight I can see the basic outlines of the shapes of his tattoos but not make them out. My eyes go lower, trace the V down to where he demonstrates just how ready he is for me, and hell if he's not packing what Luke claimed to have.

The unbidden part of me doesn't care that he knows I'm openly staring at him so I lift my eyes ever so slowly up to meet his. He walks toward me, his body announcing the predator inside him ready to take what he thinks is his. His eyes are hungry, smirk arrogant, and body made for the kind of sins I enjoy committing.

My only thought is that I need to hold on tight because I have a feeling Hawkin Play is about to take me for a ride in more ways than one, and I just hope both my body and my heart will be able to handle it. I've been able to separate sex and emotion with men prior to tonight, but I know right here, right now, with that look in his eyes and that purpose in his posture, that there's no way in hell I'll be able to with him.

"Bed's this way," he says with a lift of his chin over his shoulder as he stops in front of me and reaches out to my hips and pulls me into him. Skin against skin. His erection presses deliciously between the V of my thighs, making my mouth water and my legs weak with thoughts of everything that's about to happen.

"Rest assured, I know where my bed is, Hawkin."

"Then why are you not on it?" The heat of his breath feathers over my lips as I fight every urge in my body to continue our banter when all I want is him and me rolling around on the bed.

"Because I wanted to make you come first." I know exactly what I've said, how he's going to take it, and by the flash of the feral smile he gives me, know that he heard me.

He laughs. It's more strained now as he fights the urge to figure out what I'm trying to accomplish. "Hmm. Now, I know you may think I'm a selfish bastard but I promise you, I never come first unless it's with my own hand. So . . ." he says, fingertips tracing a line down the side of my cheek that I can't resist leaning into, "get your ass on the bed, *Trixie*, before I'm tempted to tie you to the bedposts and fuck you into explaining who this Trixie is that you pretended to be."

His words, his touch, his nearness intoxicate me so that it takes a moment for me to respond. I nod my head to the drawer of my dresser as I reach out and pull open. It has a small stash of condoms—a girl's gotta be prepared. I step away from him as he raises his eyebrows in surprised approval.

I saunter slowly toward my bed, eyes looking over my shoulder at him as he watches me. "By the way, Trixie is my naughty side. . . . She just might like that a little too much."

I hear his intake of air, see his eyes widen, right before he launches himself at me. I'm on the bed before he lands next to me and scramble away from him as we erupt into a fit of laughter laced with a tinge of desperation.

"Don't think you're going to live that comment down," he taunts as his hands find my hips and pull me toward him. I struggle playfully because when he presses me into the mattress, his body flanking mine, I can't help the sigh that falls from my lips at his closeness. Our eyes meet and our smiles remain but silence descends as he leans forward and slants his mouth over mine.

And this time he holds absolutely nothing back. He draws every last ounce of desire from me as his tongue meets mine, leading this intimate dance with skill and passion that has every part of my body lit aflame and begging for him to hurry the pace and sink into me. Even though I know the minute it's over I'll wish he dragged it out.

His knees find their way between mine and push my legs slowly apart while his mouth continues to tempt me in every way possible. A hand cups my breast before sliding farther down my body, each inch feeling like it's taking forever to cover on the way to where I want it the most.

And he kisses away the moan he coaxes from me when his fingers find me open and waiting for him. Gentle yet demanding touches on the most sensitized of flesh. I lift my hips up, physically begging him to sate the desire burning out of control within me. The motion earns me a chuckle against my lips, and the head of his dick lines up perfectly at my wetness. His fingers part me, dipping in to test my readiness for him, and I pulse my muscles around his fingers to show him I'm more than ready.

His mouth brands mine, one last searing kiss that cements emotions I shouldn't be feeling before he pushes up on his haunches like a pagan god between my thighs waiting to worship, but the only thing I'm allowing him to devote himself to is me.

He pushes into me, that slow burn of stretching as my body accommodates him the most exquisite of pain. He looks down, hands holding my thighs apart, eyes expressing the unspoken words behind his mask of arrogance, and lips falling lax as he succumbs to my wet heat. We hold each other's gazes as he begins to move, and I can see so many things flicker within his eyes. The pace he sets is slow at first. His thick crest slides over nerves I never knew I had and brings me unfathomable pleasure.

I close my eyes when the sensations become too intense, my feelings too transparent, but every time I open them back up, his eyes glisten through the darkness. I become mesmerized with the look, the feel, the subtle sounds he makes as he sheaths himself root to top before pulling back out.

I lose myself to the feeling, to the moment, and allow it all to wash over me. Yes this is casual sex, chemistry igniting between two willing people, but the way he takes his time and yet takes what he wants simultaneously is an intoxicating spell I willingly submit to.

He slides his hands down my inner thighs, fingertips adding friction to my clit, propelling me closer to the edge. "Hawke." His name is a sigh on my lips as I buck my hips up to meet his fingers and the rhythm of his thrusts.

Sounds fill the room—my plea, his praise, our combined moans, as he works us into a frenzied pace where the simple touch of flesh to flesh feels like two live wires connecting. Sparks trace from where we become one and chase their way through my body, digging in and taking hold, annihilating any hope I have from walking away from him unscathed.

My hands fist sheets and then move up to score lines into the muscles of his thighs before sliding back to the sheets again—restless movements that try to satisfy the desire unfurling within me and between us. My legs begin to tense, my muscles clutching around him so that he knows I'm nearing my peak.

Just when I want him to drive harder and faster—force me into the oblivion just beyond my reach, he slows down. My head snaps up to challenge him just in time to see the ecstasy written on his face when he slides all the way in and pops his hips in some way that needs to be patented and taught to men everywhere because whatever the hell he does, when he does it a few more times, I'm lost.

I fall under the warm rapture of my orgasm as it hits me with a savage intensity. I don't know what I say or do because I'm hidden behind the veil of white-hot pleasure that is so overwhelming all I can do is feel: the satisfying singe of his touch, the stroke of his cock over sensitized nerves, the ricochet of the orgasm as it pulses through my body. And then Hawkin begins to move again, withdrawing and plunging back in, in a fervent pace that not only prolongs my climax but pulls his from him like a tornado touching down.

"Fuck!" he cries out, his hips jerking spasmodically as he chases his release, driving as deep as he can into me, fingers digging into my thighs, my name falling from his lips.

He leans forward, crawling up my body, mattress dipping at my sides as he presses his hands there before collapsing softly on top of me with a satisfied groan. "Damn, woman," he says, warm lips pressing tender kisses against the chilled skin of my chest as our panting breaths fill the silence of the room. "You wore me out!" His chuckle rings with warmth and satisfaction and vibrates into me from our connection.

My fingers trace up and down his back, the flush and scent of the sex we just had still clinging to my skin. "Well shit . . . then you sure as hell wouldn't be able to handle Trixie," I tease, earning a quick graze of his teeth on my nipple in response.

I wiggle away from him, laughter falling around us as he slips out of me, the emptiness ringing loudly despite his hands still touching me. "Oh." He grunts out the sound. "I'm going to have so much fun playing with her."

We laugh as I find a pillow beneath my head and his lips

pressing against mine, tongue slipping between them in a slow, tantalizing kiss that cements what we just experienced. I groan in protest when he pulls back, but I love the look he graces me with, eyes hazy and a smirk softening his features.

"Silly boy," I murmur, bringing my hands up the sides of his torso, feeling the muscles bunch beneath them as I go. "Trixie's for men." I can't resist the taunt—the play off the cereal commercial—because he sure as hell just proved to me he's a one hundred percent skilled man but I need to keep this simple. The way he's touching me and not rolling over and snoring like so many others have done is making this moment a bit too intimate for me, making it a bit too real. And hell yes, I'll take something real but I also know that with the real comes the heartbreak that's inevitable and so I defuse the feelings from finding permanence with humor.

"Wow!" he exclaims in jest, eyebrows raised and fingers finding the ticklish spots on my rib cage. And at first it's innocent in nature when I writhe beneath him but as my breasts rub against the firmness of his chest and the condom he hasn't removed yet that's still slick with my arousal slides over my thigh, desire fires anew. My breath hitches when his hands find my hair and fist in it before his mouth meets mine in a kiss that surges with hunger. "Guess I better show you again how much of a man I can be then."

He pushes up off me, leaving me cold and wanting as he saunters over to grab another condom from my drawer-o-protection, his ass a sight I could stare at all day long, and all I can think is *Pretty please.*

"I thought you were going to edge me out. What happened to that?" I throw the taunt at him as I hear the telltale tear of foil, my body already stirring back awake with the anticipation of getting more of him.

He turns back and looks at me, the moonlight soft on his skin and confidence reflected in his posture. "Hmm. If I'm not mistaken, it was you just screaming my name, right?"

"It was a moment of weakness," I lie, savoring the smile he graces me with because we both know damn well it was more than that.

"I think it was a whole lot of skill," he says as he walks slowly toward me, erection bobbing with each step as I scrape my eyes over his shadow in the night. He crawls on the bed and hovers over me, our bodies void of any contact. "Skill . . . and this weakness I seem to have when it comes to you."

My heart swells at his words and the only thought that passes through my mind is, rocker trumps racer, without a doubt.

Chapter 16

QUINLAN

Through dreamy eyes and a sleep-fogged brain with the warmth of his body beside mine, I take in everything. The dark stubble shadowing his jaw that begs me to reach out and rub my fingers over its coarseness. A tangible reminder that this is real, last night was real . . . the sudden onslaught of feelings I have for him is real. The sheet is somewhere on the floor, both of us bathed only in the sunlight streaming in through the half-open blinds that were forgotten last night in our pleasured exertion.

He shifts some, turning on his back and moving his arm opposite me behind his head. I watch his biceps flex and trace the line of his body to where I can see the symbol inked into his skin on the inside of his wrist. I don't want to move too much and disrupt his sleep—this is my chance to memorize specifics about him—but I angle my head some to catch the tattoo.

The music note is clear as day sitting on the inside of his wrist but another symbol placed toward his elbow isn't easy to decipher. I stare a bit longer and as much as I want to slide a little farther away so that I can see the markings on his upper bicep, I decide this feeling is way too heavenly to leave. I can look later, ask later.

I snuggle into him, nestling my face into the crook of

his arm and torso, and return my hand to his abdomen so I can feel it rising and falling softly beneath my palm. I think of last night. Of the murmured words and how Hawke completely owned my body and every reaction he coaxed from me. How we lay spent and exhausted but riding that first-time high in comforting silence as I wondered what happens next. Was he going to call Axe to come get him or spend the night and awaken to that awkward silence?

And the best answer was neither.

After a few minutes where we let the sweat cool from our bodies and our labored breaths settle into a normal rhythm, the bed shifted some and the next thing I knew his hands were pulling me into the heat of his body.

"Hmm," he murmured into the crown of my head, followed by a kiss. "I'm exhausted."

My soul content and body satisfied, I trailed a finger over his chest and thought about how he had most definitely given me the toe-curling sex that I had been without. "Can't imagine why . . . a show, drinking with the band, a pissing match with Luke, a—"

"Rocker trumps racer every time, sweetness," he said and the smile returned, my heart swelling despite my conscience telling it not to at the endearment. "Besides, it wasn't any of those things that made me sleepy. No," he said, the pull of sleep thickening his voice, "it was you and the incredible sex we just had. And then again."

"And then again," I responded, happiness tingeing my tone and my ego preening with his compliment.

My mind drifts fleetingly to Luke and a surge of guilt riles my peace. I'm not sure what else I could have done last night. He was hell-bent on attending the after party and then the shot fest that followed was indirectly my doing but I have no claim on him and can't control his actions. Still, whatever way I try to spin it, I feel like shit that he's going to wake up sometime today nursing a wicked hangover while I'm waking up sexed and satisfied.

Hawkin stirs again beside me, mumbles softly, and I can feel the minute awareness jolts his body awake. He squeezes me tightly against him and says, "Good morning," against the crown of my head. And I used to think there was nothing sexier than a man's voice in the morning, sleepy and gravelly, but I was wrong. Way wrong.

Because Hawke's voice in particular is sex personified in every way possible.

I close my eyes and enjoy the comfort between us as he wakes up and I realize I'm screwed here. Because if I thought I was going to be able to step back, then I was sadly mistaken. This—him—me—us—is just too damn good for me not to get wrapped up in it.

"I gotta pee like a racehorse," he says with a soft chuckle as he releases me, then the sound of his feet shuffling over the floor fills the room. I scurry up and out of the bed when he shuts the door to my guest bathroom and scrub the alcohol from last night from my teeth and throw some water on my face. I meet my eyes in the mirror and even though it's been hours since we fell asleep, my cheeks are still flushed and eyes still alive with desire.

I'm sitting up in bed when he returns, his white T-shirt slipped over my head. I know it's presumptuous but if I'm wearing it then that means he's not and hell if that's not a fine sight to take in first thing in the morning. He saunters toward the bed, completely unashamed of his nakedness, and fuck if my body isn't already responding to his.

This is going to be a serious problem. I can already tell.

He bends over at the side of the bed and tosses my covers back onto the mattress. "Here, you look cold."

"No, I'm good," I reply as I notice his eyes wandering down to my chest and when I follow his gaze I find my nipples hard and visible against the flimsy white cotton of his shirt. I look back up to meet the amusement in his eyes.

"Well, if you're not cold," he says, crawling back onto the bed and leaning against the headboard behind him, "I think I need to inspect what exactly the problem seems to be beneath my shirt." He reaches his hands out to grab my hips and shift me so that I sit astride his lap.

We both emit a groan at the exquisite pain of my pussy centering over his hardening dick. And yes I'm a tad sore from last night, but the havoc he can wreak on my system is worth the momentary discomfort I know he'll take away with his mind-numbing pleasure.

We stare at each other for a moment as we control the urge even though sleepy sex—hell any kind of sex—with Hawke is top priority on my agenda. My eyes are drawn to the symbols decorating his left shoulder and top part of his bicep. With his eyes on me, I reach out to touch them, trace their lines, and I'm a tad surprised when I look back to see the flush staining his cheeks.

The man is adored, scrutinized, objectified daily by women everywhere but in the small confines of my bedroom, he's shy in front of me. There's something about that juxtaposition that's beyond endearing to me. Makes me wonder what he was like as a little boy with those storm cloud–colored eyes of his.

"So many symbols but so different from Gizmo's," I murmur more to myself than to him. Hawkin's are denoted symbols, lone and unattached, while Gizmo's are continuous drawings flowing from one into another. Giz's are like art in a sense and his are more like a statement, and I wonder what story they tell. I trace my finger down the inside of his arm to the ink I noticed on his wrist earlier but can now study. "What does it mean?"

"It's a treble clef," he answers, to which I glance up before rolling my eyes.

"I know that. What's this one?" I ask, pointing to the one lined up behind it.

"It's the Adinkra symbol for strength," he says quietly, flexing his fist so that his forearm tightens and I can look at it closer. I follow the swirl of the loops with my fingertips.

"Why this? Why Adinkra?" For some reason I know the question is going to strike a nerve, and yet I ask it regardless because I want to know more about him. Need to. I look back up at him in time to see the pain pass through his eyes before he tucks it away. We hold our gaze steady as he battles whatever it is he doesn't want me to see, silence suddenly heavy in our first morning together.

"They all have a specific meaning to me. My dad died when I was young."

"I'm so sorry." The emotion in his eyes is heartbreaking and pulls at me, makes me want to pull him into my arms.

"My mom didn't handle it well. When she looked at us,

she saw him and that made it hard for her to stay in reality for a while. So my grandparents helped her pay for a nanny to help take care of Hunter and me for a bit." He stops for a moment, staring down at my hands holding his arm, his own fingers beginning to trace the lines. "Aya was from West Africa and was our mom in a sense for over a year. I was . . ." His voice trails off, his Adam's apple bobbing with emotion, and I immediately feel guilty for asking, for casting a shadow on our morning.

"I'm sorry. I didn't mean to pry." I squeeze his hand and he returns the action.

"No, it's okay. It was a long time ago." He nods his head a few times like he's trying to tell himself to believe the statement. "Anyway, she taught us about her culture, the symbols that represented so many things. I was so lost, so alone, so I clung to her, to them . . . so . . ." He shrugs lightly as my eyes leave his and scan back over to his biceps.

Their positioning is hard to explain except for a series of symbols stacked in succession forming straight lines but making the appearance of a plate of armor from the top of his shoulder to about three inches down the top of his bicep. I lean forward to look closer, try to figure them all out without asking. I want to know their meaning but also don't want him sad since they portray a tale I don't think he wants to share with me just yet.

And I think of Colton, of his Celtic tattoos representing his journey from his childhood hell of abuse to the new beginning he's found with Rylee. So I hold back the part of me that wants to learn more, accept it's for another time, another place, when he speaks.

"Each one represents something different, a virtue. The fern is for Aya since that's the name of the symbol. Mortality," he says, pointing to another. "Bravery and strength. Hope. Change. Guardianship. Responsibility, weakness . . . a few more, but you get the gist."

"They're incredible. Thank you for sharing." I'm mesmerized as I stare at them, appreciating the strange beauty of them when I'd expect something totally different from him. And then something rings in my head about meeting Gizmo the other day. "At least yours fit you. I laughed the other day when I saw all of Gizmo's intricate designs and then that bright pink heart on the inside of his wrist."

Hawkin's body stills momentarily before he throws his head back in a loud, hearty laugh. I'm not sure what is so funny but I'm glad whatever I said was the catalyst to disperse the somberness I'd created with my quest for more knowledge about him. When he lifts his face back up, he's got a wide smile and his eyes appear much lighter than moments before.

"What?" I laugh.

"You're sitting here, cold again," he says, lowering his eyes down to my chest before glancing back up at me to meet my eyes. But this time his gaze reflects his salacious thoughts front and center. "In perfect position and fuck if I want to think about anything else but how incredible you felt last night."

"Care to feel it again?" I lean forward and murmur against his lips, my body already ten steps ahead of him.

His fingers dance up my bare hips and under his shirt to grab the back of it. He fists his hand in it, pulling it tight, covering my breasts like a second skin. And this time the moan he admits is more of a swear from the sight of my nipples behind the veil of fabric.

"Goddamn, Quin," he mutters as he dips his head down, and I savor the warmth of his mouth closing on my pebbled peak over the T-shirt. The muted feeling only causes me to grind my hips over the top of him. He looks up, eyes already darkening with need, dick pulsing, begging me to grant him entrance to my heat, and says, "You're gorgeous, you know that?"

I murmur incoherently as he twists the shirt tighter, the dual sensations an unexpected turn-on. My hands sift through his hair on my way to grab on to the top of his shoulders as he begins to drug me once again with his adept skill.

Damn. I never imagined that addiction could feel so good.

My head falls back on the armrest of the couch when Hawkin's thumbs firmly rub the instep of my foot. I'm still in his shirt and he's shirtless in his jeans, top two buttons undone, and I have to remind myself every few minutes to take my eyes off him because he's just visual porn for a one-handed spank bank.

"Talk about orgasmic," I murmur, meaning more than just the foot rub, but however he takes it, the comment earns me a soft chuckle.

"No. I gave that to you earlier," he says, aiming my way the lopsided, arrogant smirk that unravels me as he trails his fingers up and down my shin. And he sure as hell did. My thoughts flicker to the look on his face as I sank down onto him. "This is because I know I need to go, get shit done, but I don't really feel like leaving yet and going back to the real world."

"This isn't real?" The comment is off my tongue before I can help it. And hell yes, cocooned in this little bubble of my house this feels real but what about the minute he steps foot outside? Will this all be a memory? I hate the insecurity popping up suddenly when he's given me no indication that he's ready to end whatever this is between us.

My stupid comment leaves an awkward silence. I'm just about to apologize when the doorbell rings.

"Shit." I scramble up, unwilling to answer in just his shirt and my lacy boy-short panties.

"No, stay. I'll get it," Hawke offers as he rises to his feet and pushes my shoulders back down.

"Are you sure?" I'm racing to try to figure out who it can be at two in the afternoon. Whoever it is, they are going to be more than surprised at my *butler* and exactly how he's dressed.

"Yeah. You got any candy?" he calls over his shoulder, making me laugh. Him and his damn sweet tooth.

"Let me think."

But my thinking about candy gets derailed as I watch him walk toward the front door, loving the way his jeans hang low on his hips, the knowledge that he's not wearing any underwear beneath them making him seem even sexier. Like that's even needed. When he leaves my line of sight, I smile at the sound of his feet padding down the hall. It's an oddly comforting sound and I'm glad for the interruption because it just saved me from a monumental screwup with the question I asked.

Realization hits me several seconds before I hear the slide of the dead bolt. I'm on my feet and scurrying down the hall, my first thought that it might be Colton and how ugly it might get if a random man opens my front door without a shirt on. I don't care how old I am, Colton will always see me as the little girl that no guy should touch.

Unfortunately for my last date that ended up staying the night, his face met Colton's fist when he told him to butt out. And I didn't talk to my brother for a week because he needed to grow up.

I turn the corner just in time to see light framing Hawkin's body and a rather rough-looking Luke looking at him with an expression of surprised displeasure, mouth lax, eyes glaring, shoulders square.

"Hey," Hawke says with a shrug of his shoulders, hands jammed deep in his pockets. "Sorry, man." He drops his head, awkwardness rising between them. And a part of me loses a tiny piece of my heart to Hawkin in the moment. He could be a royal asshole to Luke right now, be arrogant and gloat that he got the girl, but he doesn't do any of it. Instead he is contrite and humble.

A disbelieving laugh falls from Luke's mouth as he shakes his head when he looks over and sees me walking up behind Hawkin. His eyes take in my attire, the shirt Hawke had on last night not going unnoticed. Guilt pushes the contentment I'd felt this morning away because Luke is a good guy, and he definitely didn't deserve to find out this way.

Hawke takes note of Luke's change in focus and shifts sideways to spot me. I glance his way, tell him in the visual exchange that it's okay. Hawke turns back and nods his head to Luke before walking past me with a quick brush of his hand against mine in reassurance before disappearing into the house.

Stepping into the doorway, I chew the inside of my lip as I get the courage to meet Luke's eyes now that we're closer.

"I'm sorry about last night," he says.

I snap my head up. *What?* "I'm the one who should be apologizing, Luke." I step forward, the soother in me wanting to hug him to take the sting out of all of this and the other part of me knowing I can't add insult to injury, comfort him with my body I won't offer to him in other ways.

"I . . . It kind of just happened. . . . I didn't mean for . . . I'm sorry."

I feel guilty for lying, for not telling him that Hawke and I already had a little something started because then it just makes him feel like the date I'd accepted was a consolation prize. I'm feeling about two inches tall right now, even though I know I made the right decision last night, because sometimes all kinds of right for me can still be all kinds of wrong for someone else.

"Nah," he says with a shrug of his shoulder, trying to play off the disappointment and hurt flickering in his bloodshot eyes. "I let my ego get the best of me. Got plastered trying to prove I was the guy you wanted instead of Hawke—not exactly great behavior for a first date. Sorry for being an ass."

The sadness in his voice kills me. "Luke . . ."

"No. Don't." He forces a smile as he steps in and places a kiss on my cheek, my own tears threatening because I feel so bad. "Thanks for . . . I've got to go."

He nods again and turns to walk away. "Luke," I call his name, remorse heavy in my voice.

He stops, his head hung down. "I'm here if you need me." It's all he says before he walks away.

Chapter 17

Why am I still here?

Why the hell am I propped back on the pillows of her bed watching her through the partially obscured view I have of her as she applies her makeup in that close-up mirror thingy in her bathroom?

I'm usually long gone by now: do the deed, have some niceties, and then out the door. And yet with Quinlan, the deed has been done over and over and needs to be done a few more times today if I have my way.

I glance at the drawer in her dresser, the one that she surprised me with when she pulled it open to a minimart of protection, and wonder if we could work our way through the remainder of them throughout the rest of the afternoon and into the night.

It's a pretty lofty challenge but one I'd rise to the occasion for.

And shouldn't I be freaked by the fact she has so many condoms? What does that say about her? I laugh at myself and scrub a hand through my hair at my hypocrisy. Why is it that I can have a supply of them and she can't or else it looks bad?

When I look up and watch her apply her lip gloss in the mirror, my hypocrisy is forgotten because all it means is that she wants to be safe, stay healthy. Can't blame her for that and can't blame my dick for already hardening at the sight of her.

She has on a yellow tank top, the blond curls of her hair pulled forward over one of her shoulders, and that delicate font tattooed between her shoulder blades. There's something so damn sexy about it. The words and the simplicity of its placement, not for show, but solely for her just like my tattoos are for me.

When I read the words, *Make it count*, I can't help the satisfied sigh that falls from my lips because we sure as fuck made it count last night. My dick pulses at the thought, wanting it again with her so damn close and so goddamn tempting. She shifts in her chair to grab something and the movement leads me to fixate on her sexy-ass lace panties that mold to the cheeks of her ass.

And that is exactly why I'm still sitting on her bed in my jeans, ignoring the bullshit texts from the guys asking if I *fell in and got lost*.

They can fuck off because I kind of think they're right. I think I'm lost and not sure I want to find my way back.

But I look at her and can't fathom how her independence, her strength, could make me weak if this were to continue. The idea, the notion, the possibilities begin to spiral out of control, beg me to question things and beliefs so ingrained in me that I've only ever questioned them in theory.

And yes, watching her, with the scent of her soap on my skin and taste of her pussy seared in my memory, I can't help but wonder what it would be like. How is she making me . . . *Shut it down, Hawke.*

My chest constricts as I push the notion away, the haunted promises I've lived my life by, and opt to lose myself in thoughts of Quinlan instead. The woman is all kinds of contradictions balled up into one knockout punch. Shit, she's playful and a dynamo in the sack, is feisty outside of it, and doesn't get freaked out by my name or career.

But these feelings swirling around like a man after a fourth of Jack with the room spinning around me can't be right. This is supposed to be easy, supposed to be uncomplicated, supposed to be casual.

Casual, my ass. From the get-go it's been a challenge and so many things I'd usually walk away from. And yet here I am, relaxing on her bed, radio playing softly to a rock station, and actually relaxing.

Maybe I'm just enjoying the silence. Not being in a house with three other guys, people constantly coming in, is a relief. I thrum my thumb on my leg to the beat, laughing at my crazy surreal life when one of the D-Bags' songs comes on. I don't think this will ever become old hat, being a little starstruck, a little giddy when the person I was having a beer with last night is now singing on the radio.

Leaning my head back, I realize maybe my contentment comes from the lack of incessant talking that usually follows sex with the random women I've grown accustomed to. The ones that just want the notoriety they'll get from bragging about hooking up with me. I don't care if I disappoint those women because one, they're crazy if they think I'm going to fall madly in love with them and let them have my babies. And secondly, I don't let them get close enough for there to be any other expectations that I won't deliver on.

You can't control crazy so I don't even try to.

But then there's Quinlan and shit if she hasn't gotten to me somehow, broken through the ludicrous bet I made with Vince that I could get her to sleep with me, because now that's all I want her to do.

Well, obviously I want more than that because I'm blowing off the guys, ignoring the random texts Hunter's sending my way that are escalating in pissiness, and watching her put makeup on while I kick back on her bed in and out of an oversexed fog. For the first time in forever I'm not thinking about figuring out the next lyric, the next chord, the next number one hit, losing my mother, jail, anything, because Quin's successfully pulled me into her nice little bubble and held me here willingly.

Shit, she can let Trixie out and hold me here with restraints for a while if she really wants to. And that's saying a whole helluva lot.

Living the dream, man.

I chuckle, ruining the silence I'm enjoying, which causes her to turn around on the little stool she's sitting on and angle her head as she meets my eyes. *Fuck.* My gaze flickers down to where her darkened nipples peak through the yellow tank top, the hickey I gave her last night visible above the fabric. Her tan legs make me want to spread them so my hands can run up their length to her pussy as the prize at the end of their journey. She parts those thighs some and I groan softly at the knowledge of just what it feels like to be nestled between them.

"You know you don't need any makeup. You're gorgeous without it."

She laughs when most others would be flattered by the comment. I must be losing my touch, here.

"Thanks but you're full of shit." She rises from her chair, eyeliner in one hand as she walks toward the bed. "A man will say or do anything when he thinks he might get laid."

"Is that what I'm doing? Trying to get laid here?" I feign innocence as my dick tents unmistakably against the denim of my half-buttoned-up jeans.

"Mm-hmm," she says, mischief in her eyes and desire reflected in the way she works her bottom lip between her teeth so that one side of her mouth quirks up in a suggestive smirk.

"*Anything*, huh?"

"Anything," she says as she crawls onto the bed and sits cross-legged in front of me. Her perfume—clean and not overpowering—fills my nose and makes me recall how she must put it between her cleavage because when my mouth was sliding over her perfect tits that's when I smelled it the strongest.

My eyes wander down her body, to the panties that are hiding everything I want and over and up her tits to her eyes. "I can think of a few anythings that I assure you I wouldn't do for sex."

"That so?" she asks, eyebrows raised, playful smile on her lips. "What about for ice cream?"

I chuckle softly. "Now, that? I'll do anything for," I tease in return. "A man's got to have his vices after all," I tell her, pursing my lips to fight my own smirk when I see the challenge in her eyes.

"Hm . . . ?" She angles her head, tapping her eyeliner pencil on her knee. "I do seem to have some ice cream in the freezer. . . . I wonder just what you'd do for it." She taunts me, with both her words and her body.

"Oh, sweetness, are you trying to tempt me?" Thoughts in my head turn to getting a double fill of both of the things I'm dying to have right now: ice cream and Quinlan. Talk about her being the cookies to my cream. *Damn.*

She leans forward and studies my face, suddenly making me self-conscious when I never care what others think. "I think you would have been great in an eighties hair band."

My loud laughter echoes around the room as I try to decipher what in the hell she's thinking about that made her say that. "Come again?" I ask, confused how we went from sex to ice cream to old eighties rock bands. None of these things are connected — well, maybe later I'll connect the first two if I get lucky — so what is she getting at?

Her eyes continue to scrutinize me, her nose scrunching up in an adorable way as she concentrates. "I used to love hair bands. Bon Jovi, Van Halen, Def Leppard, Whitesnake . . ."

As if I don't know my hair bands. Did she forget what I do for a living? "Yes . . . ?" I finally say. She's lost me but as long as I can sit here staring at her nipples through her tank top then I'm good.

"Well, I'm wondering what you'd look like with big hair and guyliner, shirts with the sides cut out of them, and skin-tight pants."

I can't stop the smile that blankets my lips right now because I'm clueless but this is pretty damn funny. "What? Just when I was thinking how you're the first noncrazy girl I've been with in some time, there you go and prove how certifiable you are."

She takes the dig in jest, how I intended it, and smiles so the action lights up her entire face. "Rocker boy," she says, scooting in closer, and there's something about when she calls me that term that makes me smile, makes me feel special to her when I've done nothing to deserve it, that I love. "Humor me." She holds up her eyeliner pencil and raises her eyebrows.

"No way," I laugh, batting her hands away playfully.

"You did say anything. . . ." She lets the word trail off,

desperately trying to hide the victorious smile from spreading on her lips when I realize she just backdoored me into doing this.

Fuck if that's the kind of backdoor entry I prefer.

"So I let you put guyliner on me and then I get ice cream?" I quip, leaning back on the pillows behind me as I adjust my dick that's at a constant state of semi-arousal with her around. She nods her head once. "I think I need a little more than that, Trixie," I challenge back.

"Like what?" she giggles as she climbs astride my lap with pencil ready to demasculinize me while at the same time igniting my fire with the heat of her pussy sliding over my dick.

"Like this," I say as I fist my hand in the back of her hair and pull her toward me. Her soft lips hit mine and I don't hold back as I slip my tongue between her lips and take what I want.

She responds, all tongue, hands, mouth, and fuck am I not primed and ready to go. Our breathing gets heavier, our bodies reacting to each other, and all I want is more of her. I slide my hand into the back of her panties when she drags her mouth from mine.

"You're trouble, you know that?" I laugh but it's strained because fuck if I don't want to take her fast and hard right now.

"Me, trouble?" she feigns innocence with a bat of her eyelashes, nipples front and center in my line of vision. "I'm just a challenge to handle, rocker boy, and oh how I like to be handled." The laugh she gives me is seductive and could probably make a weaker man come on the spot but I'm holding out for the whole experience.

I pull her toward me so that I can taste her, get a little fill of the temptation before she denies me with that challenge I can already see blazing in those *come fuck me* eyes. Just when she starts letting me take the lead, reacting to my every action, I tear my mouth from hers even though it kills me so that I can leave her wanting a little bit more. "Believe me, I know how to handle you."

She looks at me with her hazy caramel eyes, lips swollen from our kiss, and cheeks flushed. She sighs heavily, body tensing as my fingertips graze the slick flesh between her parted thighs. "I get what I want first," she says holding up the eyeliner, "then you get what you want."

Damn she's good. Just when I thought I was in control, she handled me like nobody's business, but that's cool. In the end I'll get everything I want.

Always do.

Living the dream.

Chapter 18

I've been running in slow motion all day—it's ridiculous. I feel like I'm ten steps behind from my first class of the day and I'm completely okay with it because I'm traveling through time on cloud nine.

And all because of Hawkin.

He kept me on the phone all morning, talking about everything and nothing until I looked at the clock and screeched at the time. He makes me feel like a damn teenager with a first-time crush. It's rather ridiculous. I know how this story is going to end but hell if this girl, who doesn't believe in fairy-tale endings, isn't going to wear the glass slipper for the short while it fits.

And this glass slipper is more the stiletto with red sole variety.

I trudge across campus, actually getting a breather for the first time all day but I'm still moving at a clipped pace. I'm eager to get to the seminar early so that I can see Hawkin before the masses claim him.

I'm a greedy bitch because as far as I'm concerned the lazy Sunday afternoon we spent playing Guitar Hero after I rewarded him for letting me make him into an eighties band lead singer wasn't enough. Neither was falling to the sofa in laughter after I beat him at the game where we then tested the couch springs, or the no shirt, no shoes dinner of Chinese takeout we had on the back porch before he left to go home.

I've prided myself on being a woman who is never needy, rather I've always been the one glancing at the clock to see how long my date-for-the-night has been at the house because he's way overstayed his welcome, and yet the other night I didn't want Hawkin to go. But after our fifth or sixth good night turned into lustful groping kisses, he finally left to go back to what he deemed to be his "fucked-up reality."

I nod to an acquaintance as I wonder just what that reality is for him. I know there's bad blood between him and Hunter causing a rift between the guys in the band but every time I've tried bringing it up to him, he conveniently changes the subject. Just as he does when it comes to the rest of his family: his mother, if he has other siblings, extended family. He's closed off but hides it well, always shifting into stories about the band or a show or a snooty celebrity he has inside dirt on.

I sense he doesn't trust easily—and that's understandable with the public position that he's in—but I get the hint that there's more to it than that. How much more, I'm unsure.

The stupid smile remains on my face even when my thoughts veer to Luke and how he proved himself to be the gentleman I knew him to be. How when I called him Sunday evening to see how he was feeling and to apologize again, he actually picked up and we talked for a short while. I explained I wasn't trying to lead him on, give him false hope by calling, but rather if he was comfortable with it, I'd love to keep him as a friend because he really is a good guy.

Axe stands at the door as I approach the theater and that causes my smile to spread even wider because that means Hawke is inside. I feel a slight relief that maybe, just maybe, Hawkin feels this euphoric giddiness that I do and that's why he arrived early when he never has before. And just maybe he's done that because he can't wait to see me.

Axe greets me warmly as he opens the door for me, and once inside I walk quickly across the atrium. I pull open the doors housing the interior with high expectations and nerves running rampant but for the first time, they're from anticipation and not from loathing the guest lecturer.

The straight punch of lust I feel the minute I see him is like nothing I've ever felt before. A ball of bound energy radiates through me, causing a slow burn of desire and a definite bang of lust between my thighs. I falter momentarily in my movements, wanting to appreciate the sight of him but at the same time wanting to run down the steps and taste his kiss again.

Hawkin sits with his Verbz on, head down, hand beating to a rhythm I can't hear, eyes closed as he becomes a part of the music. I know he's stuck on some lyrics for a song he and the guys started writing the night he left my house so I assume he's still working through his creative roadblock. Regardless of what he's doing, the man is a visual orgasm in his worn jeans with a hole in one knee and his shirt of choice today has a Van Halen logo on it.

How many old-school rock shirts does he have?

And then the memory hits me and I chuckle as I walk down the stairs unbeknownst to him. The dark eyeliner I put on him in addition to his hair I tried to tease as best I could. What the press would have paid to have pictures of him like that as we battled on Guitar Hero. As we laughed so hard until we ended up moaning together.

I hit the lowest step, my eyes trained on him, and the desire coiling tighter in my core with each step. I'm suddenly worried that maybe I'm making more of this than he is, that I'm going to be caught off guard when he sees me and then where will I be? I shake off the thought that is so unlike me, hating the insecurity it brings. And I clear my head in perfect time because Hawkin glances up and sees me.

Surprise passes over his face but the wide grin and warmth that softens his eyes the minute he sees me clears away all worry and is an aphrodisiac all in itself.

"Hey," he says, pulling the earphones from his ears and straightening up as I close the distance between us.

I step in front of him, nerves humming, hands twisting together, and his eyes locked on mine. "Hi," I say tentatively when all I want to do is step into him and press my lips to his. But I refrain, not wanting to take whatever this is somewhere he doesn't want it to be. "Sorry to interrupt . . ." My voice trails off, while his eyes darken with lust as he flicks them over the low V neckline of my shirt and down the length of my legs and back up.

"You're not interrupting," he says. *Does he still want me? Was it a one-time thing? Why aren't you kissing me?* "Do you think you could go check the PA connections? They don't seem to be working properly."

I glance over to the podium where nothing is turned on and back to him, ego and hopes confused and slowly deflating, the rendezvous I was hoping for nonexistent despite my initial surge of optimism. "It's not on. You need to—"

"No." He cuts me off in a stern voice as he reaches out to grab my bicep. My eyes flash up to meet his, catching that half-cocked smile that lifts up a corner of his mouth when he speaks. "You need to check in the room over there, Trixie. *Now.*"

Oh. OH! Took me long enough to get what he's trying to say and his eyebrows rise in amusement the minute he knows I understand what his intentions are.

And hell if I don't love bad intentions when they're of the sexual nature.

Looking up at him from the veil of my eyelashes, a diminutive smile plays over my lips. "Yes, Professor Play," I respond in the most innocent voice possible—which is harder than hell considering I passed over being innocent a long time ago. Besides, breaking the rules is so much more fun sometimes. I make sure my hips are swinging up the goods I have to offer him as I saunter to the small alcove where we shared our first kiss—and my senses are already so heightened chills race over my skin when I hear him behind me.

When I step into the shadowed alcove, my stomach flutters with excitement, my sex already moist from the thoughts of what is going to happen next. I stand still in that silent state of suspended desire as I wait for his touch to ignite my skin. The sound of his breathing fills the space around me, and I'm not waiting any longer.

Desperation has me turning to face him, and his mouth

is on mine instantly. His lips bruise and brand, tongue claims and owns the moan his hands already gripping my ass from beneath my skirt coaxes from me. His kiss shows me how hungry he is for me, the groan he emits reflects a raw carnality that says he's going to take without asking and hell if I'm going to stop him.

Because nice and slow is sometimes good but a no-holds-barred, fist in my hair, back up against the wall quickie is most definitely a good thing. And that sure as hell appears to be where we're headed.

Yes, professor. . . . Please, school me. Here. Now. Hard. Fast.

The words flicker through my mind, incomplete thoughts as we are drawn toward each other's flames, knowing damn well we're going to get burned.

"God, I want you," he growls into my mouth as my hands match his, pulling our bodies together, nails digging into heated skin, mouths meeting again with a volatile passion.

He presses me back against the wall as our fingers fumble with clothing. My hands undo his button and zipper to push down his jeans and grab his rock-hard cock as he uses his feet to knock my feet apart so that he can pull my panties aside. He dips his fingers between my folds and tightens the one hand in my hair, another groan falling from his lips as he finds me wet and ready for him from just his kiss alone.

His fingers touch me where I want them the most, the place that has ached the past few nights when I've gone to bed thinking about him while his melodic timbre speaks to me on the other end of the phone line. The pads of his fingers rub gently over my clit, adding a slight friction to the already sensitized nub there. The pleasure of his hand and his mouth on me causes my legs to slightly buckle from the sensations he's evoking in me.

"That good, huh?" He murmurs against my lips as he releases my hair to slip his arm around my waist to help support me as I succumb to his dexterous fingers. He laughs as I arch my hips out toward him in a begging motion when he removes his touch. "Gotta make sure it counts," he murmurs seductively, my lips showing the ghost of a smile.

He slips his other hand off my back and I stand there, shoulders against the wall, pelvis thrust forward, skirt askew, and body humming. My eyes flash open to catch his, their gray color burning black, lids heavy with desire. "I told myself I could wait until after class"—I hear the telltale rip of foil, my eyes widening with the sound because that means I'm getting more than just fingers . . . I'm getting all of him— "but I can't." He says the last words with a pained restraint before glancing down to jacket himself. "I just can't."

His mouth is on mine again as his fingers grip my hips and direct me to the side until my ass hits a small console behind me. I cry out, having forgotten it was there in the darkness, and then acquiesce to his physical commands as he helps lift me up on the shallow top of it. The cabinet is so narrow that my backside sits halfway off it, so I lean my back against the wall, thighs framing his muscular torso and hands gripping the edge as he lines his dick up to my entrance.

He teases me with his head, slowly pushing into me and then withdrawing several times. I groan out in frustration, my body amped up on the thought of him fucking me senseless. He kisses me again, demanding and possessive. "Quin . . . I have to have you," he moans as his hands grip my thighs, pulling them apart at the same time he thrusts all the way into me.

My cry of ecstasy drowns out his groan of pleasure as my body welcomes the girth of his dick slamming into me, nerves singing, body stretching, endorphins surging. I'm writhing against him in jerking movements, my backside half off the console adding to the depth he can reach with my weight bearing down some on where our bodies meet.

"Easy, Q," he says, his voice gravelly as it scrapes over my eardrums, his obvious pleasure a turn-on. I glance down to where his dick is slowly pulling out of me. My arousal glistens against the faint light at his back and it's sexy as hell to see the evidence of what he does to me, what he makes me want more and more.

I look back up to the salacious look in his eyes and know he's turned on by the fact that I like to watch him slide in and out of me. We hold each other's gaze as he moves slowly back in and it's like one big chain reaction of electricity from my core out to my fingers and toes with every movement of his.

Fixated on the eroticism of the moment, I glance back down to watch us. I'm so turned on by everything—the man before me, the idea of being here and doing this when we shouldn't be, the pleasure he's most definitely bringing me—that I purposefully squeeze my muscles around his dick when he begins to withdraw so that the wide crest of his head has trouble pulling all the way out.

I love the groan he emits and the way his head falls back at the sensation, giving me a glimpse of his strong jaw and Adam's apple before looking back up and straight into my eyes. "Keep doing that sweetness and I'm going to come quick and hard."

Wanting to watch him, I fight the urge to close my own eyes as I'm swamped with the sensation of him bottoming out inside me and holding there in a silent dare. "Quick and hard?" I whisper, leaning forward, muscles contracting again with the movement. "Yes, please."

His eyebrows arch and a libidinous smirk curls up one corner of his mouth. "Fuck . . ." He moans the word out as desire and my comment snap the restraint he was barely holding on to. "Hold tight, Q."

And the minute the words are out of his mouth he begins to move at a demanding pace, the cabinet hitting smartly into the wall behind me with each thrust. The small space fills with the hushed sounds of our desire, the slap of skin on skin, and the console rattling from the force. My hands grip the edge for support as I open my eyes to see his face pulled tight with pleasure, eyes closed, shoulders tense.

He obliterates everything else so that I can focus only on him, on this, and the way he's manipulating my body. All three pull me under the frenzied state of bliss so that I'm almost drugged when my orgasm hits me in an earthquake of sensation that reverberates through me and then comes back to slam into its epicenter once more.

I manage a broken cry of pleasure before suppressing it when I realize where we are. And it's almost as if the minute my sex starts contracting around him, when he knows I've had mine, Hawkin sets a punishing pace for himself to chase his own climax.

He's sexy as hell when he comes, head thrown back, fingers unknowingly bruising the tender flesh of my thighs to match the marks he left there this weekend, and he releases a feral groan that resonates in my ears and scores my memory.

He rests his head on my shoulder as we both catch our breath. "Class," he murmurs as a reminder to himself where we are before lifting his head and pressing a chaste kiss to my lips as he slips out of me. "Holy shit, you're incredible."

He shakes his head before glancing down to remove the condom and clean himself up, while my ego and emotions soar from his compliment. I slowly dismount the console, testing the stability of my legs since he's just rocked my world.

He zips up and looks at me watching him. "That was right up there with cookies 'n cream," he says with a raise of his eyebrows and a flash of a grin. I laugh that this was as good to him as his beloved ice cream. "Take your time; I've got to act like we weren't just in here doing . . ." He just shakes his head, his sudden shyness adorable in so many ways.

"Oh, I brought you something," I tell him when suddenly the irony of it hits me and causes me to smile. "It's in the front part of my backpack."

He looks at me, eyebrows knitted in curiosity. "What is it?"

"A box of Good and Plenty," I deadpan, trying to fight the smirk but failing miserably, thinking of the suggestive nature of the candy's title.

He throws his head back and laughs heartily, the sound reverberating deep within me. "Oh I'll give you good and plenty, all right," he says crossing the short distance to me before grabbing me and placing another kiss on my lips. "I believe I just did." He steps back, smug smile on his lips, and just shakes his head before he walks away.

I sag against the cabinet, a replay of the explosive and incredible sex we just had running through my mind over and over already.

Because it was that good.

Incredible really. I swear my heart skips a beat at even the thought, and I try to tell myself it has to be the newness of him, plus our inherent physicality together, that makes our sex so goddamn incredible. I rationalize that there is no way I could have feelings for him beyond the earthmoving sex we've had that makes it just seem *that much more.*

It's a futile attempt. I know I'm lying to myself. I've had good sex before—nothing like this, but still good—and I know my insides didn't twist and flutter from it like they are right now.

I'm falling for Hawkin, the epitome of everything I told myself I'd never fall for.

Shit.

Chapter 19

scrub my hand over my jaw as I contemplate how to answer the question one of the students has asked me, and I realize I can still smell the scent of Quin's pussy on my fingers. Fuck me.

Talk about a way to lighten the somber memory of today's anniversary.

And ease the anxiety over the judge sitting in the very top row of the auditorium, watching my every move to make sure that I'm fulfilling my obligation.

I force myself to concentrate on not screwing up, not on how little Miss Q just screwed me senseless in the alcove over to my right, but fuck if it's not hard to do. Especially with her scent now seared in my psyche.

So I glance over to where she sits, head down, working on whatever she works on while I lecture, and I lose my train of thought. *Well of course you did, dipshit. All you can think about is diving back beneath that skirt as soon as class is over.* And God how I love her affinity for sexy-ass skirts.

I must be silent for too long because she glances up and meets my eyes before averting them quickly. But I catch the little smile that plays on her lips as she returns to pretending like she doesn't care. Fuck if it's not sexy and calls on me to have her again.

Yes, please. The sound of her voice saying that replays in my head as I refocus despite not being able to stop my own secretive smile at knowing what only she knows happened before class. I begin to give an answer, explain just how recreational drug use in Hollywood is the equivalent to putting a fat kid in a candy store and telling him to choose just one item, when a motion at the top of the steps catches my eye.

Why the hell is he here? And of course if I didn't have Quin's pussy numbing my mind the reason would be front and center.

Hunter slides into a seat in an aisle a third of the way down the banked rows. He has a baseball cap low over his eyes so one wouldn't immediately make the connection that he was here, but I know my brother, recognize his clothes and his presence. Besides, I notice him only because everyone else is so busy looking at me.

Including the judge. How much more of a clusterfuck can this be?

As Hunter looks up and meets my gaze, the intense look on his face tells me why he's here. My brother who uses everything else to help him forget—sex, booze, drugs, pushing my buttons—is here because today of all days, the anniversary of Dad's suicide, he's going to abuse the one thing he can without risking jail time. *Me.* Deep down I know somehow, some way, Hunter is here to try to hurt me for the fate he screwed himself out of but blames me for instead.

Jealousy is a mean, nasty bitch.

He flashes me a smarmy smirk, and I know I'm right. Fucking stellar. Is he here to try to rub my face in how he succeeded in making me bend when I shouldn't have, take the blame for him, fulfill my promise to complete the seminar, to save his ass? My gut is uneasy with the possibilities and so I look away without giving him any reaction and continue on with my explanation to the class.

I don't need this shit but I pull my head back from thoughts about Hunter because if I blow this lecture with the judge here then I'm the one fucking up, the one not fulfilling my promise to Dad to protect him.

The one who is weak.

And I know it's fucked-up logic, deep down in my core I

know it is, but it doesn't make it any less powerful when history has already decided your fate today.

I trudge through the rest of the lecture, think I do pretty well considering the pressure coming at me from what feels like every angle, and roll my shoulders at the line of students waiting to speak to me after class. I'm not in the mood to be on in front of everyone, particularly not when I have the three people I don't want interacting all within fingertip range: the one person deciding my fate, the one person I want in every sense of the word, and the one person I don't want to deal with watching my every movement beneath his ball cap. My eyes keep flickering between them and the students in front of me.

Axe can tell I'm irritated and cuts the line off the same time that Quin starts packing up her bag. I make the rounds, catch sight of the judge as he pulls out his cell phone, and then look over to Hunt to find his grin wide, and eyes settling on Quinlan. When he looks back toward me, he gives me a subtle thumbs-up that causes dread to pour through me.

Vince is right, isn't he? My brother will go after anything I want except for my music because the band protects me like a shield that he knows he'll never break through. The one thing he hates the most—my success—he can't touch, so he goes after anything else he can in my life.

And by the way he keeps eyeing Quinlan I know just how he plans to go about hurting me.

So what do I do now? Cause a scene where I can't control what my brother will say and have the judge overhear something that might be damaging and fuck up all of this time I've put into trying to pay my penance? Lead him right to Quin like a dog to a bone? Neither is an acceptable option.

My mind whirls as I try to wrap my head around the smartest thing to do. Of course it would be to tell Quinlan what his modus operandi is but I can't do that right now, not with the judge sitting up there listening to every word and smart enough to conclude that I'm lying about the drug charge. On the flip side, if I show Hunter that I really am into Quin for more than the quick fuck I explained our little hallway groping at the house to be, he'll be all over her to hurt me.

To get me back for kicking him out of the band and then signing the record deal without him.

And his immediate reaction? Instead of getting the help I set up for him so that he could earn his way back into the band's good graces, he took the one woman besides our mother that I've ever allowed myself to feel anything beyond mutual companionship for and tried to ruin me by hurting her.

Because fucking our band manager's sister, my then girlfriend, and getting her pregnant and dropping her once the damage was done . . . Yeah, those were fucking stellar moves. Telling her to get an abortion or else he'd go public about one of her little fetishes was even better. Losing our manager over it was just the icing on the cake.

Whatever I have that he wants, he takes on his own terms. *At any cost* is his motto.

I glance up at the next person in line the same time I see Quinlan stand and pull her bag onto her shoulder. The judge is still staring at his phone, still within earshot, and Hunter leans forward in his chair to watch the action unfold between her and me, completely oblivious to our third-party observer. My head is a mess, striving for a course of action that will cause minimal consequences for me, plus avoid any heartache for Quin. I just hope that somehow she will get the hint, see my twin up in the audience, and figure out between his actions last time and his presence this time what I'm doing.

It's a long fucking stretch of an assumption but it's all I've got.

"Hey, Hawke," the sorority girl Quinlan called Delta Sig says as she sways her body from side to side, chest forward so that I can see just how perfectly her letters bend across her more-than-handful-size tits. I stare at her, a moment of regret causing me to pause when I see Quin walking toward us, eyebrows furrowed in curiosity how I'm going to handle perky sorority girl now that I'm having smoking-hot sex with her in the school alcoves.

And shit, I've done nothing more than kiss sorority girl, and since the exchange was less than memorable her name escapes me momentarily. Hunt is now on the move, slowly walking down the stairs, his eyes tracking Quinlan as she walks my way, her short skirt showcasing her killer legs, and fuck me because I know my brother's enjoying the sight of them right now.

I look back at Delta Sig and smile softly although I know it doesn't reach my eyes. She's so caught up in the idea of me she won't notice the difference anyway. "Hey, how's it going?"

"Good. Good," she says, twisting her hands in front of her and all I can think about is the damn candy sitting on the table behind me that Quinlan brought me. Fuck, how am I going to do this? "I brought you some Skittles since I saw you like sweet things."

Just like you, right? This isn't my first rodeo, so of course my mind fills in the blanks for her. She reaches out a bag to me. "Thanks," I say as I take it and toss it on the table behind me.

Delta Sig bites her bottom lip in a calculated move that I've seen more times than I care to count. God, the girl just tries too damn hard. When you wear a sign screaming *I want you to fuck me so I can brag about it* . . . Yeah, it's not very appealing to me. "I was wondering if you wanted to go out for a beer at Sully's Pub." She takes a step closer, bottom lip back between her teeth again. "And then we could head back to my place if you want."

And there she goes and gives me an opening and an out that I can't refuse. My head is screaming no, telling me to find another way to get Hunt to fuck off and leave me so I can drag Quin right back to that console and work some of my emotional duress out while fucking her tight, hot pussy until I feel better. But I know I have to play this game or else she'll be the consequence.

The judge clears his throat and I glance up to see his attention focused back on me. Shit.

I can feel Hunt's stare as he stands on the bottom step at Quin's back. I can see Quin staring at me in my periphery, and Delta Sig is begging me with her big blue eyes that are smoked up a bit too much for a school day. She definitely had her plan of action today and I know I'm an asshole for using it to get me out of this situation and then turn her down without giving her the other kind of action she's hoping for.

Fuck, here we go, Play.

"Sounds like a plan." The look of elation on her face is ridiculous. I hate to see what her panties look like. Shit, from my experience with desperate women, she's probably not wearing any. "Meet me outside in ten minutes, yeah?"

I hear the quick inhale of breath to my right from Quin and when I flick my eyes her way the glare I deserve is slicing into me.

"Sure. Ten. Yes," Delta Sig says as she walks back to her seat but my focus is already on Quin.

I can see Hunter over her shoulder, and I nod to him, hoping she realizes there is someone else watching our exchange. But I see the hurt flicker through her eyes, recognize the shock evident after what I just said, and know she's not paying attention to who else is in the room because that fire of hers is aimed directly at me.

I choke over the words I need to say but know I need to spit them out because I already see Hunt checking out Delta Sig as she walks away, confirming my hunch that he just wants to stir shit up for me right now.

I look at Quinlan, she's so goddamn beautiful, especially now when all I see is anger and all I want to do is leave with her, take her to her place, lay her down, and show her the shit I feel that's on continual spin cycle in my gut. Those feelings that are churning within me way too quick and way too fast. There are emotions stirring that I don't want, can't have. Hell yes, I pursued her, loved the fucking challenge she presented, and I loved the idea of Vinny boy getting another ring around his damn pink heart, but never expected this notion that just slammed into me like a Mack truck.

That this is more than just a bet. That this is more than just about sex.

I expected a fun fling but never expected to consider losing a stupid goddamn bet because one, no way in hell am I letting Vince touch her and two, no way am I letting Hunter either.

How did this get so fucking complicated? How did the

pressure of Hunter being here and the notion I'm going to hurt her make all of this fester up and slap me in the face?

Fuck. Fuck. Fuck. Way too much all at once.

I panic momentarily, force myself to see that wanting something more than sex doesn't necessarily mean love. It just means that I care for her and know I'm about to hurt her and hate myself for that look I know I'm going to put in her eyes. But I also know the kind of hurt I'll inflict will be ten times easier than what I fear Hunter would do just to get back at me.

"Ten minutes?" Quin's voice breaks through the riot in my head, pulling me back into the moment.

"Yeah." I break eye contact and start to walk toward the table where my keys and phone sit on the table, anything to not see her lips shock apart and eyes widen. Anything to act normal and get the judge to lose interest and walk away. "Can you make sure that you get this all set up for the next class for me?"

"Excuse me?" Disbelief laces her voice.

"The PA. Next class. Got it?" The less I say the better.

"Did I miss something here?" She's closer to me now, and I turn to face her. I can be a callous asshole without a second thought like the best of them but hell if I'm not going to hate myself later for this.

"Nope. Not a thing. Just gotta wrap things up here so I can meet up with a friend."

"A friend? Hmpf. You must have a lot of friends—kind of like flavors of the month." The contempt is dripping from her voice, and I see her clasp her hands to prevent them from trembling with emotion.

Shit, I know she said she was a woman okay with casual sex, but I also know that casual sex takes off the next morning once they feel it's polite to leave. I stayed the whole fucking day until night fell. She's got to know—like I just realized—that there is more than just sex between us. She has to. I just hope she remembers that right now as I utter my next words.

"That's about right. It's all good though, at least I have thirty-one to choose from at any different time. They come and go *so quick*, right? Makes them easy to sample and move on," I tell her, delivering the final blow in what I hope will get her the hell out of this room and away from Hunter.

My phone alerts a text but I don't even flinch because she stares at me a beat without speaking, jaw clenched, eyes blinking as she processes what I just told her.

"Well, this flavor just expired," she says, starting to walk toward me and for a moment I'm unsure what her intentions are but she veers to the right of me and toward the stairs there. I track her movement as she walks up the steps with determination, holding the apology back on my lips, and if the notion hadn't slapped me in the face moments ago that I care for her, it definitely would have hit home right now.

I realize that Quinlan never turned around to see my brother behind her. She doesn't have a clue why I just did what I did.

She walks right past the judge at the same time he stands, nodding a polite greeting to her but eyes still focused on me. What I'd give to tear off after her right now, clear the hurt I just put from her eyes, but at what cost since the two people who can ruin my fate are sitting here in the same fucking room? I wince at the sound of the doors slamming shut with force at the top of the theater and pull in a deep breath as I prepare to face my brother and whatever shit-storm he's hedging toward.

Today's brutal enough, can't I just deal with it my own way without him making it worse?

"Well, that was awkward," he says in that mocking tone of his. "You had her already and what, she wasn't good?"

My fist clenches and it takes everything I have to turn my back to him and walk toward the side of the auditorium and turn the PA system off. Normally talking like this with Hunter or Vince or one of the guys would be okay—our sex lives are an open book—but I don't want to hear him talk about Quinlan or about how good she was or wasn't. He doesn't deserve to know.

Hell, I don't even deserve to know. She's way too good for me.

"What's up?" I call out to him, trying to act nonchalant and ignore his comment when I'd rather shove him up against the wall and tell him just what I think of him and his bullshit. I step into the small alcove, and I swear to God it still smells of the sex we had earlier. The pang of guilt stabs again but it'll never be deep enough to inflict the pain I deserve after what I just said to her. I flip the switch and turn around as fast as I can. I don't want him ruining what happened in here between Quin and me either.

When I emerge back into the theater, he looks at me expectantly. "So what gives? Blondie's bad in bed so you moved on to sexy sorority girl? Because she's definitely more my type."

My patience is gone and my temper boils but he just said the words I needed to hear. I've caught his attention with Delta Sig.

"Yeah, something like that," I defer, running a hand through my hair in exasperation. "I need to get going. She's waiting. Do you need something?" And when I glance up to the seats now, I find that the judge has slipped out and it's just him and me. A sigh of relief flickers through me despite the tightrope I'm walking with him.

"Oh, you're going out with her right now?" he says, lifting his chin up the stairs, motioning his hands across his chest like the letters Delta Sig girl wears on display.

"Mm-hm." I stuff my keys in my pocket as my phone alerts me of another text.

"I'm tagging along with you, man. Want to see how bad you blow it with this chick so I can swoop in and save the day."

"Dream on, dude. Don't you have somewhere you need to be?" He's pushing buttons, and I'm in no fucking mood for his shit right now, especially today. Can't he get that he's not the only one who suffers from the memories this day evokes? I know I'm fooling myself thinking he does. "How's your counseling appointments going? Huh, Hunter?" I meet his eyes, the need to see if he lies to me front and center.

"Next week is my first one." His eyes dart to the left and then back to mine.

"You think I'm going to buy that bullshit lie?" I can hear the incredulity rising in my voice, the stress of the last fifteen minutes taking its toll. "You think I'm here paying a penance for something I didn't fucking do to save your goddamn ass and you get to skip out on your end of the bargain?" I step toward him, fists clenched, teeth gritted, patience gone. "You fucked up last time, lost your chance at a whole helluva lot. . . . You gonna risk more now?"

"C'mon brother, you know I'm good for it."

I just look at him as truths I push aside every day about my brother come crashing down around me. I continue to hold out hope but I don't have to ignore the anger. "Don't you dare *c'mon brother* me! I don't care what you're fucking good for because right now it seems like you're not good for a fucking thing!" I yell, my finger jabbing him in the chest. "I took the fucking fall for you. Jeopardized my freedom, my career, my band *for you*, and you stand here like it's no big fucking deal."

"You and your precious career!" he sneers.

"You bet your ass *my career*, you prick. Who do you think funds your lifestyle? Your habit? Did you forget where your monthly payoff from the band comes from? I pay you from my cut you asshole merely because the guilt eats at me that you forced me to make a decision, keep you on and ruin the band's collective career or force you out to get help and save myself. . . ."

"You're real good at saving yourself." He fists his hands. "But you sure as shit suck when it comes to saving others now, don't you."

His words knock me back a staggering mental step. I stare at him eyes wide, disbelieving that he actually just went there. I grit my teeth and take a less than calming breath. "Not everybody wants to be saved, Hunt." We stand in a silent standoff, our words doing much more damage than our fists ever could. "You included, right? You gonna save yourself? Get help for your habit? You can blame me all you want . . . but your jealousy is on you—"

"I'm not jealous!" he yells back, voice thundering around the room as I'm hit hard with his resentment. And it doesn't fall on deaf ears that he didn't refute my comment about his habit or anything else but his jealousy.

"You're not? Try again, asshole. You think I don't hear the comments, see your bullshit, know you try to undermine anything that goes good for me? You think I'm that fucking naive to your game? Undermining deals, throwing a bag of blow my way the minute you see the sirens reflected in the windows of the house? You use my guilt against me, so back the fuck off me and own it!"

My mirror image just stares at me, chest heaving, eyes glaring, and animosity pulsing off him in waves and crashing into mine. "I'm not jealous of you and your bullshit career. Daddy's favorite sure is fulfilling his potential while leaving me with the raw end of the deal, having to take care of Mom."

"Take care of her? I believe I foot the bills." I step into him, chests bumping against each other. "Besides, I didn't realize getting high was taking care of her—because you're still getting high, aren't you? Drugs more important than promises, right?"

"Fuck you!"

"Right back atcha, brother! At least my conscience is clean." I say the words but my father standing before me pressing the cold steel to his chin flashes through my mind. My conscience is anything but clean because I didn't try to stop him. I shove the thoughts from my mind. Try to step up to the plate and be the heavy hand that Hunter needs to clean up his act.

"Can't be too clean since Dad's dead, right *choirboy*?"

We circle like caged dogs waiting for the chance to rip each other apart. We're purposely trying to hurt each other, and it's going to do nothing good for our relationship but fuck if it doesn't feel good to let it all out right now. To hurt someone else for a change rather than sit back and take it.

"Clean is something you know nothing about," I grate the words out. "What's your drug of choice now? Coke? What's next? Heroin, so you can really fuck up our lives?"

"People are going to hear you. Calm the fuck down—"

"Don't you dare tell me to calm down when it's my god-damn ass on the line! Let them hear me!" I yell at the top of my lungs. "You afraid for them to find out? Huh? Are you?" I goad him. "Then do what you fucking promised. Clean yourself up! I'm taking the fall for you this one time, Hunt, but no more. I'm done. You're my own flesh and blood, man, but this is bullshit."

"Figures. You get all high-and-mighty this year with your recording contracts and your whores . . . think you've proven yourself to the world and yet the only thing you've proven to me is that you're a selfish bastard just like he was. Like father, like son."

His words cross the short distance between us and slam into me like a battering ram. In that split second I don't register that I know he's just taking a potshot to shut me up from calling his bullshit on the carpet. I don't process anything except my fist cocked back and the rage screaming through me to take the shot, do the one thing I want so badly but know will do nothing to ease the pain in my soul.

Make me be just like him.

"Can't do it, can you?" He taunts me, wants me to hit him so that he has something else to hold over my head.

My arm trembles with the rage I feel inside. At him. At Dad. At Mom. At Quinlan for looking at me with those eyes that I don't deserve looking at me. At fucking everything.

I see a flicker of regret glance through Hunter's eyes. And that tiny show of our connected DNA pulls me back from the brink because I fear that I have so much rage pent up inside me, if I hit him I won't be able to stop.

And you can't undo harm you've done to your family. I know this because I'm living proof. I can't undo what our dad did; I can only try to make it better.

Goddamn higher road. Taking it is bullshit when some days I'd rather drive off the edge.

My heart's pounding with rage and my head doesn't want to be filled with regret I can't take back, so I lower my arm. I've gotta get out of here. Got to get some fresh air and have a few beers to calm the fuck down. And then call Quinlan to try to explain why I said what I said.

"We're done here, Hunt." I put my hands out in front of me to tell him I don't want to do this anymore because I still sense his rage.

"I haven't used since that night." His voice is quiet, resigned, and laced with the only apology I think I'll ever get from him.

I nod my head in acceptance of his confession, but know that with Hunter his regret is fleeting and it's only a matter of time before he moves on to resent something else. Time and again he's proven this truth so I take what I can get when I can get it.

"She's waiting for me," I say with a lift of my chin toward the exit, keeping pretenses up. "I've got to go."

We've been arguing for so long, she might not still be there. I glance down at my phone to see how long it's been.

Oh fuck. The texts read urgent from Westbrook. I turn to Hunter.

"It's Mom."

Chapter 20

"I don't need your shit, Colton." I roll my eyes and flop back on the couch, phone still at my ear when all I want to do is pretend I have a bad connection and hang up. I love my brother dearly but on top of the crap day I've had, I don't need his two cents over him finding out about my date with Luke.

I ignore my line beeping another incoming call from Hawkin for what feels like the hundredth time since I left the seminar today. I opened up and he shut me down. I don't want to think about it or the sting from my dashed hopes and the emotions I sat thinking about during the damn lecture while all the while he was thinking about Delta Sig girl. My eyes burn with tears I refuse to shed because this is on me and ignoring my damn mandate for casual only.

"Q, you're obviously upset, you won't tell me why, which means it's over a guy, and to top it off I find out you actually went on a date with the dickwad? I mean two and two—"

"Does not equal four," I say, exasperated. "It's nothing. No one. I've already moved on." Like hell I have but he doesn't need to go into big-brother mode more than he already has.

"Fucking women," he mutters, causing me to laugh. "Are you sure you're okay?"

The sincerity in his tone makes me smile softly at that side very few get to see to his hard-assed demeanor. "Yes. I promise," I tell my brother.

"You'd tell me if it wasn't, right? I don't need an excuse to kick Luke's ass but it wouldn't hurt either."

Testosterone much? Jeez. "Colton! He was nothing but a gentleman."

"Okay, okay. Just tell me one thing," he says. "Is the asshole you're upset over a racer?"

The laugh comes freely now at his relentless and inherent dislike of Luke Mason. Hawkin's voice fills my mind despite the pang it causes. Rocker trumps racer. "No. A musician," I deadpan.

"Fucking figures," he grumbles. "That's even worse."

"Yep. You know me—I make all the wrong decisions with all the wrong guys," I say, imagining the look on his face at that comment.

"Fuckin' A, Q . . . What the—"

"Night, Colton," I tell him with a smirk on my face. I've fulfilled my little-sister duty to torment her older brother for the week.

"Night." I love the exasperation in his voice because it means I was successful.

I hang up the phone and toss it on the couch beside me and scrub my hands over my face trying to ignore my racing thoughts even though I know they are going to win in the end anyway. I glance over to the trash can, where an empty cookies 'n cream half-gallon ice-cream container sits on the top. Ironically, I ate the dessert earlier as I tried to process what the fuck happened after the lecture today. And I'm still just as clueless now as I was before the rigorous workout, the soak in the tub, and the call from my brother.

How did Hawkin and I go from hot, curl-your-toes sex before the lecture to him going out with Delta Sig girl? Something is screwy and I'm so fucking sick and tired of thinking about it—being hurt by it despite telling myself I shouldn't be—that I just want to go to bed to prevent myself from doing the one thing I've wanted to do since I walked up the steps of the auditorium: Call him.

I refuse to be the desperate groupie clinging on for one more roll in the sheets when he made it obvious he's already put me with his other dirty laundry. I could answer my phone when he calls to ask him myself but just need to figure this all out before I do that. I'm not a weak person but something tells me I could easily fall back under his hypnotizing spell.

I close my eyes, the couch beneath me a little too comfortable, and drift off. At least I think I do, because when the pounding starts on my front door, I'm startled and jump up off the cushions, heart racing, head foggy, and adrenaline pumping. My immediate thought is fear. I mean I'm still trying to clear dreams from my head as I trudge to the front door, my mind not even considering that I'm wearing my cami-tank and panties.

The knocking begins again and when I look through the peephole, I'm shocked wide awake with anger. "Go away, Hawke! You're not welcome here."

"C'mon, Quin!" He pounds again, the door vibrating beneath my cheek pressed there so I can watch him through the hole.

"No. Go away." I flick the porch light off, holding tightly to my resolve and dignity, and shuffle down the hall. I stand in the family room for a moment, indecision reigning over what to do next as he bangs on the door again. I flick the light off by the couch, certain that I just need to sleep this off and maybe like a hangover, it'll be gone in the morning.

I head to turn the light off in the laundry room, where the washing machine is running midcycle, when the door to the backyard flings open. I yelp out in fright as it bangs against the counter behind it but then it quickly turns to anger when I see Hawkin there, shoulders leaning against the wall framing the jamb, head down, looking more than worse for the wear.

"Quinlan," he slurs, head lifting slowly for his eyes to meet mine. "I need you."

My heart skips a beat at the desperation in his tone. Hurt me and want me back, shame on you. Hurt me and I take you back twice? Dream on. In theory it sounds brilliant but when the man you want is standing before you with a pout on his lips and those words falling from his mouth my tough-girl facade wavers.

C'mon, Westin. Don't cave. He was an asshole. Discarded you and now realized what he did and is looking at you like a puppy dog kicked to the curb.

I lean against the washer behind me, willing my damn heartstrings to quit tugging on everything inside me, and cross my arms over my chest in a futile attempt to keep him at arm's length. "What? Your thirty-second flavor expire and now you're coming back for more?" My tough-girl front returns momentarily with much more bravado than I actually feel.

"Q," he sighs. "I need to explain."

"You're damn straight you do. You think I deserve—anyone deserves—to be treated like that? Discarded that way?" My voice rises as the hurt overrides the anger and fires in my veins. All of the pent-up emotion of the day that I tried to pretend didn't matter bubbles up and explodes.

"There's an explanation," his voice is quiet, resigned, and I recognize the sadness but I'm on a roll here and nothing is going to stop the rejection I felt from coming out now.

"I don't care, Hawkin! You may be some hotshot rock star but you know what? It doesn't give you the right to be an asshole," I yell at him.

"If you'll be quiet I'll explain!" he yells back, stepping into my space. He reaches out to my arm and I yank it out of his vicinity.

"No! There are no excuses good enough. We're *just friends*, remember?" I shout like an adolescent throwing a tantrum. He runs a hand through his hair, eyes on mine, and muscle pulsing in his clenched jaw. "You think—"

Before I can finish my thought, his mouth is on mine. I struggle against him, arms pushing, legs moving, head darting from side to side but he holds me still: hips pinning me against the spinning washing machine at my back so that my arms are trapped between our bodies and his hands hold my head firmly in place. The fight in me rages stronger.

"No!" I yell against his lips, hating my body for betraying my mind as it begins to hum with the heat of our connected bodies, remembering just how good we can be. "How dare you!" It's a halfhearted protest.

His fingers grip my hair and pull just tight enough that I am forced to look into his eyes. "I was trying to protect you."

The sarcastic laugh takes me by surprise. "Really? Wow, you sure have a funny way of showing it, Hawke. What are you trying to protect me from? You?"

"Yes."

"Nice try, rocker boy," I sneer at his pathetic excuse. My anger drowns out the sincerity tinged with shame that is in his tone. My emotions war as what I think I should do and what I want to do clash against each other. I try to push him off me again, hating and loving and wanting and not wanting the warmth of his corded muscles against my body.

"Quin. Me. The shit in my life. All of it . . . Hunter was behind you," he grunts out as he blocks my knee from connecting smartly. "I didn't want him to mess with you. To hurt you to spite me."

And the fight leaves me. My mind spins with the comment, with how hard that confession was for him to make.

Our breaths are panting with our exertion, our faces are close and his eyes search mine to make sure I understand. Suddenly there are so many questions I want to ask and he must see them all because not a second passes before his mouth crushes to mine and takes once again without asking. The difference is this time I let him.

I open up to him as his mouth searches for the answers to the problems his own eyes tell me he can't find. I never understood when people said a kiss tasted this way or that way. I thought it was part of that fairy-tale princess world that I don't subscribe to.

But I was wrong.

When our tongues connect, when his lips bruise mine, I can taste his desperation, understand that he needs something, someone, right now to help dissipate the pain and confusion that is rifling through his eyes.

And I may not understand it, in fact I may never know the truths that lie in those depths of gray but I do know that a man rarely admits he needs anything and when he does you better sit up and listen. And I'm listening.

I let him take, let him lead so the control he seeks is beneath his fingertips, willing and wanting and tangible. Where our connection earlier today was more a mutual meeting of frenzied desire, right now I can feel his need for so much more from me. To control so that he can calm, to sate so that he can feel whole, to have the release so that he can ease some of his restlessness.

And I'm here for him. I throw my threats from earlier out the window because he needs me and right now I'll give him whatever he asks for to clear the pain from his eyes and the grief from his countenance.

"I'm sorry," he breathes into me and I just nod my head in acceptance as his mouth claims mine once again. He kicks the door shut behind us without skipping a beat. His hands palm my breasts through my tank and mine slide beneath his shirt to feel his skin heated and taut with anxiety. I pull his shirt over his head and he does mine in turn and then my fingers unbutton his jeans earning me a pained groan as my hands find him hard and ready beneath the denim.

I shove his jeans and underwear down his hips and encircle him. He tears his mouth from mine, his head falling back as my name slips from his lips in a desperate moan. As I place a trail of openmouthed kisses down his exposed neckline, his fingers tighten on my arms when I sink to my knees on the floor before him.

I look up the plane of his defined torso to study him, jaw set, eyes burning, nostrils flaring, and when we lock eyes, I take him into my mouth. His hands immediately fist into the messy ponytail at the back of my head, wrapping the hair around his hand as he hisses in pleasure. *"God, Quin."*

I may not be able to fix his problems or even know the answers to them, but this? Making him feel so much pleasure he can't think otherwise for a bit? This, I can do for him.

His grip tightens; one of my hands is on his forearm while the other is holding his cock so that I can take it in my mouth. He holds my head still and fucks my mouth so that he hits the back of my throat before grinding his hips with a moan of ecstasy and then pulling back out. Where I'd normally explore more, tempt and taunt, I can sense from the volatility of his emotions, as well as the muscles tensed beneath my hand, that niceties aren't welcome. He's in this for the endgame, for the pleasure that might dull the pain, even if for a bit.

He holds my head still and moves his hips into my face.

I know he's close, can feel him hardening in my mouth but this time he presses himself a little too hard, a little too long so that I gag on his length. I hear his curse, feel the immediate release of my hair and his hands on my shoulders dragging me up, apologies on his lips as tears burn my eyes and I cough from the intrusion.

It's really not a big deal, just a hazard of the act, but it's almost as if something breaks within him because of it. He's gone from angry and pent up to confused and regretful, trying to gather me into him and apologize. I'm sure it's a mix of the alcohol and whatever happened to him today that has pain and grief written all over him and is the cause of his emotional instability. I'm probably so far off in my thinking, but my gut check reaction is that the only way to calm these manic extremes is to put him back in charge, tell him what I want, force him to finish this out.

And I have no clue what I'm doing, but I act on instinct, and what I can read in his expression.

"No, Hawke . . ." I try to push myself out of his arms. When I look into his eyes, I see emotion swimming within them, and press my lips to his in a no-holds-barred kiss. I force my tongue between his lips, thread my fingers through his hair, wrap a hand around his cock, and begin to pump it in my hand.

At first he doesn't react but then my actions begin to spark him back to life. "Fuck me, Hawke. I need it hard, fast, rough." I breathe my demands into his mouth and nip his bottom lip as I pull back and meet his eyes again, but this time I see the haze of desire begin to darken them as need washes over him.

And from one beat to the next, Hawke grips my hips and lifts me up onto the top of the washing machine. I don't even have a moment to realize my victory because with the machine on spin cycle vibrating beneath me, he wastes no time jacketing up, parting my sex, and slamming into me in one slick, desperate stroke.

We both cry out as he bucks his hips before stilling momentarily, trying not to succumb to my wet heat. He waits a beat before pulling back out and setting a frantic, punishing pace as his hands hold my thighs apart and I press my back against the wall behind me. I watch his dick slide in and out of me and with the vibration of the machine beneath me, urging my release on, I slide a hand down between my thighs and add the friction to my clit needed to push me into the oblivion he's holding out for me to find first.

I know later I'll recall how even at his worst, Hawkin is thinking of me, but right now, I can't think. All I can do is feel: the rapturous sensations of his thickness sliding against my nerve-laden walls with each hammer of his hips, the movement of the washer, my own finger knowing just how to pleasure myself. Recognizing my body's signs that tell me my orgasm is just within reach, I hold my breath as my legs tense and my feet flex. I look up to see Hawke's face pulled tight with pleasure, the muscles in his neck and shoulders strained, his eyes squeezed tight as his body draws orgasms from the both of us.

I go first. His ability to give me the hard and fast I asked for earns me an explosive orgasm that has white-hot heat streaking down my spine and exploding in my core before ricocheting out to every single nerve in my body and holding them hostage.

I can't recover fast enough to watch Hawkin reach his, so my eyes are closed, body slumped on the machine when his harsh shout of "Fuck!" fills the small room. His fingers tighten as he rides his out.

I can feel the tension leave his grip on my thighs and open my eyes just as his head falls forward for a second before he reaches out in a move so unexpected that I hesitate momentarily when he gathers me to him and wraps his arms around me.

Our bodies are still joined in all aspects and as he holds me tight in my confining laundry room, I can also feel our souls begin to intertwine, and my heart slip a little farther down the cliff toward the ocean of love below.

"This band's got a good vibe about them," Hawkin murmurs quietly as he taps his fingers to the beat on the bare skin of my back. It's the first thing he's said since we fell in the couch after moving from the laundry room what feels like forever ago. We're a tangled mess of temporarily satisfied desire as I lie half on top of him.

"Mm-hm." It's all I murmur as our hearts beat against

each other's, and the warm night air teases our bare skin. Honestly, my mind's still thinking about the evening's unexpected turn of events. The sex that was tinged with greed and desperation on both of our parts but for different reasons.

And with the sex came the shift in my state of mind and emotions. I'm falling hardcore for Hawkin, no question. We may have walked into whatever this is between us without any suppositions to where it's going, but I doubt either of us will be able to walk away unscathed.

Obviously something happened tonight to drive him to drink, something bad enough that led him *to need me*. It had to be more than his simple explanation that Hunter was behind me today to set this off. My thoughts race but all I can determine is that only he holds the secrets to reveal.

I feel like I'm an open door to him and yet he still seems like a hallway full of locked ones. Am I walking into a dead end? I just don't know. I'm trying to keep my feelings on lockdown, trying to prevent the heartbreak I sense on the horizon because I need him to give me at least a few keys to unlock his past. It doesn't mean I'll use them, but they're necessary to feel like we're on an even playing field. And I just don't know if he's at a place in his life where he's willing to share.

Because if he can't, something like tonight is going to happen again. The silence wraps around us and I question myself, ponder whether I'll be able to live with another tonight, especially if he doesn't explain his actions any further. I wonder if letting him between my thighs when he hasn't let me in his private life makes me seem like a pushover, or a woman willing to forgive at the drop of a dime. I let the thought settle and know that it doesn't, it just makes me human.

But at the same time, I'm going to have to make sure he understands that the word "doormat" is the furthest thing from what is stamped on my forehead.

A small part of me revels in the fact that whatever he's distraught over, he came to me tonight, needed me tonight. Not one of his other thirty flavors from his past. That's a pretty heady feeling when you combine it with the emotional highs and lows of the day.

I'm so caught up in my thoughts I don't even realize that

I'm tracing the tattoos on the inside of his forearm, the treble clef and the symbol for strength, moving over them in a rhythmic movement. And something strikes me suddenly, so I shift my body so that I can look at the wrist of the arm Hawkin has resting on my back. He obliges my nonverbal request and lets me look at the skin sans tattoos on there.

"What?" he asks as I shift back over, curiosity now getting the better of me.

"You never explained the pink heart thing the other day. Do they all have them? You don't?"

He stares at me a beat before he laughs. I welcome the sound after the heaviness of our exchange, and wait for his answer. "They're . . . oh God." He chuckles, his chest beneath my chin vibrating from it. "For as long as I can remember, the four of us made bets—about anything: songs, women, you name it. We did it so much that it became a habit, but at some point we realized that there was no recourse for losing."

"Uh-oh," I say, the smile on my lips contradicting the shake of my head.

"Yep. So one drunken night we decided that loser gets a tattoo, winner's pick. More drinks, more decisions were made and we decided that it had to be a uniform image and location. We figured why not make it an image of what we love. . . ." He pauses, the self-deprecation in his laugh humorous. "Ah, I can't believe I'm telling you this. . . . Rocket said he loves the pink color of the inside of a woman's pussy. . . . And, well, our decision was solidified. A pussy pink heart."

"Well," I say, but I'm so busy laughing it's the only word I get out.

"Yeah, I know. Can you see why I make sure I can win any bet I take so I don't ruin the significance of the ones I have?" I nod my head, envisioning each of the guys' wrists and their permanent reminder, as he continues. "The guy has to get the heart outlined to make it bigger with each bet he loses . . . hence why Gizmo has the biggest one. Love the guy to death but he'll bet on anything."

"I'm afraid to ask what the bets are."

"You should be." He snickers.

"And you're just *that good*, you've never lost?" I ask, immediately assuming he has to cheat the system somehow.

"Nope, I'm just that good," he says, causing me to smile as he clears his throat. "It's hard to explain. . . . Sounds stupid, really, but my tats have a meaning; they tell my story in a sense, and I refuse to lessen their significance by scarring myself with a pink heart." His voice fades and a silence falls around us, so that even though we are lying on top of each other, I feel the distance.

"How long have you guys been together?" I ask, wanting to keep him engaged, learn more about him, and I figure this is a safe topic of conversation.

"Vince since sixth grade. Him, our other friend Benji, Hunter, and I used to be inseparable. We met Giz and Rocket in high school."

He skims quickly over his brother's name but I don't miss it. So Hunter was a part of this close-knit group of guys who are now a band and now he isn't? There's obviously more there. I've seen the animosity between him and Vince first-hand. I want to ask, want to delve but choose a safer path.

"What happened to Benji?"

"He's still around," he says, voice laced in amusement. "Ben doesn't have a musical bone in his body. He prefers being an asshole . . . so he became a lawyer." I snap my head up at him, surprised by the comment but find him smiling so I know he's teasing. "Nah, he's a good guy. Always looking out for my best interest."

I rest my head back down on his chest as the song changes. Hawke's fingers keep tapping the beat on my back, but I still feel like there is a huge elephant in the room that we need to address. I've watched my brother go through some pretty serious shit, watched Rylee break down his walls, and learned that with men patience is a virtue you need to hold on to. And I'm patient, but I'm also curious.

"So is this how you deal with all of your problems?" I ask, causing his hand to stop momentarily from playing the beat before he continues again.

"Hmm?" he murmurs. "You mean putting the spin in your machine's spin cycle?" He chuckles softly, his hand moving to tug the holder out of my ponytail and begin to play with my hair. "Because shit, that felt hella good. We might have to try that again sometime, minus the barge through the door thing."

"It was kinda hot," I tease, earning a tug on my hair that makes me laugh. "I'd hate to see what you do when it's just you and the guys on a tour bus then," I joke, wanting to lighten the mood some, give him room to breathe so that he can be comfortable enough to answer.

I love the laugh he emits; it's free and sincere and tells me some of the weight on his mind has lifted. "I assure you the guys don't get to see that side of me," he muses. "And to answer your question, no, that's not how I usually deal with shit. I take it out on Giz's drums—pound the hell out of them for a good hour or so—but I think I've found my new substitute."

"You have?"

"Yes. You." His unexpected words cause a flutter in my stomach that I try to ignore. I'll need to try harder with that because even though I'm sure he knows the right thing to say to make a woman swoon, the sincerity in his tone weaves its way into my soul and wraps around my heart. Gives me hope of possibilities that I realize I was fearing before but now really want to believe have a chance.

I don't know what to say but his comment has made me feel a little more secure in this ever-revolving world around us, and I want to give him something in return. I press a kiss to his chest, his heart beating just beneath my lips, and rest my chin there on top of my hand. "You want to talk about tonight?"

"No . . . I don't." He sighs after a moment and I can all but feel his sadness return. "But you deserve an explanation after what I did to you today."

"Hawkin—"

"I'm not that much of an asshole, Quin. If I'm going to fuck it out with you, you sure as shit deserve an explanation." There is no arguing with his tone, so I keep my eyes fixed on my fingers tracing his tattoos and nod my head in silent agreement. And of course now that he is about to talk about it, I'm almost nervous to hear the explanation.

If it's something he keeps this close to the vest, will finding out change the opinions and feelings I'm starting to have for him?

"Today is the anniversary of my dad's suicide."

I whip my head up to look at him, shocked by the confession I wasn't expecting, the key he handed me to unlock one of his doors, and hurt for him all at once. My mouth falls open and then I close it, and open it again, having everything and nothing to say to him.

He keeps his eyes averted from me though. I know he's hurting, can't imagine the pain of having to live without a dad, but don't know how exactly to soothe him besides just letting him know I am here for him in silent support.

"Hawkin." It's the only thing I say to him, his name softly spoken.

"No. Don't. . . . I gave you the short version of it the other day. I'm sorry."

"Please don't apologize," I plead.

He exhales a breath, his fingers still playing idly with my hair in a gesture so contradictory to the tumultuous emotions emanating off him. "When I was nine, I was home sick. My mom went to pick Hunt up from school and my dad stayed home with me. I went downstairs to get a toy—a Transformer—and he was there. He was ranting and pacing and nervous and the things he said confused me. . . ." His voice fades off as my heart squeezes in my chest at the sadness that begins to suffocate the room around us. "He made me promise him things about my mom, about Hunter, about how I'd live my life. . . . Then he made me stand there and watch him load the gun . . . made me watch him pull the trigger." Hawkin's voice that is usually so melodic in tone is hollow when he says the last words, and the absence of his trademark warmth speaks volumes. Tells me this man understandably still mourns the loss of his father, the loss of his innocence, and everything else his father took from him that day that I can't even fathom.

The silence around us is deafening as I reach out and lace my fingers with his, my thoughts racing over the damage that was done to his psyche that day. Questions fly through my mind: Why make your son watch? Why did he commit suicide? How can two sons left by their father end up at such odds when they probably used each other to get through it?

"What was his name?" I ask, unsure what else to ask but needing him to know I care.

"Joshua," he says softly and then falls silent for a beat. "He told me . . ." He clears his throat from the emotion clogged there and it breaks my heart. His chest stills beneath my cheek as he reins in his emotion and continues. "My dad said that he was weak, loved my mom too much, and that he just couldn't deal with it all anymore. By today's standards, I'm sure he'd be diagnosed with depression, something that might explain things, but looking back through the eyes of a child, we never saw it. . . . He was just our dad. The man I idolize."

I press another kiss to his chest, his heart beating erratically against my lips, and it's not lost on me that idolize is present tense despite the amount of time that has passed. My mind turns to thoughts of my own father, who still seems larger than life. How as a child he protected Colton and me from life's harsh realities and yet Hawkin was thrust right into them with a front row ticket.

"I'll never understand why he did it, why he called me in there. Why he left us. It's hard even now for me to admit how selfish he was for making me stand there and watch him. For making me promise to live a life by the standards he couldn't himself live out. He saddled me with the burden of proving it's possible to do what he couldn't and survive. . . ." He falls quiet, and I just lie there in silent reassurance, my eyes welling with tears I don't want him to see. Tears for the little boy he was, the damage it caused him, and for the grown man still feeling guilt over it all this time later.

Scars run so deep sometimes, the invisible ones cutting the deepest of them all.

"He ruined us that day—my mom, Hunt, me. But the fault lies on me too because I still want to make him proud somehow by doing it. I can't not. Something's wrong with me, I guess . . . I don't know." He shakes his head and blows out a breath in frustration.

"Nothing's wrong with you," I murmur, not wanting to overstep my boundaries. "You're just trying to honor your word. No one will ever fault you for standing by that."

He just falls silent and I worry that maybe I said something he didn't want to hear. All I can think about is this little boy with stormy eyes and the invisible scars he wears beneath the surface, the burden of being the man of the house after it seems like the house fell down around them.

"My mom has never been the same since. I've always said I lost her that day too. Our house was always filled with the sound of her singing or the classical music she was trying to teach us when the classics we'd much rather have been listening to were the rock variety. Then after . . . she was just this shell of herself. . . . I don't know how else to explain it."

"There's nothing I can say," I murmur; all of the words on the tip of my tongue wouldn't express even an iota of what I really mean so I just keep quiet, pulling him in tighter to me, appreciating the fact that he trusted me with his story.

"Nothing to say." He shrugs when he lifts his head up to finally meet my gaze. His eyes are heavy with sorrow and I wish I could take that away from him for a moment, a day, so that he can live free of the burden of it. "Hunter . . . I don't know." He shakes his head. "We were close for a while. We hit high school and he started to fall apart. Sports games without our dad in the stands, my mom so lost we had to turn to friends to teach us how to drive . . . He fell into a bad scene for a while." He shakes his head and lays it back down, his eyes returning to the ceiling but not before I can see the pain, the guilt he carries in his eyes.

I want to tell him that wasn't his job, his responsibility to fix because he was suffering too, but he continues before I can find the right words.

"I think a part of him thinks my dad favored me, held me to a higher standard by having me be there with him. He doesn't get the images I have to relive every time I think of my dad. Blood gushing like a fountain, pooling around my feet frozen to the floor. The echo of the gunshot slamming into my goddamn skull, haunting my dreams, and making me jerk to look when I hear a car backfire. The promises I had to make, the only things I have left to make him proud of me." He scrubs a hand over his face, his five o'clock shadow chafing his hands, and all I want to do is gather him to me, hold him tight, and try to take the memories away for him, but know I can't.

He's baring his demons to me and I'm worried what damage has occurred by him dredging up the memories I'm sure he keeps locked tight.

"Music was how I coped. I lost myself in it—the lyrics, the beat—and it allowed me to step outside the situation, allowed me to feel alive again when I was dead for so long. We formed a band sophomore year in high school—Hunter, Vince, Rocket, Giz, and me. It was my salvation, my daily catharsis from the shit fucking up my head. We kept at it and started playing clubs before we were old enough to drink. Had a couple of gigs we played regularly for a while but the lifestyle was bad for Hunter. He slipped back into the shit he delved into in high school. Started needing the drugs more than the music, I guess. Missed gigs, fucked-up chords on stage . . . The guys started getting pissed, knew he was going to blow our chance.

"Then we had a scout in the crowd one night. He talked to us after and came to a few more of our sets at different clubs. One thing led to another and then another and he wanted to sign us, but he wanted Hunter gone because he was a liability. He was right but fuck, what was I supposed to do? He promised to clean up, drop the drugs, and then he never showed for the performance we had for the record execs because he was so coked up he passed out. They offered us the deal as long as Hunter wasn't on the ticket." He falls silent, the strife raw in his tone at having to make a decision between his anchor and his life preserver. "Anyway, the guys told me it was my decision, that they understood if we had to pass the contract up."

"Wow." I don't even realize I've spoken until he speaks again.

"Exactly. That's how good of friends they are to me, willing to give up their dream so that I didn't have to leave my brother behind. It fucked me up for a while—the guilt still does, I guess, but I chose the band. Told Hunter if he couldn't get his shit together that it wasn't fair to everyone else to throw the years of hard work away."

I draw in a deep breath, trying to wrap my head around

the decision he had to make and the added weight it must be on his already burdened shoulders. And I also think he's fortunate that he has friends like the guys who offered to give up the possibility because he meant so much to them. It also explains the tension between them all to an extent.

"And then of course we hit it big and I could see his resentment eat at him. Watched as he tried to undermine situations between the guys and me but they stood firm from our shared history and always had my back. So he moved on to everything else he could fuck up for me."

By now my head is spinning at all of this information, so I just nod. His eyes reconnect with mine and give me the courage to comment. "And that's where I come in?"

"Fuck if I know." He blows out a breath, his free hand reaching down and grazing over the length of my jaw. "I couldn't save my dad, but I tried to save Hunt . . . still am in a sense. I pay him a portion of my cut because guilt eats at me, I guess. Either that or I'm stupid . . . but I promised my dad I'd take care of him and I'm trying to. Am I enabling his habit that he can kick every so often before he uses again to deal with his shit? Probably. Do I cover for him, when I shouldn't? Always . . . but it's getting old and I've started resisting more and more, causing him to become more bitter, going after anything I have to prove he's better, I guess. Restore that ego of his I damaged. Women, family, friends. Anything I want, he tries to fuck up in his own personal vendetta to get back at me."

"So then kick his ass and tell him to leave what's yours alone." The comment comes out as a reflex, and I immediately regret the inadvertent declaration. I cringe and avert my eyes knowing that's like the kiss of death to a guy, particularly one like him who's probably used to changing women like he does his underwear.

The silence kills me so when I look back up, I don't expect the lopsided grin that spreads lazily on his face and lights up the sadness in his gray eyes, but it's such a welcome sight. "What's mine, huh?" He angles his head to the side and stares, lips pursed, eyes reflecting the thoughts flickering through his mind. *"You staking a claim, Trixie?"*

Is the sky blue? If I worried that his confession was going to push me away from him, I was way off base because now I only want him more. Deciding to demonstrate, I sit up and climb over his lap so that I'm facing him, my legs straddled on either side of his. His brow furrows and lips turn up as his eyes never leave mine, questioning my actions without using words.

When I bend forward and brush my lips to his, my bare breasts skimming over his chest, and then lean back so that I can see some of that discord clear from his eyes. "If hot sex on my washing machine is part of this claim," I say pressing my mouth to his again, slipping my tongue between his lips to tempt and tease in a seductive dance before pulling back again, "then hell yes, I'm in."

He laughs softly, and the momentary playfulness makes me feel a bit more settled. But I can feel the weight of sadness begin to descend again and before it can grow roots, I slip my arms around him and pull him into me. With our positioning, his head rests just under the curve of my neck and I can feel him hesitate slightly, can feel the unease with his sudden vulnerability, but I don't let go. I know this can go one of two ways because a man's vulnerability is akin to having his heart lie on the outside of his chest, unprotected and defenseless.

It also means it's open to possibility.

My gut instinct that he needs to be comforted could backfire. I could be so off base and scare him the hell away, but he came here. *He needed me.* I feel his hesitancy, his want to rein in the emotion, be strong and not break with weakness. Fulfill his promise to his dad.

And then he reacts, tightening his arms around me, gathering me into him. An exhale of a stuttered breath, fingers pressing desperately into my back, silence settling around us as he holds on and finds the comfort I'm offering without strings or claims. And yes, I know we've had sex already, been as close to someone else as we possibly can be, but at the same time, this feels ten times more intimate in the moment than the joining of our bodies.

I run my hands up his muscular back, slide my nails in his hair and scratch his head gently in a silent show of support. His response reminds me of a little boy needing someone to comfort him so I do just that. I hold him tightly, pressing kisses into the crown of his head, fingertips grazing his skin, our hearts beating in time with each other's.

We sit like this for some time, the songs changing on the speakers overhead, the feeling of our naked bodies pressed skin to skin an added bonus.

"Did something happen tonight to upset you besides the obvious?" I murmur.

He sighs, the heat of his breath warm against my neck. "I got into it with Hunter after trying to distract his sights from you with that sorority girl. If he thought she was what I wanted, then he'd go after her, and not you." I hear the honesty in his voice, and I smile softly, the hurt he caused me forgiven. "Then we got a call—Mom was having a rough day so we went to see her and things only got worse from there. She wasn't happy to see me because . . . That's another story." He blows out a breath, the keys I need him to hand out going back into his pocket. "So I hit up a bar and drank till the anger lessened . . . but I just kept thinking about you. I needed to see you and you wouldn't respond or pick up the phone, so here I am."

"I'm sorry you had such a shit day," I tell him honestly, struggling trying to process everything. I don't have much to contribute so I'll say the one thing I can. "I'm a big girl, Hawke. I have no problem telling your brother to go to hell myself."

His laugh is low and derisive. "I know you can but Hunter's an all costs kind of guy, and I always wonder how much there is of Dad in him. They ruin someone else while self-destructing on purpose. Dad was larger than life but everything was in extremes. Hunt's the same way." He adjusts our position so that he leans back, my body now falling into his, and he sets his chin on my shoulder. "Jealousy is a nasty bitch, sometimes. I love my brother—it's just how it goes—but most of the time he uses our past as an excuse to pardon his actions, his drug habit, and the ruin it leaves in its wake. . . . And while I may love him, that doesn't mean I have to like him all the time either."

"I understand that." My thoughts whirl over how lucky I am that even though Colton had a childhood full of inexcusable things, he always protected me fiercely. And in the same breath that notion makes me understand why he wants to protect Hunter the same way. "Why not just distance yourself? Let him trip and fall and have to deal with the consequences himself? Maybe he'll appreciate everything you've done for him."

"In theory that works, but that's not the promise I made to my dad." Before he falls silent, I hear the conflicted love so raw in his voice it grates through it. "*I'm all he has, Quin.* He might be an asshole, he might try to hurt me, hell it probably makes me look like the biggest pussy in the world for not telling him to eat shit and die, but *I can't.* When it comes down to it, he's all I have left. He may be a manipulative fuck at times who deserves what he gets, but my mom would never forgive me if I cut him loose. And then what? I lose both of them and I've got no one? That scares the fuck out of me."

We fall silent again as I hear what he is saying to me. It seems to me he has no one already. The thought makes me so grateful he has the guys in the band to be there for him. But I understand the sibling bond. Colton and I are close and he's adopted, so I can't imagine the connection between two twins who underwent hell together. I don't understand what Hawkin means about his mom holding on and it's the second or third time he's implied something is wrong with her without being more specific. I want to ask, want to understand his cryptic comments, but I let it go. He's baring his emotions and there is no way I'm going to ask for more from him.

I get his loyalty to his twin, understand his acceptance of being hurt while trying to make everyone else feel better, but it's not his sins to atone for, they're his father's.

"I know it makes no sense Quinlan so don't try," he murmurs once he infers my train of thought. "It's my own fucked-up guilt over something I had no control over. I know that, but it doesn't make me feel any better about the past. It doesn't change my family dying that day. Dad was my idol—right or wrong or selfish or cowardly—he made me make promises to him . . . and I truly believe a man is only as good as his word." His voice trails off again, leaving my heart somersaulting at his confession. I think he's finished but I stay silent. Then he murmurs, "And I'm just trying to be the best man I can be."

I'm not sure if he says the words to me or to reassure himself, so I let the comment settle between us. I shift my body, our limbs still entangled, and I wonder if our hearts are slowly following suit.

Doesn't he get that he's so much more than the little boy who made promises and the man who's trying to keep them? Thousands see it. He holds them all spellbound with his music. Hopefully in time, he will too.

The emotional overload of the day and the satisfaction of sating our desire together pull the ribbons of slumber until they wrap around our bodies, slowly tying us together until we succumb.

Chapter 21

QUINLAN

"Read 'em and weep, boys!" I lay the three aces on the table to the curses of the guys around me.

"Fuck, Hawke! Why'd you bring her?" Rocket asks tossing his cards down as I make a show of pulling all the chips in the pot toward me, playing it up as Hawke throws his head back and laughs. And it's such a good sound after last night and the state he came to me in and the confessions of his past on his lips that I glance over and hold his eye, my own smile widening.

"Ah, poor sports!" I grumble with a smirk. "Good thing we're not betting on pink heart tattoos tonight or Hawkin right there just might be getting one!"

Vince howls out in laughter that turns into a coughing fit when Hawkin gives him the evil eye. "What?" Vince says innocently before turning those hazel eyes of his back to me.

Hawkin's phone rings and breaks up the moment. He furrows his brow before he scoots his chair out to take the call. I watch Hawke's broad back as he disappears into the darkness of the backyard, then turn back to three beseeching pair of eyes.

"I want to see all of your hearts," I tell them, pointing to my wrist so they understand what I'm talking about. I inspect them all, Vince's is the smallest, Giz's the largest. "What gives, Giz? You like pink or something?"

"The right kind, in the right place I do," he says with a raise of his eyebrows that causes me to blush.

"He's just gullible as fuck and will bet on anything," Vince clarifies, earning the middle finger Gizmo lifts at him.

"So tell me, boys, what's the last thing you guys bet on?" The three of them fall silent as they glance at one another, and I realize that they think I can't handle it. "Oh come on, I won't be offended."

Vince clears his throat and looks down at his tattooed heart before looking back up. "Last bet was getting a woman into bed within a certain amount of time." He purses his lips, eyes intense on mine, waiting to see my re-action.

"Well, considering it's you guys, a rock band with women who'll spread their legs for you at the drop of a dime, I don't get why it's such a big deal. Besides, it's not exactly some-thing easy to prove. Anyone can stand on the opposite side of a closed door and moan, right?"

Rocket abruptly scoots his chair back and excuses him-self while Giz leans back, effectively removing himself from the discussion to let Vince and me continue. "You make a good point. That's why this bet entailed that another mem-ber of the band be able to partake to make sure the param-eters of the bet were fulfilled."

"Partake?" I say with a laugh, my mind firing suddenly and an alcohol-fogged memory coming to the forefront. Another night where Vince talked about threesomes. Is this something that's a norm with the band? *Is that what Hawkin's used to?* Is it something I have to do if I even have a chance at being on his long-term playing field?

The idea is definitely a turn-on, no doubt—being with two men at the same time. My imagination toys with the thought momentarily before I remember that Vince's eyes are scrutinizing my reaction.

"You make a threesome sound so damn sexy," I tease to dispel the sudden awkwardness I feel because I wonder just what he and Hawkin would be like together. "So who won?"

"What are you guys talking about?" Hawkin asks as he

walks up, pulling me from my lascivious thoughts and making me realize what a lucky girl I am to be sitting here right now. And shit, I've been with him all damn day—from going out to breakfast to pretending to be tourists and walking hand in hand along Muscle Beach where we people watched and laughed all day long—and the man still makes my heart stutter at his sex appeal and good looks. Because a man can be sexy or good-looking, but when he's fortunate to possess both attributes and they're all rolled into one package? This woman's a goner.

"The last bet you guys made," I answer. Hawke coughs, choking on the sip he just took before shooting a warning glance over at Vince.

"No worries, bro," Vince says. "I didn't spill our secrets. What happens in the band stays in the band." He taps the neck of his beer against the one in Hawke's hand. "It's all good. How 'bout you?" He lifts his chin at the phone Hawkin sets on the table. "Everything okay?"

"Fucking stellar," he replies. "Hunter needs money."

"Hawkin, you can't—"

"Drop it, Vinny," he snaps, silencing the conversation despite the glances some of the guys angle his way. I can tell he's upset by something, but at least I have a much better understanding of the dynamic now. "Are we going to play or what?"

The night wears on, hands are dealt, big wins and big losses are had, but I'm enjoying the competitiveness because it's fun to see Hawkin around the people he's most comfortable with. He's definitely the closest to Vince, but the love he feels toward the other two guys is just as apparent. The band has invited me into their inner circle without the begrudgery I'd expected.

We've all had some alcohol, and every once in a while Rocket disappears and comes back with the distinctive scent of dope clinging to his clothes. I can see the distaste on Hawke's face and the random disapproving glances his way.

After the third or fourth glare, Rocket finally says, "Relax!" before tossing his cards on the table and scrapping his hand. "Don't act like you're the saint here. Back in the day you had no problem taking a toke." They stare at one another in an unstated challenge. I'm slightly uncomfortable but notice that no one else at the table is even blinking an eye so this—either Rocket smoking a joint or him challenging Hawkin—must be a regular occurrence within their group hierarchy. "I'm not him and he's not me, so knock it off, will ya?"

And my assumption that Rocket's talking about Hunter is confirmed when Hawkin's phone rings again. He spits out a curse as he shoves the chair back with force. "He's fucking everywhere," he mutters as he stalks off.

Rocket starts to stand to go after him, just like I want to. Then Vince advises, "Leave it, man. Hunter's probably pulling his shit right now."

Rocket stands there in momentary indecision before shaking his head at Vince and following after Hawke.

And the act makes me fall a little bit more in like with Rocket for worrying about Hawkin when he could have let it go. I'm not sure why it brings me such comfort. Probably because I can sense how much Hawke craves normalcy, and I love to see that he's succeeded in surrounding himself with a family of his own creation.

"Well, since it seems like we're taking a break, I'm gonna take a piss," Gizmo says as he knocks his chair backward before wandering inside.

I watch him go and when I look back toward the table, Vince is eyeing me again. We stare into the silence for what feels like forever, snippets of Hawke's conversation drifting over to us occasionally.

"You know why he's pissed, right?" Vince asks, clearly expecting an answer from me. He's overprotective of Hawkin but I feel like I'm about to be tested and I'm not sure how I feel about it. The fact that he's testing me though means he senses that I might be more than just a wannabe groupie.

"I'm assuming he's pissed about something with Hunter." It's a safe response on my part that causes Vince to drum his fingers on the table, an internal debate warring over his features as he decides how much to divulge.

"You follow the rags much?"

"You got a point, Vince? Because I'm sensing you want to get something off your chest. I'm worried about whatever is stressing Hawkin out, and honestly, I want to take him upstairs and have my way with him, so patience is not my virtue right now."

A grin spreads over his lips. "Well damn, woman. You sure know how to get a man's attention." And where a moment ago I was annoyed with him, he's already won me back with his response. "Hawke talk to you at all about his drug charge a couple months back?"

I glance down to his drumming fingers and then back up with a quick shake of my head. "Nah . . . I figured if he wanted to bring it up he would. His business."

He raises his eyebrows with a subtle nod of his head. "In a sense it's a whole lot of people's business. . . . Hawke won't admit it, but he's taking the fall for Hunter."

"What? Wait, I'm confused. How's that even possible?" I ask, but Hawke's confession about his brother last night rings in my ears, and before Vince answers, I know it's true.

"Same place, same time, identical twins although they're anything but identical." He shakes his head when I just narrow my eyes at him. "Shit, we can't even tell them apart sometimes. They have their own style now, but when we were younger each would dress up like the other one, and we'd have no fucking clue until they started laughing. They know each other's mannerisms, speech, everything . . . so as stupid as it sounds, it's easy to believe how they could pull it off." He takes a sip of his beer and tips the bottle toward where Hawke stands. "Look, Hawke's complicated, stubborn, but he's also loyal and family comes first. Always. Even if it's fucked-up family."

"He told me about his dad," I murmur and notice Vince widen his eyes and turn his head. "And Hunter and the band."

"Hm. Well, that should tell you something. . . ."

I can take his comment a few ways and I'm not sure which way I should. Is he saying it's a big deal Hawkin told me because he doesn't talk about his past and his confession means he really likes me? Or is he saying, see, he's fucked-up, a head case from his childhood, and I should lace up my running shoes and run far away?

I know which one I hope he's saying but I'm uncomfortable now, talking about Hawkin and him not being here.

The last thing I want is for a misconception to be made that I'm digging for info on him. I have a feeling that would end any chance of something more between us, so I just sit there, play with my poker chips, and wait out the silence.

"Hunter's had some run-ins with the law, a pair of drug convictions for one. Hawke won't elaborate about what happened this time other than the two of them were at a party, he laid his jacket on a chair at some point, picked it up to go just about the same time cops showed up . . . and somehow the bag of blow was in the pocket and he was busted." He waits for me to look up and see that he doesn't buy Hawke's story. "The way I see it, Hunter gets convicted again, he's tried under California's Three Strikes law and gets a lengthy sentence. I don't know the details but I know that jacket isn't Hawke's, and I seem to remember seeing Hunter having one just like it. Hawke's taking the fall to prevent destroying his family even further. Willing to risk himself to live up to the cruel promise the memory of his father makes him keep."

We sit there in silence as I gather my thoughts. "Why are you telling me all of this, Vince?"

"Because I've seen the way he looks at you, Quin. It's not a normal thing for Hawkin to let someone into this world of ours unless it's for . . ." He stops himself, scrunching his face up, and the expression alone tells me where he was going with the statement.

"Thanks but I get it. You're rock stars, right? Women are willing and in abundance. No need to sugarcoat it."

His shoulders fall when he exhales the breath he's holding. "Thank fuck you're a cool cat, Q," he says with relief. "I'll cut to the chase. He agreed to do the seminar as a way to get in the judge's good graces, hopefully a slap on the hand for his first offense after doing the lectures."

Puzzle pieces begin to fall into place for me. The answers in regard to his sudden appearance at school, his refusal to give me a straight answer as to why he agreed to do the lecture.

"The thing is, doing the lecture doesn't guarantee a lighter sentence. He won't admit to anything, but I find it odd that out of the blue he's making Hunter go to some kind of drug counseling. I swear he's taking the fall for his brother and trying to use it as leverage to get Hunter to get help. . . . It's fucked up."

Loose strings begin to tie and the picture becomes more and more clear. The only gray area is their mother but as forthcoming as Vince is being, that's not something I'm going to ask about.

So I look at Vince and twist my lips in thought. "And if Hawke goes to jail, then the band gets damaged too, right? Why are you telling me all this?" I stare at him, not liking what I think he's asking of me. "Oh. I get it. You want me to convince him to turn his brother in so that the band doesn't catch the fallout if he's sentenced. I'm not a pawn. Ask him yourself—"

"You think I give a fuck about myself or the band?" He pounds his fist against the table, which makes the chips rattle loudly as fury flashes through his eyes. "He's like a brother to me! The band will be here for him regardless of what happens, so I suggest you take that accusation and shove it," he says, his voice full of spite and his love for Hawke palpable.

Chills race over my skin as we stare at each other in a silent standoff. I don't know why I pushed that button of his when I already knew the answer. Maybe I just wanted to reaffirm what I thought about their bond. Maybe I like Hawkin way too much, and I want to make sure that everyone is looking out for his best interests since his own blood obviously isn't.

"Point shoved." He breaks out in a ghost of a smirk at my response and I know he's let my comment go. "It's not my place to say anything, Vince. If the topic arises, if he tells me about it, then maybe . . . but as of right now he doesn't even know that I know. . . ."

"True," he muses as we hear laughter. I look over to see Rocket's arm slung over Hawkin's shoulder, their heads thrown back.

They approach the table and Hawkin looks at me and then back to Vince. "You guys okay?"

"We good here, Q?" Vince asks me with a knowing smile on his face.

"We're good." I nod, our chat affirming that he most definitely has Hawke's back.

"Well hot damn! I think Trixie needs to show up and deal us a hand! What do you say, Giz? You in?" Vince asks as Gizmo walks out the back door.

"Who in the hell is this Trixie?" Gizmo asks as he takes a seat.

When he bends over to get the bottle opener for his beer, Vince leans over and whispers into my ear. "He has no clue you're Trixie. We've been telling him she's another piece that Hawke and me are playing with on the side." When I frown at him, he just continues with Hawke snickering over his shoulder. "He's the one who pulls all the pranks on us on tour, so we like to fuck with him when we can . . . so . . ."

My eyes widen as I realize he's asking me to carry on their charade, and I can't help but laugh at poor, poor Gizmo. I glance back and forth between Hawke and Vince, their eyes begging me, and hell, I've had enough to drink, why not.

"Hey, Giz?" I angle my head over to him sitting beside me. "You haven't met my twin yet?"

"Trixie's your twin?" he says, the pitch of his voice escalating and his eyes lighting up.

Turning my body toward him, I lick my tongue seductively over my bottom lip, push my chest out, and rub my legs up against his. "Yeah," I say breathlessly, my fingertip tracing a line down his throat. "We're kind of kinky and like to play together—tag team a man or two when we find the right ones. We're *a lot* to handle, Trix and me." His Adam's apple bobs as he flicks his eyes over my shoulder to the guys who I cannot believe are not bursting out in laughter. "We're identical except for one minor detail. Most men can't figure it out after searching our bodies for hours. Do you think you could?" I lean in close and whisper in his ear, "Hmm. You're pretty damn sexy. I really think Trix would like you. She loves tattoos. Loves looking up at a man covered in them while she's sucking him off."

His breath hitches, and I hope to God Vince and Hawkin were being honest about him being the prankster on tour or else I'm going to feel like shit about this next part.

"You want to join us sometime?" I whisper as he nods

eagerly, his breath coming quicker now. "Mm-kay, well, the only requirement is that you're packing some heat," I say, my voice still seductive as silk as I slide my hand down his chest to the waist of his pants. I cup him softly through his jeans, suddenly feeling the weight of the guys' eyes as I play their game for them. "Whoa!" I say as I lean back and withdraw my hand.

"What?" he says, looking at the guys and then back, expectancy in his voice.

"I'm not sure if I'd even be able to feel you stick it in," I deadpan as the guys behind me erupt into laughter. Hawkin falls off his chair and knocks over his bowl of candy he's laughing so hard, Rocket spits out the beer he was drinking, and Vince pounds the table in his laughter, the poker chips rattling with each thump.

"*Ah, man* . . . fuck you, guys!" Gizmo says, shoving back out of his chair, the sounds scraping across the patio.

"I'm sorry," I say through my own laughter. "They put me up to it."

"Dude, paybacks are a bitch," Hawkin says as he pulls himself off the ground, still laughing, and pats Giz on the back.

"Okay, okay," Giz says and shrugs Hawke's hand off him in annoyance. He looks at the four of us in our uncontrollable fits of laugher, and I can see him fighting off his own smile before lifting his hands in surrender. "I deserved that after the shit I pulled last tour." And I don't know what he did, but obviously he's conceding to it so it must have been pretty bad.

Hawkin pulls my chair backward at an angle so my feet lift off the ground and he looks upside down at my face. "That was fucking perfect, *Trixie*," he murmurs, flashing me a megawatt grin before closing the distance and kissing me backward, his chin to my nose.

And holy shit after the day we've had, this little taste of him makes me want to take him upstairs right now and get the rest of him.

"You taste good," he whispers, unshaven cheek scraping along mine.

"Hmm, I taste even better somewhere else."

I love the groan he emits at my comment, but it's short lived when Gizmo slaps him hard on the back so that he almost drops my chair. "What the fuck, dude?" Hawke yells.

"I've got the feeling, man."

"It's about damn time! Been forever since one of us has." Rocket slams his hand on the table, startling me. "Let's get on it!"

Chapter 22

The rhythm owns my soul.

Rock and Vince are playing off the beat that Gizmo's pounding out like it's a song we've practiced time and again. My lips are stretched in a wide grin as I bob my head, fingers drumming on my leg, because we haven't just jammed for the sake of jamming in forever and the music we're making off the cuff right now is fucking killer.

Just like the good old days.

I adjust the soundboard to make sure we're recording this just in case we link notes we want to keep for anything new. We've had some killer shit come out of jam sessions before. Quinlan's sitting on the arm of the couch, head angled to the side, eyes steadfast on mine, and a smile on those sexy-ass lips of hers. Goddamn, the music's calling me, but hell if that sleepy smile and those bedroom eyes don't have me wanting to say *fuck the music* for the first time ever in my life.

With my guitar in my hand, I walk over to her, needing one taste to tide me over a little bit longer. A thrill shoots through me, tightens my sac, at the sight of her sitting up a little taller when she notices my approach. I take the back of the body of my guitar and place it against her back and pull her into me. Her tits pressed against my chest, her nipples so hard it's impossible not to notice the feel of them, make me doubt my decision about the music when I could be fucking her instead.

Damn. I have a serious weakness for this woman.

When I look into her eyes, I try to read what's there but we've either had too much to drink for me to comprehend it or she's guarding what she feels. Regardless, I notice and love the way her breathing changes the minute I touch her like this. It tells me she feels whatever this is too.

I press my lips to hers and sample what I plan on taking later. Damn if the warmth of her tongue, the taste of her beer, the softness of her lips doesn't have me swearing as she pulls away from me and against my guitar still pressed to her back.

I release her, and she falls to the couch behind her. And I can't help but glance down to her tits, her legs, and what's in between before flashing her a smirk and looping the strap over my neck. Ideas of just what I can do with my favored instrument and my hot woman later flash through my head as I walk over and plug my guitar into the amp.

Fuck. I just might have to cut this jam short with that image floating in my head.

I close my eyes, feel the music for a minute—the beat, the rhythm, the notes—before I can jump in. My body rocks to it instinctively as I find my chords to join the guys. And it's easy enough to do because we've been playing together for so long that I know where Vince is going to go with his riff and how to come in when it starts to fade some. Gizmo leads me into the jam, and Rocket rolls in right after me.

I concentrate, fingers moving to hit those first notes in synch with the guys, and I open my eyes for a moment to glance over at Vince to make sure he's good with where I took it on my side. He nods his head as he chimes back in. Knowing we're in sync, I close my eyes again, let my head hang down, and allow the world around me to slip away with each passing note as I become a part of the music that has saved and comforted me most of my life.

Losing myself in the music, I let go all of my anger from the fucked-up phone calls tonight from Hunter begging for money to probably get his next fix. The beat erases my past, bit by bit, memory by memory, sadness by sadness until all that's left is the here and the now: my best friends around me, Quinlan watching me, the music cleansing me from responsibilities I never asked for.

"You built me up. You tore me down. Left me to wear your poisoned crown . . ." The lyrics I've been toying with come without warning, and I'm so in my own head that I don't even realize I've said them aloud until I notice Rocket slow down his pace to keep with what I've belted out. I keep my head down, trying to avoid feeling vulnerable as I sing the words that come to mind and tell my story, but it's no use. Putting my thoughts to words then penning words to paper before turning them into lyrics is equivalent to cutting open my soul to expose the dirty, dark, bloody secrets I hold close. Every fucking one of them.

And yet I continue the temporary purge of my misgivings.

"I am not weak. I am not strong. Just a man left walking in a world where you made sure I don't belong." My voice breaks on the last word, and I squeeze my eyes shut as my fingers still on the guitar. The room falls silent around me, Gizmo's labored breathing from drumming the only sound of life.

"Holy fucking shit, dude!" Rocket says, surprise and admiration lacing through his voice. "Was that the shit you've been working on? Just . . . wow!"

He says something else that I don't catch because I'm so busy trying to come to grips with the things I just said, the feelings I just scraped from the scars on my soul that now feel open and raw. The things everyone around me knows about already. But coming out this way, through the emotion of a song, is so much more real than a monotone blow by blow.

I sucked at school but I remember learning that Orwell said good writing is like a windowpane. Too bad my lyrics are more like tempered glass, reflecting how I'm so broken and shattered, the shards never falling because they're being held up by invisible strings. Someday though all the pieces are going to come popping out one by one, till all that's left is a gaping hole surrounded by irreparable shatters.

I feel hollow now, afraid to look up, afraid to keep my head down because more memories might come that I don't want to think about. I feel more vulnerable than I have in a long fucking time and I know for a fact it has to do with Quinlan. I've let her in when I usually keep everyone at arm's length unless it's for that quick rocking in the sheets before I roll them out the door.

The realization hits me that maybe now after hearing my from-the-heart lyrics she'll realize who I am, what I come from, and that I'm not enough for someone like her. Yes, I've told her about my past but something about music reinforces the damage within me.

The thought hits me hard because hell yes, we're fucking good together but at the same time, she's got her shit together, her life together, while my number one hits don't mean shit when my life's shadowed daily by the next phone call from Westbrook, the next request from Hunter, the continual demise of my mom.

When I pull myself from my thoughts and find the wherewithal to raise my head, Vince is making sure the recording is there and then I see him flick the switch turning the soundboard off. Rocket and Giz are nowhere to be found. He meets my eyes with a nod of his head, a shift of his eyes over to where Quinlan sits behind me, and then walks toward the door.

I track his movement, too chickenshit and embarrassed to meet her eyes just yet. Vince stops with his hand on the door and says, "You did good, man. Let's hope it feels as good for you to get out as it did for us to hear."

All I give him is a single nod in acknowledgement as I fiddle with the strap on my guitar before he closes the door. Sighing softly, I turn around on my stool, eyes still focused on my fingers as I rein in the needy bullshit I don't want to deal with right now. Hell, *right now*? Who am I kidding? How about never want to deal with.

And I feel awkward for the first time ever with her but I know it's only the mixture of alcohol and exhaustion and shit with Hunter that's making me feel this way.

"So . . ." I say, trying to find my way through the minefield I've led us into. "I'm feeling a little . . ." My voice trails off as I find irony in the fact that I've just sung lyrics so honest and telling, and yet now I'm uncomfortable saying how I feel about it.

"Did you say something?" she asks, her tone chock-full of confusion that has me lifting my eyes to meet hers. "Sorry, I wasn't listening. I was too damn busy thinking about having sex with you."

The smile comes naturally to my lips, and it matches the desire that's a constant when she's around. "Is that so?" I rise from my seat, swing my guitar to rest against my back, and walk toward her, wondering how she can know a comment like that is just what I needed to break up my sudden discomfort.

Standing in front of her, I enjoy listening to her breath hitch when she runs her eyes up the length of my body. And then those eyes of hers—liquid amber—lock onto mine, her eyebrows lifting as if to say *What are you waiting for?*

And I don't know why I'm waiting, but there is something about the moment, the lyrics, her being here that makes me want to stand here a minute and let it all sink in before I lose myself to her.

Because that's what's going to happen. I can deny it all I want, tell myself I'm a man who needs no one, let alone the same set of lips to kiss him before sleep each and every night, but I'd be lying to myself. And not very well either. Maybe it's Quin, maybe it's the idea that I'm finally so fed up with Hunter I know the last straw is about to break. Maybe it's the realization that my mom may still be here but I really lost her all those years ago. . . . I'm not sure. What I do know is that I crave the normalcy of a relationship, a home life without the constant shadow of grief and weight of a promise that's not mine to keep.

I crave the love that will make me weak and know it's not in the cards for me.

Her hands on my hips shock me from the shit suddenly clouding my head and bring my thoughts to exactly where they need to be. Right here. Right now. On her and how she's touching me and just what I should do with this guitar.

She pulls me closer and I go willingly, my dick front and center as she sits before me. I gasp, a shot of straight lust streaking down my spine when she snakes her fingers beneath my shirt and scrapes her fingernails along the top of my waistband.

I'm instantly hard—it's a thing with her—where when I've had more than my fill over the years it sometimes takes me a minute to catch up to the predictability of the moment. But when Quinlan touches me, I'm already thinking about how I'm going to want another night with her when the sex we're about to have is over.

Wanting more sex is a given, but rarely with the same woman time and again.

Her fingers make quick work of my zipper but instead of pulling my pants down, she leans forward to where my cock is now begging for attention and looks up. A slow siren's smile turns up the corners of her mouth before she darts her tongue out to wet her lips and fuck me; between the hunger in her eyes and her mouth open and willing, I know she's about to destroy me in every pleasurably painful way possible.

She leans forward and presses her mouth to the material snug over my cock and blows hard and long. The hot air from her mouth seeps into the fabric and feels like it's wrapping around my dick. It's like she's giving me the hint of a blow job, the tease of what she can do, and it feels so fucking good, I roll my head back and enjoy it.

Quinlan does it a few more times as her fingers tease the small amount of skin that she's bared. I roll my head to the side as she tugs my jeans and boxer briefs down, my dick springing up when she clears it. And before I can open my eyes and look down at her, she has me in her mouth.

Our brief conversation from earlier flashes through my mind: handing her my latest test results showing a clean bill of health, her showing me her pack of birth control pills and a promise her test results are the uneventful kind like mine.

And thank fuck for the forethought of that conversation because a blow job with a condom on is nothing compared to the feeling of a wet, warm mouth sliding over rock-hard flesh.

I hiss out a breath, maybe her name, I don't know because that would mean I'd have to think and right now there is absolutely no thought as her tongue slides across my head, dipping in to lick the drop of precum there. She wraps her lips around my crest, that fucking fantastic tongue owning me as it circles around and turns my knees to Jell-O. I'm gonna come on the spot.

I moan again, my hands gripping into her hair in reflex, gently urging her deeper although I'm pretty fucking sure I don't need to give her any hints because the woman knows how to give a blow job. And I've had a lot of blow jobs, the quintessential go-to from a groupie to try to get something more.

But Quinlan does this . . . ah . . . I forget what I'm thinking about because my eyes roll back in my head and her name falls from my lips as she takes me all the way into the back of her throat and her fingers press in that spot just beneath my balls that causes bursts of heat to ignite and that ache to burn.

"Feels so fucking good," I say in an exhale of air as she begins to bob her head onto the length of my cock: fingers stroking, mouth sucking, moan vibrating against my sensitized flesh. She looks back up, mouth full of me and her cheeks flushed, and for some reason it's that right there that pushes me to the point of no return.

My muscles tense, my balls tighten up, my dick swells to the point of painful as the coiled ache of need unfurls and explodes. I lose my mind, can't process anything except for the rush of pleasure I can only express with my jerking hips, my hands fisting her blond curls, and the cry of release sounding off the walls surrounding us.

It takes me a moment to come back to reality, for my breath to calm and my muscles to relax. When I open my eyes, I look down to see her sitting back on the couch, putting the cap on the bottle of water she just took a sip from, and a smug smirk on that mouth of hers that can own me like that any day.

We hold each other's gaze, exchanging words we don't have the courage to say aloud. And I can tell she's just as freaked as I am by it because she starts laughing at me. Fucking laughing.

Talk about going from feeling like a king to being knocked down to feel like a pauper.

"What?" I ask, smiling wide because *goddamn*, she's

beautiful. And incredible . . . in ways I never imagined when I saw those long legs of hers standing on the steps of the lecture hall as she argued with Axe.

"You look kind of funny," she laughs out as I look down at my own body and see how I look through her eyes. I have my shirt on, guitar still strung to my back with the strap across my chest, pants bunched around my shoes, and my dick just hanging out there.

When I look back up and meet her eyes, I fight my own smirk as I remove my guitar in a slow, deliberate motion over my head and lean it against the edge of the couch. I toe off my shoes and step out of my pants, hands stripping my shirt over my head, all while our visual connection never breaks.

"And you," I tell her, fumbling for the words to make sense because fuck, I never have to try at this kind of shit—have never really cared—but something about tonight, about the song, about what she just did to me, makes me want to care. She makes me want to be worthy enough to be with her.

"Me?" she asks, with that slight taunting raise of her eyebrows and purse of her lips as she waits for me to tell her what to do.

"Hmm, so many things I want to do to you, Trixie." I slide my eyes up and over her body, so many curves, so many places I want to get lost in. Leaning over, I place my hands on the back of the couch beside her head and dip down to taste that mouth of hers, the perfect combination of temptation and salvation in the simple meeting of our tongues.

Her eyes light up when she hears my comment and it's such a turn-on how her mouth falls lax when I pull back and just stare at her. "Stand up," I order and I see the slight hesitation in her movement before she slowly rises from the couch. The funny thing is that as much as I demand a woman give me the reins in bed, there's something sexy as hell in the fact that she questions handing her control over to me. It's as if she's telling me I don't need you, don't have to do this to feel needed, but *I want to.*

And fuck if that wouldn't bring this man to his knees.

Her hair falls down around her shoulders when I lift her

shirt over her head. I lick my lips and slide my eyes over the lacy pink bra, my dick already stirring and ready for round two at just the thought of what's hidden beneath. My fingers tickle over her stomach and push down her jeans, and I'm momentarily mesmerized by the matching panties underneath.

I lean into her so that I can unfasten her bra but I pull back just as she leans forward to kiss me. "Hmm," I exclaim, part groan, part protest because I want her lips on mine more than anything . . . but I want her naked first. The straps fall from her arms to reveal those hard nipples begging me to graze my teeth over them.

"I think . . ." I say, stepping back and angling my head at her. "I think it's time to test that rumor after all."

Confusion darkens her golden eyes before recognition flashes in them when she sees me reach out and pick my old guitar up by the neck. Her lips tilt up in a dare of a smile as she steps into me, taking her own lead in this seductive game. "Tell me, rocker boy," she says coyly, her tone breathless and her fingertip skimming up my chest, "is it true that you can you play this body like a guitar?"

Her fingers leave my skin and she palms her own breasts, thumbs rubbing over her nipples just like I want to, causing her head to fall back and a soft sigh to fall from her lips.

"I'm gonna bang you like a goddamn drum set if you keep that shit up," I murmur as I use every ounce of restraint not to drag her to the floor and fuck her until we're breathless and spent.

Her rasp of a laugh only challenges me further. "Arms out, Trixie," I command, causing her head to snap forward to figure out what I'm going to do next.

She holds her arms out to her sides and doesn't say a word when I stare at her body momentarily as I figure how to work this, before stepping forward. Screw it, never hurts to try new things.

I take the guitar and place it at her back much like I had earlier before the jam session except for this time, I plan on it staying in place on its own volition. I match the neck of the guitar to her outstretched arm before looping the strap around her biceps once. Next I run the strap under the swell of her tits, my mouth dipping to taste and flick my tongue over each nipple in the process. She hums in appreciation, her eyes brimming with desire when she realizes my intent after I repeat things, looping the strap around the other biceps before reattaching it to the guitar.

When I step back and look at her, trussed up on my favorite guitar, strap pushing her boobs up so that her nipples are begging for attention, I know that even though I may be the one playing her like a guitar tonight, she sure as hell is unknowingly playing with my heart by standing here so willing, so open, infiltrating every part of my life.

She's such a sight standing before me, I can't hold back any longer. I place my hands on the side of her face and brush my thumbs over her cheekbones before kissing her softly. Taking my time, I build up the kiss and the moment to try to curtail that constricting feeling in my chest as I try to accept truths about what I feel for her that I don't want to face yet. I want to give her soft and gentle before I work her into the frenzy that's coming.

I'm still moving too fast, and I want to draw this out so I drop to my knees in front of her, fingertips trailing up and down her outer thighs and then tracing the lacy edge of her panties. Goose bumps chase across her skin, visual proof of how much my touch affects her as I pull the fabric down, my lips grazing kisses here and there as I follow their descent.

"Hawke." She moans my name softly in that *please stop, please don't stop* tone that urges me on further.

There are so many things I want to say, so may things I want from her right now, but as hot as the idea of telling her them are—spread your legs more, get ready to come, how bad do you want me—I say none of them. Sometimes the use of touch to speak is all the words you need.

She gasps when she sees me take a guitar pick between my fingers and her reaction is music to my ears. I begin to trace lines very slowly up each inseam, my actions causing her to spread her legs for the access I need. She begins to writhe, pushing her hips toward my face in front of her as I reach the apex of her thighs.

I can't resist. She's just proven the chink in my armor of restraint because no man is going to forgo his mouth on a pussy when it's being thrust into his face. So I give into her temptation. I move both picks to one hand while my other hand parts her slick lips. My tongue flicks out and hits her clit, moving over the bundle of nerves before sucking on it.

She moans my name into the silence of the room, and I love the sound almost as much as watching her squirm from the onslaught of sensations caused by my mouth. Keeping her sex spread apart with one hand, I use the other to take a guitar pick and slide it softly over her clit.

"Oh God!" she groans, her hands fisting in their strapped position. I guess I don't have to worry about if she likes it or not.

"Is there something you want?" I ask, grazing her clit with another flick from the pick.

She jerks her hips forward as I sit back on my heels, my dick more than begging to get in on this action. Her tits jiggle with the motion and I wonder just how long I can draw it out, bring her to the brink and then let her fall without crossing over the edge. I have no clue but it's sure as fuck going to be fun trying to find out.

"Hey, Quin?"

She looks down to meet my gaze. Her cheeks are flushed, her bottom lip is tugged between her teeth, and her eyes are hazy with desire.

"This studio is soundproof. Make sure you scream when you come."

Chapter 23

Stretching my legs out, the sheets slide over my bare skin that still carries Hawkin's scent from the incredible sex we had last night. *Incredible?* That's an understatement. How about the kind of sex that I'll forever think of as the time that ruined me for anyone else?

The man is definitely *creative* with his instruments. Damn. He brought me to the brink and denied me so many times that when he finally granted me my orgasm, I willingly drowned in the wash of pleasure that felt like it lasted forever.

And if I didn't know the answer before, I sure as hell know it now; Hawkin most definitely lives up to his last name and the rumor.

I let my mind wander over everything that happened between us last night. Watching their jam session was incredible but when Hawke started singing, it was almost like watching him purge the emotion he doesn't think he has the right to feel or express otherwise. His lyrics were a confession, a trace of the tumult he feels on a daily basis. From the continuous glances shared between the guys when Hawke left his head hung low and eyes closed, I could tell that him baring his demons like that was unusual. And of course when he was finished with the song, I could tell he was just as surprised by his lyrical confession as the guys were.

So I did the only thing I could do. I let him gather himself for a moment before using humor to dispel the unease in those gray eyes of his. And then once I got him to laugh, I let him use my body to help him forget. Little did I know that Hawkin's way of forgetting was by working me up into such a frenzy that I would have begged, pleaded, or borrowed for one more kiss, one more touch, one more look at him as he hovered over me before sinking into me.

I may not believe in the fairy-tale ending, but who cares? I'd challenge anyone to prove to me that Prince Charming can turn a woman out better than Hawkin Play did to me last night.

Bracing myself, I brave the bright light of the bedroom and open my eyes to find the bed empty beside me. I groan with disappointment but then notice the guitar pick placed on his pillow. My smile is automatic as is the ache stirring awake inside me at the little reminder he's left me—although there's no chance I'll be forgetting last night anytime soon.

Lost in that thought, I roll back over to notice that it's eleven o'clock. A *cat ate the canary* grin spreads on my lips because I'm an early riser, so the fact Hawke sexed me up so good I slept this late is a testament to just how fantastic last night really was.

And as much as I want to snuggle back under the covers, I want Hawkin more. I rise from the bed, muscles stiff from being oversexed, and I grab Hawke's Pink Floyd shirt draped over a chair. It's long on me and with my boy-short panties, I'm comfortable enough to cruise the house and look for him even with the other guys around.

After brushing my teeth and pulling up my hair in a messy ponytail, I open the bedroom door and pad down the hallway. Music plays near Gizmo's room and Rocket's distinctive laugh startles me from a room past the staircase. As I descend, I catch snippets of conversation floating up the stairs mixed with the clink of silverware against dishes from the kitchen below.

I must be crazy because I suddenly have butterflies over the idea of seeing Hawke. It's ridiculous and silly but I love it because a man who gives you butterflies is definitely a man you can lose yourself in.

"Dude, sugar does not equal breakfast." Vince's comment has the smile spreading across my lips.

"To me it does. Now get back to what you were ragging on me about. *Please.* Nothing is better than a lecture after a great night of sex," Hawkin says sarcastically.

"Look, I haven't seen you like this about a chick in a long-ass time. If ever." Vince's words cause my feet to falter, the rational side of my brain and the curious side in an instantaneous war whether to announce my presence or eavesdrop.

Curiosity wins.

"What business is it of Quin's? She's my life, my responsibility." My ears quirk up at the same time a sinking feeling clips the butterflies of their wings. "I still love her. Regardless of everything . . . I can't not." The resignation and pain in Hawke's voice tug at my compassion while the actual words make my head spin with a slow, uneasy discord.

"Look, I like Quin a lot too. Think she brings out a side of you that I've never seen before . . . I just think she has a right to know that Helen comes first. And always will. That you're going to leave at the drop of a dime when you get the call."

Helen? Calm down. There has to be a reasonable explanation here.

"I know—it's a fucked-up situation. . . ." Hawke says and then the clatter of dishes drowns out the rest.

"That's exactly the problem though, Hawke. If this plays out, Quin deserves to come first . . . and she won't. Dude, I get the hold she has over you but fuck man, you gotta live your life and quit beating yourself up over what's happened." I can sense Vince's aggravation, can hear it in his tone, and my mind wanders to what they can possibly be talking about. I try to fill in the missing pieces that the kitchen clatter drowns out. "If Quin sticks around like she looks like she will, she's gonna find out sooner or later; it's going to be best if you tell her about everything."

"Ben's been able to keep my past zipped up so that no one knows about her, about any of it unless I want them to."

My mind connects the dots, and understanding dawns about why even though I researched him, his father's death was never mentioned. Somehow, some way, his boyhood friend used legal means to secure his past. Privacy about his father's suicide I can understand, but what the hell are they talking about now?

Once again I find myself in the dark surrounded by the secrets Hawkin keeps. And I'm not a fan of secrets or the dark.

"But there's always Hunter now, isn't there?" Vince says, the room falling silent.

My mind reels and imagination runs wild. Does Hawke have a child? Has he been married? Was he in an accident and his girlfriend was injured and now he feels he owes her? What could possibly be so stressful that he can't tell me?

My stomach churns with the possibilities and I'm not fond of any of them. Do I stay or do I leave undetected? I'd rather find out what is so horrible now before I fall even harder for Hawke than I already have. The best way to face it is head-on so I enter the kitchen just as Hawkin says, "The constant wild card in my life."

"Good morning." Vince and Hawkin's bodies jolt at the sound of my voice.

"Morning," Vince nods cautiously before shooting Hawkin a knowing glance and walking out of the kitchen.

"Sorry, was I interrupting?" I ask as I meet his eyes, hoping my eavesdropping isn't given away in them.

His answer is to tug on the hem of his shirt I'm wearing and pull me into the V between his thighs. He wraps his arms around my waist and with the height difference of him sitting and me standing, he buries his face into my chest and holds me tight.

"Good morning, sleepyhead," he murmurs, the warmth of his breath seeping through my shirt and into the sensitized skin of my breasts. And there's something so sexy about a man when he's willing to cuddle in broad daylight. It's that combination of rough and soft at the same time. The notion that he's willing to be caught by the other band members.

I wrap my arms around him in kind and try not to let the confusion over the conversation I just walked in on ruin the moment. I press a kiss into the top of his head. "Morning. Everything okay?"

I almost don't want him to answer, to ruin this, because

this feels so normal, so right that I don't want to worry about tomorrows or what most likely won't be for us. If he says yes, everything is okay, I know despite last night, he's still keeping secrets, and if he says no, then I fear he'll tell me something I don't want to deal with right now that might push me away.

The conundrum is we haven't known each other long enough for me to feel like I deserve to know the answer to the question, and yet my feelings have grown strong enough for him that I want to know.

He sighs and I can feel the tension in his shoulders. "Yes. No. Just shit I don't want to deal with right now," he says, giving me an all of the above answer that allows our ambiguous state to remain. "I know what would make me feel better, though." He looks up at me, eyes warm and inviting as his grin spreads slowly, the I'm-a-rock-god-bow-before-me one that I can't resist.

"I'm sure you do." Damn, just a few words and he already has that slow burn of desire simmering in my core.

"What instrument should we play today?" The amusement in his tone mixes with the lift of an eyebrow that has me laughing out loud.

"Oh, I'm sensing a new theme here. Working our way through the instruments now, are we?"

He slides his hands down to cup my ass, fingers sweeping ever so softly over the thin fabric of my panties between my thighs. "By the time I'm done with you, we'll have played a rock band's worth of instruments."

He keeps his hands on my backside and pulls me into him, his forehead to my midchest. I close my eyes and take a deep breath, confusion lingering within me over things I know I can't control: his secrets or my feelings. I tell myself that I need to take a step back from this paradox of a man.

I'm getting wrapped up too fast with him. And yes I think he feels similarly, but I also know there are way too many truths left untold. While I don't feel that he owes it to me to throw his soul and secrets on the table at this juncture, I know I've been completely open, and that scares me. Unfortunately I've been on the receiving end before of situations when you fall and there's no one there to catch you.

I tell myself that I need to tell him I'm super behind on

the first draft of my thesis and I need to go home to work on it. Separating myself from his sexy morning voice and addictive smile is necessary for the space I need to get a new perspective on whatever this is between us from the outside looking in.

Because falling in love is like the rain. You can't always predict it and when you do it might never appear, but you can always see the signs of it before it falls.

I know that if I take that step back, I'll see storm clouds bearing down on the horizon. I'm just not sure how I feel about that. Living in Southern California, rain isn't something I see a lot, and when I do, I love it for the first few hours . . . until I realize it's ruined that perfectly composed appearance of mine. Once it makes my hair frizzy and my makeup run, I start to drown under its dark cloud.

And then there's the thought that if it is raining, Hawke and I haven't even given an ounce of thought to what comes next. We're too busy enjoying the now, the intensity of getting to know each other in all senses of the word, and haven't even thought about the umbrella to prevent us from getting soaked. He has a tour coming up; I have my thesis. . . . Ugh. I'm beginning to overthink crap I shouldn't even be thinking about because shit, it might not even rain. Damn forecasters are always wrong.

"What are you thinking about?" Hawke murmurs, his breath heated against my skin, pulling me from my sudden and unexpected analysis.

"The rain."

Hawke leans back and looks at me with an amused expression and a lazy smirk on his lips. "I hate the rain," he says, making it hard to form a coherent response. I know he doesn't know my metaphor, but I can't stop my breath from hitching nonetheless because now that I know he hates the rain, I kind of want it to pour. "But I can think of a helluva lot better ways to get you wet."

My laugh comes freely as his fingers press with intent between the apex of my thighs, that tingling ache simmering in my lower belly at the feeling. A soft sigh falls from my lips as Hawke stands, sliding his chest all the way up my body in his ascent, making me forget all about the rain I want to fall until it falls. We stand face-to-face, lips inches apart, and senses on high alert in preparation for the wild frenzy we bring out in each other.

Your thesis, Westin. Step back and get some distance. Put this back on an even playing field.

I hear myself all right, know what I should do, but when Hawkin leans forward and presses those delectable lips to mine, tongue slipping between them to lead the seductive dance I know I can't resist, my only thought is *Later*.

Much later.

I'm about to play in the rain.

Chapter 24

"So things are looking good," I muse as I tap my pencil on the counter. The lyrics have been coming on and off all day so my pad sits in front of me, scattered prose scrawled randomly across the page. When I glance down at them, I realize they all reflect a man infatuated with a woman.

How the hell did this happen?

"Thank fuck, because for a while, there, man . . ." Vince says, pulling me from my thoughts and from my lyrics that seem . . . happy somehow rather than the angst-ridden ones I usually write. *What am I supposed to do with happy?* Vince blows out a breath and runs his fingers through his hair. ". . . I was worried it was all going to fall to shit."

"No way, man. The tour's shaping up nicely, the new single is dropping in two weeks," I say, feeling a little relief that the stress on the business side of things is under control. The front door slams from the front of the house; both of us glance at the clock, knowing it must be Gizmo going on his daily run.

"And . . ." Vince says, knowing there's more on my mind. And of course there is, there always is, but am I going to jinx it by saying it out loud?

"Hunter followed through with his promise."

"No shit."

"Yeah." I hate that my immediate thought right after I say the word is *for now*.

"Well, there's that." Vince lifts his eyebrows as we both fall silent for a moment. "So what does he want?"

"Vince." I sigh knowing he's right on target but Hunter's my brother, only I can say shit like that about him and it be okay. The sad thing is Vince has been more of a brother than Hunter has and has earned the right to make the comment so I let it go.

"I'm not trying to be a dick man but tiger, stripes," he says with a shrug of his shoulders. "There's always a calm before he causes a fucking storm. Every damn time. A few nights ago he was blowing up your phone for money, and now, what? He's behaving? Something's off there. Just be careful is all I'm saying."

"Duly noted," I say knowing he speaks the truth. I've been burned enough by the damn calm. "But I'm trying to focus on the positives here: the band, Rocket stepping up and figuring out how to twist that last riff on 'Twisted' and killing it, the—"

"Quin rubbing your dick often enough you'd think it's a genie's lamp," he says cutting me off and shifting the gears of the conversation. "I mean, if we're talking about positives . . ."

I hang my head and laugh, surprised him fucking with me hasn't started sooner. "Well, my dick does grant wishes," I quip, earning me a snort and a *"Bullshit"* from his side of the room.

"Something that small's not big enough to grant anything let alone an orgasm."

"Fuck off," I tell him, throwing my pen at him. He catches it and raises his eyebrows as in *Not bad, huh?* "You're just jealous I'm getting nightly action when you're not."

"I am too!"

"Dude, barflies and groupies don't count. If you can catch an STD standing within two feet of them, they don't count."

He shakes his head with a laugh. "Aren't we all high-and-mighty now that we're the ringmaster of her Quin-kitty."

"It's the lead singer thing," I tell him, knowing how much it pisses him off. "We get all the Grade A."

"Lead singer thing, my ass." He grabs a beer from the refrigerator and holds it out. I nod and he grabs one for himself, pops the tops of both of them, and walks back and hands it to me.

"Thanks."

"For the beer or for the push to go after Trixie?"

"Both." I stare at him and try to gauge where he's trying to direct this conversation.

"Hm . . . so your seminar ends when—this Thursday?"

"Yep." I'm so distracted by the sudden bridge that just came to my thoughts I'm scrawling it out rather than picking up the bread crumbs he's dropping.

"We should throw a party after it. A kind of *thank fuck that's over* type of thing."

"Yeah, sure . . . sounds good." I read the line I wrote, cross it out, and rewrite it. The perfect version of it is just beyond my reach, but I know it's there.

"Or should we wait until after your court date next week?"

"No, this week is fine. Next week is crazy." I blow out a breath, lyric lost at the sudden panic piercing through my concentration that all this could have been for nothing: the seminar, forcing Hunter to make empty promises I know he can't keep, my inevitable fall from grace. Shit, the only good that's come out of this whole situation is Quinlan.

"I added an appointment at Sledge's on your calendar," he deadpans, and now I'm sure as shit listening.

I snap my head up to meet his eyes when I hear the name of our tattoo artist. "Excuse me?"

"We made a deal, brother." He smiles smugly. "I'm in the mix or there's no proof."

Irritation flickers and flames. "What exactly is it you're looking for out of this besides just plain trying to piss me off?"

"You tell me, Hawke." He stares, lips pursed, telling me to figure it out myself. "A bet's a bet."

"Yeah and an asshole's an asshole." I don't have time for

his games. He's angling at a point, wouldn't take this approach if he wasn't, but I'm just trying to figure out what it is.

"I bet you'll look pretty in pink."

"And I think you'll look uglier with my fist in your face. What gives, Vin?"

"What was the bet?" I look at him like he's losing his mind.

"Tame the untamable. Sleep with Quin by lecture's end, you in on the action for proof, or else I get the tat of stupidity." I roll my eyes, exasperation setting in. "But that was before. . . ." My voice trails off as I wave my fingers in a gesture of irrelevance.

"Before what?"

"Nothing. Never mind." I bite the words off, the unspoken confession hanging there that I don't want to fess up to yet. I'm just not sure if my hesitancy is because I don't want Vince to know or if I'm not ready to admit it to myself.

"Never mind? What, you got a thing for her?"

"No. Drop it."

"Drop what?" Vince goads me with a smug smirk that irks me to no end. What the fuck is he trying to get at here?

"You wanted to know about the bet? What about it?" All I want is to change the subject.

He narrows his brow and studies me. "Did you sleep with her?"

I give Vince an *are you that fucking stupid?* look. "Nope."

It's his turn to give me the *fuck you* sigh so common between us. "Dude, the studio's walls aren't *that* soundproof. Jesus, the two of you almost got me off from audio alone."

"Damn, that was hot," I'm unable to resist commenting because fuck, *it was.* I don't think I'll even be able to play that guitar again without the image of her on it distracting me. Shit, I just might have to hang that puppy on the wall with some of my other favorites. . . . The best part is everyone will assume it's there because I wrote this or that song on it. It's none of their fucking business I wrote music on it but not the kind they're thinking about. "But wait, if you've heard us, why do you need proof?"

"Because a bet's a bet. Why not finish it?"

"Hmm. Who said I wasn't going to?" I say although my head is screaming *over my dead body*. Sharing Quinlan and the goddamn perfection she is between the sheets and the kind I'm finding out she is beyond the bed—patient, feisty, naughty, thoughtful—is out of the question.

So now of course I'm between a rock and a hard place when the only place I want to be back between is Quinlan's thighs. Do I go back on my word for the first and only time in my life with Vince, balk on our bet? Or do I just follow through, stay true to the wager, and hate myself for doing it?

But what about being true to myself?

I swear to fucking God women are like alcohol. They smell great, they taste delicious, and right or wrong, they kill you slowly, one way or another. But shit, death by the slow burn Quinlan's lit within me sounds like a pretty fucking perfect way to go.

"Well, let's see, I don't hear you inviting me into the mix to finish the bet off." I groan as Vince's words pull me from my thoughts, from the vision floating in my head of Quinlan lying on my bed, legs spread, eyes inviting, and her lips begging me to fuck her. Jesus if the image was any hotter it would be a goddamn porno.

"Could it be that Quin means more to you than a romp in bed? That for once you're seeing the one thing I've been trying to get you to see for the past . . . umm . . . forever? Might you be falling for her, Hawke? Might she actually think you're worth it?"

"No." *Yes.* He's fucking with my head in this conversation, and I'm not too thrilled about it. We're in uncomfortable territory for me. That place I don't delve except for in my own mind. The dark inadequacies I refuse to speak about must be rather transparent since Vince is calling me on the carpet over them.

My pride, my ego, everything I hold on to tightly to prove that I am not the weakling my dad was. I can't fall for anyone, because the one thing I know . . . is that love makes you weak.

I hate the bullshit pile of emotions I feel right now. That contradiction between what I've always believed and that weird stirring wanting to see Quinlan again. Gauging my days on if she's gonna come around. *Fuck, this is fucked.*

"What are you, Vince? My goddamn shrink?" I'm a little irritated and a lot annoyed. I don't like having my hand forced, especially not in this arena . . . and he knows that so why is he trying to use a bulldozer to push home his point?

"Nope. Just looking forward to you getting that tat."

"Not gonna happen. I keep my goddamn word—every fucking time—so don't you go start questioning my integrity now." Or what Q is beginning to mean to me. *Fuck.* Why did I agree to this bullshit bet?

"Oh so this thing with Quin is really all just about the bet then? Seems to me like things might have changed on your end."

"No. Yes. Sure. You'll get your proof at the party, then you can get the fuck out of my business, got it?" I shove up out of my chair, pissed and done with this conversation.

"Stubborn asshole, you're missing the point!" he yells to my back as I walk out of the kitchen only to find Hunter sitting on the bottom step of the stairs. His presence stops me dead in my tracks, but it's the smug look on his face, the twisting of his lips, and the amusement in his eyes that I need to worry about. They tell me that he heard way too much of our conversation. *Fuck.*

"So Quin was just a game, huh? One of your stupid band bets?" He doesn't hide his thrill over the opportunity that just presented itself, and I hate myself for giving it to him. "I'm sure she'd love to hear about that."

"Nah. Vince was just fucking with me," I lie to my twin, knowing if I let on how much I don't want that to happen, it'll only spur him on to tell her. My mind starts rifling back over the rest of our conversation trying to figure out just how much Hunter heard. Goddamn it. The front door wasn't Giz after all, it was Hunter and that means he might have heard everything.

"Yeah, right. Did you forget we have that twin thing going on?"

"Not very smart to bite the hand that feeds you, right, Hunt?" Vince says, stepping up behind me.

And fuck yes he says what I want to but sometimes it's a

helluva lot easier to just shut the hell up than to make Hunter go on one of his little tirades and fuck up my life some more. Sometimes it takes more of a man to turn the other cheek and appear to be a pussy than it does to plow my fist in his face and tell him I'm done.

But fuck if that time's not coming sooner rather than later. A man can handle shit dealt to him over and over, swallow his pride and bite his tongue, but involve that man's woman, and *it's on*.

And I just called her my woman. FUCK! Can anything be more of a mess right now than my head? I scrub my hands over my face as Hunter finally answers Vince.

"Not biting anything," he muses, smirk still in place. "Just making an observation is all."

We all stare at one another, the animosity vibrating between the three of us and just once I want to see my brother and be happy. Just once I don't want to question his appearance and try to figure out what he wants from me, how he's trying to stab the knife in my back while reaching his hand out with the other.

When I step closer, I can see red in the whites of his eyes, notice the delayed response of his tracking, and bite back the reprimand on my tongue. "You high?" He stares at me like he's offended I asked. Is he fucking serious? *"Answer me,"* I demand through gritted teeth.

"So a party, huh?" he says, ignoring my question and ratcheting up the tension. "That ought to be fun."

"You using, Hunter?" I ask again, the straw slowly breaking. My hands fist at my sides and I'm a millisecond from grabbing the front of his shirt and throwing him the fuck out of the house.

"Naw, man. Just drunk and wanting to party a bit myself, but I seem to be outta cash. Can you help a brother out?"

"Fucking unbelievable." Vince snorts behind me.

"Don't you have somewhere else you need to be right now, Vinny?" Hunter sneers at him.

"Nope. He lives here. You don't," I say to cut off his power play as well as his drunk tough-guy routine. "How'd you get here, Hunt?" I ask, emotion roiling inside me as I see his keys on the floor by his feet.

"Can't a guy just visit his brother when he wants?" He

laughs and it grates on every nerve I have right down to the very last one.

"You drove, didn't you?" It seems we're on the repeat-each-question-twice routine here and my patience is done.

He just throws his head back and laughs. "What's so fucking funny, Hunter? A DUI?" Vince growls as my brother keeps laughing.

"It's okay," he says, holding a hand to his gut. "My brother will take the rap for me."

And I *snap*. Every pent-up emotion I've had over the past few years, every ounce of hatred, resentment, guilt, balls up in my clenched fist and is the driving force behind it as it connects with my brother's face in an unsatisfying crunch.

He goes down for the count with my first hit. His drunk ass is sprawled on the stairs and I'm so angry, so pumped full of hatred that I want him to wake the fuck back up so that I can keep going. My body is vibrating and my mind is a constant slide show of the years and all of the shit I've let him hold over me.

"It's about fucking time," Vince murmurs.

I rock back and forth on my heels before looking over my shoulder to find him wide-eyed and staring at me, asking me with the look if I'm all right with what I just did. And fuck yes, I am, and hell no, I'm not, all in the same damn breath. "I gotta get out of here," I tell him, suddenly restless, unsettled that I've just gone against everything I've ever told myself I couldn't do.

But fuck does it feel good.

"I'll take care of him," he says. And I know he will; it's just that I feel guilty for making him. *Fuck that, Hawke. Fuck the guilt. It's not on you.*

Well, shit. Guess there's not going to be any calm before the next storm. I look at my brother and sigh.

I hit the road, drive for what feels like hours. I don't know where I'm going or what I'm looking to find, but as long as I keep moving, my past can't catch up to me.

At least it's a good idea in theory because I can't outrun this shit. The stuff I want to and the stuff I don't want to.

I end up the one place I used to go to be alone, to think,

and as I stare at the Hollywood sign from my seat on the grass at the Griffith Park Observatory, I love the feeling that I'm this little person in this big world. The idea comforts me some. The notion that on the grand scale of things my problems are minute. Someone out there has it way worse.

And no one expects a rock star to be here so with my hat pulled low on my head, I'm able to disappear.

I stare down below to the city where as a little boy, scared and traumatized, I wondered how all of the dreams inside my head could ever see the light of day when I felt like I had the responsibility of the world on my small shoulders. But I did. *And I made it.*

So why do I feel like I'm still not enough? For my brother? To make my mother better? For Quinlan to even want me beyond the killer sex we have? For the fans who scream and sing my lyrics like they live them when they have no fucking clue the meaning behind those words and the damage within from them.

I scrub my hands over my face, needing a drink, craving an ice-cream cone, and wanting the feeling of Quinlan's arms wrapped around me as she silently sits there and just *is* with me.

My mind veers to Hunter. To the look on his face as I threw my punch. I push the guilt away, hold on to my gut-check rationalization that he deserved it, and realize that's the trouble I'm having here. Going with my gut versus going with the bullshit promises I've lived by forever.

My stomach churns and my head feels like Gizmo's banging the hell out of it with his sticks. I shove up off the grass, needing to get the fuck out of here, my heart and head in conflict, and for the first time in forever I dare to think what could happen if my heart finally won for once.

After I start my car, I sit there for a moment, trying to figure out where to go next. I feel like nothing has changed in my day to day, absolutely nothing, so why when I look back do I feel like everything is different?

I exit the parking lot and begin the long descent down the hill to reality. And I know without even directing the car that I'm headed to Quin's house. She may have told me she needed to work on her thesis to get the space I saw in those panicked eyes of hers, and I might be heading there with a head fucked up and a heart still in tumult if it can actually love without ruining me, but I need to see her.

Chapter 25

When she opens the door, I feel like I can breathe for the first time in forever. Her lips part in surprise and then turn upward in a slow smile, but I also can see her hesitancy, the guard that's up in her eyes. A shudder of panic darts through me and I feel lost, unsure what has changed between the two of us. The world beneath my feet seems to be shifting—beliefs, promises, truths, all of it in doubt—and I can't have whatever is causing these changes—*her*, *us*—not be okay.

"Hey," she says and motions for me to come in but then holds her hand up in the air in a *one minute* gesture. I see the phone in her hand as I follow her into her family room. She motions for me to sit on the couch but I'm too restless to sit because all I want to do is pull her toward me and kiss her senseless. It's like I can't get enough of her, and I need to abate this burning in my gut.

She leans against the kitchen counter with a smile on her face from whatever the person on the other end of the line says. "Well, that sounds like a great idea. I'll have to take you up on that," she says before falling silent while the person speaks again. She laughs affectionately, and I can't tear my eyes away from her. "Well, I've got to get going—someone's here. . . . Uh-huh, but I'm glad you called. Bye, Luke."

What? Talk about whiplash. I stare at her as she takes her time setting her phone down before she walks toward me. "What a nice surprise!"

I don't know if it's all of the shit in my head and my fight with Hunter mixed with my sudden want for her to be only mine, but my temper flashes without forethought. "Who the fuck was that?"

"Luke. Is there a problem?" She stops and places her hands on her hips.

Quin has every right to be annoyed by my question. Hell, she's probably playing me and pushing my buttons on purpose, but I'm not in the mood for games. I've dealt with enough shit as it is today and am at that point where my confusion and emotional turmoil and need for her all crash together into a perfect storm waiting to explode.

"Yeah, there is. I thought we . . . I mean we . . . What are you talking to him for?" I grit the words out, frustrated at myself for being so flustered and playing into her game if she is in fact playing one.

"Because I want to." And the way she says it, challenge mixed with *what are you going to do about it*, has me angling my head and questioning myself again.

"Not when you're with me, you won't."

She stares at me, arms crossing over her chest and that fuck-you lift to her chin. "I'm with you? Because unless I'm mistaken being with someone means that you don't hide shit that's a need-to-know. We've never talked about being exclusive so I'm free to do what I want, right?"

"We're exclusive." I react without thought, my own answer surprising me.

Quin stares at me for a beat, eyes wide, lips parted before shaking her head in disagreement. "No we're not. Being exclusive means closet doors are open so we can peek at the skeletons inside . . . and yours? Your doors are locked shut and that's not okay with me."

Is she rejecting me? What the fuck am I missing here? Fear that I'm going to lose her when I just realized I want more with her hits me. "What are—"

"You're pissed I'm talking to Luke . . . so I can be pissed you haven't told me about Helen, right?"

Her words take me by surprise. My mind stumbles, panic

replacing my anger again—but of a totally different kind than when I knocked on the front door minutes ago. I must look like a deer in the headlights trying to figure out how she knows about my mom because she answers the question for me.

"You and Vince were talking about her in the kitchen the other morning, and I overheard," she says with a quiet, resigned hurt in her voice.

And things start to click into place for me. Her sudden departure after we had sex. The flustered excuse to work on her thesis that didn't match the deception in her eyes. Almost like she'd fallen into the lust of the sex with me and once it was over, she realized that it was all too much . . . but in reality she was thinking I was cheating on her or double-dipping or what-the-fuck-ever with the person we were talking about in the kitchen.

I've held my mom's privacy so close for so long that my chest constricts when I think of letting an outsider in. And even though that person is Quin, trusting someone to know about my mom, the one person I love more than anything, my one and only weakness, paralyzes me.

I hang my head down and squeeze my eyes shut from the hurricane of emotion that is whipping inside me. "Helen's not who you think she is, Quin." The words are so quiet I'm not sure if she even hears me but when I lift my head to meet her eyes, I know she has. "Come with me somewhere?" The offer is out of my mouth before I can stop it.

We drive in an awkward silence toward Westbrook. Quin must have sensed my distress when I asked her to come with me because she stared at me for a beat before grabbing her purse and climbing in the car beside me.

I glance over at her, eyes shadowed behind her sunglasses and hands folded in her lap, and wonder what she's thinking. Does she have any clue what my insides feel like right now? Like they're being churned and twisted and filled with acid. She can't possibly because I haven't said a word and yet she still sits there in silent reassurance, allowing me the space I need to work through my inner turmoil.

"I knocked Hunter out." I'm not sure why I choose right now to confess this to her other than to break the silence.

"Well, he probably deserved it," she says matter-of-factly and asks nothing more. No *how could you punch your brother*? No *you don't do that to your family*. Nothing.

And yet I feel like I need to explain, purge the wrongdoing from my soul, because I continue, "I lied about some shit, took the fall for him, and he made a smart-ass remark about how I'd do it again."

"Vince told me about the drugs." It's all she says and it's so soft that all I can do is nod my head in affirmation. "Everyone has a breaking point, Hawkin. One person can take on only so much responsibility without buckling from its weight," she murmurs without any judgment of the lies I've told.

I keep my eyes fixed on the freeway in front of me as I let the comment resonate, knowing its truth despite the constant tumult that burdens me. A part of me sags in relief at her observation, knowing that someone else sees the cracks in my resolve, while the other part of me begins to question again.

And the scary thing about questions are they usually result in a revolution of some sort. I'm just not sure if I can withstand an overhaul of principles without it resulting in casualties.

"Am I the reason he's like this, Q? How did this person I've been with since conception . . . how can we experience the same tragedy but be so completely different? Did I try too hard, protect him too much, throw him to the wolves when I shouldn't have and end up proving I'm just like Dad?" I speak the questions floating around in my mind aloud, throw them out there even though I know there's no way in hell she has the answers.

She does nothing more than reach over and lace her fingers with mine, staying silent, but her unconditional support is deafening. Except even with someone beside you, the quiet has a way of smothering you when you're left alone with just your thoughts. And of course mine turn to where we are headed right now.

I don't have a clue why I'm so goddamn anxious all of a sudden when my thoughts veer to my mom. It's not like I'm a monster. It's not like anyone knowing she's sick is going to ruin me. It's none of the above so why does my dad's voice still ring in my ears as prevalent as the sound of the gunshot?

It's bullshit—the fear, the worry, the sense of the inevitable—but it's the truest thing I've ever had in my life. My mom might never remember me again, she might hate me, but she's still my mom.

She's my greatest love. And my biggest weakness.

Exposing her illness to the press, who'd splash it across magazine covers and make a spectacle of her because of me would break me when Dad's death nearly did just that. I wouldn't be able to protect her anymore from the glory-hound paparazzi, who would feed their greed by taking advantage of the insults her ailing mind hurls at me. How many people would stop and look at the cover of a rag if they proclaimed "murderer," "useless," "coward" as a precursor before *lead singer*?

They'd use her up and spit her out to get dirt on me without a second thought to collateral damage. If that happened, I would have failed her twice in my lifetime, and that's something I can't let happen.

You can't remove the scars of your childhood. They stay with you forever, an indelible mark to remind you time and again what you should or shouldn't do differently next time. And fuck if my scars aren't so deep my bones are grooved by their presence. Even in my own death they will remain.

So I've had Ben ensure that it appears that she's fallen off the face of the earth, so far buried in this Google era and HIPPA privacy laws that no one can bribe a facility nurse to repeat the insults and accusations my mom hurls at me as a means for tabloid fodder. Keeping her condition private, using her mother's maiden name on her patient history, means I no longer worry about someone manipulating her to get to me.

So why am I suddenly feeling like I need to tell Quinlan about her? Letting her in my private world is like unzipping my soul and letting her climb inside to the deep, dark recesses I choose not to delve into. I'm not the only one in life who has gone through this and yet the one thing in my very public life I've fought fiercely to keep private, I want to tell someone about.

Quinlan sitting here terrifies me and frees me simultaneously. My thoughts are running a thousand miles an hour, scattered in so many directions I can't keep them straight.

Years of obligation, hours of self-doubt, a lifelong inability to accept someone's love, all boil down to this . . . letting someone in when I'm so used to shutting everyone out.

Will she think less of me when she realizes I can't even take care of my own mother? That I have her in a facility to not only protect her but to protect my own image? I mean how fucking selfish does that make me? And what if my mom is having one of her sundowning moments and hurls vile things at me? What will she think of me then? Will Quin understand that underneath it all—my continual protection of Hunter, staying true to my word—all of it is some fruitless attempt to redeem myself and not be weak like my dad was? Ever again.

I suck in a breath when I realize my thoughts have transitioned so drastically in the past five hours that a damn sprinter wouldn't even be able to keep up with them.

I'm letting Quinlan in. *I want to let her in.*

I try to shut all of the noise out for a moment, quiet my head, and let the warmth of the sun against the car's window warm the cold parts of my soul. This is all too much too fast. The truths I've always believed to be true are now pouring down around me like the acid rain in this Los Angeles smog.

I don't know what all of this means for me or for the way I live my life. Shit, if throwing a single punch can cause all of these revelations, what the hell would happen if I actually allowed myself to let someone in? If I actually let myself love?

The thought staggers me, for the good and the bad. Blows apart preconceived notions in my world that I've tried so hard to make as predictable as possible.

My past has written the path of my future and made me who I am. For the longest time I thought it would be impossible to rewrite what's laid before me. But as I pull into the parking lot at Westbrook and glance over at Quin with her soft smile and blond curls floating from the breeze, I realize I don't want to accept that anymore. I have a pencil in my unsteady hand and when I step foot from this car, I'm attempting to write on a new page.

I just hope the lead sticks.

If not, I might be erased.

Chapter 26

I don't know who I thought Helen was, but I sure didn't expect to be entering this upscale assisted living facility to find out.

Even though I'm walking beside Hawkin, I feel so incredibly far away from him with each step we take into the depths of this bright and peaceful building. To think I've let the conversation between Vince and Hawke gnaw at my sanity over the past few days until I was convinced whoever Helen was would tear me apart. And then of course when he showed up earlier, I toyed with him by using Luke, and tried to push his buttons to get an answer to a question I should have just flat-out asked days ago.

As we approach a nurses' station, Hawke glances over to me; the uncertainty in his expression and the defeat of his shoulders break my heart over the internal battle he's waging right now. I have so much to say and nothing at all, all at the same time.

With my hand in his, I can feel his body tense up as the nurse behind the desk greets Hawke by name. Her eyes flicker over to me and I can see the startled surprise at my presence.

"Hi, Beth. She doing okay today?"

Beth's eyes hold compassion as she studies him and

nods. "Better than some days, worse than others. She hasn't been sleeping well so we're trying to play with some new ways to prevent her triggers."

Hawkin glances at a door on our left before smiling tightly at her. "Thank you," he says, his voice barely audible.

"I'll let her know you're here."

We follow Beth and within moments of her entering the room, she comes back out with a smile, and holds the door open for us.

Hawke hangs his head for a beat and takes a fortifying breath before he enters the room. I hesitate, suddenly uncomfortable, feeling like I'm invading his privacy, and hating myself for forcing him into a situation with my stupid accusation.

I walk warily into the room and take a position against the wall where he motions for me to stand. My heart is in my throat and for some reason I'm nervous of the unknown here. Our gazes meet momentarily and the look in Hawke's eyes tears at everything in my soul. He looks lost, scared, apologetic, and resigned and it takes everything I have not to reach out and pull him into me to assuage his pain.

But I know I can't. There is nothing I can do to help the war inside him that's written all over his countenance besides stand right here, offering silent support. He closes his eyes for a brief moment before turning to walk over to where a woman sits looking out a window with her back to us.

"Hi, Momma," Hawke says, cautiously lowering to his knees beside her. His words float calmly out into the stillness of the room and break my heart. Despite his warm greeting, Helen continues to stare afar as Hawke looks up to her, eyes searching, body language wary.

Everything in my body constricts in despair with the revelation that Helen is his mother. And in his short life, not only has he had to deal with the death of his father but also with whatever ails his mother. And then it all makes sense, the concert to benefit Alzheimer's. How could I have not connected the dots sooner?

"How are you doing today? It's nice and sunny out. Do you want to go for a walk through the grounds?" A lump forms in my throat at the hope in his voice and yet she just sits there stoic and silent. I can feel every part of him willing her to respond, to take notice of him, like a little boy seeking attention or approval, and it kills me. The sight of my bad-boy, good-hearted rocker on his knees and the anguished rawness in his voice make me want to wrap my arms around him and take it all away. "I'd like to take you outside, like when we were little and you'd take us to the park to watch the kites fly."

"I used to like the red ones best." The sound of her unemotional voice startles me but the look on Hawke's face has me wiping the tears away before they can fall.

"Yes, and we'd lay on the grass for hours and watch them in the sky above us," he says eagerly despite the melancholy tinge to his voice. He grasps desperately for a connection with her and yet she says nothing more despite his unwavering attention.

I'm scared to breathe, afraid to move so that I don't disturb them because even though I don't know specifics, I can tell that Helen's reaction has given Hawkin something to hold on to.

"Mom, I brought someone for you to meet," he says, glancing my way, anxiety etched in his features. "She's my friend," he explains with a pause to see if it will garner a reaction, without avail. "Her name is Quinlan."

Helen's head turns slowly toward him so that I finally get a glimpse of her. She has pale but beautiful skin; her dark hair is pulled back from her face so it's more than obvious from their profiles that they are related. Hawkin's eyes hold hers, his face mesmerized with hope, but I notice the fisting and releasing of her hands. My heart begins to beat faster as unease begins to fill me.

"How dare you bring one of your dirty, filthy, homewrecking whores into my house, Joshua?" she snarls at Hawkin. I watch her words hit him with more force than a knockout punch. His eyes widen and then blink rapidly and his mouth falls lax as he tries to digest them. At first I think his reaction is a result of her calling him his dad's name, but the more I watch the shock, hurt, and disbelief play over his features, I realize that it's so much more than that.

He's realizing the man he's idolized, the man he's lived his life to make proud, is a man he didn't really know at all.

"Were you trying to prove a point?" Her even voice begins to rise in pitch and emotion with each passing second and yet Hawke sits there in a shell-shocked state. "You think I don't notice the lipstick on your shirt collars, the late nights where you put *them* before us?" She's yelling now, starting to rise from her chair, and it's such a poignant image and yet so very wrong at the same time: the mother standing tall looking down to the little boy looking up to her from his knees.

And I don't know if Hawkin isn't moving because he wants her to finish what she's saying, complete the story that he's never heard before, or because he's frozen by the truths. Regardless, everything about him—his posture, his expression, the muscles lax in his body—says he's defeated, weary from the unfounded battle he's been waging.

"How dare you flaunt her in front of me!" she shouts even louder, hand flashing out, and the sound of the slap connecting with his cheek echoes off the sterile walls of the room. "Get out!" she yells, trying to pull Hawkin to his feet, aggressive hands digging into his shoulders with force. "Get out! We're done!" she screams again, fists beginning to connect with Hawkin's torso as he stands and tries to grab her wrists. "*You just lost your boys.* I'm telling them tomorrow and then I want you and your whores out of our lives forever!" The anguish in her voice sends shivers down my spine. Having been cheated on myself, my heart clenches for the injustice done to her, the desperation she must have endured, and the panic she must have felt knowing she was about to raise two boys on her own.

I have to look away though. I can't handle the sight of Hawkin standing there taking the rage meant for the man he's held on a pedestal. The look on his face will forever be etched in my mind, his pain raw, his disbelief palpable, his agony unrelenting. It breaks something inside me and if this is how I feel just watching it all unfold, I can only imagine what it's doing to him.

I glance at the door beside me; tears I didn't even realize were falling down my face blur my vision because there's nothing I can do to help with the hurt now, the devastation I can see in him.

"Mom! It's me, Hawkin. Mom!" he says over and over,

finally snapping back to the here and now, her fists reinforcing the pain her words just created. "Mom," he says, his voice breaking, and I hear the sob catch in his throat as helplessness sets in.

The door beside me pushes open, her shouts having caught the attention of Beth and some orderlies. I remain with my back against the wall as they enter and hope they can help save Hawkin from his own personal Hell.

Within seconds they are pulling her away from him, restraining her from going back for more despite the anger visibly vibrating over her small frame. But Hawkin hasn't moved his feet; he's a broken man staggered by hidden lies. Lies most likely told in good faith to protect the mourning little boy but that are now breaking the grown man.

Beth puts a hand on his shoulder and says something to him but it's almost as if he can't bring himself to look away. The nurse urges again and he takes two steps before stopping and looking back at his slowly calming mother.

"I'm so sorry, Mom." The broken and pained grate of his voice makes my chest constrict. He moves again, head kept down, but I see him wipe an errant tear from his cheek as he walks past me and out the door without a word. I scurry after him in silence as he strides through the facility with purpose.

He shoves the exit doors open with force, and I can hear him gasp for air as his chest heaves in a futile attempt to rein in the tears he doesn't want to fall and the shout I know he wants to yell at the top of his lungs. He does neither though. He bends over, placing his hands on his knees for a few silent moments before standing straight up and walking to his car.

He holds the keys to the car out to me and says, "Just drive."

I oblige without hesitation. I start the car, merge onto the highway, and drive to no set destination as he sits in absolute silence beside me, hands gripping his thighs and eyes fixated on the world beyond the windows.

I squeeze the wheel beneath my hands to prevent myself from reaching out and grabbing one of his to give him some kind of comfort. My mind spins, thinking of all of the things every son would want his parents to be proud of and knowing that he's had none of this. He's been the rock, the support, the everything for himself, and I know that what I told him in the car on the way to the facility holds true. Every man has his breaking point, and his absolute silence makes me fear that he just reached his.

Chapter 27

My arms scream and sweat runs down my chest. I have no fucking clue how long I've been banging on the drums, but I know that a part of me feels a little more whole while the rest of me feels a lot more empty.

The beat bangs in my ears like my dad's words to me over and over and over. And as fucked up as my head is right now, all I can think about is how wrong he was. And how absolutely right he was. It makes no fucking sense though. So I pound a little bit harder, try to lose myself in the rhythm I can't find to try to cover up the pain some when all I want to do is drown in it.

He told me love would make me weak, would kill me just like it did him. Well, I loved him, I loved my mom and both of them have brought me to my knees today with their lies and made me weaker than I've ever felt in my life.

How's that for fucking irony?

Just when I'm ready to take a chance and step out of the goddamn box he put me in, I feel like I'm blindsided by the truth that I'm just as weak as he was. My mom just proved that by knocking me to my knees with the hidden secrets she's kept locked in her erratic mind. The one woman I've loved . . . just made me weak. So these fucking drums are taking the punishment I'd love to throw his way right now.

When my mom screamed those words to me—the hatred, the accusations, the hurt—I swear that the image of the aftermath of my dad pulling the trigger flashed in my mind. But along with the old ones etched there came new memories. Ones so bright and powerful, they knocked the air from my lungs and no matter how hard I pushed them away, they just kept coming.

In that split second of time, I tried to rationalize that it was the Alzheimer's fabricating lies but deep down, I knew they were true. It was almost like hearing those words opened my subconscious, allowed me to remember details that the fog of his suicide repressed: the crammed suitcase on my parents' bed, my mom's red-rimmed eyes that morning she'd blamed on allergies, the continual guilt my mom carried like a badge before she transferred it unknowingly to me.

The images spin out of control. They are so vague and yet are so fucking vivid at the same time. I can't breathe. I want to throw up. I want to scream. To cry. To slide under the haze of alcohol and numb myself. To fade away for a bit.

Must run in the family.

The thought is distracting enough that my arms give out and the drumsticks slip from my hands to the floor below with a clatter. I grit my teeth and clench my fists and yet don't even have the fight in me to want to throw a goddamn punch in the air.

I know she's there, sitting on the couch she hasn't moved from since she brought me home to bang on Giz's drums. Something about the gesture, the fact that she remembered I said that's what I do when I can't process life, breaks momentarily through the haze of my confusion.

"I'm sorry I brought you there today, that you had to see that . . . but I wanted you to know." The words are out of my mouth so softly that she shouldn't hear them and yet I know she does because I hear her shifting on the couch. She must be wondering what the fuck to do, but truth be told, I don't even know. I mean, who the hell am I? A man who has lived another man's principles his whole life only to find out they were a lie?

"I wasn't sure if you wanted me to stay or be alone. . . ." Quin's quiet voice pulls me from the goddamn tornado of incoherency in my head and heart. I can hear the hesitancy in her voice but I don't have it in me to look at her just yet because I'm afraid if I do she's going to see more of me than I can through this fog of confusion. Silence suffocates the room, both of us unsure of what step to take next.

"Do you want to talk about it?"

Do I want to talk to her about it? Fuck no. How do I explain to her that the rug's been yanked so fucking hard out from under my feet that I don't even know where to land? Between punching Hunter and now this, the goddamn ground has shifted so much I think it's going to take a long fucking time for it to feel steady again.

But at the same time, I bite back all of the words on my tongue that want to come tumbling out because for the first time in forever, someone besides Hunter was there, someone knows what I go through to an extent. And as fucking cruel as it was for me to throw her into my fucked-up situation, I feel a tinge of relief for having her there.

"I don't even know what to say." I shake my head back and forth as I pick up my shirt beside me and scrub it over my face to buy myself time. When I lower my shirt, I raise my eyes to meet hers, and I don't know what I expected when I look at her but what I see causes my throat to burn. I see compassion instead of disgust, acceptance in lieu of judgment, pride not shame, and the combination of them all is more than I can process in my already overloaded system.

Her quiet empathy makes me feel things that are wrong to feel right now in the midst of me questioning everything about myself. And yet it's still there. That need to pull her against me and just cling to her, to have someone be there when before I would have probably pushed her so goddamn hard the other way.

"You don't have to say anything."

"I know, it's just . . . fuck . . ." I run my hand back through my hair again and don't know how to explain the emotions inside me. Almost like a cargo truck has turned on its side and all of this has come spilling out all over the place. "The only way I can explain it is like this. What if my dad told me that day that the sky was green? That no matter what anyone said, he was right and they were wrong. So I've spent my whole life believing that the sky is green. Fighting against the tide to prove otherwise, wearing blinders to the obvious. Would stake my life on the claim. And then one day someone ripped the blinders off for me to find that this whole time, my entire life, I've lived fighting to believe something, love a certain way, and it's fucking wrong. The sky is really fucking blue."

Tears well in her eyes as she nods solemnly to tell me she understands what I'm saying although I know she has no fucking clue. No one does.

"I don't know which way is up right now, what to believe anymore." I don't want to talk about anything and yet I keep doing just that.

"Well, everyone's version of which way is up is different so don't try to figure that out just yet. Who cares if you're sideways for a bit? That's allowed, Hawke, and perfectly understandable."

I squeeze my eyes shut momentarily. Memories flicker and flame through my mind. The four of us happy. That horrible day, the sound of the gunshot, the blood, the smell, the scream that never came frozen in my throat forever. The three of us mourning. Hunter and me trying to survive as our mom held on to the thin thread holding her to reality. Losing my twin bit by bit. Fighting like hell to keep it all together, protect them, provide for them. The times I'd start to feel that twinge of something in my gut for a woman only to shove her away because she just might make me love her. How hard I fought against so many things, how alone I've felt . . . and it was all a lie.

Every fucking thing.

"When my dad . . . that day," I start to say, focusing on the wear patterns of the mid-tom because I can't look her in the eyes while I explain how stupid I was to believe my dad blindly. "He made me promise that I'd take care of my family at all costs. He told me that when you let someone in, you lower your guard for love, you open yourself up to the worst hurt of all. You prove you're weak . . . and when you are weak, you end up like him."

The sharp inhale of her breath at my comment followed by my name on her lips sends chills over my body. And I don't need pity for being a stupid, goddamn lemming jumping without thought, following without questioning. And

I'm ready to bend over and pick up Giz's sticks again, deal with how that just made me feel, the fucking acid eating holes in my gut and worming its way into my heart.

"Hawke," she calls my name again but I can't meet her eyes. "You were only nine; do you really think it's fair to judge yourself when what happened probably scared the shit out of you? What normal kid wouldn't have tried to make him proud by living according to the promises he made you make? You can't fault yourself for that!"

I know she's right but it does nothing to abate the years of self-deprecation, the nights spent reliving every moment, the doubt that has ingrained itself into my psyche. "Yeah, but the problem is today just proved my dad right. I let the two people I love the most blindside me."

"Anyone who loves lets their guard down—whether it be for a pet, for music, for their parent, or for a lover— letting your guard down means that you feel, that you care. And hell yes, you open yourself up to being hurt but my dad used to always say, 'Hurting is feeling, and feeling is living, and isn't it good to be alive?'"

I snort aloud, immediately writing off what she's just said because it hits a little too close to home. I feel alive and numb all at once but the feeling part is so intense I feel like I could sit down and write a thousand songs to get it all out and it still wouldn't be enough.

And she's up off her feet in an instant of my nonverbal rebuff and approaches me for the first time since we've been in the studio for who knows how the fuck long. She stands in front of me, her face pulled tight with anger, and her hands on my shoulders force me to turn away from the kit to face her. "When you write a song, when you play it on stage, can't you feel it? Doesn't it make you feel alive?" She's not backing down and I'm a little shocked that she's so in my head she's confronting me with what I was just thinking myself. "Sure you lose yourself in your music, but you also find yourself, right? It makes you feel so that—"

"Don't you get it?" I lash out, my anger resurfacing through the haze and unfortunately being directed at her, but I can't stop myself. "Right now I hate him so goddamn much for doing that to me and in the same breath still love him. How is that not fucked up?" My blood is pumping and my hands start trembling from the rage inside me, my body wanting to shut down but my head refusing.

"Your dad did what he did and it had nothing to do with you." The quiet calm in her voice stops my mind from spinning for the first time since we left Westbrook. "He may have cheated on your mom, but that's on him. Your mom may have lied to protect you, to preserve his memory for you, and that's just being a good parent. It might take a while for you to see it but do you really think she knew what he said to you that day? Do you think she knew by allowing you to keep him as an idol in your life that you'd be left with this burden?"

"It's easier to live with the guilt." I don't know where the confession comes from but it's out and I can't take it back.

"Of course it is. You're human, Hawke. Why should you deserve all of this," she says, her hands out to the side, motioning at everything in general, "when Hunter can't get his shit straight, when your mom is fighting with dementia, when your dad took his own life? Of course you feel guilt . . . but you know what? You worked your ass off to get here, you overcame odds, you do deserve it."

She might be right but fuck if I want to hear it right now. I don't care if it was for my benefit or not. . . . Maybe I do. . . . Fuck! I can't process anything right now: good, bad, truth, lies, love, hate. I've toed the edge on some of them, but have always held the few ideals to be my grounding truth to find out they were all bullshit principles he never lived by himself. So I've lived a life full of empty connections because I was so fucking scared to end up a mess of blood and gray matter and hopelessness that I never allowed myself to love someone.

I just stare at Quinlan in front of me and recall how earlier I thought it was time to rewrite my own life some. I wonder why after all of this time I finally had thoughts of stepping outside my comfort zone and was feeling like in doing so I was going to let my dad down. And then this happened.

Fate's a fickle, funny bitch sometimes.

"Hawke?" Quinlan looks at me and despite the hesitancy in her eyes she steps in between my legs and puts her arms around me, pulling me into her. I sit, kind of stunned because her touch, her compassion, physically hurts me. It's like I don't deserve this from her, don't want to accept it, yet within moments I've tugged on her torso and am clinging to her, have dragged her against my chest, and am holding on for dear life. The need to need someone is so profound I can't catch my breath.

I fight the ingrained thoughts that want to push her away, to not feel, but that's all I can do right now is feel. My hand fists in the back of her shirt, my face is buried in her abdomen as I squeeze my eyes shut so goddamn tight because I will not cry but my body shudders with the force of trying to withhold it.

And Quin just holds me tight, giving me all of the comfort I've needed from my mom for so many years. I've found consolation over the years between the thighs of a willing candidate but not like this, not making myself vulnerable, not needing someone. As unsettling as it feels, I can't let go, can't pull away from her and her quiet murmurs of soothing and the silent support of her arms.

"It's okay to need me . . ." she says and then falls quiet. I just pull her in tighter and I'm sure she can't breathe but it's okay because right now I'll be her fucking air so long as she doesn't let go of me.

And that thought . . . the immediacy of it as it runs through my head almost knocks me as far back as the confession from my mom's lips.

The funny thing is that even with all the shit I'm trying to process, I don't know why that one thing doesn't scare the fuck out of me. Why of all of the revelations I've come to today, having Quin here with me feels more right than I ever could have imagined.

Chapter 28

I watch Hawkin from the couch in the studio. He's working through the lyrics of a song while I'm on my laptop getting into the heart of my thesis. This feels good. All of it, especially where we are right now when it could have gone in so many different directions after the past couple of days.

I love the opportunity to watch Hawke work. He gets this little crease in his forehead when he jots down lyrics and reworks them on the pad. He also does this thing where he bites his lower lip as he strums out the chords on the guitar with his eyes closed before he brings the words into it. Something about his process is most definitely sexy.

Every time I see him stare off into space in thought, I wonder how he's really doing, and I can't help but remember the look on his face as he stared at his mother, the hurt and shock and devastation in his expression. It was so brutal to watch, so heart-wrenching to stand by and not be able to do anything to ease his pain.

He's shut down still, not really talking about it, and yet I know the truths he learned are making him question everything about what he's grown up believing. Maybe that's why he's poured himself into his music the last couple of days.

After this past week, I know my mom's old adage describes Hawkin perfectly: Sometimes the strongest people are the ones who love beyond all faults, only truly grieve behind closed doors, and fight battles that nobody knows about. My only hope is that by losing himself in his music, he's been able to process everything.

Besides leaving the house for his last lecture today, he hasn't really left the studio much according to Vince. But in Vince's eyes that means Hawke's coping, he's working through it with music, and that's a good sign.

Hawke glances up and smiles softly, the guitar falling silent. It takes a moment for me to realize I've been caught staring at him and the smile on my lips is out of pure reflex.

"Hey, how's your paper going?" he asks as he grabs a handful of M&M's.

"If it included a hot rocker guy writing a song, then I'd say it was going great. . . . You're distracting, Play."

My stomach flutters at the full-fledged grin he gives me in return. "I can distract you in other ways if you'd like." He raises his eyebrows and my heart squeezes at the comment because it's the first time he's pseudo flirted with me since everything happened.

Maybe Vince is right, maybe the music is helping.

"I'd like that. Maybe I can inspire you with my wicked ways to write a dirty song."

"Sweetness, every time I touch this guitar I'm reminded of you." He smirks, my eyes drawn to *the guitar* and my body reacts viscerally. "But there are plenty of other instruments in here; we can try to add another one to our sexed-up band."

I start to clear the papers from my lap, not one to turn down the look in his eyes or the hints of what they say he wants to do to me. My old, playful Hawkin has emerged from hiding and a part of me sighs in relief. He reaches me the same time I have a clear lap and drops to his knees between my legs.

Leaning forward, he bestows a tender kiss that causes that sweet, slow ache to burn in my core. He slips his tongue between my lips, and I swear to God I can taste the next sixty years when his mouth connects with mine.

The thought startles me. Shocks me enough that I break away from the kiss. A tide of panic flutters within me but at the same time, I know what I just felt was real. With our faces inches apart I stare into his eyes, my hands smoothing over his jaw as I let the idea settle some.

"I know, I'm sorry," Hawke says throwing me for a loop.

"What?"

"You have every right to question me right now with everything and how I've been acting and—"

"That's not . . . I'm not questioning . . . I just . . ." My voice trails off as I realize he thinks I'm hesitant to kiss him, to be intimate with him, because of how closed off he's been the past few days, when in reality it's because I'm so overwhelmed with feelings. How do I tell him that and not freak him out? I can't. Not with everything he's going through.

"Hawke, it's not you at all. I—"

"You guys gonna come out of your *sex studio* long enough to join the party?" Vince asks as he barges in the room. A knowing laugh falls from his mouth when he sees our positioning. "See, I knew it. Shit, I owe Rocket ten bucks. I told him that there was no way—"

"We'll be there in a minute," Hawke shouts over his shoulder. "We're kind of busy." He leans in and kisses me again, a little piece of Heaven amid the chaos that's been surrounding us as of late. I slide my hands up his torso, anxious to feel him and touch him, show him somehow, some way that his past is his past, and that his future is wide open.

I moan into his mouth as his strong hand slides up under my shirt, rough to soft, and finds my breast, thumb grazing over my nipple as his mouth seduces me. I sink into the feeling, the emotion surrounding us, and can't think of any other place I'd want to be.

Hawkin's phone buzzes with a text and we ignore it as my hands start to tease and tempt and taunt his bare flesh, loving the heat of him beneath my fingertips, the bunching of muscles, the connection being made. His hands work wonders on my breasts, his fingers finding their way beneath my bra so his calloused fingers pleasurably scrape across my sensitized flesh. My head falls back as I lose myself to the sensation and he moves his mouth to the span of skin on my neck to place openmouthed kisses there.

His phone alerts another text. "Such a popular guy. I

guess I should feel lucky to be in your presence," I tease breathlessly, my senses in overdrive.

"There's nowhere else I'd rather be than right here, right now," he murmurs with his lips against my neck. His phone alerts again and he mutters, "Jesus Christ!"

"It might be your . . ." And my voice fades off, afraid to bring up his mom, but I'm already worried.

He swears again and leans back to the table he was writing lyrics on and grabs his phone. God he looks sexy with his hair all mussed up by my hands. He looks at his phone and scrunches his face up momentarily before slamming his phone down. I cringe at the sound and worry what's wrong.

"Fucking Hunter," he grits out. "The lecture's over so he must be back on the prowl for drugs again. How is it possible he's asking for money? He gets more than enough. Goddamn it!" He shakes his head and runs a hand through his hair before raising his eyes slowly to meet mine. "I'm sorry—this is . . . this is just how it is with me. I'm trying to change this—how I need to fix him and help—so it's going to take me some time to not react . . . to not enable him. You deserve better than this. . . ." His voice trails off and he lowers his head.

I scurry over to where he sits on his knees and mimic his posture. I force his head up with my hands and stare into those gray eyes of his that do funny things to my insides, even now when he's looking at me with regret. "Hey, rocker boy . . . I don't want anybody else though, I want you." I love this hitch in his breath from my words, love knowing that it can affect him that way because maybe one day he'll be able to tell me what I see in his eyes . . . that he feels the same way about me.

"Quin . . ."

"Look . . . I'm here, okay? I'm not going anywhere. It's going to take time and I get that." I lean forward and use my lips to reinforce the words. He pulls me into him and uses his tongue meeting mine to tell me he understands.

The door at our back flings open, the noise of the party escalating tenfold from when Vince did what seems like minutes ago. "Hawkin motherfucking Play! Get your and

Trixie's ass out here now!" Gizmo says with a drunken laugh. "It's time to party!"

The tenderness of the moment is gone but I still have Hawke in my arms. "We can escape if you want. . . . After this week, you might not want to . . ."

"Nah," he says with a chuckle. "I'm okay." He kisses me one more time. "We're coming, Giz!"

Note to self: Never let Rocket mix me drinks again. Holy shit, he makes them strong!

My mind's a bit fuzzy as I wander downstairs looking for Hawkin, wanting to make sure he's okay after all of the shit from this week. And I might want to take him upstairs and have my way with him because every time I think of him, I feel that ache deep in my core and know the only person who can sate it is him.

"Have you seen Hawkin?" I ask a group of women, my buzzed mind not registering until it's too late that they're probably here angling for the man that I have and they might not be too friendly.

"Why, who are you?" The redhead sneers.

"I'm with the band," I say, my own private joke because they think I'm just another floozy on the long list of them here tonight.

"Really?"

"Is it true what they say?"

"Do they like to tag team?"

All three questions are thrown at me at once and I can't focus on a single one of them because I catch sight of Hawkin across the room. "Sure, yeah . . ." I leave them behind, on a mission to walk up and kiss him to prove to them I am indeed with the band.

About fifteen feet away from Hawke, I stop when I see him arguing with Vince. I can't hear what they're saying but can tell by the body language that Hawke's not happy. I walk closer, curious and cautious at the same time.

"Why are you pushing this so hard?" Hawke asks, his jaw clenching.

"Deal's a deal, man." He shrugs his shoulder and catches my eye, immediately standing down. He holds his hands up in mock surrender and backs away. Hawke shoots daggers at him and Vince just laughs with a shake of his head. "I'm off to the head. Let me know when you change your mind." He turns to leave the kitchen, and when he walks past me, he stops to kiss me on the cheek. "Convince your man to come and play, Trixie."

It takes a minute for his words to sink in and by the time they do, Vince is gone. I'm not sure what in the hell he means but shrug it off because I meet Hawke's eyes and even though there's underlying irritation at Vince, I can also see the desire we unleashed earlier simmering beneath it.

I walk toward him; the sight of him slightly unkempt, with a carefree smile he hasn't possessed for days calls to my libido on so many levels it's ridiculous. He brings a shot of something to his mouth and I don't even give a second thought to what it is because I know I'll taste it on my lips momentarily.

He hums deep in his throat when I step up into his body and there is something so inherently sexy about the sound — knowing that I caused that reaction — that together with the feel of his firm body against mine lets me know there will be no interruptions this time.

He looks at me, eyes darkening and one hand sliding beneath my shirt a beat before our lips meet in a hungry, no-holds-barred kiss. His empty bottle clatters on the counter behind him so that his other hand can join in the temptation. I lose myself in the taste of the tequila on his tongue, and the hypnotizing feeling of his hands on my body.

The music thumps hard around us, the noise buzzes, and the faint scent of cigarette smoke wafts in from outside but it's as if none of it hits me because I'm consumed by everything about him: his taste, his cologne, the groan I can't hear but can feel against our connected chests, the heat of his body. I don't care who's watching because it's almost as if the overwhelming emotions that he's experienced all week long are manifesting themselves into our mutual desperation.

"Upstairs. Now," he murmurs against my lips, and I've never heard more perfect words. He grasps the bottle of tequila behind him in one hand and my hand in the other without saying anything further and walks with purpose through the crowd. I can't see his face but he must have a determined look on it because not one person stops him to talk when that's been the norm for the evening thus far. At the bottom of the stairs, I catch the eyes of the three wannabe women and just smirk. Call me bitchy, but I can't help it, I'm with the one they were hoping to land tonight.

Chapter 29

We reach Hawke's room and he pushes the door open, sets the bottle down, then closes the door. The minute it shuts behind us, giving us a reprieve from the thumping bass below, we collide together in a mass of desperate desire turned into burning need. We're all hands and mouths and moans and grinds, body to body, need against want, desire fueled by lust. I can't get enough of him. Not now, not ever, and I just allow myself to feel this, feel him, and not think.

He puts his hands in my shirt and pulls it over my head, throwing it behind him without thought, his mouth back on mine. Then he pulls away, shocking me from the lack of connection despite the heat of his breath panting over my lips. "I'll be right back. I have a surprise for you," he murmurs against my groan.

"Nooo! Don't leave."

He leans in and places a lingering kiss on my lips that I try to deepen to entice him but to no avail. "You'll like it — I promise. Get naked for me and I'll be right back."

"It better be good," I grumble.

"Have I disappointed you yet?" He says with a flash of that grin that makes me want to do dirty things with him. "Here," he says thrusting the bottle toward me.

"Are you trying to get me liquored and loose?" I tease, taking the bottle and setting it down on the dresser. I've had enough to drink tonight. Besides, no amount of alcohol has the ability to intoxicate me as thoroughly as the man in front of me.

"Sweetness, I don't need liquor to get you loose," he whispers against my ear and then shuts the door behind him as he leaves.

I stand in the darkness for a moment, kind of pissed and kind of excited all at the same time because I know it must be something good for him to leave me in the middle of *I'm about to get laid* time.

I strip down and slide between the sheets suddenly leery that there are a hundred or so people downstairs and any one of them could wander up and open the door. I close my eyes, imagining Hawke's mouth on mine and all the ways he can manipulate my body, then I slide my hand into the wetness between my thighs and rub gently. It's nowhere near as satisfying as when Hawkin does it but I know it will make me more ready, allow my orgasm to come that much quicker, and man if I'm not ready to come.

The door opens, a dark shadow against the brightness of the light behind him, and I sit up in the bed, my sheet falling around my waist. "What took you so long?"

"Well, shit." The voice has me grabbing for the sheet and pulling it up around me as fast as possible despite the darkness of the room. "Hawkin actually wants to do this."

"Vince?" I ask in an unsteady voice, trying to wrap my head around what the hell he's doing in here, and then my mind processes his comment. "Do what?"

I have a surprise for you. I hear Hawke's words again from moments before as my mind recalls several times since we've met where there has been the innuendo about a threesome. I thought it was just guy talk, macho bullshit, but that mixed with the comment from the groupie girls downstairs causes my heart to start pounding rapidly. Is this really what Hawkin wants?

Vince's laugh is low and suggestive and as much as I want to say the idea doesn't turn me on, it does. What woman doesn't want to be pleasured by two men at the same time, if not just to check it off her sexual bucket list?

Of course it's crossed my mind, but does that mean I'd actually follow through if I had the opportunity . . . ?

I guess I'm about to find out the answer.

I'm not one to be talked into anything, especially on the sexual front. The idea of this threesome unnerves me and at the same time sends that tingle of desire in my core into overdrive. *Do I want to do something like this?* Is this something Hawke's used to doing? What if I start to go for it and then chicken out?

My mind wars over all of this in a matter of mere seconds while my palms start to sweat and my body trembles with indecision and the unknown. "Did Hawke tell you to come up here?" I ask with an unsteady voice, and I know it's a shitty thing to ask, like I doubt him, but I can't help it.

"Rocket said he was looking for me where he makes music because he needed me to help with something. I went to the studio and he wasn't there, so I tried here and I . . ." He whistles low and quick. "After his tiff in the kitchen I wasn't expecting this, but shit, Trix, I'm game if you are?"

I'm still unsure how I feel about this, excited yet nervous, wanting to and at the same time fearful about how the dynamic would change if we went through with a threesome. Add to that, the man I want is Hawkin, hands down. Vince is good-looking in a lot of ways but Hawkin just affects everything within me like no other man has done before.

Vince's question hangs in the air with the lingering excitement of the unknown. And then Hawke's smile from earlier tonight flashes through my mind, the ease, the relaxation; the old Hawkin that I'd missed was back, and if doing this for and with him keeps it there, then I'm good with the idea.

Besides, I'm usually open to new experiences and this most definitely would be one. . . . I just have to go into it with an open mind and defined limits.

"I . . . um . . ." It's all I can manage, glad Vince can't see the flush in my cheeks through the shadowed darkness of the room because then I'd really feel like the naive little girl right now.

"It's okay, Q. We'll take it slow. Only do what you're comfortable with. Hawke and I may have done this a time or two," he says, providing me with a strange comfort.

"Sorry, Q, I can't find the surprise," Hawkin says as the door opens and closes behind him.

"I'm right here, man," Vince says, and although I can see only Hawke's profile, I can see the double-take action of his head.

"What—"

"Can't believe both of you are game after all of the shit you've been giving me over this."

The room falls silent momentarily as Hawke walks the length of the room to where I'm perched on the bed. Nerves start to hum within me and I suddenly wish that the bottle of tequila was closer because hell if I'm not going to need some liquid courage now that this is about to happen. Hawke sinks down onto the bed beside me .

My pulse pounds in my ears, my body feels like it's been lit on fire from the flush of adrenaline that burns through me, and even Hawke's touch on my skin does nothing to abate my nerves. I liked the idea of this but now that the opportunity is a reality, my fear and anxiety and excitement all crash together. I'm going to have to act, not think, feel not worry, relax until the apprehension fades to pleasure. My every emotion is amplified in the silence of the room, and the muted beat of music down below throbs like a second heartbeat.

"Quinlan." The way Hawkin says my name as he reaches out to brush my hair off my face pulls on every emotion that the moment hasn't already churned up, because I hear the strain in it, the sadness I want to be gone. "I don't—"

And before I can chicken out, before I can tell him that I'm so nervous I can't speak in return, I yank him toward me and cut his words off by putting my lips on his. Hawke is hesitant at first, trying to pull back to make sure that I'm okay, but I don't relent. I keep my hands and my lips in constant movement so that I can lose myself in the moment.

And then he starts to finally respond. He's just as eager, just as hungry as I am. My hands are trying to unbutton his jeans but his hands slide between my thighs before I can get them undone. I don't even realize that the incoherent moan that fills the room is from me until Hawke groans in response when he finds me slick with desire for him. I arch my back as I'm swamped with the sensation he gives me when he slips two fingers inside me at the same time his mouth finds the tight bud of my nipple.

The haze of arousal owns all of my senses and is amplified by Rocket's drinks and the heady sensations of Hawke's hands on me. Our chemistry is so intoxicating that it feels like forever since he's touched me intimately even though it's been only days.

I get lost in his thoroughness as he works me into a frenzy: his warm mouth on my chilled skin, his fingers sliding in and out of me before pulling back up and adding friction to my clit. He murmurs to me, how sexy I am, how hard he wants to fuck me, how he can't wait to feel his dick in my mouth.

My muscles begin to tense as everything begins to overwhelm me, that warm, sweet ache in my core spreading from my center outward like some inexplicable paralysis due to an overdose of sensation. "Hawke, God," I moan. "Don't stop."

My body soars as I fall off the edge when my orgasm hits me full force. My breath, my heart, my emotions, all three work in overtime so that I can ride out the orgasm Hawke has given me. My body trembles as I resurface from my climactic haze, and then Hawkin brands his mouth to mine, stealing my soft mewls before I can even begin to recover.

Then I feel the bed shift, and I'm shocked back to the reality that Vince really is here, on the bed. I'm immediately pulled from our intimacy that was like a protective shield making the moment solely ours. *And now it's not.* Hawke's lips fall from mine instantly and I can physically feel the hesitation in his actions, fingers flexing into the sides of my hips and mouth denying me its taste.

I'm not sure if it's my overall hesitancy or nerves mistaken as a lack of enthusiasm toward Vince, but something about the moment shifts.

Even with Hawke in front of me, I suddenly have doubts about my decision to be okay with this. It's not Hawke and it's not Vince, it's me.

Am I trying to be something I'm not by doing this?

"Stop." My voice cuts through the lust clouding the

room. Hawkin shoves back off me, and the lack of physical connection with him immediately leaves me cold and insecure. So many things flicker through my mind in a flash and the only one I can hold on to is shame.

I know it's not warranted—I have a right to change my mind—but even with the strength of my feelings for Hawkin I feel like an inadequate little virgin who can't hang with the big boys.

And then I stop myself and wonder if I just have cold feet. That maybe my buzz has worn off and now I'm letting nerves control my thoughts when I shouldn't.

"Just go!" Hawke's voice is low and even and full of an emotion I can't quite peg, and I hate that I can't see his face to read his expression. At first I think he's talking to Vince, but he's facing me and when he doesn't move or speak and the only sound in the room is the remnants of the party downstairs, I realize Hawkin is talking to me.

I feel like he's slapped me although we're nowhere near touching. The shame I felt but told myself was my own ridiculous insecurity comes back with a vengeance. "Hawke . . ."

"We'll deal with—just go!" He bites the words out, and I can hear his feet heavy against the floor as he paces before something slams against the dresser.

What the hell? He's kicking me out because I changed my mind? Talk about whiplash. "I'm sorry . . ." I say and am immediately pissed at myself because I shouldn't be. Besides, what am I apologizing for? For being nervous? For changing my mind? Yes, but I sure as hell am not going to apologize for not being like one of the floozies downstairs who would have dived in headfirst.

"This is . . . I can't with you. . . . You're not . . ." I can hear the remorse in his voice as he tries to explain but my embarrassment has now turned into anger. I'm off the bed in an instant, hands reaching in the dark for my clothes because right now all I want is out of here and away from this mess. Hawke takes a step toward me. "Q, don't you . . . Vince . . . *FUCK!*"

"I knew that she—"

"Shut the fuck up, Vin!" Hawke shouts but my mind is still focused on what Vince said, the amusement in his voice even more confusing than the irritation in Hawkin's.

If my head wasn't so hell-bent on leaving I'd laugh at the thought of the two of them, half dressed and yelling at each other, but my focus is on getting dressed. I hurriedly throw on my jeans and shirt, bra left somewhere in the darkness, and open the bedroom door to leave.

"Quin. Wait!" Hawke's voice calls to me but Vince cuts him off.

"Dude, what's your fucking problem?" he asks, a mocking tone in his voice I never expected, and I'm so confused how I could have been so wrong about him. I'm instantly pissed at myself and my misjudgment but I can process that later because right now I'm hurt. And angry.

"You. Her. This!" Hawke shouts, but I'm so busy being upset I don't stop to consider just what he's referring to.

And I mean so much to Hawke that he chooses to go toe-to-toe with Vince rather than chase after me. The question is after everything that just happened, do I really want him to?

The notion hangs in the back of my mind as I hurry down the stairs, fighting the tears that now come with my head down, the walk of shame written all over my face, and I'm so hurt I don't care who sees it. A few people ask me if I'm okay but I just keep moving forward because if I'm moving then I'm focused on that and not the shit running around in my head: shame, anger, disbelief at my poor judgment, hurt.

I'm pulled from my internal struggle when I swear I hear my name being called but after I stop for a moment, I don't hear anything. The hope I had that I was wrong crashes back down around me because if I mattered, if whatever *we are* mattered, he would be chasing after me, right?

Pushing open the door I hurry into the darkness of the backyard and welcome the cool night air, needing some time to wrap my head around everything. I head as far as possible away from the house, into the shadows of the garden to lose myself for a bit.

People are milling around the grounds but no one gives me a second glance, so lost in their own conversations or so drunk I don't register. I find a bench and sit down, elbows on my knees and head in my hands. The eddy of chaos still remains and I just need to slow my mind down, feel my way through the fog of everything that happened, deal in concretes, not emotions.

Something is niggling at the back of my mind that I can't put my finger on and I need to calm down so that I can figure it all out.

Lying back on the bench, I straddle my legs on either side of it and close my eyes as I start to go through everything from the moment that Hawkin came into the room. At first it all seems pretty clear-cut, that there is no room for misinterpretation, but the longer I sit here with the fresh air clearing my mind and my buzz abating, my perspective starts to shift and change.

In my mind, I hear the tone of Hawke's voice again, the hesitancy, and of course I curse myself for being so nervous that I grabbed him and kissed him and never let him finish whatever he was going to say to me. Because now that I think about it without the anxiety and lust and alcohol interfering with my thoughts, I almost feel like he was going to tell me something.

My mind starts to spin now, to look at everything from another angle, and I realize that Hawkin's anger wasn't directed at me, I think it was at Vince. I replay everything over and over again, my heart starting to pound again but for a very different reason as my supposition becomes more and more concrete.

Oh my God. How stupid could I have been? I'm so used to being the one treated like crap in a relationship that I inherently assumed the worst rather than giving him the benefit of the doubt. I sit up and wipe the tears from my cheeks that I didn't even realize were there and try to steady myself. I have to figure out how to explain my overreaction when there really is nothing I can even say but *I'm sorry*.

"You're so stupid, Westin," I mutter to myself as the tiny bubbles of hope start to rise to the surface. Hawkin didn't care that I changed my mind, in fact he was probably glad that I did because now with a clear head, I realize he wasn't mad at me at all. No. He wanted me all to himself, thought enough of me that he didn't want to share. The revelation buoys me as I start back across the grounds to find him and explain myself as best as possible.

I laugh softly in exasperation as one of my mom's go-to

comments she used to tell me as a teenager flickers through my mind, "If you're not willing to sound stupid, then you don't deserve to be in love."

And then it hits me. My laugh and feet falter, my breath hitches, and my heart stumbles and falls completely off the cliff. *I'm in love with Hawkin*. The thought staggers me momentarily because my mom was right, with anybody else that I've been with, I wouldn't have even thought twice about feeling stupid. I would have laughed this all off as a misunderstanding and if it worked, it worked, and if it didn't, it didn't.

Standing here in the darkness as the awareness hits me, I feel stupid once again, but not only for my freak-out upstairs but because I never saw this coming. I've been blindsided. Hell, I've fallen for men time and again, but never like this to the point where when the awareness hits, my chest constricts and my heart thunders as every part of me wants to see him right now to right my wrong.

And then I hear him call my name. Relief surges through me and then crashes when a figure steps out of the house's shadows. It's not Hawkin, it's Hunter. I bristle immediately, self-conscious of my braless chest and the cold night air, feeling naked around him even though I'm clothed.

"Where's the fire?" he asks as he steps in my path. "You're like a woman on a mission running across the grass and I'm not going to say I mind the view." His eyes flicker down to my breasts and I immediately cross my arms in front of myself.

"None of your business," I say as I try to skirt around him. His hand flashes out and grabs my upper arm and I'm more annoyed than anything because I don't want to deal with him or his shit right now. This is only my second or third encounter and the man can take a hike. I can see why Hawkin has warned me about him.

"What's this?" he asks, pulling me into him as I try to yank my arm from his grip. I notice his lip is swollen, like he's been hit, but by the time I process the thought, he speaks. "You've been crying? What did wonder boy . . . oh, OH, you must have found out." The knowing tone in his voice has me tilting my head in question and narrowing my eyes. "I'm sorry. I told him you deserved more respect than to be the endgame of one of their stupid band bets."

The words hit my ears but don't really register. My lips open and close but nothing comes out as I try to ask what bet but I think deep down I already know, vague hints of a conversation flickering briefly through my subconscious.

"Bet?" I croak when I'm finally able to speak, and I'm not sure if I want to know more or would rather be left in the dark. I know I should write off what he's saying after the staunch warnings Hawke's given me about how his brother will try to hurt him at all costs, but that red flag warning deep down has me standing still rather than walking away.

"Yeah, it's so fucked up." He shakes his head and releases my arm now that I have no desire to run. "To bet that Hawkin can get you in bed by the end of the seminar and that Vince had to be in on it for proof to prevent him from getting one of those stupid fucking hearts? That's just fucking cruel." He says the comment off the cuff but the way his eyes bore into mine, I know he's waiting to see my reaction.

And fuck yes I have a reaction. About a million of them all at once as my mind suffers the whiplash from five minutes ago, realizing I loved him, to this. My body starts to tremble as the shock hits, and I keep telling myself that Hunter is just being a dick and trying to hurt me to get to his twin. But those memories that were on the fringe come back with a vengeance now: little comments from the guys here and there, Hawke's immediate dismissal anytime I'd bring up their band bets, the poker game where Vince told me the last bet they had was trying to get a woman into bed in a certain time frame.

And what the hell, they were mocking me the whole time? And of course I walked right into it when I said it made perfect sense to need a third person to verify that the sex really happened. The laugh they must have been having at my expense. I recall Hawkin's face and the warning glare he gave when Vince told him we were talking about their stupid, damn bets.

What happens in the band, stays in the band.

I want to scream, want to cry, want to rage, but all I do is stand here in the shadow of night with a man I don't really like and my feet rooted to the ground, afraid to run and wanting to flee. Humiliation wars with devastation to see which one will take the crown and it doesn't really matter because if I hadn't realized I was in love with Hawkin before, I sure as hell do now.

Hunter stands silently in front of me and I can't bring myself to look at him because it's like a slap in my face since he's the mirror image of his brother. But I need to move because his presence is rubbing my nose in my own stupidity, lifting the blinders I wore when I went with Hawkin willingly.

I feel so silly being hurt so deeply by the deception but after he took me to see his mother, after letting me in his inner circle, after protecting me from Hunter, I thought that we were more than this. I sure as fuck didn't think I was a crass band bet made to occupy their time.

Sniffing back the tears that burn, I just shake my head in disbelief because I will not let myself cry. I prefer the numbing void I feel right now to the pain that I know will hit sooner rather than later because the saddest thing about betrayal is that it rarely comes from the people you're expecting it from, your enemies. It comes more often than not from the ones that care about you. Or in my case the one I thought cared about me.

Everything is quiet outside as I silently fall apart and question myself in every way possible. My chest constricts as my heart takes in the finality of it all, the misjudgment, the humiliation, and without a single word, I turn on my heel and leave.

Chapter 30

If I can get the lyric to come it will be a sign that she'll talk to me today. I laugh out loud into the empty studio, my own voice coming back to me with that tinge of hysteria to it. What the fuck am I thinking? That a perfect lyric means she'll forgive me for fucking up royally when I should have come clean a long-ass time ago?

Scrubbing my hands over my face, I try to focus on the chords again but when I look down, my hands are on the neck of the guitar, the one I strapped her to before I fucked her. My mind lingers on the memory of that night: the soft, the wet, the hard, the fast, the guitar pick, and every goddamn moan in between. I can remember the look on her face, the way she made me feel, and all I want to do is chuck it across the room and hold it closer to me all at the same time. I'm a pathetic fucker but I've never been through this shit before, never knew how goddamn bad it hurts.

No wonder there are so many fucking love songs written.

My mind flickers where I don't want it to go, in those deep dark recesses where the wild things are, to my dad, and for a moment I understand his desperation that day. Shit, I'm just losing a girl when he stood to lose his wife and two sons. I'm going fucking crazy right now since she's refused to even speak to or see me in the last three days—I can't imagine how he felt.

I force myself to turn the mirror away, to stop drawing comparisons to my dad because fuck if I'm going to commit suicide and hell if I want to admit I might just understand an iota of the mindfuck he was going through. Sometimes reflections are a hard thing to face and right now I've got enough shit on my plate. I don't need to be scared to look in the goddamn mirror.

But I am.

My mind rifles over the images from that night, trying to make sense of everything. The comedy of errors that led Quin to think I was actually going to share her. No fucking way. I'd just spent fifteen minutes in the kitchen telling Vince that he could fuck off and die if he actually thought I was following through with the bet. Shit, it's not like she's some random groupie.

She's Quinlan.

And fuck—everything after that was a misunderstanding: leaving the room to look for the tuning fork so I could tease her body with the different vibrations by resting it above her clit like a musical vibrator of sorts, then telling Rocket to have Vince come and help me find it since he had it last, Vince going to the bedroom when I wasn't in the studio because I thought I'd seen it in Rocket's room. Fucking Vince thinking that when I said meet me "where I make music," he thought I meant between the sheets. And then of course everything that happened after that. I heard the trepidation in her damn voice, could feel her nerves bouncing off her so that when I knelt on the bed to tell her she didn't have to go through with this, I was surprised when she yanked me into her and kissed me like a woman starving for her last breath of air.

I should have stopped her, pushed her back right then and told Vince to get the fuck out, but the mix of alcohol, the ache in my nuts wanting to finish what we had started earlier, and the taste of her kiss . . . it ruled out any thought of stopping. And then thank fuck she said no and changed her mind, stopping everything I didn't want to happen but thought she wanted.

Then of course I was so fucking busy being pissed at

Vince for pushing the issue, and making her so uncomfortable. How did I let the situation get that far? What the fuck was I thinking?

I let her walk away when I should have fucking run after her immediately rather than five minutes later with a hurt fist and complete panic. But how she found out about the bet, I have no clue.

I rack my brain for the millionth time, even though I know who must have told her because while I was looking for the tuning fork I ran into Hunter. My fucking brother looking for a handout but instead I told him to get the fuck out.

He had to have told Quin. The only other people who knew were the guys and I know they wouldn't have ratted me out even though I deserved it. They knew without me saying it how much she'd come to mean to me. Shit, I let her in when I let no one in.

But that still makes me question Vince and his full-court press on the matter. It sucks to be committed to being in this house with the guys when one of them is someone I don't really like right now. The one who knows me better than anyone, who I'm trying to figure out what the fuck kind of game he's playing.

Add to that the shit I should be worried about, my court date in two days. My do or die. The thought of the possible outcome makes me throw back the rest of my drink. I'm surprised Ben hasn't called to prep me on yet another thing I need to do or say since I stood him up for our scheduled meeting to go over details. I stopped answering his calls so I'm sure beating down my door will be his next move.

The idea of beating down the door has me thinking of my pathetic-ass self and how I left the house for the first time last night to force Quin to talk to me. How I stood on her porch forever, waiting her out, when I should have been at Ben's office.

The fucked-up thing is my mind should really be focused on my court date on Tuesday, but it's not. It's on a long-legged, wavy-haired blonde who owns my thoughts. I know they say absence makes the heart grow fonder, but fuck that shit. Absence makes you want to drink a fifth and pass out so you stop thinking and feeling. Both make your gut twist so why not take the one that numbs you?

Living the dream, man.

"Are you ever going to leave the studio or do you plan on looking like you're homeless for the next tour?" Speak of the bastard. I look up and just glare at Vince, my frustration fueling my anger, my temper on a hairpin trigger ready to hammer forward at the slightest pull. And he's pulling. *Fucking stellar.* "Some chicks dig the unshowered, unshaven, I-look-like-shit look. It's working for Jared Leto, so I guess it's worth a shot."

"Leave me the fuck alone," I grumble, wanting to fall back under the veil of my comfort: music and my Jack and Coke.

He rubs a hand over his unshaven face and moves his lower jaw back and forth. "You gonna punch me again?"

"You gonna piss me off again?" I ask, raising my eyebrows. First my brother and then Vince. What is it about Quinlan that makes me want to defend her at all costs? It's like some switch has been flipped in my head and all of a sudden I'm thinking things I've never allowed myself to think or feel before.

And of course the realization comes now that she's not around, so I shove it back down and read it as desperation on my part, unable to accept the truth of our situation just yet.

"Doesn't take much these days," he muses.

"You got a fucking point, *Vinny*?" I ask, slamming down my pen on the pad of paper, causing the crumpled candy wrappers to fall to the ground, and then he chuckles and that makes me even more pissed off. "What is it with all of this, huh? Why are you riding me so goddamn hard? You won your fucking bet, now back the fuck off me," I shout at him, my pulse racing, my anger mounting when he just smiles that goddamn smirk that taunts and irritates me all at once.

"That all this was, a bet?"

"Yep." It's all I'll give him because one, I don't want to talk about it, and two, he doesn't deserve shit for an explanation about what this is or isn't. It's my damn business, not his.

"In all the years I've known you, man . . . like forever . . . I never took you for a pussy. Guess there's always room for one to change though, isn't there?"

As much as I want to shove my chair back and unleash my hurt on him right now, to get out all of my pent-up frustration and anger and misery on him, I just clench my fists, grit my teeth, and glare. Instead I take a deep breath and stand up, eyes locked on his, and head for the door, suddenly needing to leave the room I've used as my sanctuary for the past few days.

"You don't get the girl, Play, if you don't fight for her." His voice is low and even as it hits my ears, stopping me in my tracks, hand on the door.

So many thoughts whirl through my head and to fuck it up further, I'm just not sure which one I want to hold on to when all I want to be holding on to is Quinlan.

"Dude, I've been fighting my whole life, maybe I don't have any fight left." It's the biggest bunch of bullshit, deep down I know that, but right now I need to find the life left in me before I can find the fight there.

Vince belts out a laugh but it falls flat, telling me that as much shit as he's giving me, he's concerned about me and what deep end I'm going to jump off now. I keep my back to him, one foot out the door, because I can't let him see how lost I am right now. If he does, he's gonna say shit to me, force me to see stuff that I'm just not ready to acknowledge aloud just yet.

"Sometimes you have to fight in order to be free," he says into the uncomfortable silence, and all I can do is nod my head because there's nothing I can say. "I'll leave you be, Hawke," he says finally after a deep sigh, "but I hate seeing you like this and love seeing you like this all at the same time."

When I look over my shoulder at my oldest friend and my most honest sounding board, I realize that right now I love him and hate him all at once. I want to question what he means but know he can only be referring to the one difference in my life over the past few months, Quinlan.

"You've lived long enough by your old man's principles; maybe it's time you start living by your own." We stare at each other a beat longer before I nod my head and turn around to walk out.

I used to think that holding on to my dad and the promises he extracted from me were the one thing that made me stronger, but now I suddenly realize that sometimes letting go is when you can truly show your strength. Vince's words just reaffirmed that. The problem is, I think I'm holding on to the wrong person while letting go of the right one.

Chapter 31

QUINLAN

Open your goddamn door.

It's an echo of several texts I've gotten over the past few days but this time it's from a different person. I groan at the sight of Colton's text about ten seconds before the pounding begins on the front door.

I pull the pillow over my head and try to shut the noise out, try to shut out the things that I really don't want to talk to my brother about. And then after I get him out of my house I'm going to lay into Layla for getting ahold of him and sending him over here.

Can't a girl just wallow in self-pity for a day or so . . . ? Well, more like the five days I've called in sick to Professor Stevens, but who's counting?

"Go away," I shout to the walls of my room as if he can hear me and just keep the pillow there, my mind immediately drifting to Hawkin and his endless phone calls and texts. The first ones worried about where I was and asked me to let him explain what had happened. That he didn't want to share me with anyone because he wanted to be the only one to bring me pleasure and no one else. That the surprise was another instrument to add to our pleasure play, not a threesome. Vince had misinterpreted something he had told him, and it led to a clusterfuck of a misunderstanding. That he wasn't mad at me for stopping the situation and that he did chase after me but he couldn't find me so he sat in the studio to wait for me to come back. But I didn't.

Misunderstanding, my ass.

How can he say all of that when in the end I was a mere casualty of band fun time? But that's where things get murky for me. If I was just a pawn in their fucked-up game, why take me to see his mom? Why protect me from Hunter, who in the end, ironically, was the one who protected me from Hawkin? All of it doesn't sit real well with me, but I need to wait for the dust to clear from this disaster because right now I'm looking at the situation through my emotional goggles.

I laugh into the pillow at how damn stoic I sound when I'm still upset and . . . I miss him. I stayed strong though and ignored the texts as long as I could until my anger got the best of me. I succumbed to my emotions with a single word response: **Liar.**

Then of course he responded with a flurry of responses, each one getting more and more adamant, followed by unanswered phone calls, to which I responded, **A bet? That's all I was to you? Fuck You.** That message set off another round of calls that then turned into two random appearances at the house in which he pounded on my doors. At least this time I was smart enough to have my laundry room door locked.

I refuse to give him the time of day.

The only part I get a small amount of pleasure in is that I know the stake of the band's bets. I know that Hawke didn't prove shit to Vince. So that means the asshole has to ink a pink heart on his wrist for losing, and every time he looks at it, at least I'll know he'll remember me. That makes me happy.

And that makes me sad.

Fuck. I don't want it to make me feel *anything* and yet it makes me feel everything. I can close my eyes all I want, pretend all of this never happened, but there's no way I can close my heart off to the ache that's nestled deep within me.

The pounding continues and I know my brother—he's not going to stop until I open the door. **Go away**, I text.

The repair bill for a broken door is going to be expensive then. You've got 5 minutes. Starting now.

A frustrated groan falls from my mouth as I chuck my pillow across the room and push myself off the bed. I glance in the mirror and start laughing because I am heartbreak personified: curls wild, a pillow crease in my cheek, and a smudge of the chocolate bar I ate last night on my tank top. I look like hell.

So I shuffle into the bathroom and brush my teeth, because even I have limitations to my slumming, plus I throw my hair up in a clip so that I look less miserable for appearance's sake.

Three minutes left.

With a roll of my eyes, I pull open the front door and let it swing back on its own before turning to walk back down the hallway without even looking at my pain-in-the-ass brother.

"You look like shit."

"Yeah thanks. So do you." I raise my middle finger in greeting over my head and smile at how dysfunctional this routine of ours is and yet I love it.

I walk to the couch and plop down, grab a blanket and wrap it around my shoulders. Colton takes a seat across from me, dark hair hidden underneath his beloved lucky ball cap and green eyes assessing me. I wait for the smart-ass comment I can see lighting up his eyes but it never comes. "That bad, huh?"

"How's Ry doing?" I change the subject to tell him I don't want to discuss it.

"Taking lessons from me on avoidance, now?"

"Had to learn something from you, right?"

"Did you wake up on the wrong side of the fucking bed or what? Oh wait, my bad, it doesn't look like you've left your bed in forever."

I know he's giving me the tough love shit but don't want that right now. And at the same time I know if he were to sit beside me and pull me into a hug, I'd start bawling the tears I've withheld for five long days. The floodgates would open and that's just too much like rain and rain makes me think of how it's like love and . . . I don't want to go there.

My traitorous bottom lip trembles and his face softens. "The musician?"

I nod my head morosely.

"Did he cheat on you?"

"No."

"Dump you?"

"No."

"Be an asshole?"

"Well, he is a guy," I say, cracking a slight smile.

"I take offense to that comment," he says with mock irritation. Or at least I think it's mock.

"Well, considering you used to be the king of assholes when it came to women, you shouldn't be." I shrug, suddenly thankful for his intrusion into my misery. He grunts at my answer and accepts it without further argument. "It's hard to explain," I confess but for some reason I don't want him to know the whole extent of it. I've got to get my head on straight. *Why in the hell am I protecting Hawkin when he played me like a fiddle?*

Well shit. I guess there's another instrument I can add to our band—unfortunately this one didn't bring me pleasure.

Colton scrubs a hand over the stubble on his jaw, so out of his element right now, uncomfortable at having to give advice to a female.

"Dude, you're not George Clooney or Jason Statham so that look went out last year. Time to shave," I tease, trying to ease his uneasiness, and at least I get a chuckle from him.

"You know you're kind of being a bitch when I just stopped by because I'm worried about you."

And that comment right there knocks the snarky wind from my sails because he's right, I'm being an ass because I'm hurt. "You're right. I'm sorry." I blow out a breath and watch my fingers tracing the pattern on the couch. "This is just . . ."

"What happened?" he asks, scooting to the edge of his chair.

"I was the stake in a bet."

"Excuse me?" The pitch of his voice escalates and his posture changes instantly, going into full-force protective brother mode. I cringe; I didn't want to go there with him, but I want to confide in him at the same time. "His name." It's not a question.

"Hawkin Play," I say ever so quietly but Colton does a double take when he hears the name.

"As in lead singer of Bent, Hawkin Play?" I just nod. "Shit, I liked their music too. Dare I ask what the bet was?" He's feeling me out and I just sigh.

"No, you don't want to know."

"Fuckin' A," he growls, the muscle in his jaw pulsing as he tries to rein in the rage for my sake. "I don't need to ask. . . . I'm a guy. I can imagine. . . ." His voice trails off as I watch him struggle with the dueling emotions, to sympathize with me through anger or through comfort. I just nod when his gaze meets mine, saying yes to all of the above. "You know I'm going to kick his ass now, right?"

That first day I drove Hawke home flashes through my mind, when he commented that my brother must have gotten in a lot of fights protecting my virtue. *The irony.*

I don't say anything, just keep watching my fingers trace the fabric aimlessly. "You really like him, don't you?" The solemnity and compassion in his voice make my heart swell. My lack of an answer is one in itself. "Shit, Q, if Rylee were here she'd say some shit like 'Never give up on someone that you can't go a day without thinking about.'"

I groan, as that's the last thing I want to hear. "And you'd say?" I lift my eyes to meet his.

"Fuck, I suck at this shit."

"Yes you do, but other than 'what's his address' so you can go knock his teeth out"—Colton's face lights up at that comment—"I want to know what advice you'd give me. *Please.*"

He rolls his eyes and it looks so out of place on the bad-boy thing he has going. He leans forward and places his elbows on his knees as he twists his lips in thought. And I have to admit it's pretty damn cute that he's actually being serious and thinking of some big-brotherly advice.

"You really like the guy?" he asks.

"Yeah, I do," I murmur without even having to think about it, sadness once again owning my heart.

"Even though he fucked with you?" He stares deep within me, and even though I'm ashamed about the situation, I can't turn off my feelings.

"Mm-hmm." I want to avert my eyes, feeling ashamed, but I know Colton won't pass judgment on me since he's done a whole helluva lot worse than still care for someone who's wronged him.

"Look, the way I see it, trust is kind of like a piece of paper. Once you wad it up, tear it, mark it . . . sure you can fix it, flatten it out, tape it together, do what-the-fuck-ever to it, but it will never be perfect again. . . . So the question you need to ask yourself is can you live with the marks on the paper? Can you move forward knowing it's imperfect from here on out?"

I stare at my brother, so dumbfounded by him right now that if I didn't love him madly already, I would in this moment. His words are so poignant and hit home in places so deep inside me that my mind starts to whirl with thoughts I'd shoved away.

"But fuck, what do I know? I'm just a guy," he says, suddenly uncomfortable. "Just"—his voice fades off as he tries to figure out what to say—"whatever you decide, just make sure it's right for you, you know? Look at me—I've been crumpled up, thrown away, and taped back together more times than I care to count, but Ry's okay with that. She says it makes me imperfectly perfect, whatever the fuck that means, so I guess it must be good," he says with a smirk. I knew his arrogance wouldn't be held at bay for too long.

"Perfect belongs nowhere near your name," I deadpan, having to knock him down off his pedestal some.

"You're just jealous," he says before he falls silent again as he studies me. "You okay?"

"Better now, yeah. Thank you, Colton."

"Sure, whatever," he says, shrugging off the compliment and rising from the couch. He walks a few feet forward and stops in front of me. "If you decide to give this guy another chance . . . I plan on having a little chat with him. You need to know that ahead of time, okay? Because I don't want you giving me any shit when I show him the long walk off a short pier I'll be giving him if he fucks with you again."

I nod my head in agreement with a soft smile on my face. God, I love my brother. He leans down and kisses the top of my head. "Thank you."

"You sure you're okay?"

"Yeah, I will be."

"Okay, I've got to get into the office," he says, starting toward the door. "Ry said to call her so you guys can do the girlie shit together. That it'll make you feel better."

"Okay, sure."

"And lock the door behind me," he reminds me since I always forget.

"Yeah, yeah, yeah," I tell him as I sink back into the couch when the door slams shut.

I want to pull the blanket over my head and hide, want to grab my keys and drive to see him, but know I need to flat iron the damn piece of paper and see if I can live with the creases I can't get out first.

Chapter 32

'**ve showered.

At least I can add that to my list of accomplishments for the day. My head hurts from the significant quantity of wine and ice cream consumed last night. The problem is Hawkin's ruined ice cream for me. Sitting there eating it straight from the container with Layla made me more depressed, which led to more wine, which led to more ice cream.

Thank God it's the one day I don't have to be on campus for class or TA sessions. I've made a resolution to throw myself into my thesis and not come up for air until I have the first draft completely finished to turn in on Friday.

I'm burying my head in the sand by getting up late, blaming it on the wine headache that's no longer present, but I'm also pretending that I don't remember that today is Hawke's hearing and possible sentencing. I hate that I want to be there for him, hate that I'm still mad at him, hate that I am still falling deeper in love with him.

I guess it's true when they say instead of overlooking faults, love sees through them and to the hidden parts inside. Whoever *they* are need to consider that it still sucks trying to figure your way around them.

Colton's brotherly advice won't stop running an endless

loop through my mind. Thoughts about trust and crumpled paper, being perfectly imperfect, and whether the risk to lay my heart on the line is worth it, consume my thoughts even as I pull out my research papers.

Focus, Westin. Focus.

The knock on my door pulls me from my scattered thoughts, and I immediately get my hopes up that it's Hawkin while at the same time groaning because I don't want it to be him. But wait, it can't be him because he has a court hearing shortly. I don't want to care, want to shut my mind off but know it's no use. With my papers still perfectly neat and untouched, I head to the door wondering who is there.

Before I even look through the peephole, I'm mad at myself for wanting it to be Hawke and then I'm confused because even if it was, I wouldn't respond anyway. Or maybe I would give in once I saw him face-to-face. I don't know. What I do know is that I'm surprised at who stands on my porch.

Through the lens of the peephole I take in his buttoned-up shirt and clean-shaven face before unlocking the door and opening it. "Hi?"

"Hey, Quin," Vince says cautiously, eyes studying my re-action to his unexpected appearance. "Sorry for just show-ing up, but . . . I got your address from Hawke's phone. . . ." His voice fades off midexplanation, and I can see him trying to figure out how to say whatever he's come to say. He's obviously uncomfortable, and I'm unsure whether it's be-cause he's here clearly butting into Hawke's and my busi-ness or because he saw me naked and coming the other night.

I definitely know the reason why I'm shifting my feet back and forth in unease.

"You clean up nice. Hot date?" I ask to try to break up the awkwardness, and no sooner than the words are out of my mouth does it dawn on me why he's dressed so nicely. "I . . . Sorry. I wasn't thinking."

"It's okay. This was a knee-jerk thing to do on the way to the courthouse . . . but I had to say some things to you." The gravity in his tone is unexpected and has me immediately curious.

"Come in."

"Just for a minute," he says as he walks past me. I lead him into the family room, watching him check everything out. "Nice place you got here."

"Thanks. Is there anything I can get you?" I ask, manners prevailing despite suddenly being nervous.

"Nah," he says, but remains standing when I motion for him to sit. We stand, staring at each other for a moment. "Look, I don't even know where to start other than to say I'm really sorry." He blows out a breath and goes to run his fingers through his hair but stops when he remembers it's stiff with gel. "The whole bet thing . . . at first it was a joke . . . and then as I started seeing how Hawke was being with you . . . I kind of forced the issue to try to make him see shit about himself. . . . It was too convenient—you being there was too convenient and made it easier for me to force the issue. I . . . Shit, I'm sorry." Despite his fast-paced ramble, his last words are barely audible, but the regret laced with shame in his voice tugs at parts of me. So many questions whirl and race through my mind, and there's a tangled mix of emotions that I can't put my finger on except for one: anger.

"So . . . he's not getting any response from me so he sends you to do his dirty work for him?" I know it comes off bitchy, but I can't help it, he's at fault here too. He just confessed to using me and I'm supposed to sit here and kumbaya with him? Best friends like Vince, like Layla, go to bat for you, so how is this any different?

"No," he says quietly, his eyes pleading for me to listen. "He has no clue that I'm even here."

And why should I believe that? "What was the bet? How'd it come about?" I need to hear it from him so I can use the words as a validation for the anger I'm harboring and to withhold the forgiveness I feel.

He looks down at the floor for a moment and then back up. "It was after the first lecture. You'd given Hawke a run for his money, and I teased him that you might be the first woman he's ever met that would turn him down. He had a knee-jerk reaction, said *bet me*. I'd recently lost a really crappy bet so I took the chance to brand him with that ridiculous heart for once, betting him that he couldn't sleep with you by the last day of the seminar. Due to a bet I lost where there was no proof, he jokingly offered for me to join in if I was so desperate for it . . . so I agreed." He looks at me sheepishly.

I take the damn piece of paper I'm holding crumpled in my hand and toss it into the trash can. The decision to not flatten it out, see where I stand, was just made that much easier.

I force a swallow down my suddenly dry throat; I hate hearing the details but need to all the same to reinforce my resolve. How I felt then, how I feel now, and the tears I feared would come if Colton hugged me, all come barreling down on me. Consumed by my thoughts, it takes a moment for me to come to the here and now, to Vince standing before me trying to see how the confession sits with me.

"Quin . . . I used you and I'm an asshole for it."

"You can say that again." Sarcasm thickens my voice.

I expect him to argue but he just nods his head and wins a few points with me. "Here's the thing though—I saw something in Hawke that I've never seen before when he was around you. He's spent his whole life living by whatever his dad made him say that damn day . . . always pushed anyone away when they got too close and yet with you he struggles with it. It was like something about you made him question himself, question the fucked-up shit in his head," he says and a part of me stands up at attention, allows me to know that Hawkin did in fact care about me somehow, some way.

It's bittersweet. It pisses me off. And it makes me miss him that much more.

And it makes it that much harder to deny that damn piece of paper is out of the trash can, still balled up, but with new significance.

"I screwed this up in so many ways—"

"Look, I get that you're protecting Hawke, but he's a big boy, he can make his own amends," I cut him off, using anger to fuel my bravado, and at the same time realizing that I'm the one shutting Hawke and his attempts down, that he has tried to explain. Talk about an emotional clusterfuck.

"Just . . ." He sighs. "Quin, you have every right to be pissed but please, just hear me out." He stares, making sure

I've heard him. "At first it was funny. Watching Hawke get flustered, be off his game when he talked about you. Then I noticed every time I brought up the bet he would say no way in hell was he letting me near you and at the same time, he wasn't getting a tattoo. I realized that maybe for once in his life, he thought he just might be worthy of having a real relationship, but every time I questioned him on it, he got defensive . . . so wrong or right, I pressed him on it."

And now my fingers are toying with the edges of the paper to see just how flat it can be made again.

He's frustrated that he's not explaining this very well when in fact he is. I just think my mind is fearful of accepting what he's trying to tell me. I want to believe him, yet . . . I don't know. "But why continue? Just call off the bet, then. Let it run its course. . . ."

"We should have," he says and the adamancy in his tone tells me he's being honest. "But I've got to tell you, Quin, it was so fucking great to see Hawke struggle with wanting someone, to feel like he deserved it. . . . I just wanted him to see it, acknowledge it . . . and I thought the only way I could do that would be to force his hand. Hell, I knew you guys had slept together, no denying it with the thin-ass walls in our house, but I thought if I could push him into the situation, that he'd push back finally. He'd defend you, realize his feelings for you, and in turn acknowledge so much more about himself as a man."

It takes a moment to digest his first few sentences. I obsess over the fact that he's seen a change in Hawke and that I wasn't making all of these feelings up in my own head. And then his last sentence hits my ears and takes hold. My eyes flash back up to his, heart hoping what I heard was true. "His feelings for me?"

Vince angles his head and his expression is one of incredulity. "You have to ask? He's head over heels for you."

That damn paper is uncrumpled, my hands pressing it down, running across its surface over and over, adding pressure, trying to make it as smooth as possible.

"Oh." It's all I can manage as a sliver of hope begins to seep into the majority of the fractures in my heart, cementing it back together. Talk about throwing a perfect chord in there when everything has been playing out of tune the past few days. I tell myself to calm down, tell my pulse to stop racing so I can get a handle on everything because regardless of what Vince has said, there is still a whole helluva lot of wrong mixed in with the little bit of right he's just laid on me.

Imperfectly perfect. I shake my head, trying to clear the thought from my mind, but it doesn't budge.

"The night of the party, when we were fighting in the kitchen, he told me basically to fuck off and die if I thought he was going to let me in on the action. I laughed, told him to get ready for his pussy-pink heart. He was pissed I was forcing the issue, so that's why I was so shocked when Rocket told me Hawke was looking for me. And shit, I walked in and you were . . . how you were. And then Hawke came back and thought you wanted it to happen since you kissed him instead of let him talk you out of it." He nods with a sallow smile, my thoughts on an emotional merry-go-round. "Yes, he was trying to talk you out of it, but what man is going to resist a woman when she kisses him like you did Hawke?"

My mind flickers back to it all, the same things I have replayed over and over in my desolate misery. The gamut of emotions I felt that night, still feel now. How my stupidity made me react without thinking, clouded my judgment. The desperation I felt trying to right the wrong, and then with Hunter's words . . . the crushing sensation of being used, made the fool, played when everyone else was in on the joke. The flashback gives me a firmer grip on my anger, on the pain Hawke's actions caused me.

"Well shit, I mean so much to him, Vince, that he came running right after me, now, didn't he?" I raise my hands up in the air to emphasize my point.

"Yeah, that's because he was too busy landing a punch on me." There's a smirk on Vince's lips but the tone of his voice tells me that he's dead serious. I just stare at him to make sure I've heard him correctly. "Yep. Dead truth. I never saw it coming because the room was so damn dark. And then he stood there for a moment, shocked I think that he actually hit me, and took off after you."

The memory of thinking I heard my name being called returns—and I think about how I disregarded it, and wonder if he'd found me then, if Hunter had never interfered, would I have ever known about the bet? Would I still be the fool or would I be none the wiser and better off without the knowledge?

"Well, he didn't find me, Hunter did." I tell him, hands back on my hips and turmoil in my soul. His eyes shock open a little at Hunter's name but he nods his head up and down.

"Hawke couldn't figure out how you knew, but assumed it was his brother."

"Hunter was in on it, then?" I'm confused as a thought hits me that never crossed my mind before, and just when I was softening some. Hunter's not part of the band, and yet he knew about the bet. Who in the hell else knew about it then? The groupies by the stairs, the rest of the guests that night? I mean was I the pathetic laughingstock of the party?

Vince can see my anger rising and puts his hands up to calm me down, his head shaking side to side. "No. He eavesdropped on a conversation Hawke and I were having. That's the day he punched him, the day his mom unleashed everything. . . ." His voice trails off. "When Hawke went looking for you, he ran into Hunter, who'd been texting for money all day. After everything with his mom, with whatever you were able to get him to see, he told Hunter he was done supporting his habit when he ran out of the monthly bullshit payoff he gives him." He must sense my surprise at the comment because he nods his head. "I was surprised too. So Hunter showed up, was pissed about being denied money, angry we didn't tell him when the party was, and him and Hawke went toe-to-toe before Gizmo calmed the situation down. He must have gone outside, and then he saw you . . . and Hunter did what he always does, he tried to fuck over Hawkin."

Sinking down into the couch, I try to wrap my head around the new information, about being used by twin brothers but in ways I never expected, and worry what this all says about me, worry that I'm perceived to be someone who is gullible.

"Wow." It's all I can say.

"I know. . . . Look," he says apologetically, "I didn't mean to lay all of this on you. I know I'm partially at fault . . . and

I know it's not going to change your decision about Hawke or take away how bad you were hurt, but I thought you should know."

We stare at each other for a moment as tears begin to well in my eyes. I nod my head, letting him know I understand his reasons for being here, but I'm struggling to process everything. I can tell he's uncomfortable so I'm not surprised when he says, "I should probably get going."

"'Kay," I murmur, lowering my eyes as he walks up to me and leans over to press a kiss to the top of my head much like my brother did. The hollow sound of his boots on the tile fills the house as he walks to the door before I hear the click of it shutting.

For the longest time, I stare at the same spot on the carpet with blurred eyes and muscles tense as I contemplate what's best for me. And even when the first tear falls, I already know my answer, know that he's who I want.

My hands have worried that damn piece of paper flat, edges are folded over, creases are faint but there. Can I live with that? Will those imperfections be the weak point ready to give when the edges are strained over another issue? That's what I need to decide.

I want Hawkin on so many levels. I think I'm ready to fight for him. I just need to figure out how to go to him with a heart full of understanding rather than a fistful of resentment.

Chapter 33

HAWKIN

I tap the rhythm out to the song circling in my head, lyrics absent but beat present as I try to work through the nerves humming in my system. I've worked crowds of thousands of people but sitting here on the hard leather seat, the judge's bench in front of me, Ben to my left, and nothing but the unknown stretched out before me, I'm nervous as fuck.

Add to that he took my phone from me so that it would not interrupt or distract the proceedings, so I'm shit out of luck when it comes to trying to ease my anxiety by getting lost in mindless rounds of Angry Birds.

I'd kill for some Skittles right now. Maybe candy would help calm me.

"Relax," Ben murmurs, closing his hand over the top of mine to stop my thumb from thumping, and immediately the jogging of my knee beneath the table takes its place.

"Easy for you to say," I snap, my misplaced anger directed at him. It's not his future and his freedom on the line here. Come to think of it, it shouldn't be mine either. I sigh loudly. This self-doubt is such a new thing these days and I hate it.

"I have a feeling everything is going to—"

"Feelings don't mean shit!" I bark in a hushed whisper, and then squeeze my eyes shut to staunch my anger. I mean the comment in more ways than one, and I can't fucking think about her right now because I need to focus on this, on the here and now.

Ben sighs in resignation as I glance over my shoulder for the hundredth time since we've been sitting here waiting for the judge to arrive. I know she won't be here but for some reason I keep looking, keep hoping. I'm a poor fucking pussy-whipped sap.

Keep telling yourself that, Play, and you just might believe it. Being whipped is the least of the things I need to worry about. Thinking I'm falling in love with her is a tad bit larger.

I shake my head in shock as the realization hits me right now when I can't do shit about it. The panic I expected to feel should this day ever occur doesn't come because I'm scared, but rather because of how bad I fucked this up. I may finally have found a woman I'll let in my battered heart and then lost her all in one fell swoop.

Stellar.

My eyes sweep back over the benches and see no one, not even Vince. I told the guys I didn't want them here but despite that I still expected Vince to be here representing the band. And a small part of me is shocked that Hunter's not here. I wouldn't put it past him to want to watch his brother pay for his sin, take a little bit of joy out of me being in the legal hot seat for once. It's a fucked-up thought but it's true. Besides, he's pissed at me enough right now because I've cut off his funds, so I'm thankful he's skipping this party.

"Man you're making me nervous," Ben says in my ear, and thank fuck whatever was up his ass ten minutes ago when he walked in this courtroom has been removed because last thing I need right now is him being an asshole to the judge and jeopardizing my freedom. "There's an accident on the ten. We just missed it but that's why the judge is late. Just *relax*." He draws the word out and if I hear the term one more time I'm gonna flip my shit.

If only traffic was the reason that Quinlan isn't sitting behind me too. I'd bet a million times over that were things right between us, I could ask her to be here, but think I should refrain from doing what got me into the mess with her in the first place.

I tug on the collar of my shirt and wonder how in the hell Hunter can wear these damn shirts on a daily basis. I've got enough things trying to tighten around my throat and suffocate me, last thing I need to add to it is a shirt.

"Ben?" the feminine voice behind us says.

"What's up, Steph?"

Steph? I turn to see who she is, surprised by the tiny, eye-catching woman behind me when I'm so used to Ben's usual male aide. She holds out my phone and looks at Ben, asking if it's okay for me to take it.

"Mr. Popular," he teases. "Sure. It's not like the judge is here anyway."

"Thanks, Dad," I mock as I reach out to take my phone the same time Steph closes her hand.

She gets flustered when our skin touches and jerks it back. "I'm sorry. . . . I didn't mean to . . . Here." She shoves my phone out to me, face turning red. I realize the same time Ben starts chuckling that Steph is nervous because of who I am. Poor thing, trying to do her job and not fangirl at the same time.

"Thank you," I murmur as I give Ben a look, wondering if she has the job because he's hitting the hottie. Her skills outside of the office are presumably more important, and by the sheepish look on his face I know the answer.

I take my phone, relieved to have something to fidget with even if it's just for a moment. And then once it's in my hand trepidation floods me because I worry that it's going to be from Westbrook, something wrong with my mom.

My heart suddenly vaults into my throat when I glance down and see it's from Quinlan. **We need to talk. We hit a sour note and need to find the right chord again, decide where to go from here. Call me when you can. Good luck.**

I have to hold in a childish whoop of excitement. Relief mixed with hope surges through my system and I swear that I'm so emotional over her text because I'm inundated with anxiety right now about the trial, but shit, I'll take whatever I can get from her at this point. I need to get my foot in the door so that I can explain, prove to her that I know I fucked up and I'm not really *that guy*. I'm this guy, a man still a little out of tune but a helluva lot more in sync than I was back when I made that stupid-ass bet with Vince.

Right when I start to text her back, as I'm trying to figure how to say the million things running through my head, I hear, "All rise."

"Fuck," I mutter as the bailiff announces the judge's presence in the courtroom. Perfect damn timing.

I look at Ben, down at my phone, and know I have only seconds but at the same time I fear if I don't respond, Quinlan is going to think . . . I don't know what she might think. I shove the phone over the railing behind me to Steph. She looks at me with surprised eyes. "Go give this to Vince. He should be here any minute. Have him call her. Tell her I'll call her when I'm done." I swear I sound like a pathetic sap but she just nods. Now, I just hope I'm right in thinking he'll be here.

The severity of what the next few minutes, hour, who knows how long, may have over my life hits me again, as I stand and face the front of the courtroom. The quick reprieve I felt with Quinlan's text is gone immediately with only the lingering whisper of possibility as the judge walks in.

Just like I do before taking the stage to calm my nerves, I hang my head down, close my eyes, and take in a fortifying breath. I can pretend all I want that I'm a hard-ass, that this isn't a big deal, but when it comes down to it, the man before me with the black robe holds my fate in his hands.

The silence stretches as he sits down, and then I hear throats clearing—the press filling the benches behind me, waiting to report my fall from grace. I know if I get off, it will be a blip of a byline, but if I get sentenced it will be this week's cover of *People*. My pulse thunders in my ears and I feel like my shirt is strangling me as the pins and needles I'm standing on begin to jab their way into my confidence.

"So, Mr. Play"—I look up when the judge's deep baritone hits my ears to meet his eyes—"are you trying to fulfill the middle cliché of the sex, drugs, and rock-and-roll reputation . . . ?"

Chapter 34

Be there in thirty.

When I stare at the text once again, giddiness soars through me. I know we need to talk about things, sort out the creases, but at the end of the day, I want Hawke in my life and a chance for whatever this is to take its course.

I finally want it to rain.

Anticipation runs rampant as I look out the front window again. I'm nervous, excited, and a little unsettled at the text. I'm not sure what I was expecting in response to my text. Maybe a bit more enthusiasm? I don't know. I'm overthinking this, know he said he would be here in thirty minutes and that in itself says he hasn't moved on and wants to try to work things out.

Being cautious is okay, but it doesn't take away the toll of the emotional wringer I've been through the past few days. Plus, I just plain don't want to be hurt any further. I need to play it all by ear when he gets here, follow his lead.

Add to all of this the notion that the hearing must be over and if he's getting here this quickly, then it must have gone in his favor. At least I think that's how it works, but my clean record is proof of my naïveté of the judicial system.

Busying myself, I put some music on, and then shut it off, not wanting to appear like I'm trying too hard. In a fruitless attempt to waste time, I check my makeup, pull my hair up, and then let it back down.

When the knock sounds at the door, my breath hitches, nerves jittering through me from head to toe. I rush to the door and then force myself to stand there for a moment so that I can retain some of my dignity. I smooth my hands down my shorts and slowly open the door.

A cautious smile spreads across my lips at the sight of him in the just-setting sun's light, which halos his silhouette. My rush of nerves collides with cautious optimism. He looks different from how I've ever seen him, sans his beloved vintage rock T-shirts, and wears a button-up dress shirt and slacks. My first thought is that he needs to change because he looks nothing like my rocker boy and too much like Hunter, but I really don't care, he's here and we're going to figure out how to navigate this minefield together.

"Hey," I say softly, stepping back.

"Hey." He steps into the foyer and angles his head to stare at me a moment, eyes guarded, an impassive expression on his face. For a split second I fear that he's here to instigate more conflict but after a beat, his eyes searching for something I'm unsure of, his mouth turns up into a soft smile.

I want to step into him, hug him, hold him, kiss those lips of his, but I don't sense the same on his side. I'm confused—I should be the one who's guarded and pissed and yet I feel like he's the one acting that way. Then it hits me that something must have gone wrong at the hearing. Oh shit.

"Come in." I lead him down the hall, trying to figure out how I need to proceed, because feeling uncomfortable was the last thing I'd expected in this reconciliation. I stop just inside the family room and turn to face him. "Look, I hate that this is awkward, hate everything about this situation except for the fact that you're here and I want to try to make this work and figure out how we can move forward. Hawke," I say his name, a plea in a sense as he stands there, jaw clenched, body stiff, but then he steps toward me. And so I ramble on, unable to help myself. "When I look at this all, the bet and the night at the party, I feel like it's one clusterfuck of a misunderstanding and so we have to . . ." My voice trails off as he reaches out and cups the side of my jaw, thumb brushing over my bottom lip. My breath hitches and that electric current of our connection is still there, so much stronger after my skin has been starved of his touch.

He opens his mouth to say something and closes it again, words unspoken, and the moment is full of conflicting emotions. When he does it again he just shakes his head and pulls me into him, wraps his arms around me, and holds me tight. Our bodies fit together perfectly but something seems off to me. At first I chalk it up to the change in his cologne that makes him seem not like my rocker boy, but then realize that he's so tense, strung so tight that it's affecting me. But I hold on to him, absorbing the feeling of his body against mine and the knowledge that I made the right choice to reach out to him.

When he doesn't say anything, I become even more worried. "How did the hearing go?"

"I don't want to talk about it," he murmurs into the crown of my head with a deep breath. The heat of it warms my scalp as my mind worries itself into circles trying to figure out what exactly happened.

"Really? Please just tell me your piece of shit brother was there, stood up, and actually took the blame for once." I wince, worried I've overstepped my boundaries, but at the same time seeing him this upset is disconcerting.

He releases me the minute the words are out of my mouth and walks into the kitchen, his back toward me, and pounds a fist on the counter so that the few dishes stacked on it rattle from the force. I startle from the sound as he braces his hands on the counter and hangs his head down in silence.

"I'm sorry Hawke. I don't know what happened today." I trace the strong lines of his back, my heart lodging into my throat as I attempt to explain my comment. I know how it goes, you can bad-mouth your own kin but no one else can. Shit, I have Colton for a brother. I've bitched about him countless times before but the minute someone else does, my back is up and my mouth is on the defensive.

But then again, Colton has never tried to ruin everything I've worked for either.

"Look, I just . . ." I really want him to turn around so that I can see his expression but when he doesn't, I continue. "I see how much of a burden he puts on you, how even when you know you are doing the right thing, it affects you . . . eats at you . . . and I just want you free of that. I know you love him, Hawkin, no one would ever question that, but you work so hard at everything and you need to be able to live without the constant shadow following you of what he's going to fuck up for you next. So I'm sorry I said it but not sorry all the same."

Silence hangs heavy in the air between us, and this reconciliation feels so very different from what I ever imagined.

"I need a drink," he says, voice strained as he shoves back from the counter, eyes flicking to mine before he starts pacing like a caged animal.

I watch him for a beat, his hand pushing through his hair, jaw tense, and it's nearly impossible to tear my eyes from watching the inner turmoil eat him alive. "Sure. Of course. Jack and Coke?" I ask as I move toward the cupboards to pour him a drink.

"Just Jack."

I pull out the bottle of Jack Daniels from above the refrigerator and grab two glasses and set them on the kitchen table near where he's pacing and lost in thought. I take a seat, every part of my body aware of his nearness. It's like my nerves are a damn light switch and anytime he's near me I'm flicked on, in every sense of the word.

He stops when he pulls himself from his thoughts and approaches the table as I sit down. The clink of the bottle's neck as it hits the glasses fills the room as he pours us both a drink. I stay quiet, accept the glass he offers me even though I've never drunk Jack Daniels straight before, and just hold it in my hands. I watch him raise his to his lips and toss the amber liquid back without so much as a wince from its burn.

He finally looks up to me as his tongue flicks out to lick a drop off his lip. The smile he gives me doesn't reach his eyes, and I hate how that makes me feel so off-kilter. It's almost as if he's nervous, agitated, like a trapped animal, and I want to roll my eyes at the thought but that's the only way I can explain it to myself.

The onset of the coming night darkens the room as he

pours another glass. He sets the bottle down, sits in a chair next to me, body angled so that we face each other, knees touching. He blows out a breath before taking a sip of the Jack, and meanwhile the air has thickened with tension and the disquiet of the unknown in what lies ahead between the two of us.

"You wanted to talk?" he asks, eyes locked on mine, expression undecipherable, almost like he's detaching himself from me, and I hate it.

"I need to hear about the bet from you. I need you to make me understand why you didn't tell me when things changed between us. . . . They did change, right? I mean I'm not making that up, am I?" The silence stretches during which he grants me a slow, even nod, words unspoken but his eyes show that he's conflicted. "Hawke . . . I'm a pretty forgiving person, but you hurt me. I may have overreacted with the Vince thing, but finding out about the bet from Hunter was a blow to more than just my ego."

He nods again, the drink now gone. I narrow my eyebrows as I watch him pour another. "I'm sorry. It was a mistake, a band thing that normally I would have let run its course—"

"But you did let it run its course," I tell him, wanting to make sure that he sees my side of the argument.

"I know, that didn't come out right. Look." He scoots closer, so that one of my knees is between his. "At first it was a real thing, the bet. . . . But you're right—things changed and I fucked it all up. The thing with Vince . . . Well, that was . . ." His voice trails off as he leans forward, his eyes darkening, a sheepish smile on his face.

I meet him halfway, hungry for his kiss, his taste, to demonstrate the intimate connection between us because even when we haven't been able to communicate well in the past, our bodies have. And maybe that's what we need, this little sip of each other to remind us what we have between us so that we can begin again.

Chapter 35

Relief sifts through my body like an hourglass, slowly filling me with the knowledge that this whole bullshit charade is over and done. I've fulfilled my last promise to Hunter and now he can sink or swim on his own.

Hell yes, I love him, will help him if he asks for it, with limitations, but my days of being his father are over.

When I glance over my shoulder to where Vince sits a few rows back, there's a smile of relief on his face. He showed up even when I told him not to. Like I always say, the guy would go to bat for me in a football game if I asked him to. I lift my chin toward him as Ben nudges me to turn back around and not piss off the judge, who is finishing his parting words.

The judge knocks his gavel, locks eyes with me, and gives me a stern warning nod. I nod in kind, letting him know I understand his message, that this will be my only reprieve from getting time, before he rises and walks into his chambers.

The minute his door closes, I slump in my chair and the courtroom becomes a flurry of activity. Reporters rush out of the room so that they can call in the verdict to their boss, which will most likely squash the story because it's nothing as exciting as a conviction would have been.

"Thank fuck," I say in an exhale of breath, my head resting on the back of the chair as I throw a silent thank-you out to the universe for letting me catch a break.

"Gotta earn those big bucks you pay me somehow, now, don't I?" Ben says, throwing my comment back in my face from what feels like forever ago.

I sit up and stick my hand out to him—and it's such a formality after everything we've been through over the years, but I need him to know how much I appreciate his guidance and expertise through the whole ordeal. He glances down at my outstretched hand and just grins, knowing this is the only admission I'll give that he knows what he's doing and is good at his job. He shakes my hand and squeezes it a little too tight, before reaching out and patting me on the back.

"Thanks, Benji. I owe you one."

"I'd say anytime but if you lie for your brother again," he says, daring me to tell him that I wasn't covering for him, "I love you enough to tell you that I won't defend you. I told him the same thing right before I came in here as well."

"Told him what? That you won't defend me or him?" I ask off the cuff, so distracted by the chaos of emotions swirling around in my body that it takes me a second to hear what he has said. "Whoa, wait. You called Hunter just to tell him that?" I can't believe that with his complete disdain for my brother he even took the time to seek him out.

"First question, I won't defend either of you," he says with an arch of his brow as he starts stuffing papers into his briefcase. "Second, I ran into Hunt when I went to the bathroom before we started. It piss—"

"He was here?" What did he get, a change of heart, a conscience, or what? Because he sure as hell didn't have the guts to walk in here and watch me take the heat for him. Anger lights up within as it all hits me: my stupidity, the risks I took, being used . . . all of them simply solidifying how I already feel.

"Yeah. He was in the hallway right before I came in. We got into it. I told him this wasn't you taking the rap for him for hitting a parked car like you did in high school. Let him know he was a piece of shit for using guilt that's not yours to hold you responsible for his mistakes."

I meet the blue eyes of one my oldest friends and realize how damn lucky I am that despite my preoccupation with taking care of my brother over the years, I have all of these incredible people watching my back. Then it hits me how agitated Ben was when he first sat down, and now I know why. It was because Hunter was here.

"Dude, you're family . . . but I told him he wasn't allowed in this courtroom. As much confidence I had with how well your seminar went, it was still a crapshoot, and the last thing I wanted was to give him a chance to gloat while you took the fall for him if it went to hell."

I nod my head, the merry-go-round of emotions inside me on full throttle right now. One of the many burdens that's weighed me down has been lifted permanently and fuck if it doesn't feel good. Between Hunter and the promises to my dad and shaking this conviction, I feel so relieved. It's like I'm floating on air. And with Quin wanting to talk, shit, I might just grow wings and fly soon.

"Man, let's get the hell out of here," Vince says from behind me, interrupting our conversation the same time I feel his hand patting me solidly on the back.

"You don't have to ask me twice!" I tell him, ready to shed this stiff shirt and don one of my tees that's sitting folded on the front seat of my car. Then it dawns on me, breaks through the fog of relief, that Quinlan texted me and wants to talk. Can my day get any better? "Dude, did you talk to Quin? What did she say?"

I see the shock flicker across Vince's face before he narrows his eyes and shakes his head like he's confused. "How'd you know?"

What? "How'd I know what?" Now I'm confused. What in the hell is he talking about?

"How'd you know I talked to her earlier?"

I feel like I'm in the *Twilight Zone* all of a sudden, like we're talking about two different things. "Because I told . . . uh . . ." I look over to Ben for the name of his aide.

"Steph," he fills in for me and I can tell his interest is piqued, his eyes darting over his shoulder where she is speaking to an associate.

"Yeah, Steph. I had her give you my phone. Quin texted me. I wanted you to call her. So what did she say?" My sentences are short and clipped and I don't care that I'm kind of being an ass because I don't want to play games right now. I just want to walk the fuck out of the courtroom, which I don't ever care to see the inside of again, and go find Quin so that we can move forward somehow after my monstrous fuckup.

When he just continues to stand there and look at me like I'm crazy, I hold out my hand. All patience is lost. "Fuck it. Just give me my phone." I can tell Vince is getting irritated with me talking to him like he's a dumbshit, but if he doesn't want to be treated like one, he shouldn't act like one.

"I don't have your phone, Play. I don't know what the fuck you're talking about."

Unease begins to settle in the far reaches of my mind, and I'm brimming with frustration when Ben beckons Steph over. I can see the worry flicker over her expression as she approaches the three of us, who are focused solely on her.

"Yes?" I can hear the trepidation in her voice, the fear that she's done something wrong in her new job.

"Hawke's phone? Where is it?" Ben asks, tone stern.

Her eyes shift to mine and then back to Ben's. "I don't have it. I gave it to his brother in the hallway—"

"Oh fuck!" It's the only word that can express the dread that explodes through me right now. That and the mix of adrenaline as I'm rushing out of the courtroom like a man on a mission the minute everything registers: the possibilities, my fears, my brother's anger, his never-ending need to sabotage my life.

The problem is I've pushed him to the brink, cut off funding when I never have before, and so I fear just how he'll lash out this time.

I push through the crowd of reporters, not stopping, not worrying what an ass they are going to make me out to be in their reports. That's the least of my worries. They trail after me, shouting my name, hoping for the big scoop as I head toward the parking garage. I don't have to look to know Vince is right beside me. He always is.

It's what's waiting for me at Quinlan's house that worries me the most.

Chapter 36

Our lips meet, and I expected the softness of the kiss, but not the tears that burn the back of my eyes as emotion overwhelms me that we're going to try to work this out. I knew I was falling for him, hell I might even acknowledge that the L-word has crossed my mind in all of its ludicrousness, but I don't think I understood how much I missed him until right now with his lips against mine, the warmth of his breath hitting my face, and possibility stretched out before us.

The kiss is gentle at first, the taste of alcohol on his tongue as it softly meets mine. I scoot farther into him, my knee now against his groin, and place my hands on his thighs. He reaches out and cups my chin, fingers directing the angle of the kiss in a way he hasn't before, and I hate the fact that for a split instant I wonder if he's been with someone else. That simple streak of feminine jealousy tarnishes this moment until I push it away, but I can't help but feel that the way we are normally perfectly in sync with each other is slightly off.

I try to forget the thought, try to lose myself in the desire simmering in our kiss, and hate that the irrefutable chemistry that usually lights me on fire when we touch seems muted in a sense. And normally his bad-boy demeanor would be one helluva turn-on, but after the shit we've gone through the past couple of days, it's not. Greed is a turn-on when it's the hunger of a kiss overtaking you in your need for another, but when it's used to overshadow the amends you need to make, it doesn't do anything for me.

And I immediately wonder if I've ruined us, if learning about the bet has damaged how I feel about him and snuffed out our spark.

The fleeting thought scares the shit out of me. So I throw myself into the kiss, trying to force the feeling that I know we can find again. I try to gain some control, hands fisting in his shirt, tongue licking into his mouth, nipping his bottom lip, as I rise from my chair and straddle him.

His dick is already rock hard, straining against his slacks in a position that we always seem to find ourselves in, me sitting astride him, but there is no mistaking that Hawkin holds the control of the situation. His grip on my hair with one hand, his fingers twisting my shirt at my lower back, and the hunger on his lips tells me he wants this, and he's taking what he came for.

I slide my hands up to the crisp collar of his shirt, hoping that the feeling of skin on skin will chase all of these ridiculous thoughts from my head and allow me to enjoy our first time back together. The first time since I've acknowledged the man has won over my bruised heart.

My fingertips play with the buttons at his neck and he has his hands on mine instantly. "Uh-uh, you first," he murmurs against my lips before tightening his hand on my hair and pulling smartly on it. I yelp at the feeling and before I can react his mouth is on my neck, wet heat against chilled skin, drawing my focus from the pain.

When I grind my hips over him, a gasp falls from his mouth and his head falls back at the sensation. I do it again, loving the feeling of empowerment from hearing him want me, and I wonder if that's what I need right now. To take the lead in this round of sex so that my own psyche regains the knowledge that I am in control and won't be taken advantage of again. It's a ridiculous thought but with a mind half lost to lust, I decide to go with it.

I circle my hips over him again and within a beat of emitting another groan, Hawkin stands with my thighs still circled around his hips and walks us the short distance through the family room. The minute he lays me down on my back on the couch, his hands start pulling my tank top over my head. As I lie in the glow of light from the hallway with Hawke obscured in the shadows of the darkened room, I can't fully see the look in his eyes, but he stares at the whole of my body, covered in my shorts and bra, like it's the first time he's ever seen me. He's on his knees on the cushion, but I can hear the sound of a man appreciating my body and that helps to push me through the lingering doubts.

"Hawkin." I say his name softly, telling him so many things in that single word—take me, I forgive you, I want you, I need you—before fisting my hand in his shirt and yanking his mouth back down to mine. I feast off it, unexpectedly using the hurt and anger and shame I've had weighing me down the past five days to fuel my own greed for him.

"Fuck yeah, baby," he murmurs against my lips, and a part of me takes note that he's never called me that before, always called me sweetness, but the thought vanishes as he pushes apart my knees with his and grinds his own trouser-clad dick against the open and willing apex of my thighs.

My cell phone rings but all sense is lost as the friction hits me. My hands pull on his shirt, buttons popping off and scattering on the coffee table and floor. He tries to pull away but I keep his shirt as my need reigns, loving the knowledge that his bare flesh is exposed and mine for the taking. No way is he going to shrug out of my grip; instead I hold him close. He's not getting away from me again.

He resists momentarily and then gives in, hands over his control to me so that I can annihilate his. Our mouths brand and bruise, moans fill the air and I can scent the sex we're about to have. Then it's my hands on his button fly. His lips on my nipple through the lace of my bra. My hips pushing up into his. Instinct becoming reaction, desire becoming need.

"Take them off," I encourage, wanting him naked, wanting him in me. Desperately. Needing to feel the completeness again that I didn't even realize I was feeling until he wasn't around.

Hawkin pulls on my nipple as he sits up, my soft mewl

filling the silence of the room. I drown in the sensation but force myself to look up as he shifts on his knees on the couch to reposition us . He's in the sliver of hall light now, his body casting mine in shadow. I slide my eyes up his sexy as hell torso where that V I love is visible just above the waistband of his pants and my entire body freezes when I reach the intricate tattoo on his right pec that covers his skin to just below his collar bone.

A tattoo he didn't have five days ago and one way too detailed to have been completed in that short amount of time.

The realization takes me a split second, and the signs I've been pushing away come flooding back with validation riding the tsunami of disbelief. And fear.

What the fuck is Hunter doing here? Panic and alarms ring so loudly inside my head I'm deafened by them in the vulnerable state I'm in. *This has got to be a mistake.* I must be out of my mind. And the words are out of my mouth before I can stop them.

"What instrument tonight . . . ?" My voice fades off, hoping and not hoping that he can answer the question. If he does then it's Hawkin and I'm seeing tattoos that don't exist. If he doesn't answer then I'm in a world of fucking trouble—and the anxiety mixed with adrenaline racing through my system right now is clouding my thought process on what I should do because screaming like bloody murder isn't going to do shit in my own house with all of the windows closed. I fist my hands to prevent them from trembling as I wait for the answer, dread prematurely dropping through me like a lead weight.

"What?" he asks, confusion thick in the huskiness of his voice as the phone begins to ring again.

And I know for sure now, know that Hawkin would laugh at the comment, answer it for me, and then begin to work his way up my body.

Hunter eyes me through the shadows, sweat beads on my forehead, and my heart hammers in my ears. I wonder if I'm overreacting, telling myself that I am, but deep down I know that Hunter is going to do just what Hawke has warned me of: Take what is Hawkin's at all costs.

I begin to scoot myself into the corner of the couch, trying to contain the panic bubbling up inside, but my feet slip as I try to gain traction. Hunter's hand flashes out to grab my ankle before I can fully find my footing and yanks me back down the length of the couch.

He knows that I know.

The reaction is instantaneous, the fight-or-flight instinct so ingrained it's not even a thought as I try to scramble away from him. My free leg kicks out wildly, trying to connect and at the same time prevent itself from being pinned captive like my other leg. My pulse is pounding erratically, the blood rushing through my veins sounds like a freight train bearing down on me.

The sob falls from my mouth, and I almost can't believe that a man made of the same flesh and blood as the one that *I love* could be about to do this to me. I'm so scared and panicked that I don't even have a second to think through the truth that this whole situation has just squeezed loose from the depths of my heart. That I'm in love with Hawkin Play.

His amused and nonchalant laugh hits me like a punch as I use every ounce of strength I have to try to gain freedom: writhing, attempting to flip over and off the couch so he's forced to release my ankle, kicking, punching. Nothing works.

"Trixie," he sneers, "I'm gonna take what I want anyway, fight or not, so why not just accept it. I'm sure you'll enjoy it." The calm, even tone of his voice sends chills up my spine and even though it knocks me motionless momentarily, it makes me resist harder once that second is over.

"Get off me!" I scream at the top of my lungs, fear ruling my every reaction. Sense has been lost to fear and you can't reason with insane so all I have left is my determination and fuck if I'm going to let that fail me now.

I can hear the shouting and even though it's my voice, I don't remember thinking to yell. I lash out again in a fury of fists and my free foot that he's trying to grab on to. I know if he finds purchase around that ankle I'm screwed, so I fight with every ounce of resistance in me, finding the focus needed to quiet the panic ruling my thoughts. But this time I connect somehow with his lower torso and am granted a small reprieve when he releases his grip temporarily.

I'm up in a flash, uncoordinated and all over the place. I bang my shin on the table but I don't care. All I can think about is the front door, that there are people outside who might hear me or be able to help. I take a few steps and then his body slams into my back, him hitting me, me hitting the hallway wall face-first. My arm is wrenched behind my back, the weight of his body holding me still, my bare flesh against the chilled paint on the wall, and I try to jerk my head back and forth as his chin comes over my shoulder.

His maniacal laugh fills my ear, the tone of it telling me he is so far over the edge of reason that no matter what I do, how I reason, I won't be able to pull him back. The thought scares the shit out of me and yet I refuse to succumb to that fate.

He grinds his body against mine, a grunt of approval as his pelvis presses against my ass. I struggle against him, earning me another laugh as we stand there body to body, both of us panting with exertion, mine mixed with fear, his mixed with excitement, and the thought sickens me.

"What's wrong, Q? You don't want to double your pleasure, double your fun? Every whore wants a chance at twins, right?"

I grit my teeth, reject the taste of bile that wants to evacuate from the confines of my stomach, and squeeze my eyes shut. Thoughts, prayers, pleas run through my mind, giving me something to focus on rather than the sickening feel of his body against mine, the smell of fear in my nostrils, and the sheen of sweat coating my skin.

Chapter 37

Vince drives his truck onto the lawn and before he even has it in park, I'm sprinting to the front door of Quin's house. The only thing I need to validate my fears is here: Hunter's black BMW sitting in the driveway. My heartbeat is in my throat and the acrid taste of fear sears my taste buds with the tang I've only tasted one other time in my life.

The pent-up anxiety that has heightened with every passing mile on the way here is like a powder keg of everything in my chest waiting to explode. Her unanswered cell phone, having to call 9-1-1 because of what I fear I'm going to find, mixed with the inherent knowledge that my brother, my own flesh and blood, is the one here fucking with her. It all churns in my gut and tells me that there will be no more next time for Hunter.

Hurt me, I can deal with it. The armor I've used to protect myself over the years is worn but comfortable and I know its weaknesses. Harm someone I care about for no other purpose than to get to me, and the line I've redrawn so many damn times to excuse his actions has just been crossed and can never be erased.

I'm prepared to kick the fucking door down when I reach it, I'm so amped up on adrenaline, but the lever lowers at the press of my thumb. The door slams open and I don't know what exactly I expect, but rage the color of blood is all I see as the glow of the porch light and Vince's headlights illuminate the foyer hallway.

For that split second before they know I'm there, I feel like everything comes in a strobe light flash of images. Hunter's hand fisted in Quin's hair, yanking it back, the other trying to shove her shorts down. Quin's hands spread against the wall as his body presses her against it. The look on my brother's face, one I've never seen before—gritted teeth, muscles tense, eyes vacant—that causes chills to race up my spine. The shit from the coffee table strewn all over the floor.

I hear my yell before I even realize I'm shouting, and something snaps inside me. Fury shatters through the haze of disbelief at the same time Vince's headlights turn off. Hunter and I collide into each other, him to flee, me to avenge. We land with a crash in the darkness, brother against brother, right versus wrong, past versus future.

My shoulder smarts from connecting against the corner of the wall, knee meeting solid muscle, fists pounding into him with a disturbingly satisfying crunch. I'm exhausted, I'm exhilarated, I'm enraged, I'm heartbroken over my brother and his continual capacity to hurt everything that I care about, everything I find myself wanting to love.

I shrug Vince's hands off my shoulders time and again but still hear him shouting as Hunter connects with my jaw. The pain stuns me momentarily the same time as the light floods the room we've destroyed.

But I don't stop. Can't. Memories of the past and the here and now become a Molotov cocktail of emotion and I can't stop myself from unleashing years' worth of pent-up aggression in each action. For Quinlan. For me. For my bandmates. For my sanity.

"Hawke! Hawke!" Vince is calling my name again and for a fleeting moment I fear that if I stop, my head will quiet and I'll be forced to face whatever Hunter's done to Quinlan.

And I don't think I can handle it. Can't face it. Because if it's what I fear deep in my soul, I don't think I'll be able to live with myself. The one real, pure thing I've had in my life and he's damaged her too so that every time I look at her, touch her, I'll have to think of him.

That is if she can stand to look at me, handle me touching her again and not remember my brother.

He lands another punch but it doesn't faze me because I'm so focused on turning the hatred he's had for so long back onto him. And because I'm scared. So fucking scared so it's easier to take his pain than to deal with my own.

There are more voices as my back connects with the edge of the coffee table and it knocks the wind out of me. Steals more than just my breath as hands grab at my shoulders and now I'm fighting more than one person because I'm not done yet. I have a well of emotions to pull from and I'm nowhere near the bottom.

I'm hauled backward, fists swinging, chaos swirling, and it takes me a moment before I come out of the viscous haze holding me in my past. And when I come to, when I see the disorder of the room, the blood on my brother's face, feel the pain in my eye socket . . . all of it seems so fucking surreal that I can't process it properly.

I notice the police officer though, the red and blue lights filtering through the open front door. I can feel the vice grip of Vince's hold on me, can see Hunter pushing himself up and back against the wall as the officer approaches him. I can hear the rage of white noise in my ears as I squeeze and release my sore hands, knuckles aching.

And then I see Quinlan.

She is standing silently like a ghost in one shadowed corner of the room. The blanket from the couch that we'd snuggled under after our Guitar Hero session is wrapped tightly around her body. She has one hand up, fingertips covering her lips, but it's the look on her face as she stares at my brother that paralyzes me: shock, disbelief, confusion, all laced with a sort of innocence that I've never seen there before.

Her eyes shift some and lock with mine. My breath is knocked clear out of me even though I'm still struggling for air, and I immediately yank my arms from Vince's grip the exact same time a sob falls from her lips.

I'm across the room in an instant, my only thought, my

only goal in this moment is to reach her. She's my salvation. By the time I reach her she's sagged to her knees, the adrenaline finally abating from her system while mine is so rampant my body is vibrating with it. I drop to my knees in front of her and freeze, afraid to touch her, yet dying to hold her, desperate to feel her against me and know that she's all right.

Tears burn my eyes as we speak without words, and I can't take it anymore. "I'm so sorry. I'm so sorry," I tell her as a lone tear slides down my cheek. Her bottom lip quivers and her own tears well as the gold of her eyes glimmers through them. I reach out to touch her and pull my hand back, afraid to touch her without knowing what happened to her.

Does she hate me for bringing this upon her? Will she ever allow me to touch her again without seeing him? Is there even an us after all of this?

Her eyes flick down to my withdrawing hand and she shakes her head quickly, a slight intake of air from her swollen lips. "No. He didn't. No," she says, and every part of my body sags in relief.

I can't stand the chill between us, the loneliness, the unease I feel without her for one more second, so I reach out and timidly touch the side of her face, thumb brushing over the red mark on her cheekbone, palm framing the line of her jaw. She moves her face ever so slightly into my hand, and at that little sign, that reflex movement, fuck, *I'm lost.*

And found.

Within a beat I have her body gathered in my arms and pulled against me so that there isn't even room for air between us. I cling to her, hands fisted into the back of the damn blanket, and I can do nothing else to reassure her but use my actions, hope she feels the desperation and apology in my touch, because I can't find the words to say any of the things that are rushing through my head and then dying on my lips.

"Oh God, Q . . . I'm so sorry," I sob into the curve of her neck, needing the reassurance of the heat of her skin against my lips. I reek of desperation, of need for this woman who can't even hug me back because she is so busy holding up a blanket to cover up for the clothes my brother ripped off her.

The thought hits me hard now. What could have been. What might have happened. And so I keep murmuring to her over and over, again and again.

The world around us falls away. The cops asking to speak to me, the hands I shrug off me, the sounds of my brother calling my name, none of them register because what matters the most is in my arms and now I just hope I don't lose her because of this, because of him. Because I've enabled him for so long he felt entitled to the one person I've ever allowed myself to begin to fall in love with.

Holy shit.

My grip loosens with the realization. My breath hitches. I swear that my mind misfires because the ingrained habit to push away, to deny this emotion tries to grab hold and doesn't find purchase. Instead of finding a way to walk away, I just pull her even tighter into me.

I find an odd comfort in this moment. Not the hurt it has brought upon Quinlan, not the memories it will scar in both of us, but that after all of the shit of the past week, we're clinging to each other rather than shoving each other away.

And fuck yes I'm pissed that Hunter robbed me of the innocence of this dawning moment. He may have forced it with his fucked-up actions, but he stole something good, something special from me by doing something so unforgivable.

Chapter 38

QUINLAN

I jolt awake in the darkness, the silence around me screaming with the remnants of my nightmare.

It takes me a few moments to acclimate myself in the unfamiliarity of my surroundings, but soon I pick up the scent of Hawkin's cologne. My heart is pounding and my body aches as I shift in the luxurious bed, my mind reliving everything from earlier.

My skin crawls remembering the feeling of Hunter's deceptive hands on me. I force myself to swallow down my feelings of stupidity, my guilt, for not connecting the dots earlier before the situation went as far as it did, shame riding rampant over me that I didn't even know my own lover's kiss. I chastise myself for the harshness, tell myself to grant me some leeway, because I did notice the irregularities but wrote them off as our disconnect given the circumstances.

My stomach churns as I think of what-ifs and what-could-have-beens if Hawkin hadn't swooped in to save the day. It was like one moment I felt Hunter against me, fear holding me hostage, and then the next he was gone, the fear motivating me to flee. And as I did, as I reached for the closest thing to cover myself up, I heard a sound from Hawkin, one of pure, unadulterated rage. It stopped me in my tracks and I turned to watch Hawke not only vindicate me but I also saw years of emotions unleashed between the two of them. The brawl between two brothers, one trying to defend my honor from the one who tried to take it.

And then when all was said and done, when the police showed up and began to cuff Hunter on Vince's directive, when I looked up to find Hawke, I was found. I never knew that such a simple statement could have so much meaning behind it but it's true. Maybe it was the broken look on his face or the clarity in his eyes, but it was like he was seeing me in an all new light.

Change. Change brought on by force is not always a good thing, but for some reason I think this time, for Hawkin, it might just be what he needed to break free from the chains of his past.

I shift again, wincing from the pull on my battered muscles, and think of the look on Hawkin's face as he watched them load his brother in the police cruiser, expressionless, disgusted, done. And then there were questions and statements for the police, and reassurances that I didn't need to be seen by a medic, before I convinced them all that I was fine, would be fine, and just wanted a shower.

But Hawkin wanted me out of my house, wanted me at his place where he could watch over me until he got someone to put my house back to rights for me. And as tough as I acted, it was so nice to feel his strong arms around me, dragging me into the length of him, and drift off to the nightmares I knew awaited me while wrapped in his comfort.

But now I'm awake and cold. And I know I'm alone even before my hand hits chilled sheets when I reach out next to me. I groan softly as I push myself up and swing my legs over the edge of the bed. The night's darkness is not so welcome anymore now that I'm alone. I reach down with another twinge of pain and pick up the first thing that my hands touch on the floor.

I slide Hawke's T-shirt over my head and stop to hold the collar up to my nose and breathe him in. Use his scent to chase away the demons in my memories until I can find him in this maze of a house.

I know it won't take long though because I have a feeling I know exactly where he'll be.

I pad down the hallway and stairs, surprised but thankful that one of the guys isn't still up somewhere at this god-awful hour, living up to his rock-star reputation. I reach the studio door and see the light through cracks around the jamb. A soft smile I can't help plays on my lips, knowing that I was right, that I know him so well. That Hawkin turned to his one constant, his one true love, to deal with everything that happened today.

The hearing that went in his favor, the loss of his brother in a sense, and my assault. A lot of things for one man, who was already dealing with enough change to make most men buckle, to handle. Pressure can push only so far before one implodes.

I turn the knob slowly and stop immediately when the door cracks open, and I hear his melodic voice, scraped gravel worn smooth over velvet. I like to think I don't want him to know I'm there just yet because I don't want to disturb his work, but really it's that listening to Hawke sing is as much a therapy for me as it is for him.

The music he creates on the piano against the wall is melancholy, haunting, poignant, and it begs me to walk in the room and listen from a closer distance even though I know it's already woven into my soul and wrapped around my heart in just this first listen. I look through the crack I've opened and watch him play: head down, shoulders relaxed, fingers flying over keys without a second thought. He's in his element, lost in his therapy, coping the only way he knows how.

This poisoned crown has lost its shine, time to cut the ropes he tied with twine. I looked up, and I saw you. I looked up, and then I knew. My armor sheds, my truths revealed, for your honor I now have bled.

He sings the lyrics so softly but I hear them clear as day, know exactly what he's talking about, and it's never been more apparent that I have no chance in hell at winning my heart back from the hold he has on it. And I know for a fact that I don't want to. His fingers move flawlessly into an interlude and I don't even realize I've moved farther into the room, his pull on me so inexplicable, my draw to him irrefutable.

Take me as I am. Help me be a better man. Help me find

the path to choose, as long as it keeps me beside you. This empty heart is yours to keep, take my hand, let's take this leap. Falling soft, landing hard, happy ever after is not too far.

I can't move as his words, his heart, speak to me through the song. He sounds so lonely, so pained, and at the same time there's hope there, for whatever we are together. And after the events of the day, I cling on to the hope, desperately needing that ray of light in this incredible man to pull me through.

The music fades softly as he hums along with it and the room fills with silence. His head remains bowed, and I hold my breath, feeling once again like I'm intruding on him and his lover. It's an odd feeling but it's the most accurate way that I can explain how it feels to watch him create his music.

"I've never done this before, Quin," he says, voice strained. I startle a bit, surprised that he knows I'm here.

I take a step toward him, holding on to a ray of hope that he's saying what I think he's saying.

"Never done what before?"

"Today. Tonight. You. Me. Any of this." I try to follow what he's saying. He's got a habit of sharing what he's thinking without explaining at first so I grant him the moment to formulate just what he wants to say. I step up behind him and place my hands on his shoulders, ghost my body to his back and just wait him out.

He blows out a loud breath and shakes his head ever so slightly, fingers tinkering softly on the keys. "What I just said in those lyrics . . . By now I'm usually shoving someone away, but you . . . I don't want to do that with you. And not because I feel guilty about Hunter—which I do and always will and—"

"Shh. Shh," I murmur into the top of his head, not wanting to rehash the seven other times tonight that I told him Hunter's actions aren't on him. And riding right alongside of that is the damn hope again causing my heart to squeeze in my chest in anticipation. "Even when you push me away, Hawkin . . ." He starts to shake his head to tell me that he's not and so I continue so that I can explain. "It's going to happen. It's all you know. I'll be patient, I'll wait you out as long as you fight harder to keep me than you do to push me away."

He drops his head forward, nodding. "I will fight harder. . . . I'm pretty sure the bruises on my knuckles are proof." He snorts out a laugh and now I feel like shit because that's not what I meant. I reach down and lift one of his hands up to my lips and press a kiss to the bruises there.

He draws in a deep breath. "What I'm trying to say Quin is that I almost fucked this up by not telling you about the bet. I'm sorry. I was too busy holding on to who I thought I was to recognize the man you saw in me." Tears spring to my eyes instantly, and I squeeze his shoulders for him to continue. "But I see him now. You've allowed me to see him, to want to become him. I know that the promises I made to a desperate man when I was nine are not mine to keep. It's time to start living life for me, so I can prove those theories wrong, and the first step for me is trying to make this work with you."

He looks up to me now with a steady gaze, our eyes lock, and my smile spreads automatically. How can it not when I'm looking at this incredible man, trying to be the person so many of us have seen for so long? He's always denied it about himself, but now he's stepping forward. His eyes ask the question I think he's afraid to voice aloud. I lower myself gingerly to the bench beside him.

I take in his handsome face, black eye and all, his sculpted lips, and those gray eyes holding mine captive. His unease is palpable; the vulnerability radiates off him as if he cut open a vein, and my need to soothe his worries takes over. I reach out to press my fingertips to the softness of his lips and hold them there. He kisses them gently and my heart melts at the intimacy of the action.

"Sometimes first steps entail a helluva lot of tripping and falling," I tell him, hoping he really hears what I'm saying because I need to let him know he's not alone here in how he feels. "But it's okay because I promise I'll be there to catch you when you fall." I lean forward and replace my fingers with my lips, in a gentle reinforcement of my words. "You see, I can catch you because I already tripped and fell head over heels a while back."

I wish I could capture the look on his face, the quick intake of air, the sudden off-chord press of the piano keys, as record of the moment, but I don't think I need to because it's burned into my mind without a doubt.

"Really?" he asks me, incredulity in his tone and expressed in his face. He looks to me, eyes wide, lips wanting to smile but fearful he's misinterpreting what I'm saying. He makes me think of a little boy searching for an answer with cautious optimism.

I nod my head shyly, wanting him to see this is possible. That we can figure it all out, take everything that's been wrong and turn it into our own kind of right. We don't need to be perfect—we are never going to be and I'm okay with that. Bumps along the road are expected, misunderstandings and miscommunication are a given, but it's how we move on from there that will make us last.

A shy smile starts to spread on his lips. "Well, if I'm gonna fall, there's no place else I'd rather land than on top of you," he deadpans, with such relief in his eyes that I want this with him, whatever this ends up being, more than ever.

The laughter falls freely from my mouth, the one thing I can always count on when it's him and me.

I guess I took an iron to that piece of paper after all, got rid of most creases. And the ones that remain? I will love them for being there, adding in a little history, telling our story, and reminding me where we've been and how we got here.

And when he taps out the beginning notes of Tom Petty's "Free Falling" on the piano in front of him, the gravity of our day fades away and the poignancy of the moment we're sharing right now hits both of us. We erupt into another fit of laughter.

He leans in and brushes a tender kiss on my lips, so paranoid to touch me anywhere else for fear it might hurt me. I fist my hand in his hair and as much as my muscles scream, I can't resist pulling him in closer so that we can lose ourselves in each other, sear the commitment of this moment in our minds and weave it around our hearts.

"When you feel better," he murmurs against my lips, "I'm taking you on this piano."

"Still working on finishing the band, are we?" I arch an

eyebrow, feeling such a surge of emotion and love for this man before me.

"Sweetness, we've got a whole helluva lot of instruments to play yet."

He places a lingering kiss on my lips that causes that ache to settle deep in my belly. I lean back and look into his storm-cloud gray eyes. "The only Play I want is the one right in front of me."

Chapter 39

"So here's the schedule." Hawke lays a calendar on the table in front of me. The ocean breeze rustles it some so I take it in my hands and hold it up to look at Bent's tour schedule over the next few weeks. The cities and venues are marked on each day and then every few days feature bright red asterisks in pen that have no rhyme or reason.

"Thank you," I say distractedly to the waitress as she sets down my drink. After gazing at the calendar for another minute, I still can't figure out the red marks that bleed all over the page. "What are . . . ?" My thought trails off when I lift my eyes and meet Hawkin's.

He's staring at me beneath the shield of a baseball cap, the bruise on his face almost gone now, and I can see the amusement mixed with love in his eyes clear as day. A soft smile curls up one side of his mouth as the moment stretches on. "Figure it out yet?"

"The red?"

"Mm-hm." He nods his head and tips back the bottle of beer to his lips. There's no specific pattern and the closer I scrutinize the dates, they cover over two-thirds of the days on the tour. I look back up at him, eyes narrowed, and shrug. Hawke leans forward and kisses me. "I'm making it count, Trixie," he murmurs against my lips before leaning back to see my reaction. "I thought you might want to come cause trouble with me."

My heart squeezes in my chest because my love for him has grown stronger with each passing day. I can feel my mouth fall lax in surprise before spreading into a beaming grin. "Really? You want me to come visit you on tour?"

"Yep," he nods. "You'll be on winter break most of the time and I thought you might want to get away. That and . . . well, I figured if we're making a band together, it's only natural that it travels a bit."

"Of course. Every band has to tour," I tease, but I'm also blinking back the tears that burn in my throat. His admission that he wants me with him makes me feel like I'm walking on air. For a man so used to pushing everyone away, he sure as hell is doing a great job of keeping me close. It's my turn to press a kiss to his lips. "I think I can manage being one of your groupies for a bit."

"Well, you did dress me up like an eighties hair band," he teases, "so I get to dress you up as a road ho so that you can fit in."

"Hmm, you'd like that, wouldn't you? Short skirts, high heels, no panties, teaching me the soundboard in small alcoves," I murmur as the memory of our tryst fills my head and turns me on.

"I like alcoves," he groans under his breath and I love that I do that to him.

I point to a day where there is no asterisk. "Why not this day? This day works for me too."

"Well, I have another groupie signed up for that day," he deadpans, earning a punch in his shoulder. He dodges me with laughter and grabs my hand, pulling me close to him.

"No you don't, Play!" I struggle against him in jest but I surrender willingly when he uses his kiss as the means of negotiation. "I just might have to get a thing for lead guitarists then."

His mouth opens in shock and I take full advantage. My hand is fisted in his shirt in an instant and my tongue slips between his parted lips. Damn the man can kiss me senseless.

Hawkin's fingertips slide over my thighs and pull my chair so that my knees fit between his legs. He leans back and looks at me with that rock god smirk that turns me inside out. "Lead singer trumps guitarist any day."

"I thought it was rocker trumps racer?" His fingers grip my hips in a hint of what he wants to do to me when we leave the Surf Shack where we're eating our lunch.

"Sweetness, I'll trump anything you like as long as—" I cut him off with my kiss again.

"Is this the asshole *rocker*?"

My brother's voice shocks us apart and every part of me wants to whirl around and tell him to take his protective-brother bullshit down a notch because I've got this handled, but I don't because I'm too busy watching Hawke. And God how I love the fact that even though my heart feels like it was jump-started from cardiac arrest, Hawkin's hands stay firmly in place on my thighs and his eyes meet mine before slowly shifting to the voice behind me.

"Colton." He nods his head, the *back the fuck off* warning apparent in his stare.

"Oh chill out!" It's Rylee's voice that has me turning with a wide smile on my lips. Of course I love my brother, love how he takes care of me, but I love how Rylee puts him in his place even more.

I shift out of my chair and stand to wrap my arms around her. She leans back and raises her eyebrows in approval when her eyes dart over to Hawke. "What is it with you and hot men?" she whispers with a devilish smirk on her lips.

"You must be Hawkin," she says as she releases me. I turn to face Colton. He angles his head and looks at me before watching Rylee take a seat next to Hawkin and start up a conversation.

"The paper flattened out enough, I take it?" he asks in that gruff voice that tells me he's trying to be a hard-ass but at the same time is glad I figured my shit out and got the outcome I wanted.

"Yeah," I whisper in his ear as I pull him into a hug. "Thank you." He just squeezes me a bit tighter in response.

"Remember what I said?"

When I lean back and stare at him, his warning about having a talk with Hawkin should things work out comes flooding back. As much as I dread the idea, I know that it's

Colton's way of showing he loves me. "Go easy on him." My request earns me a wry chuckle.

Rylee doesn't break stride in chatting up Hawkin about his upcoming tour when we take a seat at the table. I'm far from blind and so I catch the intermittent glances that Hawkin and Colton share, each one laying claim to my protection.

As the topic comes to a close, Hawkin shifts his attention completely to my brother. "So Colton, lay it on me, man."

Holy shit. Both Rylee and I startle and whip our heads at Hawkin, who's going boldly where no man has gone before. And the fact that Colton chokes on his sip of beer makes it that much sweeter.

Colton sets his beer down and his eyes are locked on Hawkin's. "Wanna get something off your chest, man?"

I roll my eyes at Colton's testosterone-laced question and love how Ry quirks her eyebrow at him in a *come on* gesture.

"Nope." Hawke shakes his head a couple of times, and I love that he's not backing down and is playing Colton at his own game. That I mean enough to him to take a stand. "But I think you do."

Silence stretches, and both Rylee and I are fighting smirks over the invisible battle the two men that we love are waging. "Q's need to protect you from me is a first and tells a whole helluva lot about what she thinks of you. . . . But no bullshit, man, no one's ever going to be good enough for her, so sorry—but I'm not sorry because that's the breaks. You've got a lot to prove." Colton pauses to reinforce his words. And as much as I hate this, I love this. Love that Colton is laying down the law and being a big brother, and that Hawkin's letting him. Colton glances over to me and then back to Hawke. "My sister's a big girl, she can take care of herself, but flat out, if you fuck with her again, you'll have to deal with me."

"Colton!" I kick him under the table and enjoy the grunt he emits in return.

"Nah, it's cool," Hawke says as he stands and reaches across the table and holds out his hand. "I understand. Deal?"

Colton eyes Hawke's hand for a moment, working his tongue in his cheek before standing to shake his hand. Their hands grip tightly, gazes lock, and trust is passed from begrudging brother to a worthy lover.

I glance up at my sister-in-law across from me and she mouths, "So he's the one, huh?"

I nod subtly and feel stupid for the tears that suddenly spring to my eyes when I realize that she's absolutely right. Hawkin is the one. He's my one. I guess I believe in fairytale endings after all, so long as I can write my own ending. . . .

And I sure as hell am going to make sure this ending counts for us.

Epilogue

HAWKIN

"You didn't have to come here with me," I tell her as we stand at the nurse's station. I look over at her, blond curls piled on top of her head, pink lips, hand in mine, and fuck, I just stare. She's absolutely gorgeous.

And I don't understand why under these fluorescent lights surrounded by the medicinal smell, it hits me. I've looked at her hundreds of times before—naked, clothed, blushing, moaning, pissed, sad, sleepy, coming—and yet maybe it's me that's changed because right now as clichéd as it sounds, it's like I am seeing her for the first time. When I brought her here before, I was trying to prove a point. She called my cards to the table, thought I was cheating on her, and little did I know that taking her to see my mom would shift my whole goddamn world off its predetermined axis.

But now, the first time I've brought her back here since that day, things have changed. *I've changed.*

Every woman is beautiful in some way or another, it just takes the right man to see it in them. I guess I've finally become that man now because when I look at her, I'm absolutely smitten.

And that's a fucking scary thought for me.

But I've realized that the burdens I've carried on my shoulders for a lifetime weren't mine to bear. Hunter and I will both continue to live with demons from the day our dad sealed his fate, but my brother's problems are not mine to deal with. I can't fix things for him anymore. Fuck yes it hurts having him out of my life, but looking at Quinlan I know how much more it would hurt if I hadn't made it to her house in time.

His love is supposed to be unconditional but what I see in Quin's eyes and know from the guys is ten times more absolute than I've ever felt from him.

She smiles softly at me, telling me with her eyes that she remembers what happened the last time we were here together, and that she was there for me then and will be here for me now. She reaches out and links her fingers with mine. "I know I don't have to be, but one, you had to put up with my brother the other day. And most important, I want to be," she says, answering my question. "I need to get all the time with you I can. You're going to be gone for way too long. Like, three days before I join you in Seattle, and I'm gonna miss you like crazy . . . You're going to be sick of me by the time your flight leaves." She presses a soft kiss to my lips and I can't describe the feelings that stir within me at hearing her say that.

With Hunter serving time now and my mom most likely not able to remember me, it's such an incredible feeling to know someone here wants me home while we're on this quick mini-tour.

"Hm, don't think that's possible," I tell her, the stupidly silly grin on my face feeling strangely normal.

"You can go in now, Hawke," Beth says as she walks back toward us, interrupting our conversation.

"Thanks." I nod to her and take a deep breath, trying to prepare for the unknown that's always prevalent during these visits. Our past few visits, just mom and me, have been uneventful, but it is still heartbreaking for me to love a woman who has no idea who I am. But I can't leave town without seeing her. I have to say good-bye to her every time because if I didn't and something happened, it would be my biggest regret.

Quinlan rubs a hand up and down the length of my back in silent reassurance as I turn the handle and enter her room. She's sitting by her beloved window, staring at the world outside. I force a swallow down my throat as I step toward her cautiously.

"Mom," I call to her gently as I let her see me standing there before I slowly lower myself into the seat in front of her.

"Hi there," she says, a smile lighting up her face as she turns toward me. "My Joshy and I are going to have babies soon. Twins. And then you can call me that but for now I'm Helen. How do you do?" she asks me, extending one hand while the other hand rubs protectively over her nonexistent belly.

My heart squeezes and the smile is bittersweet on my lips as I see a glimpse of the mom I used to remember before the suicide. I reach out and take her hand, savoring the rarity of her gentle touch. "I'm well, thank you. Twins, huh?"

"Yes, two boys. I'm thinking Hunter and Hawkin after their grandmothers' surnames but I'm not sure. I told Josh, that's my husband"—she says with a beaming smile, her love for my dad so evident that the pang hits me, knowing now what he did to her. But I also find an odd sense of peace with the fact that they did in fact have a real love once. And maybe, just maybe, he realized it after he had strayed and couldn't risk losing it—"that it's a rather unique name, Hawkin, and do we really want to burden a boy with that? He said it's a unique name because he's going to make a name for himself with it one day. Only time will tell but I have no doubt he will be something, the way he kicks me." She laughs softly, completely mesmerized with her love for her sons.

For me.

"I think Hawkin is a great name," I murmur captivated, trying to fight back the tears welling in my eyes over a small piece of my prior life that I never knew. I'm filled with so many things right now, most of all gratitude for having this moment with her after all of the ones packed with spite. A little bit of the real her to hold on to.

"I do too. Kind of funny, though, when you think of it, Hunter and Hawke—predator and prey. One who attacks and one who protects. Hm. No matter." She waves her hands in a gesture of irrelevance and I love getting the chance to hear her thoughts. "I love them dearly already. I can't wait to hear them call me 'Mommy' someday." The hope in her voice and excitement in her eyes overwhelm me so the word slips out before I can catch it and potentially ruin the moment and cause her confusion.

"Mommy." It's barely a whisper, and for a split second I freeze but when I see her face light up, I can finally breathe. I glance over to Quin who is standing by the doorway, observing from afar, a slight smile on her face.

"Exactly," she says, not understanding the significance of what I said, that she just in her roundabout way told me she loves me. I feel a little more whole, a little less empty.

She glances over my shoulder at the clock on the wall, and pats at her hair. "I'm sorry, you'll have to excuse me, but you need to be getting on your way now. My Joshua is taking me out for a date tonight and I need to get ready for him. Besides, you don't want to keep that pretty lady of yours over there waiting," she says, flicking her eyes in the direction of Quinlan. "Us women like to be paid attention to."

"Yes ma'am," I tell her, our eyes meeting for a beat, before I stand from the chair. And I can't resist, something in her eyes, in the moment, has me squatting down in front of her. Her eyes narrow for a moment, but she doesn't pull away from me when I reach out and place my hand on top of hers. "I think your boys are going to love you more than you'll ever know. I think they already do." I choke on my own words, on the emotion that clogs in my throat, and the need for her to know in the hopes on those days when her brain allows her to be present, she can carry the knowledge with her.

"What a sweet thing for you to say," she says, angling her head. It takes her a moment but she slowly lowers her eyes to my hand on hers and then places her other hand on top of mine, sandwiching it in between her palms. We sit there for a beat, me absorbing the gentle and longed-for touch from my mother and recommitting it to memory.

She raises her eyes back up to mine and there is a clarity in the gray color that I haven't seen in what feels like forever. In that moment our connection feels so real I almost believe she can remember me. I lean forward and press a kiss to her hand on top of mine, half expecting her to slap me, half not sure what to expect.

I keep my lips there for a beat, desperately wanting her to wrap her arms around me, pull me close, but know I have to take what I can get and this . . . this is ten times more than I've gotten in so very long. I just want it to last. But I know it won't because she has a date with her beloved Joshy.

And the thought hits me that the date she has might have significance. That she might be communicating to me she knows her body is failing her. I hate the thought that creeps through my mind but I can't shake it. Can't get it out of my head.

I look up to my mother and say the words I need her to know, that I need to know I told her. "I love you, Mom. More than you'll ever know." I choke back the sob that tries to force its way out as all of the need for a mother's love comes flooding back with a vengeance.

She gets the strangest look on her face, almost as if I'm crazy. "Oh, Hawke, don't be silly," she says, shooing me away, but I'm rooted still as her words hit my ears, as she tells me she remembers me. "You act like you're not going to see me again. I'm just running to the store. You know I love you, you silly boy. To the moon and back."

The tear leaks over and slides down my cheek, the smile tasting bittersweet on my lips as my mom gives me the only thing I've needed from her in the past five years. She may still think of me as a little boy in her mind but she's just given me the greatest gift. She's stitched closed the wounds in my soul with those simple words, made me the most complete person I've been in the longest time.

Has given me the capability and hope to love someone else.

I nod my head and selfishly force my feet to move, afraid if I stay too long she's going to revert back and ruin this moment I so desperately needed. "Bye, Mom."

"Mm-hmm," she says and smiles softly before looking back out her window. I stare at her for a moment longer, memorizing this feeling I have, the lighter heart and clearer head.

Quinlan reaches over and links hands with me as I leave

Westbrook for the first time with a fuller heart than the one I entered with. With each step we take into the parking lot I feel a rush akin to the one I get after being on stage. It's a bittersweet emotion but shit, I'll take it. I'll take anything that doesn't leave me with that churning in my gut.

Once we reach my car, our hands still linked, it feels like there's so much possibility stretched out before us that I'm looking forward to the tour now. I'm excited to be trapped on a tour bus with Quinlan.

Damn. The thought takes hold as I look over and meet her eyes and that fucking jolt hits me just as hard as it did the first time I laid eyes on her. I'm riding my high of the present and possible future. Hell if I'm waiting for the tour bus when everything I want is right in front of me.

I pull her into my arms, lift her feet off the ground, and I'm already spinning her around when my lips meet hers to quiet her laugh.

Rocker trumps everyone when it comes to her.

QUINLAN

Hawke moves inside me.

My head drops back and his hard cock slides against my tensed muscles to heighten the pleasure starting to rock my world. The piano keys fill the room with a mangled sound when our bodies hit against them, my feet and his thighs.

We move at a demanding pace yet there is an underlying tenderness to it that resonates within me. Even if he tied me up and blindfolded me it wouldn't hold a candle to how much he owns me, mind, body, and soul, right now. His intensity, his reverence, his rough edges turned smooth just for me pull on so many emotions that I can't process them right now. I'm so overwhelmed, consumed by him, and saddened that he's leaving in a matter of hours and I'm just not sure how I'm going to cope with him thousands of miles away even if it's for just a few days.

I push it all away. Allow the moment to exist, the emotions to flow, and the pleasure to pull us into its addictive haze. It's only us, only him, only this, and hell if that doesn't make me the luckiest girl on the face of the earth.

"Quin." He calls my name in that liquid sex rasp of a voice at the same time he stills his hips. Our eyes connect, sensations tackling me from every angle as we sit in the silence of the room. It's a fleeting moment because we're both chasing the pleasure the other one is offering, but it's enough for me to see what I need to see in his eyes, even if he's unable to say it.

He leans forward and tempts my mouth, tongue fluttering, our moans expressing the pleasure we both feel. And then he begins to move again, to generate flashes of pleasure with his body that own my every nerve.

Hawke lets out a wild groan as he presses as deep as possible into me, strong hands holding on to my soft curves while he continues to drive us toward the razor-thin edge of desire. I want to close my eyes, succumb to the pleasure dragging me under, but our eyes are fused in an intimate conversation that's just as intense as the union of our bodies.

"Hawke," I moan, teeth biting into my lower lip, breath raw and ragged, errant notes filling my ears.

He flashes me a dirty smirk at the call of his name, as if I'm issuing him a challenge to bring me to the cusp quicker, harder, faster. He takes his hand from my hip to hold my neck for a beat before sliding his palm down between my breasts. Every ounce of skin he touches alights with an insatiable fire that I know only he can put out. A small reprieve in the onslaught of sensation—but I know it's temporary because I can see his muscles tensing, can feel his dick swelling, and his restraint holding on like an unraveling string.

I shift my hips up, milking his cock in my own move that has him calling out my name in a curse the same time I begin to disintegrate, powerful shivers coursing through my body. I buck my hips, hands reaching out to hold him still because the pleasure is too much, too absolute, but I'm a second too late because Hawke's head falls back as his hips buck wildly, dragging him over the edge with me.

The piano sounds a complaint to the two of us using it to make a different kind of music when Hawkin picks me up and carries me over to the couch in the studio. He sits down and then shifts us so that he's lying down on it and I'm lying on top of him, my heartbeat trying to jump out of my chest and join his.

"Wow," he says, blowing out a breath of satisfied exhaustion.

"You can say that again."

"Piano, *check*!"

I laugh with him at our endless quest to mark off instruments as sex props. "What are you trying to do, kill me before you leave me?" I say off the cuff and then immediately fall quiet as it hits me that in a few hours he will be gone.

I try to push the sadness away, not wanting it in this moment, not wanting it to overshadow the good mood seeing his mom today put him in, but it still lingers.

"Uh-uh. Don't be sad. C'mon," he says, pressing a kiss to the top of my head and pulling me in closer to him.

"I know." I shift to put my chin on his chest so I can look at his face. "I'm just going to miss you. Besides, I planted sexy panties all over your suitcase to find."

"You did?" He laughs, eyes lighting up.

"Yep. You have to find them all and show them to me via text . . . and then once you show me yours, I'll show you mine," I explain with a devilish grin, pretty damn proud of myself for thinking up this one.

"Come again?"

"Already? Jeez . . . I know you're good but that's a supernatural recovery time," I tease. Hawke just rolls eyes at me and begins to speak when I catch a glimpse of something on the inside of his wrist where there was nothing before. "What the . . . ?"

I'm scrambling to sit up astride him, grabbing his wrist and turning it over so I can see his forearm. A freshly inked bright pink heart the size of a quarter looks back at me. I know my mouth is agape and my eyes are wide at the sight. I start to say several things but nothing coherent comes out.

I itch to reach out and trace it, make sure it's real, but it's pretty obvious that it is. And of course I suddenly feel horrible because I'm the reason he has it. "But you told me you'd never degrade your other tats by putting something meaningless . . ."

He looks at me oddly, and as I look back and forth between his eyes and his wrist, it feels like I'm missing something. "Look closer."

It's the only explanation he offers and I immediately lean in closer, noting that up close the outline is fuzzy. But then I realize it's not fuzzy at all, rather it's letters intricately curved as an outline. "Hawkin? W-what?" I sputter as I connect the letters to form words. My lips fall lax. My heart skips a beat. My soul sighs with hope.

The letters form a single saying: *Make it count.*

My breath catches as a smug smirk lights up his face. I still can't speak and the astonished look on my face must be hilarious because he starts laughing at it. "Don't you get it, Quin?" he asks me and I think that I do, I really do, but I want to hear it from him. Need to hear it from that desire-inducing mouth of his. "This is the next lyric of my life's song. You're the bridge, the chorus, the final chord. This heart," he says, eyes softening and smile widening, "brought you to me. Was the catalyst that forced me to see so many things I probably otherwise wouldn't have. This heart represents you, represents me, and is my promise to you that I'm going to make it count."

The silence that echoes around us is deafening. My heart tumbles endlessly as the love I feel for this man surges to new heights. I start to speak and he brings his fingertips to my lips to quiet me so that he can finish.

"I know my life is crazy, unpredictable, and chaotic with tours, endless hours in the studio, crazy groupies, paparazzi, you name it. . . . I know that with your schoolwork and my music we'll be apart some, but I don't care. . . . I want to make this work any way we can because you've helped me find myself. I love the man you've brought out in me." He shakes his head, his words stunning me silent but causing my heart to race. "Don't get me wrong, I'm still fucked up, still have a sick mom and a whacked brother, but being with you makes it all bearable. I've done this all alone for so long that I didn't know how lost I was until I found you. . . . And I don't want to be alone anymore. I just want you, with all of your flaws, your mistakes, your smiles and giggles, sarcasm and bad habits, the way you play instruments, singing off key, everything. I just want you."

The simplicity of the last line and the conviction with which he says it melts my heart. Simple terms that mean so much to me. I look at him, my bad-boy rocker who's such a good man, and I know there is no one else I'll ever want to be wanted by. Just him.

"Whew," I tell him, my smile so wide I feel like my cheeks are going to crack. "And I thought you were going to say you just want me to be naked."

He bursts out laughing, his fingers tickling over my ribs momentarily before he brings his lips to mine. "Oh, I definitely want a lot of that. I mean that's a requirement of this thing we have here."

"Oh it is, is it?"

"Mm-hmm," he murmurs in that melodic way of his that turns me inside out. "Who else is going to be the star to my burst?"

I just shake my head at him and his ludicrous sweet tooth. "I thought I was the fruit to your loop?" I tease, loving the feeling of his hands on me, of our bodies pressed together, the feeling of his heart pounding so hard against mine.

"Sweetness, I'll take you any way I can get you. All I want is to make it count, make this count, make us count." He pleads with me like he's making a case. And I don't think he realizes that he doesn't have to tie in my *no regrets, make it count* motto to convince me to pick him because there is no need.

This girl is already madly in love with him, tattooed pink heart and all.

And for some reason I've been so afraid to voice it, have held back the words on my tongue so many times. I was afraid that if I let him know how much I cared for him we would fall to the fate of my many other relationships. That the pushing-away defense mechanism that was ingrained in him would take over and I haven't wanted to rock our boat.

But sitting astride him naked, hearing his confession, his reasoning, while he makes a case for me to choose him tells me how stupid I've been to wait. That he needs to hear it too. If he believes in us enough to permanently ink a tattoo when he's only ever chosen symbols of all that he holds close, I know it's time.

I can't resist any longer. I lean forward and press a kiss to his lips as tears swim in my eyes. My heart swells with love for him and I need him to know. "I love you, Hawkin Play."

He pulls back and now the tables have turned, his eyes are shocked wide and his expression becomes one of surprised enamorment. The image will be forever burned on my mind, the feeling ingrained in my soul.

"I've never fallen in love before, Quin. . . . I've never allowed myself to, but I know you are the only one I want to write the next song of my life with."

I meet him halfway, fingers sifting through his hair, lips sealing our connection, hearts entwining with each other's in a lazy decadent kiss teeming with emotion. He brings his hands to frame my face tenderly as he leans back and looks in my eyes, his breath still feathering over my lips.

"*Love* is nothing more than a meaningless word in a lyric until someone comes along and makes the music to bring it to life . . . and sweetness, you're helping me make music for it, *one instrument* at a time." The smile spreads wide on my lips, my body reacting to the thought of being *played* by Hawkin. I laugh softly and need to sate my simmering desire with another kiss, but he holds my face firm. My eyes flick back up to see a new intensity in his gaze.

"I love you, Quinlan." He murmurs the words but to me it sounds like he is shouting them from the rooftops. And damn it feels good to know we're both going into this on an open playing field with clear eyes, full hearts, glitches expected, and vulnerability exposed.

"Hey, Hawke?" My heart overflows with so much joy I can hear it in my own voice.

"Mm-hmm?" he murmurs, eyes locked on mine but dick stirring back to life beneath me.

I angle my head and a lascivious smirk turns up the corner of my mouth. "I finally know the answer to the question."

"The question?"

"If it's true you can play my body like a guitar."

He shifts his body some so that he can look at me better, and I love the mischievous smile that lights up his face.

"Hmm," he murmurs as he runs a finger up and down my arm, my body reacting instantly. "So?"

"Well, you sure know how to pluck my strings right," I say, brushing a soft kiss against his lips that garners me a low hum.

"And?"

"You can make my body sing," I say, the smile that comes to my lips so natural it's ridiculous but feels so good.

"We do make beautiful music together," he says with a snicker.

"Oh God!" I roll my eyes and laugh, breaking the moment. "That was totally corny."

"It was, wasn't it?" He leans up and presses his lips to mine. When he lays his head back down, our eyes meet, and there's something in them that makes my heart beat faster. "I have a bet for you."

"I thought you swore off bets?"

"Yeah, but there's no chance in hell I'm gonna lose this one." He raises his eyebrows in challenge, mouth spread in an arrogant smirk.

"You're so sure of yourself considering you lost the last one." I trail my finger up and down his collarbone as if our bodies lying on top of each other weren't enough of a connection.

"I may have lost in one sense, but I sure as hell won what matters." And I know he's just trying to butter me up for whatever bet he wants to make, but it doesn't stop the ridiculous hitch in my breath from the sentiment.

"Lay it on me, rocker boy."

"Blind bet," he asserts and just puts his finger against my lips when I start to disagree. "Loser gets a pink heart on the inside of their wrist in Bent fashion."

"Hawke . . ." I look at him as if he's crazy despite the small thrill that just courses through me over the thought that not only does he love me, but he considers me one of the guys. That's pretty damn cool. "What are . . . ? I don't . . . You already have one! That's not fair."

"Agree? Yes or no," he says, continuing with his little display of authority, which is kind of hot.

I narrow my eyes and stare at him, knowing full well I'm going to agree despite not knowing the terms of this bet.

When I don't respond quickly enough for his liking, he starts tickling me.

"Stop! Stop!" I cry out and try to wriggle away from him to no avail.

"Agree, then." He laughs.

"Okay! Okay! I agree!" And the minute the words are out of my mouth, he stops his tickle torture.

Our residual laughter fills the room as we both take a second to catch our breath. "I knew you'd see my way of thinking." When I just roll my eyes, he continues. "So, loser gets a pink heart, right? You get one or I make mine bigger. Agreed?"

"Yes." I nod my head cautiously.

"Sweet. I guess we better get a future appointment lined up for you with Sledge, then," he says, making a show of smacking his hands together and rubbing them back and forth in triumph.

"Wait! You're already declaring victory and I don't even know the bet yet!"

"Yep!" He falls silent to torture me on purpose.

"The bet, Play . . ." My patience is waning.

"You have your career to build and we have so much more to experience together first, so not in the immediate future . . . " He pauses, and we stare at each other for a beat as that slow, shy smile I love lights up his face. "But I bet you that you'll say yes."

"Say yes?" *What is he talking about?* "I say 'yes' all the time, so you're going to have to be a little more specific. Say 'yes' to what?" And as the last comment falls from my lips, it dawns on me just what he's saying to me. The lump forms in my throat instantly, followed by goose bumps blanketing my body. My mind tries to catch up with my heart, but for the first time in forever I don't want it to. I want to live in the moment. I search his eyes, the emotion in them giving me an answer way before he speaks.

"When I ask you to marry me."

It's funny. I figured this was what he was going to say, but hearing it out loud still causes my heart to skip a beat. My smile is so wide my cheeks hurt. "That's a good question," I murmur with a calm composure that completely contradicts my racing pulse and overload of happiness.

He pulls me tighter against him, and I hum in contentment as I settle into the comfort of him, knowing the answer I'll give when the time comes, without a doubt in my mind. It may be a long time off, and we might have more sour notes to face along the way, but Hawkin Play has definitely claimed my heart.

And then it hits me. I snap my head up and look at him as if he's crazy. "Wait a minute. You're betting me that I'm going to say no?"

"Took you long enough." He laughs and presses a kiss to my forehead. "Gotta hedge my bet somehow and your reaction just let me know that I'm going to win this one hands down."

He stops my sigh of exasperation by pressing his lips to mine. It's so easy to slip into the kiss with him, so damn natural I feel like everything that has been lacking in my love life for so long finally clicks into place.

And I know that bet or no bet, it doesn't matter, because this man has wrapped himself around my heart, and I don't ever want to let him go. I can't wait to see our future unfold.

Note by note.

Beat by beat.

Song by song.

Instrument by instrument.

Continue reading for a preview of
K. Bromberg's next steamy standalone romance,

HARD BEAT

Coming from Signet Select in November 2015

A hand slaps me on the back firmly. It's one of many in an impromptu celebration to greet me in the bar of the hotel.

"Welcome back, you crazy fucker!"

Burn out, my ass.

I turn to see Pauly: broad grin, hair falling over his thick glasses, and belly protruding. "Man, it's good to see you!" As I turn to shake his hand, I'm instantly pulled into his arms for a rough embrace.

He pulls back and cuffs the side of my cheek. "You okay?" It's the same look that everyone has been giving me and it's driving me fucking insane. Pity mixed with sadness. But Pauly is allowed to look at me like that since he was there before all the shit hit the fan. And coming back here, I feared this moment, meeting him face-to-face—as if he'd judge me, think it was my fault . . . but all I feel right now is relief.

It feels so damn good to be back here, with people who get me, who understand why I'd return to work when so many others think I should have given it up to stay home for good. They don't get that once you're a nomad, you're always a nomad. Or that home isn't where your house is necessarily; it's where you feel comfortable. And, yes, that comfort can alter over time—your needs shift and your wants change—but I feel more like myself than I have since Stella's death.

I pull my thoughts back to the here and now, to Pauly and the stale cigarette smoke that hangs in the air around me and the pungent scent of spices coming in through the open windows of the bar.

"I'm better now that I'm back here." I motion for him to sit down on the barstool next to me .

"Thank God for that. Took Rafe long enough."

"Almost four months."

"Shit," he says in sympathy, knowing what a big deal that is to someone like me.

"Yeah. Tell me about it. The first two months were a mandatory leave of absence, but then, once I threatened to go to CNN, he said he was speeding things up. . . . Then, fuck, they made me go take another Centurian course." The Centurian course was a class for foreign correspondents about what to do in hostile environments and how to handle the multitude of things that can go wrong at any given time. "And then I was told they couldn't find a photographer who wanted to travel to this *paradise*. . . . It was one damn thing after another."

"So in other words he was dragging his feet so he could get you back here on his time frame."

"Exactly." I nod my head and bring my bottle up to my lips. "He thought I needed a break—probably afraid that I'm going to burn out. . . ." I motion for the bartender to bring us another couple of beers.

"We're all going to at some point. In the meantime"—he taps the neck of his beer bottle against mine—"might as well get our fix."

"Amen, brother. So, tell me what the hell has been happening while I've been gone." The need to change the subject is paramount for me right now. I know Stella is going to be everywhere here, but I need a way to make her not so present in my mind so I can focus on doing my job.

At least it's a good theory.

"I'm hearing that some new players have moved into the game and that there's a high-official meet in the works, but we can talk shop later. Right now we need to welcome you back properly." Pauly raises his voice to shout the last few words, and in agreement the crowd of people around us, mostly men, raise their glasses and call out a few "aye, ayes."

The excitement around me is palpable. It doesn't take much in this place to give people a reason to celebrate. We all live on that razor-thin edge of unpredictability in this godforsaken land, so we take the chances we get to party, because who knows when we'll get another one? For all we know, tomorrow we could be on air-raid-siren lockdown in the hotel or out in the field, embedded on a mission with a military unit.

When I turn back around the bartender is busily filling the row of shot glasses on the bar in front of me with Fireball whisky. History tells me that this row will be the first of many in tonight's welcome-back celebration. My inclination is to chug back the first shot and then slowly work my way out of the bar and to my room.

It's been a long-ass few days. Between flights through multiple time zones and then a transport into the heart of the city, plus trying to reconnect with my sources to let them know I'm back in town so I can grease their palms some, I'm exhausted, exhilarated, and feeling a little more like myself, back in the thick of things, doing exactly what I love.

"C'mon, T Squared," Carson yells as he slaps his hand on the bar. Hearing the nickname, which refers to my initials, is like a welcome mat laid before me, and right then I know there is no way in hell I'm skipping out on this party.

"I'm game if you're game!" I hold a glass up for him and wait for everyone close to us to grab a shot. The jostling of more people patting my shoulders, accompanied by "Welcome back" comments, causes the amber liquid to slosh over the side of the shot glass.

"Shh. Shh. Shh," Pauly instructs our friends as he stands on his chair, holding up his own glass. "Tanner Thomas, we are so glad to see your ugly ass back in this shit hole we can't seem to leave. I'm sure once you hand our asses to us time and again by getting the stories first, we'll want you to leave, but for now we're glad you're here. Slainte!" As soon as he finishes the toast, the room around us erupts into cheers before we all toss back the whisky.

I welcome the burn, and before the sting even abates, my glass is already being refilled. When I look up from the glass my eyes lock on a woman I hadn't noticed at the other side of the bar. The momentary connection affords me a glimpse of dark hair and light eyes as she lifts her drink and nods to me, but as soon as I register she's doing it on purpose, someone moves and blocks my view of her.

But I keep my eyes fixed in that direction, wanting another glance of the mysterious woman. She doesn't look familiar to me, but at the same time, something more than curiosity pulls at me. It's been four long months — she could be anybody — but it bugs me that I don't know who she is.

"Ready, Tan?" Pauly's glass taps against mine, pulling me from my thoughts.

"Bottoms up, baby." God, it feels good to be back in the swing of things. Listening to the guys' war stories, getting up to speed on the shit that's happened on the grassroots level that no one back at home has any clue about.

The whisky goes down a little smoother the second and third times while our crowd gets a little bigger as people are coming in after fulfilling their assignments. And each wave of people joining us ushers in another round of shots.

Maybe it's the alcohol, or maybe it's the familiar atmosphere, but soon I feel like I can breathe easier than I have in months. I think of Stella intermittently through the night, how much she'd have loved this show of unity between all these people competing for the next big story, and for the first time in forever I can smile at her memory.

"So, how long are you here for this time?" Pauly asks.

"I don't know." I blow out a long breath and lean back in my chair, my finger tracing the lines of condensation down the still-full glass of water in front of me. Whisky tastes so much better tonight. "This might be my last time — I don't know." My own words surprise me. A confession from the combination of the nostalgia and my own mortality examined through an alcohol-tinted microscope.

"Quit talking like that. This shit is in your blood. You can't live without it."

"True." I glance across the room fleetingly while I nod my head slowly in agreement. "But, dude, a dog only has so many lives."

"I guess that's why I prefer pussies. They've got nine of 'em."

"Christ, Pauly." I choke on the words. "I prefer to eat it rather than live it."

His arm goes around my shoulder as his laugh fills my ears. "I missed the fuck out of you, Thomas. Speaking of . . ." His hand grips me tighter before he lifts his chin to direct my line of sight. "The hottie at two o'clock has been eyeing you all night."

I shrug the comment away, even though a small part of me—one that I'm not too happy with right now—hopes that he's referring to the woman I'd glimpsed earlier. I'd told myself that she'd left. But secretly I'm hoping I was wrong. "I'm sure as hell hoping when you say 'hot one,' you're referring to a woman and not an IED."

"Cheers to that truth. Scary shit," he says, again tapping his glass against mine, "and no, I'm referring to dark hair, great rack, killer body—"

"No, thanks," I cut him off but my eyes dart to where I saw her sitting earlier and immediately chastise myself.

"You still seeing what's-her-name?" he asks with the same indifference as I felt toward her.

"Nah . . ." I let my voice drift off, my thoughts veering to our last fight, when she accused me of cheating on her with Stella. "She took an assignment monitoring North Korea."

"She thought you and Stella were messing around?"

The thought brings a bittersweet smile to my face. Memories of Stella and me, young and in love, flash through my mind. It feels like forever ago. Probably because it was. Two young twentysomethings on our first assignment with no one else to help occupy our time. Lust turned to sweet love, and then the slow realization that we weren't any good as a couple. Then came an awkward phase in which we had to get over the bitterness associated with lust gone wrong, but through it all we really were a great team, reporter and photojournalist. But eventually, after enough time passed, we realized we were really good at the best-friend thing. We were inseparable for almost ten years, except for the odd assignment that parted us by pulling us to different places, and despite the introduction of significant others.

"Yeah, I get it. I'd probably think the same thing, but"—I shrug—"you've seen us together. Know how Stell and I were—"

"Mutt and Jeff," he mumbles as we both fall into a short

silence, thinking of her. "I'm sorry about what's-her-name. I liked her."

"No, you didn't." I laugh loudly because his statement is the furthest thing from the truth. He just nods his head in agreement—everyone knew they didn't get along. "But thanks. I think it had run its course before she changed assignments. You know what relationships are like with what we do."

"Man, do I know it. What am I on here? Wife number three? Four? You've got the right idea with the let's-have-fun versus the let's-get-hitched mentality . . . but, uh, she just looked over here again and, fuck me, I'd make her wife number five for the night if she'd let me."

The deep belly laugh he emits pulls a reluctant chuckle out of me, and it takes everything I have not to glance in the woman's direction. Resistance is futile. Eventually I give in to curiosity and glance up, planning to avert my eyes before she looks our way again.

Green eyes meet mine and her dark hair is pulled back into a messy knot that should look unkempt but makes her sexy somehow. When our eyes connect, her lips fall open in surprise before they slowly correct themselves into a soft smile. I nod my head at her acknowledgment and then casually look away, hating and loving the pang in my gut that stirs to life.

I'm a man used to living on instinct, and something about her—yet nothing I can put my finger on—tells me I should steer clear. So why the fuck do I glance back up to see whether she's still looking? And why do I care?

"I'm sure you would," I finally say in answer to Pauly, a little slow in my response.

"She's hot. I mean, how often do we get someone that fine in this neck of the woods? Damn, dude, her eyes are back on you now. She's seriously checking you out." He snickers.

"Yeah, and she's probably some sheik's wife. No, thanks—I'll keep the hand they'd cut off just for looking at her." I toss my napkin on the bar at the same time the barkeep slides another round in front of us.

"Better your hand than something else," Pauly deadpans.

"Got that right." I laugh.

"I might take the risk for her." I glance over and look him up and down. He can't be serious. "Okay. Maybe not."

"Maybe not." I scrub my hand over my clean-shaven face, knowing the smooth skin will soon be replaced by the scruff that just kind of happens when you live here. "She one of us?"

"She's been here about two weeks. Freelance, I think. Don't know much about her, but heard she's a loose cannon of sorts. Always off on her own, taking unnecessary risks and getting into people's business. I've steered clear other than a nod in the lobby."

I grunt in response, because that's just what I intend to do: steer clear of her. Too many newbies come in gung ho, trying to get the next big story, and end up getting someone hurt. *Just like what happened to Stella.*

"Well, for what it matters, loose cannon or not, I think you should go for it. She'll probably be gone sooner rather than later, which is always a good thing—prevents attachment, and, shit, you never know when your next chance to taste those nine lives will be." He winks at me and I can't help but snort.

"Thanks, but I've got enough to worry about with how to figure out my new photog coming in tomorrow." I roll my eyes and bring the shot glass back to my partially numb lips. My mind veers back to the fact that it's been ten years since I've had to break in anybody new. I'm not looking forward to it.

"Well, tough shit, man," he says, patting me on the back, "because she's making a move for you."

The resigned sigh falls from my mouth at the same time she slides onto the stool next to me. Gone is the distinct smell of this crowded bar, replaced by a clean and flowery scent as her perfume surrounds me. I keep my head down, eyes focused on the scratches in the wood bar, knowing that I don't want the small zing I feel to flourish. At all.

But of course the longer we sit here, with me looking down and the full weight of her stare on me, I know I'm in a losing battle. I've got plenty of fight in me, just not for her right now. I need to head this off at the pass.

"Whatever you're looking for, I'm not him." I try not to sound too hostile, but my voice lacks any kind of warmth.

I've been here, done this before. The newbies try to butter me up to get the scoop on everything inside town—and coming on the heels of the mess with Stella, I'm not giving anything to anybody.

"I don't believe I'm looking for anything." Her voice sounds as smooth as silk, with a hint of rasp. Why did I know she was going to have a sexy voice?

"Good."

"Whiskey sour," she says to the waiter, and I have to admit the order kind of surprises me. "And put it on his tab."

I immediately look up to see the smirk on her face and the taunting glimmer in her green eyes. Intrigue has me keeping my gaze on her because I admire the fact she came back at me with her own line instead of scurrying away to lick her wounds. Can't say the freelancer doesn't have some chops.

"I don't believe I offered to buy you one." And the truth of the matter is I don't give a flying fuck about the drink. I would've bought it anyway out of plain manners, but something tells me I just walked right into her well-maneuvered game, and fuck me if I'm going to stay here.

"Well, I don't believe I asked you to be an asshole either, so the drink's on you." She raises her eyebrows as accepts the drink from the bartender, then brings it to her lips. And of course my eyes veer down to watch her run the tip of her tongue over the drop of liquid that falls there.

My mind drifts to the pleasure she could bring with her mouth and her tongue . . . purely out of male fascination.

"Then I guess you should steer clear of me and neither of us will have to worry about me being an asshole." I grunt out the words, unsure why I'm pushing her away so hard when she's done nothing wrong.

"So you're the one, huh?"

Her comment stops me with my drink midway to my mouth, and my thought process falters as I slowly look over to her, trying to figure out what she means. "The one?"

"Yep, the one who every reporter in this room hates and wants to be all at the same time."

I take in the glossy black hair pulled back so that little pieces fall down to frame her face and soften her strong cheekbones as I mull over her comment. When our eyes meet, there's defiance laced with amusement in hers, and as much as I want to face her challenge head on, I won't. Not here, not now—and definitely not with a room packed with other journalists who are watching my every move to see if I'm going to fall apart in some way or another.

I motion to the bottle of Fireball sitting across from me and look at the bartender as I slide my money toward him. He picks up the bottle and sets it in front of me at the same time that I scoot my chair back. When I grab the neck of the bottle, I look back and give her a half-cocked smile. "Yep, I'm the one."

And without so much as another word, I head out of the bar. The guys give me shit as I walk past about being a pansy-ass until I hold up the whisky bottle to show them I'm not really turning in early. Pauly catches my eye and nods, knowing where I'm headed and that I need the solitude I can find there.

The fucking problem, though, is even as I ascend the steps in the dank stairwell, the only thing I can think about is her.

LOVE
ROMANCE NOVELS?

For news on all your favorite romance authors, sneak peeks into the newest releases, book giveaways, and much more—

"Like" Love Always on Facebook!

f LoveAlwaysBooks